How m

Tchazzar vanished during the Spellplague. He ventured into Threskel and never returned. Perhaps he was looking for a way to protect Chessenta from the blue fire; no one truly knows.

Recently, rumors have come out of the northeast. While wandering in the mountains, people have reported hearing a dragon roaring on the darkest nights. A few even claim to have seen one sprawled on the ground, with flames flickering from its mouth and nostrils.

The reports say the dragon is huge and old, like Tchazzar. They also say he's emaciated, crippled, or imprisoned somehow. That would explain why he never returned.

I don't simply assume the dragon in question is Tchazzar. But it could be.

Will you help me find him?

Tchazzar was a living god.

BROTHERHOOD OF THE GRIFFON

Book I
The Captive Flame

Book II
Whisper of Venom
(November 2010)

Book III
The Spectral Blaze
(June 2011)

THE HAUNTED LANDS

Book I
Unclean

Book II
Undead

Book III
Unholy

Anthology
Realms of the Dead

R.A. SALVATORE'S WAR OF THE SPIDER QUEEN

Book I
Dissolution

THE YEAR OF ROGUE DRAGONS

Book I
The Rage

Book II
The Rite

Book III
The Ruin

SEMBIA: GATEWAY TO THE REALMS

The Halls of Stormweather
Shattered Mask

THE PRIESTS

Queen of the Depths

THE ROGUES

The Black Bouquet

RICHARD LEE BYERS

BROTHERHOOD OF THE GRIFFON • BOOK I

THE CAPTIVE FLAME

Brotherhood of the Griffon
Book I
THE CAPTIVE FLAME

©2010 Wizards of the Coast LLC

All characters in this book are fictitious. Any resemblance to actual persons, living or dead, is purely coincidental.

This book is protected under the copyright laws of the United States of America. Any reproduction or unauthorized use of the material or artwork contained herein is prohibited without the express written permission of Wizards of the Coast LLC.

Published by Wizards of the Coast LLC. FORGOTTEN REALMS, WIZARDS OF THE COAST, and their respective logos are trademarks of Wizards of the Coast LLC in the U.S.A. and other countries.

All Wizards of the Coast characters and the distinctive likenesses thereof are property of Wizards of the Coast LLC.

Printed in the U.S.A.

The sale of this book without its cover has not been authorized by the publisher. If you purchased this book without a cover, you should be aware that neither the author nor the publisher has received payment for this "stripped book."

Cover art by: Kekai Kotaki
First Printing: May 2010

9 8 7 6 5 4 3 2 1

ISBN: 978-0-7869-5396-7
620-25153000-001-EN

U.S., CANADA,	EUROPEAN HEADQUARTERS
ASIA, PACIFIC, & LATIN AMERICA	Hasbro UK Ltd
Wizards of the Coast LLC	Caswell Way
P.O. Box 707	Newport, Gwent NP9 0YH
Renton, WA 98057-0707	GREAT BRITAIN
+1-800-324-6496	Save this address for your records.

Visit our web site at www.wizards.com

FOR CORWIN

ACKNOWLEDGMENTS

Thanks to Susan Morris and Phil Athans
for all their help and support.

PROLOGUE

12 Eleint, the Year of the Dark Circle (1478 DR)–
14 Hammer, the Year of the Ageless One (1479 DR)

Ananta woke. From a nightmare, surely, although nothing remained of it but a choking sense of dread. Heart pounding, she took a deep breath and looked around the dark cave.

Two luminous red eyes looked back from the entrance.

The body in which they were set was big enough to fill the space and occlude the night sky behind it. Rattled as she was, Ananta had to remind herself that the newcomer's hugeness wasn't cause for alarm. To the contrary. It likely meant the creature belonged in this place.

She rose and bowed. "Hail, my lord."

"Good evening." The dragon's sibilant voice was surprisingly soft for something so huge, virtually a whisper, and to her surprise, she'd never heard it before. "Do you live here all alone? I couldn't sniff out anyone else."

"I'm the only guardian, yes."

"Well, that has its good side. There's plenty of room for both of us."

She blinked. "My lord?" she asked.

"Come outside and we'll discuss it at a more comfortable distance." He backed out of the entrance.

Ananta wrapped herself in her cloak, glanced around for her staff, then hesitated. A dragon would surely recognize the length of carved blackwood for the weapon it was, and might conceivably take offense.

She picked it up anyway. The staff was the symbol of her office, so from that perspective, it would be disrespectful *not* to carry it when palavering with a wyrm. And in any case, she didn't know this particular dragon, and she sensed something strange about him. Or was that merely the residue of her nightmare still jangling her nerves?

The ledge outside the cave was spacious enough for several dragons to perch there comfortably. A thousand stars glittered overhead, and the crags rising all around looked like broken teeth. The air was cold with altitude and the coming of autumn.

Up close, the newcomer smelled of combustion. His scales were dark, although Ananta couldn't make out the true color in the gloom, and mottled with specks and streaks. His dorsal ridge looked black as ebony.

Ananta felt even more wary and uncertain. Her duties had given her abundant opportunities to study the shapes and markings of dragons, but she'd never encountered one like this.

The stranger's smoldering eyes widened, and she realized he was examining her as intently as she was scrutinizing him. Taking in a head, scales, and talons rather like his own, but married to a wingless, tailless, bipedal frame not a great deal taller or heavier than a human's.

"You're one of the dragonborn," he whispered.

"Yes, my lord."

"Interesting. The world truly did change while I was away."

"Away, my lord?"

The stranger stretched his gigantic batlike wings, then folded them again. "Perhaps I'll tell you the story later. For now, let's attend to business. I need a lair. Something roomy yet defensible. Where do you suggest?"

Ananta hesitated. "My lord, the word *lair* suggests permanence."

"Indeed it does."

"Perhaps my lord is unaware that Dracowyr is the common ground where the dragon princes hold their conclaves. No wyrm makes his home here."

"Customs change, Guardian. I'm about to turn this place to a higher purpose."

"I fear I'm not making myself clear. My master, Prince Skalnaedyr, would wish me to treat you as an honored guest. But you can't lay claim to Dracowyr. The princes already have."

"I suspect you have a way of contacting them, or at least of summoning this Skalnaedyr. Get him up here, and I'll explain the situation."

Ananta took a deep breath—and a firmer grip on her staff. "The greatest ruler in Murghôm won't come rushing just because you want him to. With all respect, my lord, I fear you may be ill. And since you refuse to behave as a guest should, I must also ask you to leave."

The dragon snorted, intensifying the sulfurous stink in the air. "Or you'll make me wish I had? All by yourself? And you claim *I'm* addled."

"I understand the strength of dragons, my lord. But it was a circle of dragons who gave me the might to defend this place." She drew a tingling surge of power from the staff into her body, then took another deep breath and blew it out again.

As it left her mouth, it became a spew of dark liquid so prodigious that her body could never have contained it. The acid spattered the front of the dragon's body and, sizzling and smoking, ate into it. Holes opened in the membranous wings. Scales and flesh on the wedge-shaped head dissolved, exposing the bone beneath. One shining scarlet eye melted, and the wyrm jerked in pain and shock.

Ananta brandished the staff. Invisible force slammed down on top of the dragon, squashing his body against the ledge. Bones cracked.

But then, despite the harm he'd taken and the power still pressing down on him, he lifted his head. He spat his own breath weapon, and smoke and embers filled the air.

The vapor blinded her and seared her, and she hissed at the sudden stinging. At the same instant, she heard a dragging sound. The dragon was crawling despite the magic shoving him down.

She hurled darts of green light at the noise, and the missiles vanished into the smoke. The sliding sound continued, proof that the new attack hadn't incapacitated the dragon either. Worse, the reptile would haul itself clear of the zone of pressure in just another moment.

Ananta wouldn't have believed that anything, even a dragon, could weather the punishment she'd just meted out. She felt a pang of fear, then strained to quash it and think instead.

She shouldn't stay where she was, not with the smoke blinding and choking her and the drifting sparks burning pocks in her scales. Better to retreat back into her cave, where her colossal opponent would have trouble getting at her. Praying that he couldn't see her any better than she could him, she backed in that direction.

Cold stabbed into her torso like a knife. The magical attack staggered her. Insanely fast and silent for a creature so enormous, especially one with broken bones stabbing out of its leathery hide and with limbs twisted askew, the dragon lunged out of the smoke.

She only had an instant to react. Somehow that was enough. She drew warmth from the staff to melt the frigid pain from her body, then heaved the weapon high. When she swung it at the dragon's head, it boomed like a thunderclap.

The blow crumpled the left side of the reptile's face. Ananta felt a surge of elation, for surely the pulverizing impact had driven shards of bone into the wyrm's brain. Surely he would finally collapse.

In fact, he faltered for an instant. But then he struck. Like a door coming loose from its hinges, his lower jaw no longer aligned with the top one properly, but his fangs still clashed shut on the blackwood staff. He yanked it out of her grasp and, with a toss of his head, sent it spinning over the cliff.

He raised his foot and whipped it down, catching her beneath it. He crushed her flat against the limestone shelf and ground her as her magic had ground him.

"I'm in considerable pain," he said, his soft voice garbled, "and your blood would help me heal. I'm also curious as to the taste, as well as annoyed with you."

She struggled to cling to her courage. "Do your worst." She

had trouble speaking too, in her case because he was squashing the breath out of her.

To her surprise, he lifted his foot off her. "Don't tempt me. *Do* you have a way of communicating with your master?"

Warily, waiting to see if he'd stop her, she stood up. "Yes."

"I hope it doesn't involve the staff, because I'm not giving it back anytime soon."

"No. Skalnaedyr taught me a ritual."

"Then it's time to perform it. In one of the larger caves, where we'll both fit comfortably. I believe there's one over there." He jerked his head to the right. "After you."

She felt ashamed, allowing him to order her around. It seemed like a betrayal of Skalnaedyr's trust. But it would be suicide to continue resisting without the staff.

So she built a little fire in a depression on the cavern floor, then cast the sharp-smelling incense into the blue and yellow flames. She chanted the incantation, invoking the Binder, god of knowledge. The first line was the same as the last, and she repeated the spell over and over without a break, meanwhile visualizing Skalnaedyr.

Until suddenly she *saw* him, as clearly as she could see her burned and battered vanquisher or the shadows dancing on the walls. An immense blue dragon with the horned snout and big frilled ears characteristic of his kind, Skalnaedyr was soaring above the dark waters of the Rauthenflow.

My prince, she said, speaking not aloud but mind to mind, *an intruder has come. He seems deranged, but he defeated me in battle. He wants to see you.* She wished she could go into more detail, but the magic only allowed for brief messages.

I'm coming, Skalnaedyr said, and with that the contact ended.

"I spoke to him," she told the stranger. "He's coming. But he was flying over the river, probably near his city—"

"So it might take him a while to reach an earthmote floating five miles above the Great Wild Wood. I understand."

"Understand that it gives you time to run away. You're strong, and you bested me. I acknowledge it. But you're not strong enough to best the mightiest wyrm in Murghôm."

"Then we'll hope it doesn't come to that."

With that, they settled themselves to wait, and the dragon set about sliding the protruding ends of broken bones back under his hide. The process looked painful enough to make Ananta wince.

But the stranger never flinched, and it soon became apparent that his efforts were simply facilitating an extraordinary recovery. His body made popping and scraping sounds as his bones knit back together. His twisted limbs straightened. New flesh seethed forth to seal his wounds, and new scales grew to cover it. A new eye glowed in the socket her breath had emptied.

By then her little fire had burned down to embers, and the mouth of the cave was gray with dawn light. The dragon retreated several yards deeper into the chamber, and then Ananta was all but certain what manner of creature he was.

Not long afterward, a familiar voice deeper than any dragonborn's called from the ledge outside. "Ananta! Are you in there?"

"Yes, my prince! Be careful! The stranger is a vampire!"

"Yes, I am," her captor said. "So it would be inconvenient for me to come out into the daylight. Will you come inside instead? Your servant can attest that I haven't set a trap."

"I wouldn't care if you had," Skalnaedyr answered. "I don't fear anything you could do."

Head lowered and wings furled tightly to fit through the opening, the dragon prince stalked into the chamber. The smell of thunderstorms surrounded him as the stench of burning clung to the intruder, and he crackled as he moved. Sparks danced on his blue and indigo scales. Together, he and the vampire all but filled the cave, spacious though it was.

Skalnaedyr stopped short when he took a good look at the other reptile. Not out of alarm, Ananta was certain, but in surprise. "You're not even a true dragon!" her master exclaimed.

"Now, that's unfair," the vampire said, a trace of humor in his low, insinuating voice. "I may have started out as a lowly smoke drake, but I've earned the right to call myself a dragon many times over, if not the veritable savior of our race. Karasendrieth never liked me, but surely she told the story even so."

Skalnaedyr blinked. "You claim to be Capnolithyl?"

"Brimstone, to my friends."

"The songs and stories say you perished in the final battle."

"Killing the undead and making it stick is a notoriously tricky business."

"Well . . ." To Ananta's surprise, Skalnaedyr seemed flummoxed. "If you are who you say, naturally I honor you. Still, Dracowyr belongs to me, and Murghôm has no room for another dragon prince."

Brimstone snorted. "I don't aspire to rule one of your little city-states, and I wouldn't seek to make my home in your territory without a good reason. After my allies and I destroyed Sammaster, I embarked on a search for long-lost secrets. I found one."

"What was it?"

"The answer to every dragon's prayers."

* * * * *

The short man had simply knotted a red kerchief around his neck. The woman beside him wore a white tabard with the shape of a scarlet sword stitched to it. The youth on the other side of her sported the most elaborate costume of all, a vermilion robe with voluminous scalloped sleeves to suggest wings and a stiffened cowl shaped to represent a horned, beaked head with amber beads for eyes.

All three marchers smiled and beckoned, urging Daardendrien Medrash to join their procession. And he hesitated.

Because the celebrants with their torches, banners, drums, and martial hymns belonged to the cult known as the Church of Tchazzar. They worshiped the red dragon who had once ruled Chessenta and allegedly presided over an era of pride and plenty. Now that times were hard, they prayed for his return.

But like most of the dragonborn of Tymanther, Medrash hated wyrms. Well, more or less; he himself had never actually seen one. But the creatures had oppressed his people for centuries, until his ancestors finally won their freedom by force of arms. To say the least, it would feel peculiar to participate in the veneration of any dragon's memory.

Yet Medrash was one of the ambassador's retainers. It was his duty to win friends for Tymanther, not give offense. And besides, since coming to Luthcheq, he'd discovered that human culture interested him. Here was a chance to experience another facet of it.

So why not? He nodded and stepped forward, and—slightly to my dismay—his new friends grabbed him by the hands and conducted him to the front of the march. He hadn't expected to take such a prominent position, but perhaps he should have. With his russet scales and reptilian features, he was as potent a symbol of Tchazzar as any of the placards and badges. It was what had attracted the marchers to him in the first place.

"Draw your sword," urged the woman in the tabard.

Again, why not? He pulled the blade from its scabbard and flourished, tossed, and caught it in time with the beat of the drums and songs. For a warrior who'd studied sword play ever since he was old enough to stand, such tricks were easy enough.

They were fun too, as was the procession as a whole. The attitude of the onlookers helped. Some cheered or sang along with the hymns. Others watched with tolerant amusement. Only a few scowled, shouted insults, or turned away.

When Medrash took a break from brandishing his sword, the woman in the tabard wrapped an arm around him, squeezed him tight, and held on thereafter. He wondered if she could possibly be excited enough—or have such exotic tastes—as to want what she seemed to want, and how to decline gracefully if she did. Then a sudden sense of vileness knifed through his feelings of bemused good cheer and well-being. It was like a spasm of nausea, except that his guts had nothing to do with it. He only felt it in his mind.

He faltered, and his companion peered up at him. "What's wrong?" she asked, raising her voice against the clatter of the drums.

"I don't know," he replied. But maybe he did.

For he wasn't simply a warrior. He was a paladin, pledged to virtue and granted certain abilities by Torm, his god, and the esoteric disciplines he practiced. And there were old stories of paladins sensing the presence of extraordinary evil, although it had never happened to him or any of his comrades.

On the other hand, maybe he was simply overexcited himself. He certainly didn't see anything amiss on the night-darkened avenue the parade was traversing, a cobbled thoroughfare whose several gymnasiums, baths, and schools of fencing bespoke the Chessentan enthusiasm for physical culture and military arts.

He took another step, and the feeling of revulsion seized him again. But this time it was directional. Whatever it was that was so sickeningly wrong, it lay somewhere to the north.

Medrash told the woman, "I have to go." He disentangled himself from her arm and—ignoring the several marchers who called out, imploring him to remain—jogged down a side street.

The boulevard he'd just forsaken was relatively straight, probably one reason the cultists had chosen it for their parade route. The cramped little streets, alleys, and dead ends in which he now found himself decidedly were not. From what he understood, the layout of Luthcheq was labyrinthine even by human standards. Maybe that was one reason people called the place the City of Madness, an old nickname its citizens employed with perverse and jocular pride.

In any case, the frequent turns, combined with the darkness and his relative ignorance of the city, disoriented him. One moment he was facing the towering black slab of a cliff that stood at one end of Luthcheq, and the next—or so it seemed—he was striding down the slope that ultimately ran to the River Adder. He might have despaired of finding his objective, except that pangs of loathing recurred periodically to guide him on.

They were becoming weaker and less frequent, though, as if a new talent was becoming fatigued. Or as if the spirit who'd decided to inspire him was losing interest.

Please, he prayed, if this isn't just my imagination, take me the whole way. Whatever's wrong, give me a chance to set it right.

Another stab of hatred made his muscles jump. This time the source was overhead.

He looked up. A shadow hurtled over him and the street in which he stood, springing from one rooftop to another. It was gone so quickly that he had no idea who or what it had been.

Lightning seething painlessly and uselessly in his throat, he wanted to give chase but knew it would be pointless. He had no hope of tracking his quarry over the rooftops. He was no acrobat—and even if he were, by the time he got up there, the leaper would have too long a lead.

Maybe he could at least glean some hint of what was going on. He scrutinized his surroundings.

The perceptions of ill had led him to one of the shabbier sections of the city, where tenements jammed to bursting with the poor leaned drunkenly, one against the next. The phantom he'd barely glimpsed had jumped from one such structure, a wooden building several stories tall, with layers of scrawled graffiti blemishing the base.

A pair of shutters on the top story swung open partway. There was a flicker of movement in the darkness beyond, then nothing. It was like someone had tried to open the shutters completely—to lean out and cry for help?—but something had prevented him.

Medrash ran to the tenement and opened the front door.

He'd never been inside this type of human habitation. But Tymanther had its own paupers, and in his limited experience, the places where they dwelled tended to be noisy.

In contrast, this building was silent—like the residents knew trouble had paid a call, and were keeping quiet for fear of attracting its attention.

Medrash found a shadowy stairwell and headed upward. The soft risers creaked and bowed alarmingly under his weight, but he didn't let it slow him down.

The uppermost floor smelled of onions. All the doors were closed, and he couldn't tell which corresponded to the half-opened shutters he'd observed outside.

He rapped on the nearest. "Are you in trouble?" he called. "Or are your neighbors? I'm here to help."

No one answered.

He knocked and shouted at the next, and once again nobody answered. Then it occurred to him that if an intruder had broken into one of the apartments and then fled via the roof, the door to that room would likely be unlocked and unbarred.

So he worked his way down the hall, testing each handle in turn. Sure enough, one door was unsecured. Holding his sword ready, he swung it open.

The space on the other side smelled of charred flesh, spilled blood, and the overturned chamber pot. The wavering light of a single smoky oil lamp revealed several bodies strewn around the room. Two of the children had burned to death, and it was a wonder the flames hadn't spread to consume the room as well. The other corpses were slashed and torn.

Except that one of them wasn't a corpse after all. The skinny, dark-haired man sprawled beneath the window proved that by groaning and stirring feebly.

"Hang on," Medrash said. "I can help you." He kindled the

warmth of a paladin's healing touch in his empty hand, then started forward.

At the sound of his voice, the human oriented on him, and his eyes opened wide. Despite the deep gashes running down his torso, he somehow managed to flounder to his feet.

Medrash realized the wounded man had mistaken him for another assailant. It was a natural mistake, especially if—like many humans—he knew little or nothing about the dragonborn.

"I swear," Medrash said, "I'm a friend. See?" He stooped and set his sword on the gory floor, then eased forward again.

For a moment, it seemed he'd succeeded in reassuring the man. Then the fellow wailed and flailed his arm, and Medrash belatedly noticed the knife in his hand. The blade was clean; he hadn't succeeded in stabbing or cutting any of his real enemies.

Medrash jumped back, and the wild attack fell short. Then he lunged, hands poised to disarm and immobilize the wounded man. It seemed to be the only way to make the poor addled wretch submit to his ministrations.

The human recoiled, and the windowsill caught him across the back of his thighs. He pitched backward, knocking the shutters completely open.

Medrash snatched at him, but caught only air. The injured man tumbled out of sight. A thud announced his collision with the ground below. Barring extraordinary luck, that drop would have killed anyone. It had surely killed a man who was almost dead even before he fell.

Medrash clenched his fists so tightly that his talons sank into his palms. At that moment, he hated whoever had perpetrated this atrocity, and he hated himself as well for failing to prevent it.

Why hadn't he run faster, or been more clever about finding the way here? And if he couldn't arrive in time to stop the attack, why hadn't he at least had the wit to use his preternatural powers of persuasion to calm the survivor?

He was still reproaching himself when he noticed the daub of fresh pigment on the wall.

ONE

11–16 Ches, the Year of the Ageless One (1479 DR)

Griffons hated the confinement of a sea voyage. You could make it a little more tolerable for them by flying them on a regular basis, but even that was no panacea. They were creatures of the mountains and the plains, and they felt ill at ease soaring over vast expanses of salt water.

Now that the cogs had finally docked, the winged mounts were frantic to get off, and their masters were having a difficult time controlling them. Their screeching spooked the horses, with the result that they too were difficult to manage. One chestnut gelding had already stumbled off a gangplank to splash down in the brown water below. It was a miracle the idiot beast hadn't injured itself.

In short, the process of debarkation was a tedious, aggravating chaos, and Aoth Fezim regarded the muddy, rutted road that ran away from the docks with equal disfavor. "Before the sea retreated," he said, "Luthcheq sat on the Bay of Chessenta. We wouldn't have needed to march from the river to the city."

Well-brushed shoulder-length auburn hair, jeweled ornaments, and the golden threadwork in his sky blue jerkin gleaming in the morning sunlight, Gaedynn Ulraes grinned. "Oh, I'm certain of it, Grandfather. As you've explained so often, *everything* was better before the Spellplague. It was always summer, the streams ran with wine, and every woman was beautiful and eager to please."

Aoth's lips quirked upward. "Do I really talk like that?"

"Only when your mouth is moving."

"I suppose it's a hazard of longevity." Or conceivably of actual immortality. The blue fire had touched him less than a century before, and it was too soon to tell if he'd stopped aging entirely or was just doing so very slowly. "Or maybe of being in a foul mood."

"Difficult as it may be to believe at present, I suspect we'll get all the men, beasts, and baggage off the boats eventually. Probably without taking *too* many casualties."

"It's not that," Aoth said. "It's Chessenta."

"Well, you're the one who decided to come," Gaedynn said.

"Did I have a choice? If so, I wish you'd pointed it out at the time." Aoth tried to drag his thoughts away from gloom and bitterness. "You, Khouryn, and Jhesrhi can handle things here. I should call on our new employer."

"As you wish," Gaedynn said.

Aoth turned toward Jet. The black, scarlet-eyed griffon, big even by the standards of his kind, stood watching the awkward confusion of the debarkation with an air of amused superiority. Altered by magic while still in the womb, Jet was Aoth's familiar as well as his steed, and possessed an intelligence equal to, though subtly different from, a man's. For that reason, his master could trust him to wander loose and unsupervised, even in proximity to horses.

Although, in a sense, Jet was never unsupervised. The psychic link they shared precluded it, just as it now enabled him to sense that Aoth wanted him. As he padded toward the pile of baggage with his saddle perched on top, he said, "It's about time."

Aoth draped the saddle over the griffon's back, then stooped to buckle the cinch. "I said we'd fly by midday, and we are." He swung himself onto the animal's back and stuck his spear in its boot. Jet lashed his wings and leaped skyward.

From the air, it was possible to view the entire Brotherhood of the Griffon all at once, and thus to see how much smaller the company was than it had been a year before. Once again Aoth tried to hold somber thoughts at bay and share Jet's exhilaration at getting airborne instead.

It wasn't too difficult. He wasn't glum by nature, or at least he didn't think so, and he'd loved flying ever since he was a youth. Winter was dying but not dead, and a cold wind blew, but the magic bound in one of his tattoos warmed the chill away.

The grasslands beneath him were more brown than green, though that would change with the coming of spring. When he and Jet climbed high enough, he could just make out the mountains to the east. A wisp of smoke crowned the volcano called Mount Thulbane.

They reached their destination sooner than he might have wished. Jet swooped lower over the rooftops of Luthcheq. Someone noticed and gave a shrill squawk of surprise.

Aoth guided the griffon toward the towering cliff and the carved structure partway up, half jutting from the rock to overlook the city and half buried inside it. It was the citadel of the War Hero Shala

Karanok, ruler of Chessenta, and—like many of the prominent folk in the city—the Brotherhood's new patron lived more or less in its shadow.

Specifically, he lived in a mansion with a red tiled roof. Yellow banners emblazoned with crimson double-headed eagles flew from all the turrets, and the stones paving the paths outside were of the same colors. Aoth set Jet down in front of the house, dismounted, scratched amid the feathers on the familiar's neck, and then climbed a short, broad flight of stone steps and knocked on the front door.

After a few moments, a servant in livery opened it. His eyes widened when he saw who was waiting on the other side.

Nature had made Aoth homely to begin with. He was short and barrel-chested, with features that were strong but coarse. Outside his native Thay, few folk viewed his shaved head and abundance of tattooing as flattering or aristocratic. In particular, strangers often considered his facial tattoos outlandish and grotesque, and of course the luminous blue eyes at the center of the pattern were overtly freakish.

So he was accustomed to his appearance attracting startled second glances and curious stares, and people's reactions rarely troubled him. But now it occurred to him that if the doorkeeper understood what he truly was, his response would likely be more unfavorable still, and that irked him.

"I'm Captain Fezim," he rapped. "Nicos Corynian is expecting me. Is he here?"

The servant swallowed. "Yes, sir. Please come in, and I'll tell him you've arrived." When Aoth entered, the other man hesitated again. He'd just noticed Jet.

"It's all right," said Aoth. "He won't eat anyone who doesn't bother him. Well, not unless it's somebody who looks particularly meaty. You might want to keep all the fat servants indoors."

The doorkeeper eyed him. "Sir is making a joke," he said uncertainly.

Aoth sighed. "Yes. A joke. Now take me to your master."

Predictably, it wasn't quite that easy. The rich and powerful always made a man wait awhile, like it was necessary to demonstrate their importance. But eventually the servant ushered Aoth through an antechamber, where two halfling clerks hunched over the documents they were writing, and into a larger study where their master sat behind a much larger and tidier desk.

Nicos Corynian was a trim, middle-aged man with graying brown hair. His general air of patrician sophistication contrasted oddly with a broken nose and cauliflower ear. Aoth inferred that in his case, the Chessentan enthusiasm for athletics manifested as a love of pugilism, or at least it had when he was younger.

Aoth bowed slightly. "My lord."

The counselor rose and extended his hand. At the same time, a huge green shape with a wedge-shaped head and shining yellow eyes peered over his shoulder. Startled, Aoth froze.

The apparition vanished. Nicos peered at Aoth. "Captain?" he asked.

Aoth had no idea what the vision meant. But it didn't seem to be a warning of any sort of immediate threat, so he pulled himself together and took Nicos's hand. The nobleman had a firm grip.

"Welcome," Nicos said. "I was hoping you'd turn up before this."

"Winter voyaging is always unpredictable. We hit foul weather while still north of Aglarond."

"Well, the important thing is that you're here now."

"I am. My men will arrive within a day or two. I trust you've arranged for our quarters."

"Certainly." Nicos gestured to a chair. "Please, sit. Shall I ring for some refreshment?"

Aoth sat. "Thank you, my lord, but I'm all right. We can get right to business, if that's acceptable to you. Where do you mean to use the Brotherhood—against Threskel or High Imaskar?"

Nicos cocked his head. "You're well informed for a man just off the boat."

"The ships put into port periodically on the voyage south, and whenever they did, I asked for news of Chessenta. So I know you're contending with two problems at once. Brigands and beasts are raiding out of your breakaway province, and Imaskari pirates are harrying your shipping and eastern coast."

Nicos hesitated. "Ultimately, I can see using your sellswords against both threats. But first I need your help with another problem."

Aoth frowned. He hated getting caught by surprise, and that seemed to be happening now. "Tell me."

"For the past two months, someone has been murdering people in Luthcheq. About all we know is that he possesses supernatural abilities and always leaves a handprint in green pigment at the scene of his atrocities."

"Chessentan law requires wizards to submit to having their palms tattooed with green sigils."

"Yes, it does. And the victims had only one thing in common— they were particularly . . . vehement in expressing antipathy for sorcerers and the like. At my urging, the war hero has tried to suppress that particular fact, but even so, people suspect mages are responsible for the murders. They're harassing them in the streets."

"More than usual, you mean."

Nicos made a sour face. "I'm aware that the Chessentan prejudice against wizards is unjust. I also know that you, a war-mage, have more reason than most to view it with disfavor. That's part of the reason I hired you."

Aoth snorted. "You thought the local mages' plight would appeal to my sympathies? My lord, I'm a professional. I'd persecute them myself if the price was right."

Nicos looked slightly taken aback. "Well, the fact is, we need someone to keep order and protect them. Even the war hero, who in large measure shares the common bias against them, agrees. And we can't depend on the city guards to do it, because *they* hate wizards too. So I offered to hire the Brotherhood of the Griffon at my own expense."

"To take up the slack for the watch? My lord, we're *soldiers*!"

"I understand that."

"Actually, this would be worse than simply filling in for the watch in normal times. Our job would be to stand between the mob and the people they hate. It wouldn't be long before they hated us too."

"You have my word that this isn't the only reason I brought you to Chessenta, although frankly—in light of your arcane abilities and dubious reputation—it is the only task Shala Karanok is willing to entrust to you. But if you prove yourself, that will change. Once the city calms down, she'll give me permission to send you to the border or the coast. Where you'll find your work more congenial and, no doubt, with ample opportunities for plunder."

"Just as soon as I live down my 'dubious reputation,' " Aoth said bitterly.

Not long before, it had been as bright as that of any sellsword commander in the East. But then the previous year, he'd broken a contract for the first time ever and fought his former employers, the Simbarchs of Aglarond. Then he'd spearheaded the forces of the Wizards' Reach in a costly and seemingly failed invasion of Thay, losing many of his own men in the process. And then—

"You have to admit," Nicos said, his tone mild, "what happened in Impiltur doesn't inspire confidence."

"What happened in Impiltur," Aoth said, gritting his teeth, "was not my fault or the fault of anyone under my command. There was a band of demon worshipers marauding in the north. More a rabble of madmen than a proper army or even a proper gang of brigands, but there were a lot of them, they had actual demons fighting among them, and they were doing a great deal of harm. The Brotherhood marched out to hunt them, and so did Baron Kremphras with his household troops. He and I agreed that whoever found the enemy first would notify the other, and then we'd trap the bastards together.

"Well, my scouts found them first, and learned they meant to massacre a nearby farming village at the dark of the moon. I sent a messenger to let Kremphras know there was just enough time to intercept them, and that if he brought his force to a certain position, we could catch the advancing cultists between us. He sent back word that he would."

"So what happened?" Nicos asked.

Aoth laughed without mirth. "You've probably guessed. The demon worshipers came, and the count didn't. We Brothers of the

Griffon had to fight them by ourselves, and it cost us dearly. Still, I think we would have won anyway, except that creatures came out of nowhere to attack our flank."

"What sort of creatures?"

"In the dark and the confusion, it was hard to tell. Some, I think, were drakes, and others kobolds. There may even have been a true dragon spitting some sort of caustic slime. Whatever they were, I had the feeling the cultists were as surprised to see them as we were. But they were happy to accept their aid, and once they did, we couldn't hold. We had to retreat or we all would have died."

"It sounds like you were lucky you were even able to retreat."

"I still don't understand why the enemy allowed it. But once we opened up the path to the village, the reptiles and such simply melted back into the night, and the cultists rushed on in to butcher the farmers." Aoth recalled the screams and the inhuman laughter, the leaping flames and the smell of burning flesh, and a pang of nausea twisted his guts.

"And how did it fall out," Nicos asked, "that you bore the blame?"

"Kremphras claimed he marched to the wrong spot because my message wasn't clear. That makes sense, doesn't it? After all, I've only been a soldier for a hundred years. Scarcely time enough to learn how to give simple instructions. But he's a peer of the realm, and I'm just a renegade Thayan who came to Impiltur with an already tarnished name. So the Grand Council believed him. They blamed the massacre on my incompetence and terminated my contract."

"Their foolishness was my good fortune."

Aoth grunted. "I still lie awake nights wondering *why* it happened. Kremphras wasn't an imbecile to misunderstand a simple dispatch, and I didn't take him for a coward who'd shirk battle. Was he a demon worshiper himself, out to sabotage the campaign? And what was the other force that attacked us?" Suddenly he felt tired. "At this point, I don't suppose I'll ever know."

"Probably not. So you'd be wise to focus on your new opportunity."

"With respect, my lord, if your emissary had been clear as to precisely what that opportunity was, I might well have passed."

Nicos's mouth tightened. "No, you wouldn't. You needed a new source of coin, you needed to get out of a realm where you'd become unwelcome, and who else was offering to hire sellswords in the dead of winter? Look, I've indulged you. I've listened to your grumbling. Now tell me whether you mean to pledge to me or not. If not, I suppose the cogs are still docked where you left them. Just don't expect me to pay your passage this time around."

Aoth took a deep breath. "I won't consent to having my palm tattooed. Nor will Jhesrhi, my wizard." His sole remaining wizard. Two of her assistants had survived the desperate foray into Thay only to perish in Impiltur.

"I can understand that," the nobleman replied. "In fact, I anticipated it. The war hero is willing to agree to a temporary dye."

"Well, I'm not. I can't exert authority wearing the mark of a pariah. You're a leader yourself. You know it's so."

Nicos grimaced. "All right. I'll persuade her somehow."

"In that case, my lord, the Brotherhood of the Griffon is at your service."

* * * * *

Jhesrhi Coldcreek wrapped herself in her charcoal-colored cloak, pulled up the cowl, reached for the door handle . . . and froze.

She silently cursed herself for her timidity. *This isn't even where it happened*, she thought. But this was where it had begun.

She jerked the handle and yanked the door open. Gaedynn and Khouryn Skulldark were just coming up the night-darkened street.

The lanky, foppish redhead carried his longbow, and the burly, black-bearded dwarf had his urgrosh—a battle-axe with a spike projecting from the butt—slung over his back. But neither wore armor or the scarlet tabards proclaiming them auxiliary members of the watch. That was because the three of them had decided to take a closer look at Luthcheq, and they were apt to see more if the inhabitants didn't realize who they were.

Khouryn smiled at her. "No staff?" he asked.

"No point proclaiming she's a wizard," Gaedynn said, "not when we're just supposed to be three friends out for a ramble. Actually, I was thinking of putting you on stilts. Some Chessentans don't care for dwarves either. They suspect you of practicing earth magic, whatever that's supposed to mean."

Khouryn spat. "I can't believe this wretched job is the only one the captain could find. We beat Szass Tam himself! Well, sort of. We saved the East!"

"But alas," Gaedynn said, "most people haven't heard the story and wouldn't believe it if they did. Anyway, this might not be so bad. Think of all the satisfaction you'll derive from breaking the knees of the dwarf-haters." He waved a hand to the narrow, unpaved street. "Shall we?"

They started walking. Gaedynn put himself on Jhesrhi's left, and Khouryn stationed himself on her right. Both knew her quirks and kept far enough away to ensure they wouldn't accidentally brush up against her.

The night was cold, and the houses looming to either side were dark and quiet, closed up tight. They reminded Jhesrhi of cities besieged by plague.

"Generally," Khouryn said, "when a town has a wizards' quarter, it's full of interesting things to see. Of course, the wizards usually don't live in mortal fear of provoking the neighbors. Are you sure you don't mind being billeted here? We could find you someplace cheerier."

"It's fine," Jhesrhi rapped. "One of us should sleep here in case something happens late at night."

"Buttercup," said Gaedynn, sounding less flippant than usual, "bide a moment and look at me."

Reluctantly, she turned and met his gaze.

"Are you all right?" the archer asked. "You seem strange."

Everyone already thought her strange. She didn't want to give them additional reason, or to have her friends regard her with pity. Gaedynn's solicitude would make her especially uncomfortable.

"I'm fine," she said.

He studied her for another moment, then said, "I rejoice to hear it. Plainly there's nothing to learn hereabouts, and I've always heard that for all their appalling bigotry, Chessentans know how to enjoy themselves. Let's find a tavern and drink the chill out of our bones."

The prospect held little appeal for a woman who detested crowds. But the best way to gauge the mood of the town was to mingle with its inhabitants, and so she offered no objection.

The wizards' quarter was home not only to full-fledged mages but also to any citizen with the bad judgment to reveal even a smattering of arcane ability. Yet it wasn't especially large. Jhesrhi and her comrades only had to stroll a little farther to reach a district graced with cobbled streets and the occasional lamppost. Voices clamored from the tavern on the corner, almost drowning out the music of a mandolin, songhorn, and hand drum. The establishment had a sprawling, ramshackle appearance, as if diverse hands had haphazardly slapped on additions over a period of decades. The sign hanging above the entrance displayed a red dragon wearing a jeweled crown.

"Perfect!" Gaedynn said. Jhesrhi gathered her resolve to endure the place as best she could.

If anything, the tavern proved to be even more crowded and raucous than it had sounded from outside. Gamblers crowed and groaned over clattering dice. A dog in a ring caught rats and broke their backs with a toss of its head. Whores with bare limbs and midriffs flirted, trying to lure men upstairs.

But it wasn't all bad. No one seemed to take any special notice of Khouryn, and the newcomers found a vacant table in the corner, where Jhesrhi could sit without people jostling her and rubbing past her.

Gaedynn waved to a barmaid and made attracting her attention look easy. Maybe it was, if a man was handsome in Gaedynn's smug, preening sort of way and dressed like he had more coin than sense.

"Once I get a beer," Khouryn said, "I'll join the lads throwing knives."

Gaedynn turned to Jhesrhi. "I wouldn't mind sticking here and sipping wine with you."

Apparently she hadn't really convinced him she was all right. "Don't be stupid. I can eavesdrop from here. But if you try, you won't hear anything."

"All right," he said. "Just don't get caught reciting charms." And before long, he and Khouryn were on the other end of the common room.

Almost immediately, a fat man with a plumed cap tried to take one of the vacant seats, but she dissuaded him with a level stare. Her basilisk stare, Gaedynn called it. Maybe the pudgy man found her amber eyes unsettling. Some people did.

Next she whispered a spell, and the wind—or the memory and potential of wind, caged for the moment in the indoor space—answered. Wherever she directed her gaze, she heard the sounds from that quarter clearly, while the rest of the ambient noise faded to a nearly inaudible hum.

A carpenter with big, grimy hands, whose wooden box of tools rested at the foot on his chair, said, "You get a snakeskin. One molted off natural-like. You keep it with you. Then no filthy wizard can hurt you."

"Why would that work?" asked a youthful companion, quite possibly his apprentice.

"I don't know, but that's what I heard."

Jhesrhi looked elsewhere.

A squinting mouse of a man whined, "I promise to pay you triple next time."

A half-naked woman with a magenta streak in her brunette hair shook her head. "Sorry, darling."

"It's just that the ship is late—the cloth hasn't come yet, and until it does, there isn't any work."

"Maybe the pirates got it, and it's never going to come."

"You know I'm good for the coin! I visit you every tenday!" But the woman was already turning away.

Jhesrhi did the same.

"It's wonderful," said a smirking man. "The wife doesn't *know* they raised my pay."

Jhesrhi looked elsewhere.

"This ham is good, but have you ever had it with cherry sauce?"

Elsewhere.

"Nobody dared to cross Chessenta when the Red Dragon was king. They say he'll come again. I don't know if it's true, but wouldn't it be grand!"

Elsewhere.

"I did too swim the Adder. When I was younger. And I can still outswim you any way you care to race. Any stroke, any distance . . ."

Elsewhere.

". . . boy asks, do the gods have gods that *they* worship? Where does he get . . ."

Elsewhere.

". . . came back different, all cold and dead and thirsty for blood. I have kin on the border. I wish they'd move to Luthcheq, but how would they live if they did? Farming's all they . . ."

Elsewhere. Specifically, to a pair of dragonborn occupying a little round table like her own, pewter goblets and an uncorked jug before them. They were sitting just inside one of the extensions that ran away from the central space like the legs of a flattened spider, which was probably why Jhesrhi hadn't noticed them right away.

Curious, she leaned forward. She'd encountered dragonborn a time or two, but not often. A century after their sudden arrival in Faerûn, they were still a rarity outside Tymanther, Chessenta, and High Imaskar.

The six bone or ivory studs pierced into the left profile of each indicated they belonged to the same clan, although she had no idea what clan that was. Their broadswords denoted esquire status or higher. Dragonborn of lesser rank would perforce have carried either blunt arms or weapons with a shorter cutting edge.

The larger of the pair had rust-colored scales and wore a steel medallion in the shape of a gauntlet around his neck. It was the most common emblem of Torm. She'd heard that dragonborn didn't worship the gods, but apparently this one was an exception. "We should get back out into the streets," he said.

His ocher-scaled companion, a runt by dragonborn standards, no taller or heavier than the average man, sighed. "I'll be stuck and roasted if I see why."

"Because the Loyal Fury prompted me to take a hand in this affair, and because I'm still the only one who's seen the murderer and lived."

Now even more interested, wishing she had a better idea how to read their expressions, Jhesrhi studied the dragonborn's faces. She assumed they were talking about the Green Hand killer, and no one had informed her that anyone had actually seen him.

"Maybe so," said the smaller Tymantheran, "but has this god of yours spoken to you since?"

"No."

"And when you say you saw the murderer, was it anything more than just a sense of motion in the dark?"

"Not really."

"So when it comes to hunting him, you don't actually have any special advantage over anybody else?"

"No."

"On top of which, you understand it isn't our job to catch the wretch. We came to Luthcheq to serve the ambassador. Despite that, I've spent night after cold, weary night prowling the city with you. We've had plenty of time to spear a fish if it was going to happen, and now there's no disgrace in giving up."

"I can't. A paladin has to answer the call to duty no matter what form it takes, and no matter the difficulties. But if you don't want to accompany me anymore, I understand."

The smaller dragonborn showed his fangs in what might have been a reptilian grin. "Right. When reason fails, break out the guilt. Well, it's not going to work this time. I . . ." His voice faded out as he craned, peering past his companion.

Jhesrhi followed his gaze. Several genasi were coming through the door, each marked by the elemental force with which he shared a kinship. The one in front was a windsoul with silvery skin crisscrossed by glowing blue lines and jagged gray crystals in place of hair. The one behind him was an earthsoul. His head was bald, and a mesh of gleaming golden lines etched his deep brown flesh.

They caught sight of the dragonborn, froze for a moment, then headed for their table.

"Akanûlans," said the smaller dragonborn. "If not for bad luck, we'd have none at all."

"Are you sure they're looking for trouble?" asked the paladin.

"For a fellow who pretends to have mystical insights, you're not much good at perceiving a danger right in front of your nose." The ocher-scaled warrior scooted his chair back from the table, no doubt so he could get out of it quickly. His companion looked around at the advancing genasi, then did the same.

The procession fetched up in front of the dragonborn. "Having a drink?" growled the windsoul in the lead.

"As you see," said the paladin.

"No doubt toasting your realm's most recent victory," said the windsoul, a little louder. Recognizing the belligerence in his tone and stance, nearby folk started edging away.

"I don't know what you mean."

"When you sneak into another realm, butcher defenseless villagers, and then run back across the border before anyone who knows how to fight can catch you, why, that's what Tymantherans consider a glorious triumph, isn't it?"

The ocher-skinned dragonborn started to rise. His friend gripped his forearm and held him in his chair.

"If you've had news that someone slaughtered some of your countrymen," said the paladin, "you have my condolences. Also my word that my countrymen aren't to blame."

"Of course," sneered the windsoul. "How could you be, when our peoples bear such love for each other?"

"We don't love you," said the paladin, "but when have we ever fought you except in an honorable fashion? You have less scrupulous foes. Look to them if you want to punish the guilty."

"Rot your lying tongue!" snarled a firesoul, his skin red-bronze and its web of lines a lambent orange. Tiny flames danced along the ones on his face and scalp. "One child *saw* your raiders and lived to tell the tale!"

"I say you're the liar," said the smaller dragonborn. He tried again to rise, but his friend still held him in place. Unfortunately, no one was holding the Akanûlans, and they reached for the hilts of their daggers and swords.

"Don't!" snapped the paladin, and the genasi faltered. Jhesrhi perceived that the russet-scaled dragonborn had infused his voice with a preternatural eloquence. "Whoever's right, we're in Chessenta, a valued ally to both our realms. Would you jeopardize her friendship by committing mayhem in the very heart of her capital? Let's at least defer this quarrel to another place and time."

For a moment, Jhesrhi thought his powers of persuasion had prevailed. Then the firesoul shouted, whipped his sword from his scabbard, and cut. The paladin jerked backward, and the blade just missed his reptilian face.

He and his friend sprang to their feet, scrambled back, and snatched for their swords. The other genasi, seven of them altogether, drew their blades as well.

It didn't matter that Jhesrhi and her comrades were out of uniform. They were peace officers, and it was their duty to stop the brawl. She wished she'd brought her staff—wished, too, that the tavern weren't so crowded. There were more than a dozen people between the combatants and her—the majority seemed eager to watch exotic outlanders slash one another to pieces—and if she wasn't careful, her spells would strike them instead of their intended targets.

She finessed the problem by jumping up and stamping her foot. The ground under the floor bucked. Some people fell, and others staggered off balance. Jugs and bottles lurched from the shelves behind the bar to smash on the floor.

"I'm an officer of the city guard!" she cried. "Put up your weapons now!"

"Where's her insignia?" someone asked.

"Forget that," replied somebody else, "why isn't the bitch's hand *marked*?"

Recovering their balance, some of the Akanûlans peered at her. Then a watersoul, his skin sea green with turquoise lines running through it, barked a laugh. "You think you can make elemental magic work against *genasi*?"

She drew breath to repeat her command, but she never got the chance. A windsoul flew up into the air and toward her. Unfortunately, there was just enough space between the ceiling and the crowd's heads to accommodate his passage. A firesoul whipped his hand up and down in a gesture that suggested leaping flame. Twisting back and forth like a serpent, a streak of yellow fire raced across the floor. Recognizing that they hadn't achieved a safe distance from the violence after all, the people between Jhesrhi and her attackers screamed and tried to scramble out of the way.

Straining to exert enough power without her staff, in the enclosed space, Jhesrhi whispered words of power to the wind. It forsook the flying genasi, and, deprived of its support, he crashed to the floor. It blew out the fire serpent like a candle. And in the moment afterward, before her opponents could gather themselves to assail her again, she peered to see what was happening elsewhere.

His medallion and the blade of his sword both shining like the moon, the dragonborn paladin was trading cuts with the windsoul who'd first accosted him. His fellow Tymantheran was fighting an earthsoul and a purple-skinned stormsoul at the same time.

Khouryn had somehow managed to engage the three remaining Akanûlans—a firesoul, an earthsoul, and a watersoul—simultaneously, and without drawing his urgrosh from its sling. Evidently hoping to subdue the genasi without causing them irreparable harm, he was wielding a chair as a combination club and shield.

The dwarf was as able a hand-to-hand combatant as Jhesrhi had ever seen. But the genasi were competent too, and had the advantages of numbers and real weapons. The firesoul slashed with his dagger, and it flared like a torch in midstroke. Khouryn shifted the rapidly splintering chair to block the attack. That left him open to the earthsoul on his flank, who instantly raised his broadsword for a head cut.

An arrow appeared, transfixing the earthsoul's forearm. Jhesrhi turned her head. As an archer, Gaedynn had faced the same problem she had—how to attack at range in the crowded room without hitting a noncombatant. He'd solved it by climbing up on a tabletop amid the remains of somebody's sausage-and-beans supper.

The earthsoul snapped the arrow off short so it wouldn't get in his way. He also stamped his foot as Jhesrhi had. Another shock jolted the tavern, and one of the legs of Gaedynn's table broke. It pitched over, spilling him to the floor amid a rain of dirty, clattering pewter plates and cups. The earthsoul rushed him.

Jhesrhi wanted to help Gaedynn. But then the windsoul she'd knocked out of the air picked himself up off the floor. He and his partner the firesoul charged her together, and she had to look after herself.

She spoke to the wind. It picked up the table in front of her and threw it. The missile smashed into the windsoul and knocked him flat on his back. But it missed the firesoul.

Backsword exploding into blue and golden flame, he closed the distance, cut, and curse it, she was caught in the corner! Somehow she dodged anyway, one searing, dazzling stroke and then another, meanwhile rattling off an incantation.

She thrust out her hand with three fingers curled. Green mist steamed from the firesoul's pores. He staggered and fumbled his grip on his sword, nearly dropping it.

The magical weakness would only last a couple of heartbeats, but she intended to make good use of the time. She grabbed a chair, heaved it high, and smashed it over the firesoul's head. He collapsed.

Panting, she looked for her other opponent. He was still down. While beyond him, Gaedynn had his Akanûlan down on the floor and was hammering punches into his face.

Khouryn had felled both his remaining opponents and moved to help the smaller Tymantheran. The dwarf had engaged the dragonborn's earthsoul opponent, leaving the stormsoul for him to battle. As the latter genasi feinted and stabbed with a knife in either hand, sparks danced and crackled across his skin.

The paladin and his windsoul adversary circled, blades clanging. The air howled, lifted the genasi off his feet, and whirled him widdershins. The paladin spun barely in time to parry the thrust that would otherwise have plunged into his back.

In other words, one instant, everyone was in furious motion. And the next, or so it seemed, before Jhesrhi could even decide where to intervene, everything was over.

Gaedynn paused, considered his adversary, and then, evidently satisfied, left off punching him.

Khouryn stabbed the tip of a chair leg into his earthsoul's groin, then bashed him in the face when his knees buckled.

The ocher-scaled Tymantheran stooped low, dropped his opponent with a drawing slice to the knee, then pulled back his sword for a thrust to the guts.

The paladin slipped a cut, shifted in close to his windsoul foe, and pounded the pommel of his sword against the genasi's temple.

Then, not slowing down an iota, he lunged and caught his friend's arm, preventing him from delivering the deathblow he intended.

Gaedynn stood up, retrieved his longbow, and then set about brushing off and straightening his garments. "We really do represent the watch," he announced to the crowd at large, "even if we hate wearing those ghastly tabards. In my judgment, the genasi started this quarrel, so we're placing them under arrest."

Khouryn moved to join him. So did Jhesrhi. The silent scrutiny of the crowd weighed on her as she crossed the room.

"What are we supposed to do with people we arrest?" Gaedynn murmured.

"I assume the town has a lockup someplace," Khouryn answered.

"The town is full of all sorts of fear and hatred," Jhesrhi said. "This brawl didn't have anything to do with the Green Hand killer or the prejudice against mages."

Gaedynn gave her a grin. "Well, not until you got involved."

* * * * *

"It isn't fair," said Daardendrien Balasar. "The genasi started it."

"We're in Luthcheq to practice diplomacy," Ophinshtalajiir Perra answered. The ambassador was an unusually tall and gaunt dragonborn, with the two jade rings of her clan glinting in the loose hide on the right side of her neck. Age had bent her back a little and speckled her brown scales with white. "Fairness and reason have relatively little to do with it. The war hero is upset. Accordingly, you and Medrash will apologize."

A servant thumped the butt of his staff on the floor. The arched double doors, ornately carved from the living sandstone of the citadel, swung open to reveal the audience chamber beyond. Walking with a slow and stately gait, Balasar, Perra, and Medrash headed inside.

Balasar could wield a sword better than most. Better, even, than most of his fellow Daardendriens, initiates of a clan renowned for its prowess. Still, he occasionally found his people's focus on the martial virtues tedious. For better or worse, the war hero's hall reflected similar preoccupations. The gorgeous tapestries depicted the clash of armies, and most of the statuary portrayed mortal combat, although here and there a sculpture of a runner or discus thrower suggested that even in Chessenta it might be possible to contend without shoving a blade through the other fellow's guts.

Shala Karanok looked at home amid the depictions of slaughter. She was a scowling, solidly built woman in her middle years, with a ridged scar on her square jaw and dark hair chopped short. The bits of polished steel adorning her masculine garments apparently symbolized armor.

An assortment of her counselors and officers stood before her throne, and—to Balasar's disgust—so did Zan-akar Zeraez and some of the lesser members of his delegation. The Akanûlan ambassador had remarkably long and slender silver spikes projecting from his scalp, and skin the color of the duskiest grapes. The pattern of argent lines etched into his face was so intricate that he looked like he was wearing a wire mask. Sparks tended to crawl on him even when he was in repose, and judging by his glower, that wasn't the case now. Balasar felt an impulse to make a funny face at him, just to see if he could elicit a glowing, popping shower of them, but it probably wasn't a good idea.

When they reached the customary distance, the dragonborn stopped and bowed. "Welcome, my lady," said Shala, her tone no warmer than her expression.

"Majesty," Perra said. "I've brought the guards involved in the confrontation."

The war hero turned her cold stare on them. "And what do you have to say for yourselves?"

"Majesty," said Medrash, "I regret the disturbance. If a similar situation arises again, we'll do everything in our power to avoid violence."

Trained to lead, paladins studied etiquette and rhetoric, and Medrash's tutors would have approved of his performance. It was deferential yet dignified. It gave Shala what she wanted while somehow subtly asserting the dragonborn's fundamental lack of culpability.

Balasar didn't try to match it. He just inclined his head and said, "I'm sorry too."

"As well you should be," said the woman on the throne. "It's unacceptable for any outlander to foment disorder. But the Akanûlans you fought were simply traders from a caravan. You two are gentlemen attached to your kingdom's embassy. I expect you to conduct yourself according to the highest standards."

"Yes, Majesty," Medrash said. "We demand no less of ourselves."

Well, give or take, within reason, Balasar thought.

Perra waited, making sure that she and the war hero wouldn't speak at the same time. When the human offered nothing further, the ambassador said, "If Your Majesty is satisfied, these two have duties awaiting—"

"I'm not satisfied!" snarled Zan-akar. His anger, the ire of a stormsoul, darkened the air around him and made the room smell like a downpour was on the way. The sparks jumping and crawling on his skin looked especially bright inside that smear of gloom. "With respect, Majesty, I thought you called these ruffians here to conduct an inquiry."

"Surely," said Perra, "the facts are already clear."

Zan-akar sneered. "Oh, there's a story we've all heard. But does it account for the facts? Does it explain how the Akanûlans—even with the advantage of numbers and even though allegedly the aggressors—ended up with broken bones, while these two escaped unscathed?"

"I can explain that," said Balasar. "Your traders fought like hatchlings from spoiled eggs."

Perra elbowed him in the ribs.

"Isn't it likely," Zan-akar persisted, "that in fact, as the genasi assert, these two dragonborn attacked them by surprise?"

"No, my lord," said Medrash, "it isn't. Balasar and I emerged from the fight unharmed because officers of the city guard came to our aid. And any fair-minded person would accept that as the truth because the watchmen say so too."

"But their involvement," said a plummy bass voice, "raises other questions."

Balasar turned. The speaker was Luthen, one of Shala's counselors, a big man running to fat in his middle years. His round head with its receding hair and neatly trimmed goatee looked small atop his massive shoulders.

Apparently he meant to take Zan-akar's side, which puzzled Balasar a little. He hadn't heard that Luthen was any great friend to Akanûl, although he supposed he could have missed that particular nugget of information. His mind tended to drift when his associates discussed the labyrinthine alliances and rivalries of Shala's court.

Lean, broken-nosed Nicos Corynian gave his fellow advisor a level stare. "What other questions, my lord?"

"For starters, why weren't they wearing their tabards?"

A man Balasar hadn't seen before stepped up beside Nicos. He was muscular and thick in the torso like Luthen, but short rather than tall. His head was as hairless as a dragonborn's, and a mask of tattooed marks surrounded his weirdly luminous blue eyes.

"Because they were off duty," he said. "But they still recognized their responsibility to restore order. Would you want them to stand idly by while blood spilled?"

Balasar inferred that the tattooed stranger must be Aoth Fezim, commander of the sellswords who'd just entered Nicos's service.

"I would wish the sorceress," Luthen replied, "to obey the laws of Chessenta and carry the mark of her essential nature at all times. And frankly, war-mage, were it up to me, I'd require the same of you."

A goodly number of the assembled retainers murmured in agreement.

"We're not going to stay in Chessenta forever," said Aoth, "and Her Majesty has given us a dispensation."

"What she's granted," said Luthen, "she can rescind. And she might want to consider doing precisely that. She might want to reconsider whether having you in Luthcheq is a good idea at all."

"We discussed this," Nicos said. "Until the unrest subsides, we need additional watchmen on the street."

"Why?" Luthen said. "To protect wizards?" He waved a contemptuous hand. "To skulk around in disguise and spy on your behalf?"

Nicos directed his gaze at Shala. "Majesty, that insinuation is preposterous."

"How so?" Luthen said. "The fact of the matter is, you've brought a private army into the capital—a force commanded by a Thayan mage and with other Thayans, wizards, and dwarves among the ranks."

"Actually," said Aoth, "I'm a Thayan renegade, with the torture chamber and the block awaiting me should I ever return. The other 'Thayans' in the Brotherhood are the descendents of men who came with me into exile a century ago. And at the moment, I only have one true wizard and one dwarf. Too bad—I could use more."

Luthen kept his glare aimed at Nicos. "You claim to have placed this band of reavers and sorcerers at the service of Her Majesty. But the reality is that since you pay them, and rogues of their stripe care only for gold, they answer to you alone."

"Well, I answer to Her Majesty," said Nicos, "so even if your assessment were true, all's well."

"Far be it from me to impugn your loyalty, my lord. But history abounds in nobles who insinuated an excessive number of their personal troops into their sovereign's capital, then turned them to some treasonous purpose. It's simply poor policy to permit such maneuverings."

Nicos looked to the throne. "Majesty, I know it takes more than empty prattle to make you doubt a vassal who has always served you loyally. Or to make you doubt your own decisions."

Shala grunted. "I'll consent to keep Captain Fezim's sellswords patrolling the city until they prove unworthy of the trust."

"Then if it pleases Your Majesty," Zan-akar said, "may we return to the true business of this meeting? It's vital that we discuss the crimes Tymanther has committed against both our realms."

Perra snorted. "Get a grip, my lord. A scuffle in a tavern, however deplorable, scarcely warrants such a description."

"That particular outrage," said Zan-akar, light seething along the silvery lines in his skin, "was the least of it. Dragonborn are slipping into Akanûl, slaughtering the inhabitants of remote settlements, and retreating back across the border."

"That's ridiculous," Perra said.

"We have witnesses," said Zan-akar. "Your marauders didn't quite manage to murder everyone. And as Your Majesty knows, Akanûl and Tymanther lack a common border. The only way for dragonborn raiders to reach us is to cross Chessentan territory. In light of the vows of friendship between our two realms, I assume you haven't given them permission to do so."

"No," said the war hero, "of course not."

"Then they're trespassing on your lands just as they are on ours."

"If these raiders actually existed," said Perra, "then that would be a logical conclusion. But they don't."

"I repeat," said Zan-akar, "we have witnesses."

"Where?" replied Perra. "Not anyplace that Her Majesty or anyone else impartial can question them, apparently. Let's be rational. If companies of dragonborn warriors were crossing Chessenta, then some of her own people would have noticed. Akanûl wouldn't need to tattle on us."

"Western Chessenta is sparsely populated," Zan-akar said, "and the hills and gullies offer excellent cover. Tymanther could sneak a whole army through."

"Be that as it may, my lord," said Perra, "since you didn't bring any witnesses along with you today, in the end, this matter simply comes down to Akanûl's word against ours."

"Perhaps I'll send for the witnesses," the stormsoul said, with such malevolent assurance in his tone that for just a moment, Balasar wondered if rogue dragonborn might actually have committed the alleged atrocities. "Meanwhile, I'm more than willing to discuss which kingdom's word a sensible person ought to trust."

Perra snorted. "Surely you aren't going to suggest that the genasi's reputation for honesty and steadfastness compares favorably to that of the dragonborn."

"What I'm saying," Zan-akar replied, "is that since the day we arrived in Faerûn, Akanûl has been purely and unequivocally a friend to Chessenta. Tymanther *claims* to be her ally, but you also profess the same to High Imaskar. The same degenerate horde of wizards and slave-takers currently sacking villages along the Chessentan coast and sinking her ships up and down the length of the Alamber Sea."

For once, Perra seemed at a loss, at least momentarily, and Balasar didn't blame her. Zan-akar, damn him, had landed a shrewd stroke. The war hero had made no secret of the fact that she resented Tymanther's continued friendship with High Imaskar.

Maybe the dragonborn should pick a side. Or maybe Balasar simply thought so because at heart he was more a fighter than a diplomat. A person could certainly make a case that when a realm only had two allies, it would be a mistake to relinquish either.

"When you put it that way," drawled Aoth, "the choice seems clear. But actually, Majesty, Lord Zan-akar is claiming a difference where none exists."

"What do you mean?" Shala asked.

"I spent the first part of last year working for the Simbarchs," the sellsword said, "and Aglarond and Akanûl are friends. So there were genasi hanging around Veltalar. I didn't make any special effort to pry into their affairs, but I didn't need to in order to hear that not long ago, the queen of Akanûl forged an alliance with High Imaskar. It's no secret—except, evidently, when Lord Zan-akar and his associates are talking to you."

Zan-akar smiled contemptuously, although the space in which he stood darkened a little more. "At a moment like this, it's good to know that Her Majesty is far too shrewd to heed the forked tongue of a mage."

Shala glared at him. "*Is* the sellsword lying? Answer honestly! You know I can find out the truth for myself."

Zan-akar hesitated, then said, "Majesty, you know as well as I that the ministers of a realm receive envoys from here, there, and everywhere. I believe that Akanûl has talked to High Imaskar, and possibly even worked out an arrangement or two regarding trade. But nothing that compromises our friendship with Chessenta!"

"Go," Shala rapped. "Diplomats, counselors, the lot of you. We'll take up your spite and accusations another day, when I'm in firmer control of my temper."

It seemed to Balasar that thanks to Aoth, Tymanther had at least held its own in the battle of words, so that made two debts Clan Daardendrien owed the sellswords. As they all filed out, he caught the Thayan's eye and gave him a respectful nod. Aoth responded with a smile that, though cordial enough, came with a certain sardonic crook.

* * * * *

Khouryn combed through Vigilant's bronze and white plumage, checking for broken feathers and parasites with the two-tined iron fork designed for the purpose. Smelling of both bird and musky hunting cat, the griffon lay flat on the stable floor so the dwarf could reach all of her. In fact, she looked like she'd melted there. The grooming had produced a state of blissful relaxation.

"It sounds like everything went all right," Khouryn said.

"Maybe," Aoth replied. He'd already finished with Jet's aquiline parts and started brushing his fur, first against the grain and then with it. The black steed's eyes were scarlet slits. "But I hate talking to zulkirs—or lords or whatever—and getting mired in their lies and intrigues."

Khouryn worked his way along Vigilant's limply outstretched wing. "Such is the lot of a sellsword leader. But I don't blame you. I'm not even sure I understand, from your account, what the palaver was fundamentally about."

"Nor do I. The brawl? Our presence in Luthcheq? Some rivalry between our employer and Lord Luthen? The hatred between Akanûl and Tymanther? Or between Chessenta and High Imaskar? Take your pick. It was all tangled up together."

Khouryn spotted a nit lurking at the base of a feather. He set down the fork, took up his tongs, pulled the larva out, and crushed it. "Why do all these people despise one another anyway?"

"Aside from recent transgressions, you mean? As I understand it, everything goes back a long way. The dragonborn and genasi fought when they lived wherever it is they used to live. When the Spellplague scooped them up and dumped them in Faerûn, they brought their quarrel along with them."

"Now, the Chessentans," Aoth continued, "started out as slaves of the old Imaskari Empire. Who were notable wizards, which accounts for the Chessentan hatred of magic. I've heard the new realm of High Imaskar isn't really the same animal as the old one. It doesn't keep slaves, for example. But the name is more or less the same, the people look the same, they have the same gift for sorcery, and that's close enough to stir up the Chessentans. They've been poking at the new Imaskari since the latter first announced their presence to the world. You could actually argue that the current 'piracy' is justified retaliation, although I wouldn't say so to the locals."

"In other words," said Khouryn, "it's all stupid."

"Well, of course *you'd* think so. Who ever heard of a dwarf holding a grudge?"

Khouryn strained unsuccessfully to stifle a chuckle. "Fair enough. It's simply that there's something to be said for fighting in a righteous cause."

Aoth swished his brush down the length of Jet's tail. "We did that in Thay and again in Impiltur, and look at the shape we're in."

"I recognize it's a luxury, not a necessity. Still, it would be nice if those eyes of yours had given you some insight into *why* Nicos and Luthen are at odds, or whether Zan-akar was telling the truth about anything."

The Spellplague had done more than extend Aoth's years. It had sharpened his sight to a preternatural degree. He could see in the dark and perceive the invisible. No illusion could deceive him. On rare occasions, he even saw hints of a man's true character or intentions, or portents of the future.

Aoth hesitated, scowled, and then said, "To be honest about it, when I first met Nicos, I glimpsed the form of a green dragon."

"What? What does that mean?"

"I have no idea. We can be reasonably sure there's no big green dragon living in Luthcheq, so it must have been symbolic, which is another way of saying it could have meant any damn thing. Maybe just that my three lieutenants were going to get involved with a couple of dragon*born*."

Khouryn tilted his head. "You talk like you didn't even bother to think about it. Since when do you discount the value of information, no matter how cryptic? How many times have I heard you say, 'Collect all the facts you can; any one of them could mean the difference between victory and defeat'?"

"In the field, yes. At a royal court, it's different. Knowing people's secrets is dangerous, and so is meddling in their business. In retrospect, I feel stupid for telling the war hero that Akanûl has ties to High Imaskar. I spoke without thinking."

"You may have earned a measure of her trust. Or gratitude."

Aoth grunted. "I suspect it takes more than that, and I certainly made an enemy of Zan-akar. All the more reason to keep our heads down, play constable with as little fuss as possible, and then head out to fight Threskel or the Imaskari as soon as Shala will allow it."

TWO

18–29 Ches, the Year of the Ageless One (1479 DR)

With his mail, shield, spear, and other weapons, Aoth looked like a warrior and had hoped the citizens of Luthcheq would take him for that and nothing more. But almost immediately they'd started whispering behind his back and making signs to avert the evil eye. He suspected that Luthen or Zan-akar had put out the word that he was actually a war-mage.

He stopped leading foot patrols thereafter. No point agitating the locals more than they were already. Instead, he and Jet had taken to monitoring the city from the sky.

An easterly wind carried them to the religious quarter, where the gilded dome of the temple of Waukeen, goddess of trade, gleamed at one end of a mall. At the other stood the colonnaded house of Amaunator, lord of the sun, with an enormous sundial out in front.

Drumming and chanting, Tchazzar cultists paraded past the instrument. Some carried crimson banners.

Others had combined forces to animate a dragon made of red cloth. Capering inside it, they made it weave back and forth in serpentine fashion.

At first no one seemed to mind. Then half a dozen priests in yellow robes strode forth from Amaunator's temple. The stout sunlord in the lead, his vestments trimmed with gold and amber, started haranguing the marchers.

"Fly lower," said Aoth. "Let's hear what he's saying."

Jet swooped and set down on the roof of the Red Knight's house, a comparatively small box of a building that, with its battlements and barbican, looked more like a fortress than a shrine. Aoth hoped the patron of strategists would forgive a fellow commander the intrusion.

Nobody mortal appeared to notice his descent. The sun priests, and the dragon cultists' reaction to them, had already captured everyone's attention.

"Dragons aren't gods!" insisted the chief sunlord, his voice raised so everyone could hear. "And your display, in these sacred precincts, is an affront to the true gods!"

"Tchazzar saved his people," replied the skinny adolescent girl at the head of the procession. She'd daubed scarlet symbols on her forehead and cheeks, and had a fervid, feverish cast to her expression. Someone had given her a fine vermilion mantle to throw on over the shabby garments beneath. "He also rose from the dead. That's what gods do. And now that we need him, he'll come back again. We only have to believe."

"Child, you don't understand these matters. You can't. You lack the education."

"I'm glad. Because I see that all learning does is blind you to the truth."

The high priest took a breath. "Put your faith in the Keeper of the Yellow Sun and the other powers of light. And in the war hero they've appointed to rule us. That's who will save you."

"When?" called a man with a pox-scarred face. "Threskel and High Imaskar and the filthy wizards are destroying us! What are your gods and Shala Karanok waiting on?"

"Perhaps," the cleric said, "they're waiting for their people to stop behaving in a manner that's both blasphemous and treasonous."

The marchers shouted back, jeering at him.

"My children," said the priest, "I tried to counsel you. As you refuse to heed me, I'll have to resort to more drastic measures."

He beckoned for the lesser sunlords to gather in. A couple hesitated or looked alarmed, but they all obeyed. Their master started chanting, and they joined in.

"They're not," said Jet in disbelief.

But apparently they were. Trying to perform some ritual of chastisement with the targets standing unrestrained just a few strides away. Did they imagine Tchazzar's worshipers would simply wait idly for them to finish?

If so, they were doomed to disappointment. The thin girl—the cultists' prophetess, apparently—shrilled, "Stop them!" She lunged forward, and the marchers surged after her.

Jet perceived what Aoth wanted through their psychic link, or else he simply recognized himself what was required. As he sprang into the air, he gave a screech that froze some of the folk below in their tracks. Aoth pointed the long spear that served him both as warrior's weapon and mage's staff, rattled off words of command, and cast a wall of leaping, crackling yellow flame between the cultists and the priests. That brought the rest of the rushing men to a sudden, stumbling halt. It startled the sunlords into falling silent too.

Then Jet made a couple of low passes over the crowd, like he was deciding whom to snatch up in his talons and devour. Scowling, Aoth tried to look equally intimidating.

When he judged that their little pantomime had done as much good as it was likely to, he had the griffon land on top of the sundial. Evidently it was just his day to take liberties with the property of the gods.

"Captain!" called the chief sunlord.

Aoth dismounted. "If anyone makes a move," he said, ostensibly to Jet but loud enough for everyone to hear, "kill him!" The griffon crouched and glared as if he'd like nothing better than to pounce over the blazing barrier and down into the marchers. Aoth then strode to the edge of the sundial and looked down at the man who'd hailed him.

"I'm Daelric Apathos," said the sunlord, "steward of the Keeper's house. Thank you for holding back the rabble."

To Aoth, the fellow sounded more stiff than grateful, but it seemed best to take the statement at face value. "That's why I'm here, Sunlord. To keep the peace."

"Hold them back for a few more moments, and my clergy and I will complete the malediction."

"That won't be necessary."

Daelric blinked. "I assure you, I only intend a mild rebuke. It won't be that much worse than the average sunburn."

"And I assure you, if you start praying again, I'll snuff the fire, climb back on my griffon, and leave you and the Church of Tchazzar to sort things out for yourselves."

The high priest sneered. "I should have known better than to expect piety from one of your kind. The war hero will hear how you denied me in my hour of need."

"I bet she will." Aoth paced to the front of the sundial. Peering out across the wall of hissing flame, still burning hot and bright with no fuel but magic to sustain it, he located the prophetess. "As long as I'm collecting names, I may as well get yours."

She drew herself up even straighter, as though to assert that she wasn't afraid. "Halonya."

"Well, Halonya, you and your friends go march somewhere else."

"It's our city as much as it is that priest's. We have the right to walk the street. Any street, including this one."

"I'm an officer of the watch, which means you have the right to walk where I say. Now go, or the next fires will drop right on your heads."

Halonya held his gaze for another moment, then nodded curtly. She pivoted and started to lead her fellow cultists away. They followed, but not without some glaring, spitting, and obscene gestures to demonstrate their dislike of Aoth.

The sunlords were more restrained about it. But their stony faces conveyed the same sentiment.

"This is nice," said Jet. "At least they agree on something."

* * * * *

Gaedynn spotted three lights shining close together in the dark street below. He sent Eider, his griffon, named for a love of swimming unusual among her kind, swooping lower.

The lanterns belonged to a patrol, but not one of the Brotherhood's. The men were locals. Their lights revealed an eviscerated corpse. A circle of spectators, some in their nightclothes, had assembled to gawk at it. A couple cried out when Eider touched down. The griffon gave them a disgusted look.

As Gaedynn dismounted, he caught the smells of spilled blood and waste. Judging from the fallen wooden bucket and the communal well just a stride or two away, the dead man had ventured out for water. The killer had left a green handprint on the brickwork surrounding the hole.

Gaedynn looked for the sergeant in charge. That appeared to be a blunt-featured man who was evidently putting on weight, since even with the bottom buckles left unfastened, his leather cuirass was too tight for his flabby body. His face pale in the lantern light, swallowing repeatedly, he stood and stared at the dead body.

"When did this happen?" Gaedynn asked.

The pudgy man shook his head. "Who knows?"

Gaedynn stooped to examine the remains. He'd spent most of his youth as a hostage among the elves of the Yuirwood. It had been an alarming experience at times, particularly when his father's continued misbehavior made his captors think they really ought to kill him in retaliation, or what was the point of having a hostage in the first place? But it had taught him woodcraft, and to him it looked like claws rather than a blade had ripped the victim. Which didn't necessarily mean that a human wasn't responsible for the crime.

Gaedynn rose and waved a hand at the gawkers. "Have you questioned them?"

"If any of them had seen the murderer, they'd be dead too."

"Not if the killer didn't see them," Gaedynn said. "Now, have you questioned them?"

"No."

"Well, someone should start, or at least make sure no one wanders off. The rest of us need to try to pick up the killer's trail. I'll look from the air . . ." He belatedly noticed the watchman's scowl. "What's wrong?"

"Maybe your flying beasts and fancy gear impress Nicos Corynian. But you're no better than us, and we don't take orders from you."

"My friend, I realize I'm not your commanding officer, and I would never presume to tell you how to proceed, except that you don't appear to *be* proceeding. And how will that look when you report to those who do command you?"

The sergeant somehow managed to look nettled and sheepish at the same time. "It's just . . . we're used to dead bodies, but not like this."

"I understand." Gaedynn glanced around, taking in the several streets and alleys snaking and forking away from the central point, then turned his gaze on the rest of the watchmen. "We'll need to split up to have any hope of catching the murderer."

"We don't all have lights," a watchman said.

"Then commandeer them," Gaedynn said. "Quickly! For all we know, the killer is only a few moments ahead of us."

And that, he realized, was what they were afraid of. No one actually wanted to catch up with the fiend. Not by himself and in the dark.

"The whoreson probably headed back to the wizards' quarter," said another man. "We'll have the best chance of spotting him if we all head in that direction."

"We have no idea where he's headed." Gaedynn turned back to

the sergeant. "But search as you think best. Just look *somewhere*, and we'll rendezvous back here."

He hurried back to Eider and swung himself into the saddle. The griffon trotted, lashed her wings, and sprang skyward.

Gaedynn laid an arrow on his bow and, guiding Eider with his knees, flew a spiral course away from the well. He looked for motion atop the roofs and in the air.

For a while he was optimistic about spotting it. As he understood matters, the sole witness claimed the killer had fled the scene of his first atrocity by traveling over the housetops, even if said witness wasn't clear whether he'd jumped like a squirrel or flown like a bird.

But all Gaedynn found were bats, owls, scurrying roof-dwelling rats, and an elderly astrologer leaning on a gnarled cane as he studied the moon and her trailing cloud of glittering tears. And when Eider had wheeled her way over a good quarter of the city, it was time to admit their quarry had eluded them.

He hoped the watchmen had had better luck. But he doubted it, and when he returned to the well, he found them loitering around empty-handed.

"Useless," sneered an onlooker to his companion, just loud enough for Gaedynn to overhear.

* * * * *

"We need to run them off," Randal said.

"Yes," and "Right," said some of the other boys.

But Theriseus asked, "Why?" Towheaded and gangly, not much good at games, he was just like that, always asking questions. Sometimes it made him seem clever, and sometimes stupid.

Either way, Randal had an answer for him, because he'd listened to his father talk—well, yell, really—about that very subject.

"They strut and push people around like they conquered the city or something. But they're just sellswords, which means they're just animals who kill for coin."

Theriseus shrugged. "That doesn't sound too different from the regular watch. They clubbed that one drunkard to death after he wouldn't put down the knife."

"Oh, it's different," Randal said. Even if he was vague on exactly how. "So, are you up to it, or are you too scared?"

"I'll help," Theriseus said, as Randal had known he would. The lanky blond boy might think a little differently than his fellows, but he prized his membership in the Black Wasps just as highly. In the rookeries where their families lived, if you weren't in a gang, you weren't anything. And you couldn't belong to the Wasps if you were scared to take a dare.

Randal led his fellows down an alley choked with slippery, ripe-smelling refuse. Up ahead, the passage met a street. Having studied their routine, he knew a sellsword patrol would march across the intersection in just a little while.

Sure enough, here came the clink of armor and the thump of feet striding in unison. The other Black Wasps pulled stones from their pockets and the bags and pouches on their belts.

Randal could go them one better because his father had taught him to use a sling, and he'd borrowed it from the chest where the old man kept it. And a sling could throw a stone *hard*. His father said it was a genuine weapon of war, although Randal suspected that had been truer in olden times than it was today.

The soldiers tramped into view. A dwarf with a spear in his hand

and some sort of axe strapped to his back was in the lead.

Randal's father said dwarves were as evil as wizards. They practiced the same sort of diabolical arts. So Randal whipped his rock at the small warrior, and his friends threw theirs too.

The missiles clattered on shields, helmets, and mail. Some of the sellswords staggered, although to Randal's disappointment nobody fell down.

"There they are!" said the dwarf. He reversed his grip on the spear—so he could strike with the butt, presumably. Then he and several of the human soldiers charged.

Randal and his friends turned and ran. He felt excited, not scared, because he was sure they'd get away. They weren't carrying the weight of armor, and they knew the back alleys of the ropemakers' precinct like no outsider ever would.

They rounded several turns, and then he glanced back. The sellswords were nowhere in sight. He waved the hand with the sling over his head and gasped out that the others should stop.

Everybody grinned and, once they caught their breaths, slapped their comrades on the back. Even Theriseus, who also asked, "What now?"

"What do you think?" answered Randal, pushing sweaty hair back from his forehead. "The same again!"

They sneaked through the alleys, staged a second ambush, and once again escaped. If anything, the new assault was even more exhilarating, yet still not entirely satisfactory. Because even after two volleys, some of the armored warriors were bruised and bloodied, but every one of them was still on his feet. Surely the sling could do better. In practice, it had smashed chips loose from a stone wall.

"Once more," Randal said.

"Are you sure?" Theriseus asked. "This time they'll be expecting us."

"It doesn't matter," Randal said. "We're smarter and faster than they are." And that really did seem to be the case. It made you wonder how these Brotherhood of the Griffon ever won a battle.

He and the other Wasps crept through the narrow, shadowed space between two tenements. Up ahead, the first rank of outlanders prowled into view. Randal kissed his stone and offered a curt, silent prayer to Loviatar, goddess of punishment, for luck, then let the missile fly.

His target clapped a hand to his eye. Blood welled between the soldier's fingers, and then he pitched forward.

Randal whooped. He and the other Wasps whirled to flee, then faltered. Somehow the dwarf and three of his men had sneaked up right behind them.

It would be useless to turn back around, because the rest of the sellswords were blocking the other end of the passage. All the Wasps could do was try to dart by the dwarf and his allies.

Theriseus and another boy made it. The outlanders beat others to the ground. Some swung the same sort of truncheons as the regular watch. The rest struck and jabbed with the shafts of their spears. It seemed unfair that they wielded the long weapons so nimbly in the crowded space.

Randal faked left, then lunged right, but the sellsword in front of him wasn't fooled. He kept himself in the way, dropping his cudgel and snatching a long, thin dagger from his belt.

He and Randal slammed together. A sort of shock jolted Randal. His legs gave way and dumped him on his back in the dirt. He heard a rattling, whistling sound. Something wet was in his throat and mouth, choking him, and he coughed a glob of it out.

The dwarf discarded his spear and shield, kneeled down, and pressed his hands against Randal's torso. Randal, whose thoughts seemed murky and slow, realized the human sellsword had stabbed him, and the dwarf—the evil, magic-loving dwarf!—was trying to stanch the bleeding.

"Curse it!" snarled the dwarf. "They're just boys. How do you think the town will react to this?"

"That's the little bastard who put Fodek's eye out," said the warrior gripping the bloody blade. "He had a sling, and a sling is a deadly weapon."

As he retched more blood, Randal was glad that his father had been right about something.

* * * * *

Jhesrhi tossed and turned until she couldn't bear it anymore. Then she cursed, rose from her narrow, sagging bed, winced at the chill that pervaded her room, and dressed quickly.

Now what? The shabby little house was silent except for the snores of one of the family who had billeted her at the war hero's command. Jhesrhi hesitated to busy herself inside their home for fear of waking them. Her presence was enough of an inconvenience without that.

But the only alternative was to go outside, and the prospect made her mouth go dry and her fingers tremble. And then she hated herself for her fear.

Luthcheq was a genuinely dangerous place despite all the Brotherhood was trying to do to keep the lid on. And it despised her kind. But she wasn't a helpless child anymore. She was a master wizard and veteran soldier who'd survived the horrors of Thay itself, and she wouldn't let this miserable cesspit daunt her.

She put on her tabard, wrapped herself in her cloak, and picked up her blackwood staff with its inlaid golden runes. Then she took a deep breath and opened the door.

Scar, her griffon, slept curled beneath an overhang on the side of the house. She felt an urge to wake the steed and go flying, but she realized that would be a way of hiding just like cringing inside the house. And she was done cringing. She meant to walk the streets all by herself until they didn't frighten her anymore.

She set forth beneath a brilliant scatter of stars that made the shuttered grime and decay of the wizards' quarter seem even sadder. The iron cap on the butt of her staff thumped almost inaudibly against the frozen mud. She asked the wind to warn her of anyone moving around outdoors anywhere nearby, and it whispered that it would.

And after another heartbeat or two, it did. It didn't speak in any mortal tongue or even think in mortal concepts, but after years of practice, Jhesrhi had no difficulty understanding it.

And she liked what it had to say. Because while it might be a sad commentary on human nature, one effective remedy for fear was instilling a dose of it in someone else.

The wind led her to a narrow three-story house at the edge of the wizards' precinct. Two dark figures were just climbing out a gable window.

Some might have thought it odd that the burglars of a town that supposedly feared mages would choose them for their victims. But the skilled professionals of Luthcheq's thieves' guild likely knew which residents of the quarter wielded true power and which only possessed enough to turn them into outcasts. They also knew that the city's homegrown watchmen rarely investigated crimes against wizards with any particular zeal.

Standing unnoticed in the darkness, Jhesrhi was eager to strike. But she recognized that a three-story fall could kill or cripple a man. So she waited for the burglars to climb partway down the wall before telling the wind to gust hard enough to knock them from their perches.

One of the thieves squawked as he fell. They both thudded down hard, lay still for a moment, then started clambering to their feet.

Jhesrhi murmured a charm, twirled two fingers in a circle, and wrapped herself in a shroud of silvery light. It ought to turn a thrown dagger or a dart from a blowpipe, but she mainly wanted it for the glow. She knew that with her willowy frame, amber eyes, tawny skin, and golden tresses—often stirred by a breeze that no one else could feel—she cut a reasonably impressive figure. Perhaps impressive enough to persuade a pair of robbers to surrender without any fuss, provided they could see her clearly, along with a manifestation of her power.

But no. They turned and ran, and she realized she was glad. Now she had a reason to knock them around a little more.

She leveled her staff, and a pair of blue-white beams leaped from the tip, diverging to catch each thief in the back. They staggered and fell.

She walked closer as, shaking uncontrollably, they tried to stand up again. "You aren't badly hurt *yet,*" she said, her aura of protection fading, "but my next spell will freeze you to the marrow."

"F-f-f-filthy w-witch," said the thief on the right, a scrawny specimen with a black goatee, a sharp nose, and the hint of cropped ears just visible inside his cowl.

"I guess not everyone can be as worthy and upright as the two of you," she answered. "Now, did you hurt anyone inside the house?"

"N-no."

"Lucky for you. So this is what's going to happen. You're going to drop your weapons and return your plunder, and then I'm going to march you off to jail."

At first it happened just that way. The burglars were sullen, but she thought she had them properly cowed. Still, she maintained a safe distance between herself and them, and stayed watchful lest they spin around to rush her or simply try to run.

They did neither. But when they passed beyond the confines of the wizards' quarter, the knave with the cropped ears abruptly shouted, "Help us!"

A dozen figures pivoted in their direction. Intent on her prisoners, Jhesrhi hadn't quite realized how many people were out roaming that particular section of street, nor was she certain why. Maybe there was a tavern or festhall nearby.

"It's all right," she said. "I'm an officer of the watch. These two wretches tried to rob a house, and I'm going to lock them up."

"She's a wizard!" said the bearded thief. "Just look at the staff! She attacked us for no reason, and she means to feed us to her demons!"

"I am a wizard," Jhesrhi said, "but also a member of the watch." She pulled open her cloak to display her tabard. "See?"

"That wasn't there a moment ago!" cried the thief. "It's an illusion! She's making you see it!"

The onlookers muttered to one another.

"That's ridiculous," Jhesrhi said. She flicked her fingers, and the wind moaned and blew back the thief's hood, revealing his mutilated ears. "You can see that this rogue has faced the war hero's justice twice already."

The thief peered around wildly. "What is she talking about? What did she do to me?"

Jhesrhi had to admit it was a good imitation of confusion. But she thought she'd demonstrated her credentials and the trickster's duplicity to any reasonable person's satisfaction, and despite the city's prejudice against mages, she expected the bystanders to lose interest and turn away.

They didn't. In fact, though it was difficult to be certain in the dark, it looked like their expressions had hardened. It belatedly occurred to her that her demonstration of her powers, petty and harmless though it had been, might have heightened their mistrust.

A woman bigger than most men shouldered a man aside as she stepped to the front of the crowd. Judging from her buckler and her short, heavy cleaver of a sword, she might have been a member of Luthcheq's underworld too, or conceivably even a sellsword. "Let these fellows go," she said in a startlingly sweet soprano voice.

"I told you," Jhesrhi said, "they're robbers, I belong to the watch, and it's my duty to turn them over for judgment."

"If you are a part of the watch, you shouldn't be. Not when your kind are skulking around murdering decent people. And we're not going to let you take these lads off to who knows where, and then maybe *they* turn up torn to scraps before the night is through."

"If that's what you're worried about," said Jhesrhi, "you can tag along and watch me hand them over."

"Don't!" said the thief. "For your own sakes! For all we know, there are more of them lurking in the dark! She could lead you into a trap!"

"Oh please," sighed Jhesrhi, addressing herself to the crowd. "Surely you people know where the guard station is. It's just a couple of blocks farther on."

"Who's to say they'll do justice there?" demanded a dandy with a rapier at his hip, a mail glove on his off hand to catch and hold an opponent's blade, and a brooch adorned with a red wyrm pinning his cape. "The folk in charge of the watch—and the folk over them—are stupid or worse. That's why they can't catch the Green Hand. That's why the realm is falling apart."

"I think," said the enormous woman to Jhesrhi, "you'd better let these fellows go and slink back to where you belong."

Not moving her head, just her eyes—she didn't want to appear apprehensive—Jhesrhi glanced up and down the street. There had to be a watch patrol somewhere in the vicinity, but none was in sight.

"The thieves are going to the guard station," she said. "And if you people don't want to join them in their cell, you'll disper—"

A clay flowerpot smashed at her feet, dashing shards, dirt, and the twiggy, leafless remains of a dead plant across the ground. Someone had thrown it from an upper-story window.

Startled, she recoiled a step. Her prisoners bolted. She pivoted and pointed her staff at them. The huge woman lunged and cocked her fist.

Jhesrhi glimpsed the threat from the corner of her eye. She dodged and the punch only glanced across her cheek, although that was enough to sting and to infuriate her as well.

She jabbed the head of her staff into the big woman's stomach and spat a word of command. A burst of force like the kick of a mule flung her attacker back and dumped her on her rump.

But by then, the dandy's rapier was whispering clear of its scabbard. He extended his arm and charged.

Jhesrhi jabbered rhyming words. Sleep claimed her assailant, and his momentum smacked him down on his belly.

Still, that wasn't the end of it. The huge woman clambered up and drew her sword. With fists clenched or with knives and cudgels in hand, the other meddlers spread out to flank the object of their hatred. More missiles showered from overhead.

Jhesrhi raised her staff high and cried out to the wind. Howling, it exploded out from her in all directions, like she was a bonfire shedding a tempest instead of heat and light. Her attackers reeled, unable to make headway. Some fell down. The missiles raining from the windows blew off course.

Now she had to decide what to do next. The gale wouldn't last forever. She surveyed her adversaries, and the answer came to her.

She snarled an incantation in an Abyssal dialect and jerked her staff through short, stabbing passes. Hate buttressed her will and lent additional power to the magic taking form around her, swirling green fumes that stank like carrion.

Because she'd hated Chessenta for her entire adult life, and now she knew she'd been right to do so. Certainly she had every right to despise the idiots before her, brutes and bullies every one.

She was almost at the end of the incantation before something—perhaps the pure concentration required to perform a complex spell with the necessary precision—cooled her fury a little. Then she remembered that she hadn't gone to war, and that her employers didn't consider these folk to be their enemies. She mustn't slaughter them wholesale for fear of repercussions.

Even then, it was difficult to alter the spell so close to completion.

The magic was eager to manifest the pattern the opening phrases had defined, and the final words were flowing automatically. Straining, she regained control of her tongue, then recited a line that completed the conjuration—but in an attenuated form, like music played an octave lower.

With the last of its strength, the wind she'd made caught the malodorous vapor seething around her and blasted it into the faces of her foes. Those who had somehow remained on their feet doubled over or collapsed, and then they all started puking their guts out.

The sickness wouldn't kill them. The diluted poison was too weak. But they were likely to wish it would.

She tried to enjoy their misery, but she couldn't. Except for their retching, the street suddenly seemed too quiet and too empty. At first glance, she didn't see any watchers peeking down at her from the windows or the rooftops, but she felt the pressure of their stares.

Her instincts told her what was coming, and she retreated toward the wizards' precinct. She'd only gone a few yards when, as though evoked by a spell potent as any at her command, the first shadowy figures swarmed out of the doorways. Her heart thumping, she whispered a message for the wind to carry to her comrades.

* * * * *

Working as fast as they could, Khouryn and his spearmen hauled furniture out of the houses—or just tossed it out the windows—then piled it across the street to make a barricade. The householders with their tattooed palms stood watching in distress, either because they disliked seeing their meager belongings so mistreated or because they understood the reason for it.

If it was the latter, then that made them shrewder than some of the sellswords. "I don't think anything is going to happen," grumbled Numer, a beak-nosed fellow with a limp, a missing finger, dozens of scars, and a clinking collection of "lucky" amulets that never left his grubby neck. "We're doing all this work for nothing."

"If Jhesrhi says it's going to happen," Khouryn answered, "then it will. Didn't you see the crowds gathering as we rushed over here?"

"I've seen plenty of crowds since we came to this stinking town. Marching around with their dragon banners or whatever. Doesn't mean they're going to do anything."

Khouryn scowled. "Just keep stacking."

They had time to make the barricade a little stronger. Then a mob surged into the mouth of the street. Forged by All-Father Moradin for life underground, dwarves saw well in the dark, and Khouryn had no difficulty making out the faces of the newcomers. He almost wished it were otherwise. He didn't like the wildness, the edge of hysteria, that he found there.

"Present!" he snapped, and, acting as one, his men leveled their spears over the top of the makeshift fortification. Khouryn hoped the martial precision of the action—and the rows of rock-steady, razor-edged points reflecting Selûne's light—would give the insurgents pause.

He climbed up on top of the barricade. "You see how it is," he called. "We're trained men-at-arms, and we're ready for you. Go home, or you'll wish you had."

"Give us the wizards!" someone shouted back.

"Go home," Khouryn repeated.

"The spears don't matter!" cried another voice. "There are only a few of them, compared to all of us! Just get them!"

The mob didn't respond with an eager shout. Instead, it gave an odd collective sigh, as though accepting a wearisome chore. But then it charged.

"Clubs!" Khouryn bellowed, because the spears had been a bluff. Aoth said they had to protect the wizards' precinct without killing too many of those who hoped to butcher the residents. Khouryn understood the reason, but even given the Brotherhood's advantages of training, discipline, and armor, it was going to make the job a lot harder than it should have been.

He jumped back down behind the barricade, unsheathed his truncheon, and settled his shield more comfortably on his arm. Then the first howling rioters tried to scramble over the barricade. It was tricky for a dwarf to fight behind an obstruction as tall as he was, but he stabbed up with the end of his club and caught an attacker in the mouth. Broken teeth pattered down on his hand.

* * * * *

To his irritation, Gaedynn's archers were still climbing onto the rooftops when the mob—or mobs, really, since they didn't seem to be acting in a coordinated fashion—converged on the wizards' precinct from three directions. The bowmen could have formed up on the street, but then it would have been difficult to obtain a clear shot at the rioters.

A pair of hands reached up from below the eaves to grip the edge of the roof, and then, as the sellsword started to clamber up, the left one slipped. Gaedynn dived down the pitch and grabbed the loose, flailing arm, risking a fall himself to keep his man from plummeting.

Well . . . boy, actually, for when he pulled the lummox up, it turned out to be Yuirmidd, a half-grown, pimply youth who'd joined the Brotherhood during their brief time in Aglarond. As usual, Yuirmidd wore a tawdry assortment of trinkets in seeming imitation of his superior's fondness for adornment.

"How difficult is it to climb onto a roof?" Gaedynn asked.

"I'm a bowman, not a mountain goat," Yuirmidd replied.

Gaedynn suspected he might be the model for the lad's impudence as well, and he had yet to make up his mind on how he felt about it. "You're not much of anything yet. Perhaps after a few more years' campaigning, in the unlikely event you live that long."

"It's starting!" someone shouted.

Gaedynn scrambled up and looked to see for himself. Sure enough, rioters were rushing the barricades Khouryn's spearmen had erected across the streets and alleys leading into the precinct. It was an idiotic, suicidal thing to do—but then, this was the City of Madness, wasn't it?

Aimed in a sensible way, a few volleys of arrows would do wonders to blunt the mob's enthusiasm. Such a tactic would also slaughter them by the dozen.

"If it looks like they're breaking through anywhere," Gaedynn shouted, "kill them! If you see someone who looks like a ringleader, kill him! Otherwise, discourage them! Put your shafts into the ground in front of their feet or the walls above their heads!"

"You're joking," growled Orrag, a half-orc with the hulking frame and jutting lower canines characteristic of his kind.

"Just do it." Gaedynn nocked an arrow, pulled the fletching back to his ear, and let it fly. It punched deep into a rioter's torso, and he dropped.

"You shot that one," Orrag said, his tone accusatory.

"He had a torch." Gaedynn laid another shaft on his bow. "If we let them set fire to the wizards' precinct, they win. Now, are you going to start fighting, or are you waiting for the captain himself to pay you a call and humbly beseech your assistance?"

* * * * *

Straddling Scar's back, Jhesrhi wheeled above the wizards' precinct. Other griffon riders soared to either side.

Most of the rioters probably hadn't even noticed the sellswords swooping and gliding through the darkness overhead, and the vast majority had no bows or crossbows anyway. The aerial cavalry were relatively safe.

Jhesrhi couldn't say the same for her comrades on the ground, repelling wave after wave of attackers. Is this my fault? she wondered. If I'd known the right words to say to calm those idiots in the street, could all this have been avoided?

But it was useless to speculate, especially when she had work to do. She hurled spells into the masses of rioters, forcing them to keel over fast asleep or snaring them in gigantic spiderwebs.

* * * * *

Before the mob arrived, Khouryn had hurried from barricade to barricade, overseeing all the warriors under his command. Once the enemy appeared, it had been necessary to stay in one place, even though that limited him to directing the men in that location.

Now he wasn't leading anyone at all. He was too busy catching blows on his shield and swinging his club, and couldn't spare a glance or a thought for anything but the next attacker rushing in at him.

Someone on his right yelled, "Watch out!" The men on either side lurched backward, and a bench fell off the top of the barricade to crack down beside his boot. Both layers of the Brotherhood's defense—the tangled mass of furniture and the lines of sellswords behind it—were giving way before the ferocious pressure of the mob.

It shouldn't have been happening. Not to expert soldiers. But Aoth had forbidden them to fight to best effect, and perhaps the Foehammer had seen fit to remind them that in battle, nothing was certain.

Dripping sweat, his chest heaving, Khouryn sucked in a breath to bellow new orders. But just then, the barricade shattered. Stools and tables tumbled and slid, knocking soldiers off balance and fouling their legs as they tottered backward.

A wooden box with brass corner guards crashed down on Khouryn's head. Then he was on his hands and knees amid a scatter of furniture, with a fierce pain under his steel and leather helmet and no recollection of falling down. The mob was racing at him, and his men were nowhere in sight. Because they'd dropped back. Presumably only a couple of paces, but they might as well be sailing the Trackless Sea for all the good they were likely to do him in the next few heartbeats.

He heaved himself to his feet. It made his head throb, and he gasped.

The stains on her leather armor reeking of vomit, a truly enormous woman cut at Khouryn with a short, heavy, single-edged sword. He blocked with his shield, tried to riposte with his truncheon, and discovered his hand was empty. He must have dropped the weapon when he fell.

His opponent attacked again. A well-dressed man armed with a rapier and a mail gauntlet maneuvered to flank him. Other foes, mere shadows in the dark and confusion, were surging forward too.

Khouryn kept warding himself and snatched a dagger from his belt. He would much rather have grabbed his urgrosh, but it took two hands to wield. If he discarded his shield, his foes would kill him in the naked instant before the axe was ready.

They stood a fair chance of doing that anyway, but a warrior could only select what seemed the proper strategy, then fight his best. He sidestepped to keep the enemy from encircling him and looked for an opening that would enable him to shift in close and use the knife on someone.

Behind him, two voices roared. Lightning flared above his head. It crackled over the faces of the big woman and her comrade with the rapier, charring flesh and making them shudder in place. A blast of white vapor painted other rioters with frost.

All the foes in the immediate vicinity halted, either because they'd just been hurt or simply because they were startled. It gave Khouryn a chance to unlimber the urgrosh and retreat.

Which put him between the two dragonborn who'd just spit their breath weapons at his assailants. From the white studs pierced into their faces, he recognized Medrash and Balasar from the tavern brawl.

He wondered what they were doing here, but now was not the time to ask. He had a battle to salvage. "Make a new line!" he shouted to his men. "And get out your blades!"

* * * * *

Peering down from Jet's back, Aoth cursed. One barricade had already given way, although the Brothers who'd manned it were still fighting to hold the rioters back. Another was on the verge of collapse. And there was no sign of any of Luthcheq's homegrown watchmen. Evidently they'd decided to sit out this particular confrontation.

If the insurgents got inside the perimeter of the wizards' quarter, they'd be impossible to stop. They'd loot, burn, and murder the residents at will.

"And so," said Jet, discerning his thoughts, "you know what you have to do."

"Yes, damn it."

He'd kept the griffons out of the fight for one reason. No matter how well trained the beasts were, if you took them into combat, they were going to kill. But because they were so frightening, they might only need to slaughter a few rioters before the rest turned tail. And in any case, the situation on the ground suddenly looked uncertain enough that he was no longer willing to trust the outcome to half measures.

He unstrapped the ram's-horn bugle from his saddle, lifted it to his lips, and blew the signal to attack. Jet screeched, communicating the same message to his kindred.

* * * * *

The sellswords were now wielding spears, axes, and swords. Morric would still have fought them if necessary, but he was glad it wasn't. Once the barricade and their initial battle lines had broken, the soldiers had formed a couple of ragged little circles to keep anyone from striking them from behind.

As far as self-protection went, it was a sound tactic, but it left an opening between the sellswords and the row of houses on the right-hand side of the alley. People were scurrying through the gap, and Morric figured he might as well be one of them. The outlanders were scum—that went without saying—but why waste time on them when it was mages he'd come to kill?

A fool in a tavern had once jeered that Morric didn't even know why he hated wizards. He answered the taunt with his fists and boots, but after he sobered up, he realized he could have used his tongue if he'd wished. For of course he knew.

Wizards trafficked with demons. It was the source of their power. They spread disease and misfortune to amuse their evil masters. They used their secret arts to control all the merchants and guilds and steal a dragon's share of all the coin, and as a result, a simple man couldn't earn a decent wage.

They must be spying and otherwise aiding Chessenta's enemies too. Nothing else could explain why the news from the north and east was so bad, even though the war hero's troops were the bravest in all Faerûn.

And obviously, the Green Hand slayings were the vilest crimes of all and made retaliation a matter of simple self-preservation. The honest people of Luthcheq had to get the mages before the mages got the rest of them.

Morric had noticed arrows falling from overhead, and the fear of them kept his head down and his shoulders hunched as he darted through the opening. But no shaft whizzed out of the dark to pierce him—or any of his companions either.

The bowmen must be looking elsewhere.

Which meant they'd missed their chance at Morric. Once he broke into a mage's house, no sellsword would even know where he was, let alone have any hope of stopping him. He glanced around, deciding where to start—and then, above his head, something shrieked. Shadows swept across the ground. He froze.

A winged beast plunged down in front of him, right on top of one of his fellow avengers. The creature's talons stabbed deep into its victim's body, its weight smashed him into a crumpled heap, and he died without making a sound.

The griffon flapped its wings and leaped onto a second man. That one did manage a truncated yelp, but only because he saw death hurtling at him. The beast ripped him to pieces a heartbeat later.

As it did, Morric noticed the armored warrior on its back. In other circumstances, the sellsword likely would have seemed fearsome, or at least formidable. Astride his eagle-headed steed, he was inconsequential.

Morric's adz slipped from his grip. He'd brought it to serve as his weapon. Still, now that he was numb and slow with dread, it didn't seem to matter that he'd dropped it. He couldn't imagine such a puny instrument hurting the griffon.

But it mattered in a different sort of way. The adz clanked when it hit the ground, and the noise made the creature's head with its gory, dripping beak snap around in his direction.

Morric still couldn't move. Or scream. He needed to, but the cry felt jammed in his clogged throat and dry mouth.

The griffon gathered itself to pounce. Then a madman ran at its flank with a leveled spear. The beast spun to defend itself.

When the beast turned away, it broke Morric out of his paralysis. It occurred to him that he could try to help the man with the spear as the fellow had saved him, but the thought was just a chain of words that scarcely even seemed to have a meaning. He whirled and ran.

Others did the same. Tripping and trampling over fallen bodies he couldn't see, but only felt thrashing beneath him, he struggled to bull his way through the press. A griffon dived and slammed a man to the earth. The creature was almost close enough for Morric to reach out and touch, and as it ripped its victim apart, warm blood and gobs of flesh spattered him.

He was so frantic to avoid the griffons that he nearly flung himself onto the point of an outlander's sword. But he somehow twisted away from the thrust and floundered onward, and then people weren't packed together quite as tightly. He could run faster, and he did.

He started feeling his exhaustion not long afterward. Still, he wouldn't allow himself to halt until the wizards' precinct was several blocks behind and he'd separated himself from everyone else who'd fled the battle.

Then, legs leaden, heart hammering, he flopped down in an alley and wheezed. He remembered the man who'd saved him—and whom he in turn had abandoned—and felt a pang of shame.

But curse it, it wasn't his fault the wretch was dead! It was the fault of the despicable Thayans and the war hero who'd given them authority. Who'd sent them to slaughter her own people when they'd risen up to cleanse Luthcheq of a canker.

THREE

30 Ches–6 Tarsakh
the Year of the Ageless One (1479 DR)

The rain pattered down from a gray sky. It made the task of picking up bodies and tossing them onto carts even more cheerless, if that was possible.

Since she was an officer, Jhesrhi didn't have to dirty her hands with such labor. Since she didn't have any men under her direct command, she didn't even have to supervise it. But she watched it for a time, then stalked back to her billet and stuffed her grimoires and spare clothing into her saddlebags.

Then she hauled them and her tack to the overhang at the side of the house. So named for the long, livid ridge that marked his flank from feathers to fur, Scar spotted the gear and knew they were going to fly. He gave an eager rasp and leaped to his feet.

And Jhesrhi faltered. Because while the griffon was hers in one sense, in another he belonged to the Brotherhood. Did she have the right to take him away with her, particularly when, in the wake of the

Thayan campaign, the pride was so diminished?

She scowled and set her burdens down while she weighed the question. Scar padded over and nuzzled her, almost hard enough to knock her off balance. He was expressing affection, but also urging her to get moving.

As she should have. For a moment later, someone whistled a jaunty tune, a song whose lyrics she considered particularly tasteless and offensive. Looking like he'd enjoyed a full night's sleep and like the rain had no power to plaster down his feathered copper hair or otherwise mar his debonair appearance, Gaedynn sauntered toward her from the street.

He glanced at the little pile of her possessions. "Ready for a change of scene?"

"War is one thing, but I don't have the stomach for this."

"Just because we killed civilians? At least they were Chessentan civilians. And I was under the impression that you detest this place."

"I do. But . . ."

He arched a trimmed eyebrow. "But . . . ?"

"If I'd handled myself better when those meddlers accosted my prisoners and me, this wouldn't have happened."

"Yes, I agree with you there."

She blinked. "What?"

He shrugged. "Admittedly, some might compare last night's unpleasantness to an avalanche. Given your intimacy with the ruling spirits of earth and stone, you no doubt understand better than I how at the start of such an event, one rock bumps another, and that one jostles a third, until an entire mountainside is falling. Here in Luthcheq, the various pebbles were the Green Hand murders, the news of pillage and piracy, the resulting disruption of commerce, the bad blood between dragonborn and genasi—and what have you—all knocking into one another to create a surge of violence that inevitably targeted the outcasts Chessenta loves to hate.

"In this analogy," he continued, "your little confrontation in the street was only one pebble among many. Still, it was your duty to pluck it from the air before it could do any harm, and you failed."

She sighed. "I know what you're doing. You want me to say that if that particular pebble hadn't triggered the avalanche, another one would have. But I don't know that for certain. What I do know is that someone else—someone like you—could have sent those louts on their way with cogent words and a jest."

"Oh, undoubtedly. After all, I am exceptionally charming, and clever too. But Aoth didn't hire you for your ability to placate the dull and ignorant. As I recall, it has more to do with your gift for knocking down walls and setting enemy troops on fire."

"No matter why he hired me, I'm a liability in this place."

"Perhaps. Or perhaps it's Aoth who's the liability to you and me."

"What?"

"He was a great war leader once, but his time has passed. Look at the state the Brotherhood is in, torn to shreds and reduced to doing this dreary job."

"You know the mission we undertook in Thay was absolutely necessary, and that no one else in the East could have done it as well."

"What about Impiltur?"

"Impiltur was just bad luck."

Gaedynn grinned. "And when a sellsword leader's luck sours, nothing else matters. His lieutenants have no choice but to desert him before he leads them to their deaths. Or before their collaboration in his debacles so tarnishes their own reputations that, like him, they ultimately become unemployable."

"You've threatened to leave before. You never do."

"Which is not to say I never will. Last night's fight upset me as it did you, albeit for a more sensible reason. We were in far more danger than was necessary, because Aoth refused to let us fight to best effect."

"You know the reason why."

"Yes. But I consider it insufficient. And why shouldn't I leave if I see fit? I don't owe Aoth anything."

"Well, I . . ." She took a breath. "Once again, you're trying to maneuver me into saying what you want me to say."

"To the contrary. I'm agreeing with you. Telling you that if you desert, I'm inclined to go with you."

It felt like something twisted in her chest. "We both know that wouldn't work."

"But if you go alone, won't you *be* alone? It's always appeared to me that the Brotherhood is your only home, and as you demonstrated last night, you don't have much of a knack for making new friends."

She lashed a hand like she was batting away a gnat. "All right! I'll stay! Just stop prattling at me!"

"Whatever you say. I respect your judgment, of course."

Her fingers tightened on her staff. "Gaedynn . . ."

To her surprise, his face became more open, his smile less superior and teasing. "Lady, for what it's worth, I truly do think the company will climb out of this cesspit it's in eventually, just as I know Aoth needs you to make that happen." His smile crooked into a smirk. "Instead of leaving, you should hold his nose in the hive for a bigger share of the spoils."

* * * * *

Pacing through the tall doorway at Nicos's side, Aoth didn't see any dragonborn, genasi, or other nonhumans standing amid the bronze and marble martial sculptures. Still, Shala Karanok's hall was more crowded than on his previous visit, and none of the occupants looked happy to see him.

When Aoth and Nicos reached the proper spot, they halted and bowed. "My lord," the war hero said. "Captain." Her voice was ice.

"Majesty," replied Aoth and Nicos in unison.

"Seventy-eight of my people are dead," said the woman on the throne.

"Don't take that for the final tally," said Aoth. "A couple more corpses will turn up someplace, and a few more of the wounded will die of their hurts."

Shala scowled, and Nicos shot him a warning glance. But he intended to be businesslike and unapologetic. He had a hunch it would be a bad idea to accept any blame or show any hint of weakness.

"Are you *proud* of your score?" demanded a familiar masculine voice. Aoth looked around and saw Daelric in his jeweled yellow robes. The stout high priest of Amaunator stood at the forefront of what appeared to be a group of the city's ranking clerics, clad for the most part in regalia as costly as his own.

"I'm proud," said Aoth, "that my men did their job efficiently and with a considerable degree of self-control. I assure you, our 'score' could have been much higher."

"The fact remains," the sunlord replied, "you slaughtered dozens of good men who only wanted to purge the city of evil."

Nicos snorted. "That's a pretty epitaph for a pack of mad dogs."

Aoth returned his gaze to Shala. "Majesty, you and Lord Nicos both told me my job is to maintain order with a special eye to protecting the residents of the wizards' precinct. I did it. What's the problem?"

Shala's eyes narrowed. Aoth braced himself for an outburst. But in the end, the war hero chose to overlook his bluntness—his insolence, some would say—and simply answer his question.

"In my mind, your task was to prevent a riot from starting in the first place. Perhaps that was unrealistic. But in the aftermath, I find I'm the ruler who set vicious sellswords under the command of an evil war-mage and a witch on her own subjects. And why? To protect other devil-worshiping wizards. To shield the Green Hand murderer himself."

"Majesty," Nicos said, "I'm sure most people understand that your agents did only what was necessary. Had they done less, all Luthcheq might have burned."

"Some people understand that," Shala said, "but as we speak, there are hundreds of Tchazzar cultists marching in the streets. Now, don't mistake me. I revere the Red Dragon as much as anyone. But it's bad to have the common people praying for the return of a long-lost savior because they think their current lords are hopelessly incompetent and corrupt. It's bad for every one of us assembled in this hall."

Luthen stepped forth from between a pair of his fellow courtiers. "Indeed it is, Majesty. Fortunately, I believe we can fix the problem."

"How?" Shala asked.

"For starters, get rid of the sellswords. We've already discussed some of the reasons why allowing any noble to maintain such a force in the capital is a poor idea. Now we see that the Thayans' swaggering, bullying presence enflames the populace like that of an army of occupation."

Aoth took a deep breath. "My lord, any fair-minded person would agree that some bad luck and unavoidable friction notwithstanding, my troops have acquitted themselves admirably in Luthcheq. But we'd be happy to go to the border or the coast and help Chessenta fight its enemies."

Luthen gave his head a little shake. "I'm not talking about reassigning you, Captain. I'm talking about discharging you and throwing you out of the realm. That's the least it will take to satisfy those whose kin your griffons tore apart. And Chessenta doesn't need mages and ruffians to stand tall against its foes."

"Indeed," the sunlord said.

Aoth could joyfully have tossed a thunderbolt or a barrage of ice at both of them. If the Brotherhood had to move on under these circumstances, it would drain their coffers and further blemish their reputation. And without another offer of employment, where could they even go? Nowhere the local authorities wouldn't view them as a threat—glorified marauders hoping to live by banditry and extortion.

"Majesty—," he began.

Shala ignored him. "What else do you recommend?" she said to Luthen.

"Arrest, try, and execute the residents of the wizards' quarter," the noble said. "If not all, at least some."

"For what?" Nicos asked.

"Who cares?" Luthen answered. "They're mages, so we know that each and every one of them has done evil deeds. And it will give the common people what they want. You never know, we might even get lucky and burn the Green Hand killer."

Nicos looked to Shala. "Majesty, you directed me to bring Captain Fezim to the capital because 'even wizards deserve justice.'"

"And it was a sentiment worthy of a war hero," Luthen said. "But the situation has worsened since then, and Your Majesty must weigh the interests of a few"—he waved a meaty hand as though trying to pluck the proper term from the air—"deviants against the welfare of the realm as a whole."

"All right," Nicos rapped, "let's do that. Let's keep our eyes on what's happening throughout Chessenta, and not just here in the city. The Great Bone Wyrm and the Imaskari are pressing us hard, and contrary to Lord Luthen's assertion, we need wizards to help stem the tide. The same wizards he wants to condemn and kill!"

Luthen made a spitting sound. "So you'd strengthen our armies by bringing the depraved and degenerate into the ranks."

"Yes," Nicos said, "if you insist on putting it that way. Our armies have always used sorcery when necessary. With proper supervision, of course. Just look at our history!"

"Magic gives an army a big edge," said Aoth. "Too big to ignore if you can get it. You Chessentans pride yourself on being a race of soldiers, but if you don't even understand that, you don't know anything about war."

"We have magic," the sunlord said. "The untainted blessings of the gods."

"And that's something," said Aoth. "I fought alongside the Burning Braziers and saw what they can do. But show me the priest versatile enough to conjure darkness one moment, a cloud of poisonous smoke the next, and rust the enemy's armor an instant after that."

Luthen turned back to Shala. "Majesty, surely you recognize this talk for the self-serving rubbish it is. For after all, you won your own extraordinary victories without stooping to wizardry."

Nicos, the sunlord, and a druidess of the Great Mother clad in a green gown and a holly wreath all tried to talk at once. Shala raised her hand, and everyone fell silent. The war hero then sat for a while, glowering at nothing—or everything—and fingering the scar on her chin.

"Lord Nicos," she said at length.

"Yes, Majesty?"

"I don't want you to think that my decision means you've lost my ear or my trust. It's just that—"

It was obvious what was coming. "Majesty!" said Aoth.

Shala scowled. "Captain, I'd already noticed that you lack the aptitude for courtly speech. But I'm still, let us say, *impressed* that you would interrupt a monarch pronouncing judgment from her throne."

Aoth inclined his head. "Majesty, I'm sorry. But I have one more thing to say before you make up your mind."

"What's that?"

"You want Luthcheq peaceful. You brought the Brotherhood here to make it that way, and you're thinking of sending us away for the same reason. But in the short term, there's only one thing that will truly calm the people down. Someone has to catch the Green Hand killer, and if you let me stay, I'll do it for you."

"I've been laboring under a misapprehension," Luthen drawled. "I imagined you were trying to do that all along."

"Of course," said Aoth. "But I had to gather intelligence before

I could make a plan that goes farther than the obvious tactics."

"What plan?" the nobleman asked.

"If I told, you all might decide that you don't need me."

"Captain," Shala said, "when you suggest such a thing, you implicitly impugn my honor."

"Then I'm sorry again," said Aoth. "But I am just a sellsword. I don't claim to understand honor like barons and royalty do. And I've heard a few things said today that make me wonder if you and your advisors truly would deem it all that ignoble an act to cheat a despicable war-mage. Now, I'm asking you for a tenday. If I trap the murderer, then give me your trust. Send the Brotherhood to war. If I fail, then send us down the trail."

"A tenday," Shala said, "and if you fail, you'll also pay wergild for the folk who died last night. To keep the people from feeling that I allowed you to commit outrages and then escape unpunished."

Aoth swallowed. "Agreed."

After they left the hall, Nicos whispered, "What is this brilliant scheme?"

Aoth chuckled with only a grim approximation of mirth. "I'll let you know when I think of it."

* * * * *

Aoth had packed every citizen of Luthcheq possessed of genuine arcane power into the shabby candlelit common room, and Gaedynn surveyed the collection with interest. Their demeanor was noticeably different from that of most of the wizards and warlocks he'd known, a self-assured if not arrogant lot on the whole. These men and women had a morose, guarded air.

Gaedynn supposed it was understandable, given the life they led, and wondered why they hadn't all fled Chessenta long ago. He supposed it was because it was the only home they knew, and because the fires of hatred didn't always burn so hot. In better times, people paid these folk for the services only a mage could provide, and mostly left them alone if they conducted themselves with circumspection.

Aoth waited for everyone to help himself to beer or wine, then claim a chair, flop down on the floor, or find a spot to stand or lean. Then he said, "Thank you for coming."

Clad in a dark leather jerkin and breeches with a dagger in each boot, greasy black hair hanging over his eyes, a sharp-featured adolescent slouched in the corner. If not for the tattooed symbols on his hands, Gaedynn might have mistaken him for an apprentice thief. The youth made a derisive crowing sound. "As if your ruffians gave us a choice!"

Aoth cocked his head. "Did they truly have to force you? In your place, I would have been eager to join in."

Thin as a straw with lank gray hair, a wrinkled old woman quavered, "It's against the law for so many of us to meet indoors, Captain." She cackled. "It forms a coven, don't you know? So by gathering us, you officers of the watch have given yourselves all the justification you need to whisk us away to Shala Karanok's dungeons."

"Well," said Aoth, "that's not why you're here, and if it makes you feel any safer, the war hero has given me a special dispensation to hold this meeting."

That, Gaedynn knew, was an exaggeration. Shala Karanok had simply given Aoth permission to put some sort of plan into effect. He hadn't told her the details, and probably that was all to the good.

"So we can help catch the Green Hand murderer," said the knavish-looking youth.

"Yes," said Aoth, "and thus persuade the town that it doesn't need to rise up and slaughter you."

"But haven't you heard?" the adolescent replied. "One of us *is* the Green Hand. And the fiend will surely sabotage any attempt to unmask him."

Perched on a narrow windowsill with hardly an inch of clearance on either side, his stumpy legs dangling, Khouryn wiped foam from his moustache. "We doubt that the killer's truly a mage and fool enough to proclaim it to the world. It's more likely he's not, but wants to divert suspicion in your direction. To help cover his tracks—or because he hates you and wants to make trouble for you."

"But he could be a wizard who hates Luthcheq for the way it treats us," said the adolescent. "He could feel a need to declare that hatred. A compulsion so intense that he *has* to leave the prints, even though they somewhat increase the risk to himself."

Gaedynn grinned. "Conceivably. But if he's here among us, he'll have to subvert the ritual without any of us or his fellow mages noticing. I'm no wizard, but I suspect that would be difficult. So, with a little luck, we catch him either way."

The youth sneered. "You're right, archer. You're no wizard. If you were, maybe you would have studied the Five Blank Scrolls of Mythrellan, and then you'd understand—"

"Hush," the old woman said.

To Gaedynn's surprise, the adolescent immediately fell silent.

"Oraxes is a good boy at heart," the sorceress continued, now addressing the officers of the Brotherhood, "but he's contrary and loves to argue. I think your idea is a good one, and obviously we have ample reason to help. So why don't you tell us exactly what you intend?"

"I practice a specialized form of magic," said Aoth. "So I'll defer to my lieutenant Jhesrhi Coldcreek."

Jhesrhi was standing against the wall next to Khouryn. Her frown was even more forbidding than usual, a sign that she was uncomfortable. Perhaps because she never liked being the center of attention, or perhaps simply because there were too many people stuffed into the room.

"I'm no expert diviner either," she said, "but I propose we pool our strength to create Saldashune's Mirror."

Oraxes snorted. "We'd need a vessel."

"We have one." Jhesrhi waved to the pair of dragonborn filling up a bench. "It isn't generally known, but Daardendrien Medrash there is the one living person ever to catch a glimpse of the Green Hand."

And, Gaedynn understood, the russet-scaled dragonborn had been hunting him ever since, out of some lofty paladin sense of obligation. That was why he'd been wandering the wizards' quarter on the night of the riot. But if he still suspected the killer was a mage, no one could have told it from the courteous way he rose and bowed to the specimens who were peering at him curiously.

"Unfortunately," Jhesrhi continued, "he only saw the killer in the dark, at a distance, and for an instant. But that's the sort of problem Saldashune invented her ritual to solve. I've made the necessary preparations in the conjuration chamber in the cellar."

The stairs creaking and bowing beneath their weight, they all trooped down to the space in question. By the standards of anyone who'd grown up in Aglarond with its rich tradition of sorcery, it was a miserable excuse for a mage's sanctum—just a squared-off hole that smelled of dirt like anybody's cellar.

But Jhesrhi had made the place seem considerably more magical. Floating orbs the size of fists shed a golden glow, while a complex geometric figure made of lines and arcs of blue phosphorescence covered most of the floor. Luminous green handprints spotted the design.

With no role to play in the conjuration, Gaedynn and Khouryn sat down on a couple of the bottommost steps. Balasar, the smaller dragonborn with the red eyes and yellow-brown scales, clasped Medrash's shoulder, then came to stand with his fellow spectators.

"Where do you want me?" Medrash asked.

"Here." Jhesrhi escorted him to a circle at the center of the figure.

"Now what?"

"Just stand and remember the moment when you saw the murderer. If your thoughts wander, that's all right. Simply bring them back to where we want them."

Jhesrhi then took a position two paces to his right, and—after some discussion and a little squabbling—Aoth and the Chessentan mages chose stations for themselves. Jhesrhi looked around like a conductor making sure all her musicians had their instruments ready. Then she spun her staff through a flourish and started chanting.

Brandishing their own rods, wands, or orbs, her fellow mages joined in, one or two at a time. Remarkably, given that they hadn't practiced together, the wizards managed to speak exactly in unison. And when the incantation became a responsory, they seemed to know instinctively who should perform the verse and who the refrain.

Gaedynn suspected that the magic, in some sense willing its own creation, was guiding them. For certainly it was present almost from the moment Jhesrhi started speaking. It made his joints ache and filled the air with a smell like rotting lilies.

Medrash had his eyes closed and his steel medallion clasped in one hand. He was whispering too, perhaps a prayer or meditation to aid his concentration. Gaedynn assumed it wouldn't interfere with the ritual, or Jhesrhi would have stopped him.

A disk of silvery luminescence appeared near Medrash. At first it was so faint that Gaedynn wasn't sure he was actually seeing it. But the mages chanted louder, more insistently—and it clotted somehow, becoming more definite if no more solid.

The disk darkened, as though reflecting a place more dimly lit than the cellar. Stars glittered in a stripe down its center. The borders were the facades of buildings rising toward the sky.

A shadow leaped, or conceivably flew, across the open space between them.

After a few heartbeats it sprang again, exactly as before. Then a third time and a fourth. But it was so tiny and fleeting that even repeated viewings didn't enable Gaedynn to determine anything more about it.

Then, however, by almost infinitesimal degrees, it started slowing down. At the same time, and just as gradually, it grew larger. Closer. Before, the magic had in effect put Gaedynn on the street, where Medrash had stood in actuality. Now it was like he was rising into the air.

"They're doing it," Khouryn whispered.

Then Medrash grunted and lurched like someone had struck him a blow. A white crack zigzagged through the mirror's darkness.

After a moment the jagged line disappeared, like the wizards' chant had repaired the damage. But now the shadow wasn't drawing any closer, or making its jump any more slowly either. And Medrash was shaking.

"I don't like this," Balasar said.

More cracks stabbed across the mirror. The wizards chanted louder still and spun their instruments through circular figures. The wands and other talismans left trails of sparks and shimmers in the air.

The cracks kept disappearing. But they lasted longer than they had before. Then a gash split the scaly hide on Medrash's forearm. Blood welled forth. An expanding stain on the front of his tunic revealed that something had slashed his chest as well.

"Stop!" Balasar shouted.

The mages kept on reciting. A forked cut burst open among the white studs on Medrash's face.

"I've seen this before," said Gaedynn, springing to his feet. "The wizards can't stop. They're in a trance. But if we get Medrash out of the pentagram, that should halt the ritual."

"Then come on," Balasar said.

The three observers strode in among the wizards. If any of the mages even noticed, Gaedynn couldn't tell it.

But Medrash did. He turned his reptilian head so the yellow eyes under the protruding brow could regard them. Praise be to the Great Archer for that, anyway.

"Go to the stairs," said Balasar, raising his voice to make himself heard above the chanting.

"No," Medrash said. "I can do this, and it's my duty."

"You can't and it isn't." Balasar turned to Gaedynn and Khouryn. "We'll have to move him."

"Fine," said the dwarf. He grabbed Medrash's forearm. Gaedynn and Balasar took hold of him as well, and they started to manhandle him away from the spot where Jhesrhi had put him.

Medrash resisted, but more feebly than Gaedynn expected of such a hulking warrior. It was like he was partly entranced himself, or dividing his attention between struggling with his would-be rescuers and reliving the instant when he'd glimpsed the murderer.

Unfortunately, the magic resisted on his behalf. The air seemed to thicken around them until it was like they were trying to walk while submerged in mud. Even Khouryn, the strongest soldier in the Brotherhood, had trouble making headway. Meanwhile, Medrash's hide split and split again, up and down the length of his body, until it seemed likely he'd bleed to death before they hauled him to safety.

As he shoved and dragged, Gaedynn caught glimpses of Jhesrhi and Aoth, oblivious to the struggle, prisoners of their own conjuration. For an instant it reminded him of the day his father's warriors came to deliver him to the elves. He'd promised himself he'd be brave, but he was only seven. When the time arrived, he begged to be spared, but his parents and everyone else he loved and trusted simply stood and stared.

Khouryn let go of Medrash and, his hands red with the Tymantheran's blood, snatched the urgrosh from his back. He chopped at one of the glowing blue lines composing the figure. The edge sheared deep into the earthen floor beneath. But when he yanked the weapon free, Gaedynn saw that enchanted though it was, it had failed to cleave something made of intangible light.

Balasar spewed frost at the same patch of floor. Dragon breath was inherently magical, so Gaedynn supposed dragonborn breath must be also, but it too failed to mar the pattern.

Still, he thought Khouryn's idea was a good one. Spoil the figure involved in raising a supernatural effect and you generally ended said effect, even if the tactic had failed dismally in Thay.

Even indoors, even in relaxed circumstances, Gaedynn usually carried a few arrows riding in a slim doeskin quiver on his belt. He felt incomplete without them. And by good fortune, he currently had one of the special shafts Jhesrhi had enchanted for him. He snatched it out and stabbed the head into one of the luminous green handprints.

The charge of countermagic in the narrow arrowhead sent nullification surging outward in all directions, an expanding ring that wiped the figure of light away. The floating mirror vanished too, and Medrash's skin stopped splitting. The wizards' chant stumbled to a halt. The cellar seemed profoundly silent without it.

Until Medrash drew a deep breath. "I don't know whether to thank you or rebuke you."

"Thank them," said Aoth. He let his spear drop to hang casually in his grasp. A blue-green glow faded from the head. "That was completely out of control."

"And heal yourself," said Balasar. "You're bleeding all over everything."

"What just happened?" Gaedynn asked. "*Is* the murderer in the room? Did he subvert the magic?"

Jhesrhi brushed a stray strand of blonde hair away from her

golden eyes. "I don't think so. It seems to me that he has a powerful ward in place to keep anyone from using divination against him." She glanced around at her fellow mages. "Do you agree?"

All speaking more or less at the same time, they indicated that they did.

"So what does that mean?" Gaedynn asked. "The killer is a wizard unknown to us or the authorities? Someone who never had his hands tattooed?"

"Maybe," said Aoth, "or he could be a practitioner of divine magic."

"That sounds promising," Khouryn growled, returning his axe to its harness. "I can just see a bunch of Chessentan mages trying to pin the murders on a Chessentan holy man."

"There are other possibilities," Jhesrhi said. "Maybe the killer simply possesses a formidable talisman or receives aid from a supernatural entity. Or is a supernatural entity himself."

"In other words," Gaedynn said, "finding out about this defense doesn't point us at any one suspect or group of suspects. So we still need magic to track the whoreson down. Now that you know about the ward, can you punch through it?"

"I'm game to try," Medrash said. Gaedynn saw that some of the dragonborn's wounds looked halfway healed, and the rest had at least stopped bleeding.

Aoth smiled crookedly. "Considering that we damn near killed you, I don't know whether to praise your courage or doubt your good sense. But I have no idea how to get around that ward. Does anybody else?"

"I wouldn't want to try to improvise a method," Oraxes said. "Next time it could be me getting sliced to pieces."

"But given time and study," said the elderly witch, "we may well find the key."

"How much time?" asked Aoth.

She shrugged her bony shoulders. "A couple of tendays. Perhaps a month."

"I have eight days left. That's the bargain I made with the war hero."

"So where does that leave us?" Khouryn asked. "We just keep patrolling and hope to catch the killer at his work?"

"No." Gaedynn picked at a tacky splotch of blood on his sleeve. Futilely; the garment was rather obviously ruined unless he could persuade Jhesrhi to remove the stains with magic. "That hasn't worked any better than the ritual. For whatever reason, we aren't able to stalk or track this particular beast. But there's another way to hunt. You set out bait and wait for the animal to come to you."

"Interesting," said Medrash. "But is it practical in this situation? The Green Hand doesn't kill any particular sort of person—"

"Rumor has it," Oraxes said, "that he kills people who have a particularly strong hatred of mages. Unfortunately, Luthcheq possesses those in abundance."

Medrash gave a quick nod. "Indeed. And given that he prowls the entire city and kills the highborn and the low, the prosperous and the poor alike, how would we go about luring him into a snare?"

Jhesrhi frowned. "There might be a way. Places can have a spirit. An atmosphere. Often it derives from their history. They attract a certain sort of person, and certain events tend to happen there.

"Generally speaking," she continued, "it's a very weak effect. So weak we never feel the tug. So weak that if you mean to go one way instead of another, you will. The influence can't change your mind. But if you kept track, you'd find that over the course of a year, or a hundred years, the groups that took each path differed at least slightly."

"Maybe I see what you're getting at," Khouryn said. "But if the effect is as subtle as all that, how can we count on it solving our problem in the next several days?"

"The effect as it occurs in nature is subtle," Jhesrhi said. "We wizards should be able to infuse a particular location with a negativity more potent than that found in any of Luthcheq's dueling grounds, slaughterhouses, torture chambers, or what have you. That will cause the Green Hand to gravitate toward that area when he chooses his next victim. And we'll be waiting there to catch him."

"But what about the people who live and work in that area?" Khouryn asked. "If I understand you correctly, the new atmosphere will poison their thoughts. They might end up hurting or even killing one another."

Oraxes sneered. "To the Towers of Night with them. If somebody doesn't catch the Green Hand, those bastards will come back here to burn and butcher all of us."

Medrash gave him a level stare. "It's unlikely that all the people whose minds you'd corrupt hate mages, or would try to slaughter you in any case. But even if they are your enemies, this is a dishonorable way to strike at them."

"Oh, sharpen your claws," said Balasar. Gaedynn had never heard the expression before, but he assumed the smaller dragonborn was telling his clan brother not to be so squeamish. If so, then he thoroughly approved.

"If a person isn't depraved to begin with," Jhesrhi said, "the influence won't make him so in just a few days."

"What about the man who's right on the edge?" asked Khouryn.

"And what about angry blows and spiteful words?" Medrash asked. "A person doesn't have to fall into outright fiendishness to make mistakes that will mar his life forever afterward."

Aoth frowned. "There's no point debating the morality of it unless we're sure it's even possible. In the time we have left, I mean."

"I think it is," the aged sorceress said. "It's not really that complicated, just funneling the raw essence of malice into a place—and this time there shouldn't be resistance to overcome. We can probably proceed with a ritual as early as tomorrow night."

"Then I say we go ahead," said Aoth. "The Green Hand murders people every tenday. The city's in a panic. Every wizard's in danger, and the future of the Brotherhood's at stake. If we can fix all that, it will more than make up for whatever incidental nastiness we cause along the way."

Oraxes grinned. "Unless somebody finds out about it. Because what we're really talking about is laying a curse on a part of Luthcheq and the people who live there. And there's no way of justifying that to fools who already hate sorcery."

"Then it's a good thing we all know how to keep our mouths shut," said Aoth. "Now, I've already committed the Brotherhood to this plan. Do the rest of you agree?"

The Chessentan mages exchanged glances, then murmured or nodded their support.

"I still don't like it," Medrash said. "But promise me a place among the hunters, and that you'll lift the curse as soon as we catch the murderer, and I'm with you."

"Done," said Aoth. "Now let's decide where to center the spell."

"The ropemakers' quarter," Khouryn said. "It's a poor district, with all the ills that go along with want, and a boy died a bloody, pointless death there just a few days back. If you want a place to stink of misery and anger, your work's already halfway done."

* * * * *

Aoth and Jet glided over the rookeries and the narrow streets and alleys snaking between them. Aoth was the only rider in the air. Griffons were magnificent beasts, useful for many purposes, but you couldn't expect ordinary ones to circle endlessly without screeching to one another.

It likely didn't matter that no one else was aloft. Clouds shrouded the moon, and few lights burned below. Even a dwarf like Khouryn couldn't have seen much from such a height.

But with his fire-touched eyes, Aoth could. He could even see the taint he and his fellow mages had cast over a portion of the ropemakers' precinct. It revealed itself as a slow seething inside the deepest shadows.

He wished they could have confined it to a smaller area. That would have made it easier to spot the Green Hand if the magic actually succeeded in drawing him in. It would also have reduced the number of innocents obliviously immersing themselves in filth.

But Aoth didn't find it all that hard to disregard their plight. He'd done worse things in war. And as far as he was concerned, he was at war now—a war to save the Brotherhood from ruin.

A dark form skulked across a canted tenement rooftop. "There!" said Aoth.

"Where?" Aoth felt his psychic connection to Jet deepen as the familiar availed himself of vision even keener than his own. "Oh, right, I see him. But is that the Green Hand?"

"I don't know. Fly lower."

Crouched, clad in a voluminous robe and a hood that covered his entire head, the man below certainly looked like anyone's notion of a fiend. But like most slums, the ropemakers' precinct harbored a diversity of outlaws, and a masked man could lurk on a roof for a number of reasons. Aoth didn't want to reveal his presence until he was sure he'd found his quarry.

The hooded man stalked to the edge of the roof and then crawled over it, clinging to the wall head down like an insect or lizard. He scuttled along the top tier of shuttered windows, seemingly peering through the cracks.

Aoth's doubts fell away. A thief who could climb like that, whether by dint of skill or magic, would steal from wealthier folk than paupers in a tenement. The man below was here to kill. Come to think of it, it was in just such a setting that he'd committed the first murders in his string.

Jet perceived his master's certainty. "I can peel him right off that wall."

Aoth snorted. His steed could perform amazing maneuvers in flight, but the prospect of plunging into the narrow space between buildings, mere inches away from one of them, was enough to give any rider pause. "Just swoop low enough to give me a shot."

"Where's the fun in that?" But Jet did as he'd been instructed.

The hooded man dug his fingertips between the laths of a shutter like he meant to rip the barrier off its hinges. Aoth aimed his spear and considered whether to hurl frost or darts of light.

Then Jet went rigid and plummeted toward the street. His spread wings caught just enough air to keep Aoth from breaking bones when they crashed down. It was only then that Aoth spotted the arrow buried deep in the feathered part of the griffon's flank, just behind the foreleg.

Aoth looked up just in time to see a second hooded figure, this one armed with a bow, step back from the edge of a roof and out of sight. The man on the wall was gone.

At that moment, Aoth hated himself for failing to spot the archer, even though no one had ever even speculated that the Green Hand might have an accomplice. "How bad is it?" He started to swing himself out of the saddle to take a better look.

"Stay where you are!" said Jet.

"You need—"

"Stay where you are!" The griffon ran and leaped. His wings lashing, he rose into the air.

Just high enough to thump down on a rooftop, where Aoth felt his exhaustion and fatigue almost as if they were his own. "Now you can see which way they went," said Jet.

He was right. The Green Hand and his lookout were fleeing to the north, bounding like grasshoppers from building to building. "Will you be all right here?" asked Aoth.

"I won't die on you. Get them!"

Aoth dismounted, yanked his bugle from the saddle, and blew it. Then he waited for what seemed forever, although he knew that in reality it only took a few heartbeats for Jhesrhi to answer his call.

She arrived flying on the wind, garments flapping, hair whirling around her, the gold runes on her black staff pulsing. When she spied Jet and the blood dripping down the shingles beneath him, her eyes widened in dismay.

"It's nothing," snarled the griffon. "Why does everyone think I'm so delicate?"

Aoth pointed with his spear. "There are two Green Hand killers, and they fled that way."

Jhesrhi squinted. "I can't see them."

"Luckily, I still can. Just. We need to get after them."

Jhesrhi lifted her staff in both hands and rattled off words of command. The wind howled and lifted Aoth in its embrace, and he and his lieutenant soared together.

It didn't take him long to realize he didn't like it. He loved flying on griffonback, but then he was in control and had something solid under his arse. Here, the unreasoning, instinctual part of his mind kept insisting he was going to fall. Of course even if he had, the magic bound in one of his tattoos would have enabled him to float down to a soft landing, but remembering that only helped a little.

Fortunately, he was too intent on the quarry for anxiety to claim much of a hold on him. He had to redirect Jhesrhi as the murderers veered this way and that. Meanwhile, she had to maintain the pursuit and also pick up their comrades hiding in the shadows of chimneys or in doorways and stairwells at street level.

Even for a mistress of elemental magic, it had to be taxing. But one by one, Khouryn, Balasar, Medrash, and Gaedynn bobbed or whirled up into the sky. Aoth found a bit of amusement in the fact that the dwarf and the smaller dragonborn looked even more uncomfortable than he was. The paladin, though, appeared so intent on righteous vengeance as to barely even notice he was flying, while the auburn-haired archer smirked as usual.

Gradually, they narrowed the killers' lead. Gaedynn tried a couple of shots, but even he couldn't hit a moving target in such difficult circumstances. Jhesrhi's conjured wind was just too strong, as well as unpredictable from one moment to the next.

The murderers leaped onto the roof of a fair-sized but dilapidated box of a house at the edge of the city. They threw open a trapdoor, scurried through, and closed it behind them.

"Half through the top and half through the bottom!" yelled Khouryn.

"I agree!" Aoth replied.

Jhesrhi spoke to the wind. Aoth recognized one of the languages of Chaos, although he wasn't fluent enough to understand all the words. Fortunately, the wind did. Khouryn and the two dragonborn hurtled toward the ground. Aoth, Jhesrhi, and Gaedynn flew onto the roof, and then the air stopped supporting them or fluttering their clothes.

Jhesrhi panted and swiped back her hair with a shaky hand.

"Are you all right?" asked Aoth.

"Fine," she said.

"There are only two Green Hands," said Gaedynn, nocking an arrow, "and six of us. If—"

"I said I'm fine," she said, gritting her teeth.

"Then let's get to it," said Aoth. In theory, with them coming in from the roof and Khouryn and the Tymantherans entering on the ground floor, they had the killers trapped between them. Still, he didn't want to give the bastards time to do anything clever.

He tried to pull open the trapdoor. The Green Hands had barred it behind them. He jabbed the point of his spear into the wood, spoke a word of command, and released a bit of the power stored in the weapon. The trapdoor exploded into scraps and splinters.

Below the hole was a ladder. Aoth didn't bother with it. He simply jumped and thumped down on a dusty floor. He pivoted, spear and targe poised for defense.

He was alone in a lightless attic festooned with spiderwebs. It smelled of age and abandonment. A steep staircase descended to the story beneath.

Aoth stepped aside, and Gaedynn jumped down after him. The air moaned and surged, and Jhesrhi floated down, as though to allay her comrades' concerns that she was too tired to use more magic. She brightened the glow of the runes on her staff to serve for a lantern.

Gaedynn sniffed. "I smell smoke."

Aoth realized he did too. But they needed to stay focused on catching the murderers. "Keep moving."

Peering for some sign of the Green Hands, he led his lieutenants down the rickety stairs. The smell of burning grew stronger. From what he could see so far, the building looked like any derelict house. It had probably belonged to some prosperous burgher, with servants and apprentices consigned to the stark little rooms on this floor and the family sleeping in nicer ones below.

The darkness burned white, and something crackled. Aoth shuddered, his muscles locking, and the staircase shattered beneath him. As he and his comrades slammed down amid the wreckage, he realized that someone standing behind the steps, where even spellscarred eyes couldn't see, had struck them all with a blaze of conjured lightning.

Fortunately, it hadn't killed him. The protective charms bound into his tattoos and gear, his own innate hardiness, or Tymora's favor had preserved him, and he prayed the same was true of his friends. Starting to feel the hot pain of his burns, he floundered around to face his attacker.

Then, at the very periphery of his vision, he glimpsed a robed, hooded figure stepping out of a doorway. Liquid sprayed him and his companions, searing them once again.

Aoth's eyes burned and filled with tears. Something hit his chest—not, he thought, penetrating his mail but slamming the breath out of him. He was too blind to have any idea what it was.

* * * * *

For a long moment it felt to Medrash like he, Balasar, and the dwarf were simply falling. But at what was surely the last possible moment, the wind gusted upward to slow their descent. They still bumped down hard, but without injury.

Balasar drew his sword. "Appearances to the contrary," he said, "maybe your wizard friend does have a sense of humor."

Khouryn spun his axe through a casual practice swing. "No, she just set us down the easiest way, without caring whether it would make us think we were about to meet our ancestors." He strode to the door of the derelict house and broke it open with a kick. The door banged against the interior wall, and the impact echoed throughout the building.

"Subtle," Balasar said.

"They already know we're chasing them," Medrash said. "I doubt it matters."

It was even darker once they entered the house. Medrash murmured a prayer and infused the blade of his sword with pearly light.

The glow revealed a ground floor that had, in its time, served the purposes of commerce, with empty shelves and counters near the door and worktables farther back. He couldn't tell what the long-departed shopkeeper had manufactured and sold.

Nor did he care. All that mattered was bringing the Green Hand—or rather Hands—to justice and completing the task the Loyal Fury had entrusted to him. Ridding Luthcheq of a loathsome evil, further cementing the bonds of friendship between Chessenta and Tymanther, and bringing honor to Clan Daardendrien in the process.

A rat scuttled into a hole at the base of a wall. But except for vermin, the ground floor seemed deserted. "Let's find the stairs," he said.

Balasar pointed with his sword. "There."

They started up, the spongy steps bowing under Medrash's weight. Ruddy light flickered at the top. He wondered if something was on fire, and then two figures, mere shapeless silhouettes against the glow, abruptly stepped into view. Dark vapor streamed down at him.

Medrash's nose and mouth burned. He doubled over coughing and could tell from the sounds behind him that his companions were similarly afflicted.

They had to exit the poison cloud and come to grips with their attackers. Despite his inability to catch his breath, and the fiery pain crawling down his throat into his lungs, he started running up the last few risers.

Then he faltered and found that he simply couldn't continue. His attackers were exerting some sort of psychic compulsion to prevent it.

That meant he and his comrades had to escape out the other

side of the fumes. "Back!" he croaked.

They turned and staggered downward. Until Khouryn, who was now in the lead, froze. An instant later, the dragonborn did too. Medrash could just distinguish other figures at the foot of the stairs. He had no idea where they'd been hiding when he'd first entered the shop. But somewhere, obviously, and now here they were, exerting the same influence as their accomplices on the floor above. Caging the intruders inside the toxic vapor.

Still coughing uncontrollably, Balasar collapsed.

* * * * *

The lightning, the fall, and the spray of vitriol, all coming within the span of a heartbeat or two, had stunned Gaedynn into a dazed passivity. But a part of him knew it and screamed for him to move.

He glimpsed motion in the direction from which the lightning had come. The possibility of a second such attack broke the impasse inside him. The part that wanted to act became the whole.

He rolled to one knee. Thanks be to old Keen-Eye, his enchanted bow was still intact despite the abuse it had just sustained. In fact, it seemed to have come through better than he had, considering the ugly chars and blisters on his skin.

But he didn't yet feel the pain, not really, and praise the Great Archer for that too. He couldn't afford to feel it.

His teary eyes could just make out a robed figure. He drew back an arrow and let it fly. The shaft buried itself in the robed man's torso, and he toppled backward.

But at the same instant, Gaedynn heard rushing footsteps. He jerked around. All he could discern were vague flickers of motion, and this time, his smarting, watery eyes weren't the problem. The oncoming foes were invisible, at least most of the time.

And they were already too close for any more archery. He leaped to his feet, crossed his arms, and snatched out the two short swords he'd brought along for backup weapons.

Unable to see his foes except for a moment now and then, hoping sheer ferocity would daunt them, he slashed madly. Once, he felt his left-hand blade slice something solid. Another time, he parried a stroke by pure instinct. Twice, an attack thumped him but failed to penetrate his brigandine.

He knew his luck couldn't hold, but he was less afraid than outraged by the sheer unfairness of his situation. He and his companions had ventured forth to catch one murderer. Then they'd learned to Jet's cost that the one was really two. Now it appeared two had multiplied into a whole houseful, and they could throw lightning and acid around and turn invisible.

The invisibility at least should have posed no problem for Aoth, and the war-mage had in fact regained his feet. But, eyes compressed to streaming slits in his blistered, mottled face, the man who could famously see everything didn't seem to be doing any more damage with his jabbing spear than Gaedynn was with his swords. Apparently the acid spray had had an even more deleterious effect on his sight.

He and Gaedynn fought side by side, in the hallway where the staircase had come down, to prevent any of their unseen foes from slipping around behind them. Aoth growled a word of power, and frost leaped from the head of his spear. It painted the entire space before them white, and the hooded men as well.

Since he didn't instantly follow up, it seemed that he still couldn't see their foes, or at least not clearly. But Gaedynn could. He sprang, beat a short blade like his own out of line, and drove the point of his right-hand sword into an opponent's guts.

He jerked the weapon free, and the Green Hands disappeared. "Again!" he shouted to Aoth.

But no more frost came. Gaedynn glanced around and saw that Aoth's helmet was dented and askew, and, though he kept the spear shifting and thrusting in one of the basic defensive patterns, he looked unsteady on his feet.

And because of Gaedynn's aggression, the two of them weren't even in line anymore. Cutting and stabbing, he tried to retreat.

Then, behind him, Jhesrhi croaked words of command. Water splashed down over his head and everything else in the hallway like hundreds of buckets had overturned at once.

It washed the stinging acidic residue from his skin. It evidently washed it out of Aoth's eyes too, and roused him from the daze induced by the knock he'd taken on the head. His eyes snapped open wide enough to reveal their blue fire. He stepped, stabbed, and the power in his spear blasted to pieces the man he'd just impaled.

Aoth then turned and hurled darts of green light in Gaedynn's direction. They stopped short of him, vanishing as they pierced the two invisible foes between the sellswords. Who became visible as they crumpled to the floor.

Aoth pivoted again and hurled three lightningbolts down the hall in quick succession. The flashes dazzled Gaedynn, and the booms hurt his ears.

Afterward, Aoth lowered his spear and turned away from the steaming, twisted corpses he'd just created and the several small fires he'd started. Evidently this particular fight was over.

Gaedynn wiped the blades of his swords, returned them to their scabbards, and retrieved his bow. "That was quite . . . enthusiastic, there at the end."

Aoth grunted. "After the Spellplague touched me, I was blind for a while. I suppose it's the kind of experience that leaves a mark. Is everyone all right?"

"Not too bad," Jhesrhi said. "I have an elixir to numb the pain and keep us on our feet." She took a little pewter vial from her belt pouch, unscrewed the stopper, and took the first swallow herself. Gaedynn knew why. She would have found it difficult to drink from the container after someone else put his mouth on it.

As she handed the vial to Gaedynn, Aoth stooped over one of the Green Hands, then cursed. Gaedynn peered at the corpse and felt like doing the same.

Aoth possessed inhumanly keen sight, but even so, this was the first clear, close, unhurried look that he or his comrades had had at one of the killers. And now the unexpected shape of the hood was apparent. Or rather, the shape of the head inside it.

Aoth ripped the cowl away.

"We have to get to Khouryn," Jhesrhi said.

* * * * *

Medrash's helpless coughing made it impossible to recite any of his prayers. The pain burning throughout his respiratory system, and the knowledge that he could easily die breathing the poisonous vapor, further impaired his ability to focus his will.

But he *would* focus it. He had to help his comrades—and besides, the body and its distress were not the ultimate reality. Torm and his glory were.

He reached out to the god, and power like frigid spring water poured into him. He infused it with righteous fury, shaping it into a weapon, then brandished his sword. Flares of white light leaped from the blade to stab at the figures at the bottom of the stairs.

The attack rocked the Green Hands backward. Nearly tripping, Medrash staggered over the fallen Balasar, tried to slip past Khouryn, and again discovered he couldn't advance any farther. He'd hurt the Green Hands, but not enough to make them lose control of the psychic wall they'd created.

He channeled more power, though it was even harder this time. He fixed his gaze on one of the killers and willed him to climb the stairs and come within reach of his sword.

The Green Hand took one lurching step. Another. Then, however, he gave a harsh, wordless cry, stopped, and retreated to his original position.

Blackness swam at the edges of Medrash's vision. His legs started to give way, and he had to drop his sword and clutch the banister to keep from falling.

Torm's glory was limitless, but a mortal's capacity to draw from it was not. Medrash judged that at best, he could channel power one more time before he collapsed. He groped beyond himself, beyond the physical world into a brighter, purer realm, and the god granted a final gift of strength.

But how to use it, when his previous expenditures of power had accomplished nothing? He gripped Khouryn's massive shoulder, which jumped repeatedly as the dwarf coughed, and employed the energy to bless him. To strengthen his body and mind alike.

Khouryn stumbled down one riser, almost losing his balance in the process. Then he hefted his axe and charged.

Unfortunately, his lungs were still full of poison, and his continued coughing slowed him and made him clumsy. Though caught by surprise, the Green Hands managed to recoil from his first strikes and ready their short swords.

But they evidently couldn't do that and maintain the psychic pressure too. For when Medrash, still gripping the handrail, tried to head down the steps, he found that now he could.

He reeled toward one of the Green Hands to keep them both from attacking Khouryn. The murderer turned and lunged. The move was all-out aggression. Because after all, why worry about defense when his target was unarmed and all but spastic with pain and weakness? When the coughing would prevent him from even using his breath weapon?

But at least Medrash wasn't breathing poison anymore, and he'd spent his whole life training for combat—first with the masters of arms of Clan Daardendrien, then with his paladin mentors. Feeble and awkward though he was, he found the right instant to slip the swordsman's initial thrust, step beside him, and claw away the side of his throat. Blood sprayed from the severed arteries.

Medrash turned just in time to see Khouryn chop the remaining Green Hand's leg out from under him, then cleave his ribs before he hit the floor. Clearly he too could hold his own even in adverse circumstances.

The dwarf nodded to Medrash, and he returned the gesture. Then a clatter of hurrying feet on the staircase reminded them the fight wasn't over. Their other enemies were coming down. Evidently the lingering vapor wasn't toxic to them.

Worse, after stepping over Balasar, they stopped partway down the steps. Medrash realized that however they'd created the smoke before, they meant to make some more. And he had no idea how he and Khouryn could contend with another dose.

But Balasar, who'd appeared unconscious—or as good as—raised the sword in his shaking hand and sliced the back of a killer's leg. The murderer dropped, and his companion turned to look at him in surprise. Balasar thrust the sword up at him. The Green Hand flinched back from it, but in so doing lost his balance and tumbled down the steps.

With what was surely the last of his strength, Balasar repeatedly stabbed the man he'd hamstrung. Khouryn sucked in a deep breath, made a hiccuping sound as he kept himself from coughing it right out again, and charged back into the fumes—where he smashed the skull of the remaining Green Hand.

Medrash hoped that by now perhaps he'd taken enough breaths of relatively clean air to do something comparable. He'd better have, for he was sure Balasar couldn't wait. He ran up the stairs, grabbed his clan brother's arm—he hadn't yet regained sufficient strength to lift him—and dragged him down and out of the cloud.

Then they all flopped down on the floor, coughed, and watched for other threats, although at first it was questionable whether they could do much about any that might appear. Gradually, though, the ache in Medrash's chest subsided, and his strength started trickling back.

"You banged my head on every one of those steps," Balasar wheezed.

"Sorry," Medrash said. "Next time I'll leave you swimming in poison."

Three thunderclaps, or something that sounded like them, boomed somewhere overhead.

"I know that sound," Khouryn said. "Aoth or Jhesrhi conjured lightning."

Medrash looked at the staircase. The cloud was dissipating. "We should find out why. And I think I can cast a blessing to strengthen us so we're fit to help them if they need it."

"Good," said Khouryn. "Do that. But before we move on . . ." He rose, reached for the hood on one of the corpses, and hesitated. Medrash peered at the body and realized what about it had surprised him.

Khouryn pulled off the hood to reveal the dragonborn head underneath. "By the Watchful Eye!" he growled, astonished. He unmasked another Green Hand. That one was a dragonborn as well.

The dwarf turned to his companions. "What does this mean?"

Medrash shook his head. "We have no idea. Let's worry about it after we find our comrades." He gripped his amulet and recited a prayer.

An exhilarating coolness tingled through his body and soothed the hot rawness in his throat and chest. He lifted the medallion and it shed a soft white light over his companions. A tautness went out of their faces as the healing eased them too.

"Thanks," Khouryn said. "Now let's go."

Medrash retrieved his sword as they prowled up the staircase. At the top was the communal room that likely took up most of the second floor of the human habitation. And it was on fire, albeit burning in the leisurely way of damp, rotten wood. Flames licked across a portion of the floor and up one wall, devouring the designs and symbols painted there. Papers charred in the hearth. Smoke drifted through the hot air, irritating Medrash's nose and almost making him cough again.

Aoth, Gaedynn, and Jhesrhi came through a doorway. Each had suffered what looked like blisters and burns, and for some reason each was dripping wet. But none looked seriously hurt.

Medrash was glad to see them. But the feeling turned to dismay when the humans aimed their weapons and spread out to flank their allies.

"Move away from them, Khouryn!" rapped Aoth. The head of his spear glowed crimson.

"It's all right," said the dwarf. "We know—the Green Hands are dragonborn. But these two dragonborn aren't Green Hands. They fought the ones we met downstairs."

"You're sure?" The point of the spear shone brighter, and Medrash could have sworn that the strange blue light in Aoth's eyes did the same. "It couldn't have been some sort of trick?"

"No," Khouryn said. "They saved my life and came close to dying themselves."

Aoth mulled that over for a heartbeat, then gave a nod. "All right. Medrash, Balasar, my apologies. Jhesrhi, can you put out these fires?"

"Yes." Her voice rising and falling, the wizard chanted. The quick, soft words resembled the whisper of dancing flames. As she recited the last one, the fires guttered out.

Arrow still resting on his bow, Gaedynn turned and peered around. "We seem to have cleared the house."

"Yes," Khouryn said. He turned to Aoth. "Dragon, dragon-born . . . Now we understand your vision."

"I suppose," said Aoth. "Unfortunately, we understand too late to give our friends from Clan Daardendrien advance warning of what's to come."

FOUR

7–18 Tarsakh
the Year of the Ageless One (1479 DR)

Jhesrhi looked at Aoth, whose tattooed face was shiny with the pungent ointment he'd rubbed on to help heal his burns, and thought, Look at us. Not one but two evil mages, veritable demons in mortal guise, in the war hero's audience chamber. I imagine it's been awhile since that's happened.

Unless, of course, the mages in question were facing execution or something like that.

Hatred welled up in her, and she struggled to quash it. She'd managed to serve the zulkirs, despicable tyrants though they were. No reason she couldn't fight for Chessenta too. And fortunately, her resentful fancies to the contrary, she and Aoth weren't the ones in trouble today, even if the hostile stares of some of the courtiers might have led one to imagine otherwise.

But Zan-akar didn't look hostile, even though, from what Jhesrhi understood, Aoth had undermined him when they met before. In fact, the stormsoul approached with a warm smile on the dark, narrow face so intricately etched with silver lines that it put Aoth's tattooed mask to shame.

"Captain." Zan-akar shifted his gaze to Jhesrhi, Gaedynn, and Khouryn. "Lady and sirs. Heartfelt congratulations on your achievement."

"Thank you," said Aoth.

"I want you to understand, we genasi cherish the Chessentan people like our own kin. And so, by aiding them, you've likewise earned the gratitude of Akanûl."

"That's good to know."

As they chatted on, Jhesrhi noticed Medrash, Balasar, and Perra staring. She could hardly blame them for their concern. It was a bad sign that Shala Karanok had even invited an enemy of Tymanther to attend the council. It no doubt seemed a worse one that said enemy was talking to the witnesses to whom the dragonborn looked for help.

But it would have been stupid for Aoth to be anything less than cordial. The Brotherhood might want to work for Akanûl someday. It didn't mean he or his lieutenants would slant their testimony. She wished she could reassure the dragonborn, but just then, horns blew a brassy fanfare and Shala entered through a door in the back of the hall.

Men bowed, and held the pose while the war hero mounted her throne. Women had to curtsey. As usual, this particular lady-like gesture of respect made Jhesrhi feel awkward and ridiculous.

"Rise," Shala said. She surveyed the crowd arrayed before her dais. "First, let's rejoice in our good fortune. The Green Hand—or rather the Green Hands—are dead, and for that we thank Captain Fezim and his soldiers."

Aoth bowed again.

"How did you find the killers?" Shala asked.

"We just searched—on griffonback, mainly—until we got lucky," Aoth replied. It was safer than admitting they'd convened an illegal conclave of the local arcanists and laid a temporary curse on a portion of the town.

"Well, I'm certain it took skill and valor as well as luck," the war hero said. "Which is to say, you promised you'd earn my trust, and you have. I'll gladly send you to defend the border. Provided, of course, that Lord Nicos is still willing."

"Completely, Majesty," said the nobleman with the broken nose. Since he employed the Brotherhood, their triumph reflected well on him. But to Jhesrhi's surprise, he seemed less delighted by it than Zan-akar.

"Excellent!" Shala said. "Now, however, we must deal with the troubling aspect of last night's events. It turns out the murderers were dragonborn."

"As I warned you, Majesty," Zan-akar said, "Tymanther is High Imaskar's friend, not Chessenta's."

"That's a lie!" Perra snapped. "Majesty, I swear, the vanquisher's government had nothing to do with this."

Shala sighed. "I'd *like* to believe that. An alternative explanation would help."

"And I don't have one," Perra said. "What I can tell you is that my embassy keeps track of all the dragonborn who visit Luthcheq. Yet I don't recognize any of the ones who died last night."

Medrash took a step forward. "Majesty, may I speak?"

Shala gave a brusque little nod.

"As the ambassador said," Medrash continued, "we don't know any of the dead dragonborn. What's more, I noticed that none of them had clan piercings like these." He touched a claw to one of the white studs in his left profile. "The piercings every Tymantheran carries."

"So they took them out," Zan-akar said.

"I doubt it, milord," Medrash replied. "I couldn't find scars to show where any had ever gone in."

"This is a transparent attempt to obscure the truth," said Zan-akar, pale sparks dropping from his markings. "Where do dragonborn come from except Tymanther?"

"Majesty," Perra said, gritting her teeth. "Is Lord Zan-akar here to serve as your inquisitor?"

"No," Shala said. "But I want to hear what he has to say. Because we now share similar concerns."

"Majesty," Perra said, "your concern should make you want to understand what's really been happening in Luthcheq these past several tendays. And it's obvious we still don't."

"How so?" Shala asked.

"When we believed there was only one killer," the stooped old dragonborn said, "we could ascribe his crimes to madness. That can't explain the actions of an entire conspiracy. So what was the point of the murders?"

"To create unrest and undermine confidence in Her Majesty's rule," Zan-akar said. "An end to which any foe might aspire."

Perra kept her gaze fixed on the war hero. "Sir Balasar and Sir Medrash tell me the Green Hands started fires."

"When discovered, spies and assassins often try to destroy their papers," Zan-akar said.

"They also tried to obliterate esoteric symbols painted on a wall and floor," Perra said.

Somewhat to Jhesrhi's dismay, Shala turned to her. "Witch, I understand you saw these symbols."

Jhesrhi took a breath. "By the time I put out the fires, the marks were mostly gone. I believe they had mystical import, but I can't tell you anything more."

"We already know the dragonborn used some form of magic," Zan-akar said. "We can also assume they have their creeds and observances the same as anyone else. I don't see how this is relevant."

"Then ask yourself this," Perra replied. "If they were all going to make a stand against their pursuers, kill them or die trying, then why bother destroying their arcana? Isn't it possible that some people escaped the house while their fellow murderers kept Captain Fezim and his companions busy? And that the conspirators burned their documents and pentagrams so they wouldn't provide clues to the identities of those who remain at large?"

Shala turned to Aoth. "Is it possible?"

Though it didn't show on his face, Jhesrhi could almost feel Aoth wince. If he admitted there might still be killers running loose, would that keep the Brotherhood in the capital?

"We found a cellar," he said. "It connects to tunnels, probably used to move goods in the days when Luthcheq was a port. Someone could have gotten out that way. But there's no evidence anybody did."

"Still, Majesty," Perra said, "you can see how many unanswered questions there are. Let me help you find the answers."

Zan-akar sneered. "Or bury them."

Khouryn cleared his throat. "Majesty?"

Shala didn't look at a dwarf with much more warmth than she showed a wizard. But her tone was civil when she said, "Yes?"

"Whatever remains hidden," Khouryn said, "there's one thing we do know with certainty. Not all dragonborn are complicit in the murders. Sir Medrash and Sir Balasar helped bring the Green Hands to justice. I'd be dead if they hadn't."

"The covert agents of a hostile power," Zan-akar said, "must occasionally act against their own cause to conceal where their true allegiance lies."

By now, Jhesrhi had spent enough time with dragonborn to learn how their reptilian faces worked, so she recognized it when Balasar sneered. "You seem more than knowledgeable about the techniques of spying and treachery," the Tymantheran said.

Points of light crawled and sizzled along the silver cracks in the genasi's skin. "I had to become knowledgeable to protect my people from the likes of you."

"I'm curious," Balasar said. "When all those sparks start falling off you, is that like a real person losing control of his bladder?"

"Enough!" Perra snapped. "Majesty, I apologize for my retainer's lack of decorum."

The war hero frowned and fingered one of the bits of symbolic armor adorning her jerkin. After a moment, she said, "It's clear that we—" She broke off to peer at the back of the hall. Jhesrhi turned to see what had captured her attention.

One of the tall sandstone doors had opened. Looking as out of place as Jhesrhi felt among the finely dressed courtiers and heroic statuary, a disheveled soldier in spurred, muddy horseman's boots advanced and bowed low before the throne.

"Rise," Shala said. "What is it?"

"I'm sorry to interrupt, Majesty," the newcomer replied, stammering ever so slightly, "but the officer outside said I should. The pirates raided Samnur." Jhesrhi had studied maps of Chessenta and knew that was a village on the coast. "But I don't think they knew about the temple of Umberlee. The waveservants used their magic to help us soldiers fight, and we won."

"That's good news," Shala said, "and it's plain you rode hard to bring it. I'm grateful. But it could have waited until I finished my current business."

"Excuse me, Majesty, but there's more. There were dragonborn among the Imaskari."

The courtiers babbled.

"Majesty," Perra said, raising her voice to make it heard above the clamor, "I swear on the honor of Clan Ophinshtalajiir, the vanquisher would never allow such a thing."

"Did the dragonborn have piercings?" Medrash asked, but the question got lost in the general din.

"Shut up!" Shala snapped, and the room quieted. She fixed her gaze on Perra. "You and your people will have to leave Luthcheq."

Zan-akar somehow managed to keep his expression grave, but Jhesrhi suspected he was whooping with joy on the inside.

"Majesty," Perra replied, "let me be very sure I understand you. You're expelling us from Chessenta and breaking off relations with Tymanther?"

"I'm sending you away," Shala said, "to avoid another riot when the city hears this news. For your own safety, in other words. I'll have to ponder further to decide whether to sever ties with your kingdom."

But with Zan-akar urging her to do precisely that, and no one left to speak for Tymanther, Jhesrhi figured she knew what decision the war hero would ultimately make.

Perra surely assumed the same, but maybe she also judged it would be impossible to change Shala's mind. Because she simply bowed and said, "As Your Majesty commands."

* * * * *

Resplendent in a new suit of silk and brocade, the candlelight glinting on his jeweled ornaments, Gaedynn related the story of the taking of the Dread Ring in Lapendrar. Apparently he'd done it more or less single-handedly, with every arrow piercing a vampire or some other undead horror through the heart.

It was a tale told on two levels. His comrades were meant to take it as a joke. The pretty young ladies seated to either side of him—Nicos's nieces, or was it cousins?—were supposed to *ooh* and *ah* at his heroism, and they did.

Aoth was glad someone was enjoying the victory feast. Jhesrhi had begged off, as she often avoided such occasions. Khouryn grew quieter with every cup of Sembian red. Even their host seemed subdued.

So was Aoth, and it annoyed him. So what if the dragonborn had suffered a misfortune? No one was paying him to look out for their interests. By the Black Flame, for all he knew, it might even be true that Tymanther was the secret enemy of Chessenta. Old Perra wouldn't be the first envoy who didn't know what her own government was up to.

Seated at the head of the table, Nicos turned his head in Aoth's general direction. "Numestra, could you possibly spare the captain for a little while? He and I have matters to discuss."

Aoth's buxom, freckled tablemate had gamely made conversation throughout the five-course meal, but he had the feeling she was happy to be rid of him. His weird eyes, copious tattoos, and reputation as a bloodthirsty Thayan sellsword intrigued some women but repulsed others, and she was probably in the latter camp. And his dourness had offered little to win her over.

Nicos led him toward the same study in which they'd had their initial conversation. But the nobleman stopped short in the antechamber where the halfling clerks labored by day. Aoth caught a whiff of a distinctive sweet-and-sour smell hanging on the air.

"Wait," Nicos said. "I have a particularly fine apricot cordial. We can share that as we talk." He waved for Aoth to precede him back the way they'd come.

Maybe the aristocrat really did crave another drink. But Aoth wondered if he was trying to keep him from catching the lingering aroma of a rare aromatic gum burned in certain rituals.

Fine. If he didn't want Aoth to smell it, he wouldn't let on that he had. Kossuth knew he didn't blame the nobleman for not wanting anyone, even one of his own agents, to know he possessed a modicum of occult knowledge and ability. Not in Chessenta.

They ended up in a game room with one table for throwing dice and another for spinning tops at arrangements of little wooden pins. It was in an offshoot of the house, with no floors above it, so Aoth could hear the rain pattering on the roof.

Nicos served the sweet liqueur. Aoth assumed it probably was every bit as good as his host claimed, although he couldn't really tell. His palate was so lacking in discernment that he could drink almost anything with relish.

He waited for Nicos to tell him the purpose of their discussion, but the Chessentan seemed to be having trouble getting started. In hopes of moving things along, Aoth said, "I noticed that neither Lord Luthen nor his proxy Daelric said a word in council today. I suppose they realized they'd look like idiots speaking out against you now that you truly have stopped the Green Hand killings."

Although now that he thought about it, it was odd. Luthen hadn't looked unhappy. He'd had a little smile on his round, bearded face.

Nicos grunted. "We did stop them—or rather, you and your people did. It needed doing, and you succeeded brilliantly." He hesitated.

"But?" Aoth prompted.

"It didn't work out the way I hoped. I'm afraid the provocations from Threskel and High Imaskar, outrageous and damaging as they are, are merely the precursors to actual invasions. In large measure, that's why I wanted to catch the Green Hands. To allay the common suspicion of mages enough that the war hero and her commanders would consent to use them in our defense."

Aoth nodded. "And we did. But now Chessenta won't have dragonborn allies fighting alongside her soldiers. You're worried you came out behind on the trade."

"Exactly."

"Of course, if Tymanther really is your enemy, you wouldn't have had their help anyway."

Nicos waved a dismissive hand, as if to convey that Tymanther's guilt was an impossibility. Aoth had his own doubts, based more on intuition than the facts, but he wondered how the Chessentan could be so sure.

"In any case," Nicos said, "our situation remains more complicated than anticipated. Shala's right—Perra and her household are now in much the same situation as were the wizards two days ago. The people despise them and may well try to harm them, and we can't trust native Chessentan troops to protect them. Can you provide an escort to see them safely back to Tymanther?"

Aoth sighed. He would have preferred to have all his strength to contend with whatever Threskel sent south. "I can spare a few men."

"Good. There's something else as well. But first, I have to ask you, are you truly *my* agent? Will you follow my orders in preference to any others?"

Aoth stared at him. "By the Nine Dark Princes! Was Luthen right? *Did* you bring us here to help overthrow the war hero?"

"No! Of course not!"

"Well, that's a relief, because I don't think that at our current strength we could pull it off. We might kill or imprison her, but we probably wouldn't fare well in the dung storm that would follow."

"I'm not a traitor!"

"Clearly not, milord. I was just speaking hypothetically. To answer your question—yes, I'm *your* man, as long as you keep paying me."

"All right. Then how much do you know about Tchazzar?"

Aoth cocked his head. "Very little. I'm old enough that I actually could have seen him, but I never did. I was a little busy up in Thay the last time he was around."

"I assume you've at least heard that he vanished during the upheavals of the Spellplague."

"Yes."

"Well, there's a little more to the story. He ventured into Threskel and never returned. It's possible he was looking for a way to protect Chessenta from the blue fire, although no one truly knows."

"So, if he was in enemy territory, it's also possible his greatest enemy managed to kill him at last."

"Yes, but recently, some rumors have come out of the northeast. Allegedly, certain folk, while wandering somewhere in the mountains, have heard a dragon roaring on the darkest nights. A few even claim to have seen one sprawled on the ground, with flames flickering from its mouth and nostrils."

"Threskel's full of wyrms, isn't it? There's a dracolich running the place, and a bunch of living wyrms who pay homage to him. I imagine some of them are fire-breathers. So what makes you think this particular dragon is Tchazzar?"

"The reports say the dragon is huge and old, like Tchazzar. They also say he's emaciated, and looks like he can't stand up for some reason. If he's crippled, or imprisoned somehow, that would explain why he never returned to Luthcheq."

"But it doesn't explain why, over the course of nearly a century, Alasklerbanbastos never found him and finished him off. Or why, if he's been lying helpless for all that time, you just heard about it 'recently.'"

Nicos scowled. "I don't simply assume the dragon in question is Tchazzar. But it could be."

"And you want to find out for sure."

"Yes."

"Without Shala realizing you have someone looking into it. Because she'd take it to mean you lack confidence in her rule."

"Yes. Although it would be completely unfair to take it that way, considering that Tchazzar was a living god. *Obviously*, he could provide for his people in a way no mortal sovereign could. And he might not even want to resume the throne. It's possible he's beyond such things."

And possible he's not, thought Aoth, in the highly unlikely event he's still alive. "I have to say, I never spotted you for a member of the Church of Tchazzar."

"I'm not. But you don't have to be to revere Chessenta's savior. Or to look into every possible source of aid now that our enemies are pressing us hard. Will you help me?"

Aoth deferred the necessity of answering by taking another sip of liqueur. The cordial suddenly tasted *too* sweet, and burned in the pit of his stomach.

He had an unpleasant sense of being caught up in matters he didn't understand. There were too many anomalies. The unanswered questions about the Green Hands and the apparent treacheries of the dragonborn. Nicos's unexpected mystical skills, and his claim that after almost a hundred years, rumors of Tchazzar's survival had reached him only now, just when Chessenta was in urgent need of its champion. To say the least, it was a remarkable coincidence.

But did Aoth need to understand? Did he even want to? Or did he want to keep to his . . . well, definitely not his *place*. Though he observed the proper forms of respect to the lords of the world, particularly if they were employing him, he'd long since forsaken true subservience to anyone. But his *role*, the one he'd freely chosen for himself, was to be the sellsword captain who fought for gold and reputation without caring or having to care about the plots and maneuvers that sent realms to war in the first place.

That role was in jeopardy now. If he pushed Nicos for further answers, gave the nobleman reason to suspect his loyalty, it might slip from his grasp forever.

"You realize," he said, "that even if a spy did find Tchazzar alive, that doesn't mean a mere man could fix whatever problem is holding a dragon helpless."

"I wouldn't expect him to try," Nicos replied. "He just needs to report his findings, and then I'll decide what to do next."

Aoth grunted. "All right. I'll send someone to run this errand too. If anyone notices, I'll just say I'm dispatching scouts across the border to gather intelligence on Alasklerbanbastos's forces."

* * * * *

Khouryn sat with his feet stretched out toward the campfire and his back against Vigilant's flank. The griffon's body heat prevented the chill of the evening fog from sinking into her rider's bones, and keeping her close discouraged her from taking an inappropriate interest in the horses and mules.

Naturally he wouldn't have done it if any of his companions minded having such a big, potentially deadly animal lounging close at hand, but none of the dragonborn did. In the main they seemed to be hearty, practical folk like dwarves or sellswords, and he liked them more every day they traveled together.

And that had been long enough that he was starting to feel like he could relax and enjoy their company. They'd journeyed at a good pace. Maybe fast enough to outrun the news that Tymanther had supposedly betrayed Chessenta.

Balasar, who justly took pride in his camp cooking, handed him a grilled trout fillet wrapped in a big leaf from some aquatic plant. The best route from Luthcheq into Tymanther ran along the northern shore of the Methmere. The frequent mists were one of the inconveniences. The fresh fish were one of the advantages.

Khouryn took a bite. Too quickly—it burned his mouth. But it was tasty, sweet, moist, and spiced with something he didn't recognize. Vigilant gave a little squawk, begging, and he told her to shut up. "You had your supper before the sun went down."

"Yes," said Balasar, grinning, fog blurring his features even though he was just a few feet away. "Do be quiet, Vigilant. Your master has to keep up his strength to protect us poor, helpless dragonborn from harm."

Khouryn chuckled. "Peace. I think you realize we didn't tag along because anyone doubts your prowess. It's just that a few extra spears are never a bad idea. And if we run into angry peasants, well, it's you they hate, not us. So maybe we can persuade them to back off without needing to kill any."

Medrash scowled. "I still can't believe it's come to this. And, stuck back in Tymanther, we'll have no way of uncovering the truth."

"It's not your fault," Balasar said. "Although maybe that god of yours is to blame. If he's what really set you on the trail of the Green Hands."

Medrash glared. "Torm charged me to further the cause of good. But somehow I bungled the task, and because I did, the alliance fell apart."

"How?" Balasar asked. "How would any sane person say you botched the job?"

"Perhaps stopping the Green Hands *wasn't* the job. Maybe I misunderstood Torm's prompting from the start. I just don't know!"

Khouryn decided he didn't want to watch two friends quarrel, or Medrash wallow in self-recrimination either. Hoping to divert the conversation, he asked, "How did you get to be a paladin, anyway? I always heard that dragonborn don't worship the gods."

Medrash smiled like he too was glad of a distraction. "Back in Abeir, where we lived before the Blue Breath of Change hurled us across space, none of us did. But we've been in Faerûn for a while now. We're picking up some of your ideas."

"A pointless craving for novelty that corrupts the old traditions." Balasar's tone was severe past the point of pomposity, but then he grinned. "Or at least that's what the clan elders say. Me, I just think all this praying and such is silly. As far as I can see, all it does is fill fools like my clan brother here with fretting and discontent."

A coil of the steadily thickening fog billowed across Medrash's face, half obscuring it. "It gives us purpose."

"What better reason to avoid it?"

Once again, Khouryn intervened. "All right, that explains how some dragonborn come to embrace the gods. But how did *you* receive the call to be a paladin?"

"I suppose I heard it," Medrash said, "because I needed to. As a youngling, I was the shame of my parents and of Clan Daardendrien. Weak, clumsy, and—worst of all—timid in a kindred famous for its warriors."

Khouryn snorted. "That's hard to believe."

"Maybe, but it's true. All the other youths despised me. Everyone but Balasar."

"Ascribe it to my kindly nature," Balasar said. "Or maybe my contrariness."

"Anyway," Medrash continued, "I was well embarked on a wretched life. It was even possible Daardendrien would cast me out. But then I started dreaming of a warrior with a steel gauntlet.

At the start, I didn't even realize he was Torm, or a god at all. But I could feel his magnificence, and when he urged me to put my trust in him, what did I have to lose?"

"Clarity of mind?" suggested Balasar.

Medrash gave him an irritated look.

"I take it," Khouryn said, "that after you pledged yourself to the god—or something like that—things changed for you."

"Not all at once," Medrash said. "I didn't stop being afraid, but I found the willpower to try things even though I was. I threw myself into my warrior training, because for the first time I truly believed I could improve."

"And that's the tooth that cracks the shell," Balasar said. "Attitude. Confidence. I don't need to believe that a god truly took a personal interest in one sad, puny little child to explain what happened next."

"After half a year," Medrash said, "I was stronger, quicker, and a better fighter than a number of my fellow students. After two years, I was better than nearly all of them."

Balasar swallowed a mouthful of trout. "Except me. Obviously."

Medrash snorted. "Oh, obviously. Later still, I happened across a Tormish temple. I looked at the paintings and statues and recognized the protector from my dreams. I took instruction from the holy champions and asked them to train me to be a paladin."

"What did your clan think about that?" Khouryn asked.

"They tolerated it," Medrash said. "Most dragonborn believe that those who pay homage to the gods are a little odd, but they don't scorn us the way the Chessentans do their mages."

"The clan realizes," Balasar said, "that wherever Medrash's special talents come from, they're useful. Anyway, you can't hate everybody at the same time, and well before any of our folk took an interest in the gods, Tymanther had already chosen targets for its bigotry."

"I wouldn't put it that way," Medrash snapped. "So, Khouryn, you've heard my story, such as it is. Now you answer a question for me. I understand why Lord Nicos wanted Perra to have an escort. I don't understand why one of Aoth Fezim's senior officers is commanding it. Doesn't he want you with him when he fights the marauders out of Threskel?"

Plainly, Khouryn thought, I'm not the only one who knows how to change the subject. But fair enough. I don't need to know who it is that Tymantherans spit at in the street. "I asked to lead the escort. During the riot and again in the fight with the Green Hands, you fellows saved my life."

Medrash shrugged. "We three simply watched out for one another, as comrades do."

"Maybe," Khouryn said, "but I felt like helping you get home safely. Besides, there's another reason I wanted to come. Tymanther's not that far from East Rift. My wife's there, and I haven't seen her in a couple of years. I'm hoping to travel on down the Dustroad and visit. On griffonback, it's not that long a trip."

"Why don't you live with her?" Medrash asked.

Khouryn grunted. "That's not as happy a story as yours. Nor one I'm much inclined to tell, except to friends. When I was about as young as the two of you—which is damn young, for a dwarf—"

Vigilant sprang to her feet, dumping her master on his back. Balasar chuckled, but his mirth died away when he saw how the griffon was looking around.

Khouryn scrambled to his feet. "Something's coming." His mind raced: What did he have time to do? Pull on his mail? Saddle Vigilant? Quite possibly neither.

"We have sentries," Balasar said.

"Who don't see what's sneaking up on us," Khouryn said. Mace and boot, now that he was belatedly paying attention, he realized that except for the other campfires, reduced to mere smudges of glow, he could barely even make out the rest of the camp. He raised his voice to a bellow. "Something's in the fog!"

In response, voices cursed. He could picture his fellow wayfarers hastily rising from their ease and grabbing their weapons, even as he was snatching up his urgrosh.

Balasar and Medrash took up their shields and drew their swords. The paladin rattled off an invocation, set his blade aglow with silvery light, and grimaced when he saw that the luminescence only helped a little to reveal what lay within the mist.

Then, closer to the lake, someone screamed. One of the pickets, maybe cut down before he even realized he was in danger. An instant later, Vigilant gave a deafening screech and charged in that direction.

Khouryn ran after her, and Medrash and Balasar pounded after him. Still, the griffon outdistanced them and vanished into the fog. Then wings snapped, bodies thudded together, and hissing cries rasped. She'd found the enemy.

When Khouryn caught up, he nearly faltered in surprise, for Vigilant was fighting creatures unlike any he'd ever seen. At first glance they somewhat resembled lizardfolk, but with limbs and torsos foreshortened from human- to dwarf-length, and flexible, whipping necks stretched more than long enough to make up the lost height. Their scales gleamed orange-yellow in the glow of Medrash's sword.

Despite their fangs and claws, they were no match for Vigilant in close combat. She'd already shredded two and was gutting another with her talons. But four more, keeping their distance, spat what looked like water at her, and she screamed and jerked.

Khouryn charged the closest one. It spat the same spray at him. He dodged, but some of the jet still caught him.

It felt hot instead of wet. A wave of sickness surged through him. He stumbled, and his foe rushed him. The fanged head on the long neck struck at him like a snake.

Refusing to be weak no matter how wretched he suddenly felt, he swung the urgrosh and lopped it off. Then he pivoted and chopped a second such creature in the chest.

He looked around and saw that Medrash and Balasar had killed a couple too. That seemed to be all of them in the immediate vicinity. And to his relief, he didn't feel as miserable as he had a moment before. Just parched, like he'd marched under the hot sun all day without a drop of water.

"Where now?" Balasar asked.

It was a good question. Khouryn could tell from the battle cries and shrieks that the whole camp was under attack. But since he couldn't see the battle, how could he judge where he and his companions were needed most?

He tried to swallow away the dryness clogging his throat. "We go to the ambassador. Protect her."

Medrash gave a brusque nod, and they headed for the center of the camp and Perra's fire. With luck, maybe she hadn't strayed far from that location.

When they blundered into more of the hissing, long-necked creatures, they killed them. Once or twice, Vigilant shot Khouryn what he would have sworn was an annoyed glare. Maybe she considered it beneath her dignity to fight on the ground. But he was afraid he'd see even less if he rode her up into the air.

Finally Perra came into view. Cutting and parrying with one of the greatswords that only the highest-ranking Tymantherans were allowed to wield, the gaunt old diplomat was holding her own. So were the several warriors, some dragonborn and some human members of the Brotherhood, standing with her in a defensive circle. Still, Khouryn judged that he and his friends had been wise to come to her aid. There were dozens of the long-necked creatures attacking the formation.

He started forward, and Medrash said, "Wait." The paladin spat bright, crackling lightning, and his clan brother, silvery frost. Blasted from behind, several of the orange-yellow creatures collapsed.

"Now," Balasar said.

The newcomers rushed in. Vigilant leaped into the air and came down on top of two of the attackers. Her aquiline talons pierced them through, and as they crumpled beneath her weight, her beak nipped and beheaded another.

Khouryn hacked a creature's leg out from under it, then stamped in its ribs. Another foe caught the urgrosh in its fangs and tried to yank it away. He hung on and gave the weapon a twist and jerk that snapped the reptile's neck.

"Toad-sniffer!" Balasar yelled.

Khouryn had never heard the oath before, nor did he know why a dragonborn would consider it obscene. But he recognized the tone—shock and disgust blended together. Balasar sounded like many a warrior who'd just noticed a nasty surprise appearing on the battlefield.

Khouryn whirled in time to see the last bits of an enormous creature waver into visibility. The tops of its batlike wings and its left forefoot painted themselves on the foggy air. Its glowing golden eyes fixed on Perra, and it sucked in air. Since its scales were the same topaz color as those of its servants, Khouryn assumed it was about to spew a similar attack. But dragon breath would be far more hurtful and harder to dodge.

He yelled and charged. No good. It didn't distract the wyrm. It vomited that strange, debilitating antiwater at Perra and her circle.

Just before the spray reached them, Perra vanished, and Medrash appeared in her place. Apparently the latter had used his particular form of magic to make the switch.

The dragon breath washed over Medrash and the other warriors in the ring. Some of them tried to catch it on their shields, but that didn't save them. Khouryn winced as they all collapsed.

The topaz dragon's crested, wedge-shaped head turned, no doubt seeking Perra. Vigilant lashed her wings, rose above the enormous reptile, then plunged, talons poised to pierce the fiery eyes.

But the dragon perceived the threat. It twisted its head and spread its jaws wide. Vigilant's own momentum threatened to hurl her in.

Fortunately, she managed to veer off. The dragon struck at her, and its huge teeth clashed shut on empty air.

Then Khouryn reached its foreleg. He chopped it like it was a tree. When he pulled the urgrosh free, blood gushed.

He struck again. Then the dragon raised its foot high, nearly jerking his weapon from his grasp. It stamped.

He dodged underneath its belly to avoid being squashed. As the impact jolted the ground, he tried another blow at the expanse of scaly hide above him. The angle was awkward, and the axe blade glanced away without penetrating. He reversed his grip and stabbed with the urgrosh's spearhead. That punched through. For a moment, his desperation gave way to a fierce satisfaction.

Then pain ripped through his head. It was a psychic attack, like the one So-Kehur, autharch of Anhaurz, had used to paralyze him during the battle beside the River Lapendrar.

He refused to let that happen this time. Though half blind with tears and sheer agony, he kept moving and jabbing.

Until the topaz wyrm pivoted and darted a few strides, distancing itself from him. He started to pursue, and its lashing tail whirled out of nowhere and bashed him broadside.

The next thing he knew, he was sprawled on the ground, the throbbing in his skull replaced by a general ache down one side of his body. He tried to lift himself up and was relieved to find that he could. The impact might have cracked a rib or two, but it hadn't completely shattered any bones.

The topaz dragon was still trying to kill Perra. Khouryn wished she'd retreated. But either she'd never really had the chance, or she was as disinclined to do so as a dwarf noble would have been.

At least she wasn't battling alone. Sellswords had formed into two squads and were fighting as Khouryn had taught them to fight something huge. One team jabbed with its spears, assailing the dragon while still maintaining a little distance. When it oriented on them, they fell back and the other group took advantage of the creature's distraction to attack.

Standing right in front of the wyrm's snapping jaws and raking foreclaws, depending on his skill with sword and shield—as well a nimbleness unusual in a dragonborn—to keep him safe, Balasar cut, blocked, and dodged. Other Tymantherans ran out of the fog to assault the dragon with the same reckless daring.

Surely all that skill and courage ought to count for something. But the topaz dragon feinted a strike with one foot, then slashed with the other. Balasar still managed to catch the claws on his targe, but the raw force of the blow hammered him to the ground. Then the wyrm spewed more of its breath weapon. Caught in the spray, half a dozen warriors fell, and afterward there was nothing between the dragon and Perra. It gathered itself to spring.

Vigilant dived at the dragon. The griffon had evidently been circling overhead, waiting for another chance to catch the gigantic reptile by surprise.

Once again the wyrm somehow perceived the threat. It jerked its head aside and so saved its eyes. But Vigilant compensated and at least managed to slam down on the dragon's neck just behind the skull. Her talons stabbed deep into the leathery orange-yellow hide. Her gnashing beak tore away chunks of flesh.

The dragon gave an earsplitting scream. It whipped its neck back and forth but failed to dislodge Vigilant. It clawed with a forefoot. Still clinging to her perch, the griffon shifted sideways and dodged the stroke.

It looked to Khouryn like the dragon was finally in real trouble, and he wanted to help Vigilant make the kill. Gritting his teeth against a fresh stab of pain, he scrambled to his feet and charged.

But before he could close the distance, the dragon flopped over onto its side. Its fall shook the earth, and he staggered. Then it rolled around, grinding Vigilant beneath its bulk. When it drew itself back to its feet, the griffon wasn't holding on to it anymore. Crumpled in the dirt, her wings folded in the wrong places, she wasn't doing anything at all. Not even breathing, no matter how intently Khouryn peered at her and willed her chest to rise and fall.

The topaz wyrm twisted toward Perra. Khouryn sprinted past a hind leg and cut at its flank. "Moradin!" he bellowed.

Maybe the god heard and saw fit to help, because the axe head all but vanished into the dragon's dense flesh. And when Khouryn heaved it free again, the blood sprayed out and spattered him from head to toe.

The dragon ran, unfurled its wings, leaped, and soared up into the air. It disappeared into the fog almost immediately.

Khouryn stood panting, peering, and listening, waiting to see if the creature had simply decided to continue the fight from the air. Apparently not. Coming on top of its other wounds, especially the terrible ones Vigilant had inflicted, his final stroke must have convinced it to run away.

It was only when he was sure it was gone that he remembered its minions. The greater threat had driven the lesser right out of his head. But they must have all died or run away as well. He didn't hear any fighting anymore.

He hobbled to Vigilant and looked down at the broken, flattened husk that was all that was left of her. Grief welled up in him, and he clenched himself to hold it in.

Next he checked on his men, and there the news was better. The sellswords hadn't sustained too many casualties, and even a couple of those scorched by the dragon's breath looked like they might recover.

Then he turned to his new friends. Plainly the wyrm hadn't seriously injured Balasar, because he sat holding a leather waterskin to the supine Medrash's mouth. The paladin guzzled, and his friend took the container away.

"Just a little at a time," Balasar said.

"Once I get a little strength back," Medrash croaked, "I can heal myself. Then I can heal others."

"Well, you won't get it back by making yourself puke." Balasar looked up at Khouryn. "I'm sorry about your steed and the men you've lost."

"As I'm sorry for your losses," Khouryn said.

"By the first egg!" Balasar exploded. "I would have understood if the stupid Chessentans had ambushed us. Or if the accursed genasi had come after us. But what in the name of Arambar's arse was *that*?"

Khouryn shook his head. "I wish I knew."

"Just a random attack?" Balasar persisted.

"No," Khouryn said. "The dragon wanted to kill Perra specifically. When it decided it needed to take an active part in the fighting, it went straight for her."

* * * * *

Soolabax was no city, but it was a fair-sized market town. Nor was it an impregnable fortress, but it did have walls. The combination made it the linchpin of Shala Karanok's border defenses and obliged Aoth to deal with Hasos Thora, baron of the place and its environs.

Tall and muscular with a long-nosed, imperious face, swaggering around his own keep in half armor even though nothing in particular was going on, Hasos appeared yet another embodiment of the Chessentan martial ideal. Aoth might have expected such a paragon to rejoice at the arrival of reinforcements. Yet that didn't appear to be the case.

"No one told me you were coming," Hasos said.

"That's unfortunate," Aoth said. "But the war hero didn't decide until a few days ago, and then no one could bring word faster than we griffon riders travel ourselves."

"How much meat do those beasts eat?" the baron replied.

"Lots."

"And is it true they need to be stabled away from horses?"

"That depends on how fond you are of the horses."

The baron scowled. "And then, when the rest of your sellswords arrive, I have to house and feed them as well. Winter's just ended. Food is in short supply. I—"

Aoth tipped his spear so it leaned over the table between them, casting its shadow on the maps and documents there. He drew a little crackling flare of lightning from the point. Startled, Hasos flinched.

"I don't need you to remind me of the time of year," said Aoth, "or that your people have the same needs as mine. Together, you and I will see to it that everyone has a full belly and a roof over his head."

Hasos made a spitting sound. "It's easy to give assurances, often hard to follow through."

Aoth took a deep breath. "Milord, I'm not sure why you're giving me such a cold welcome. Maybe because I'm a mage, or a Thayan. Maybe just because you're used to being the only one giving orders inside these walls. But I don't care why. I don't need to. You've seen I carry credentials from the war hero, and if you know what's good for you, you'll honor them."

He wished those documents gave him complete, incontrovertible command of the local defense. They didn't. They ordered Hasos to provide food and shelter for the Brotherhood, but beyond that merely urged him to cooperate with Aoth.

It was stupid to muddle the chain of command that way, but Aoth had gotten used to it. Monarchs often hesitated to give a coin-grubbing outlander sellsword clear authority over their own chivalrous homegrown nobles, lest the latter take it as an insult. No doubt Chessentan lords would particularly resent deferring to a man with arcane gifts.

Hasos made a sour face. "Of course I'll honor Shala Karanok's writ."

"Glad to hear it. As you'll be glad to hear that as much as possible, I mean to put the burden of feeding my men and animals on Threskel. The problem is, these"—he waved a hand at the several maps—"are short on detail. I need you to tell me where to raid."

Hasos shrugged. "How should I know?"

Aoth frowned. "Surely you conduct your own raids, milord. Surely you at least scout."

"Naturally, my rangers keep watch along the frontier. But I need all the troops I have just to defend my own lands."

"Well, I assume defense includes chasing marauders back across the border."

"Certainly." Hasos hesitated. "But the pursuers know not to go too deep into enemy territory. They can't risk blundering into a trap or leaving our own fields unprotected for too long."

Aoth closed his eyes for a moment. "With all respect, milord, you'll never gain the upper hand playing such a passive game. When Threskel commits an outrage, you need to punish them. They have to finish worse off than they started."

Hasos laughed a joyless little laugh. "That sounds sensible. But have you ever been inside Threskel?"

"Once, briefly."

"Apparently so briefly that you didn't pick up on what a dangerous place it is."

"I lived and fought in Thay, milord. I doubt I'll be impressed."

"How many dragons did you kill in Thay?"

Aoth smiled. "That's a fair hit. Not many, I admit—and like any sane man, I have a healthy respect for them. Still, we need to retaliate."

"It's possible the raids are just the precursor to an actual invasion."

"More than possible. The war hero and Lord Nicos think it's very likely."

"That means we should conserve our strength for the siege to come."

"No, it gives us even more reason to strike first. We can gather intelligence. Steal or destroy supplies and kill soldiers before the Great Bone Wyrm has a chance to use them against us."

"You do what you like," Hasos said. "But I won't lend any of my troops to such a mission."

Aoth swallowed a bitter retort. "I understand. You have to do what you think prudent. Can you at least lend me a couple of horses?"

FIVE

19–28 Tarsakh
the Year of the Ageless One (1479 DR)

Gaedynn disliked riding horses. He liked the animals themselves well enough, but he preferred to refrain from an activity unless he did it well. And he'd never learned to sit a horse with exceptional grace or skill. His elf captors hadn't kept such animals, and after his release he'd generally ridden griffons.

But a griffon would have been far too conspicuous a mount for a spy, especially since griffon riders were about to start raiding Threskel. Gaedynn's black mare and Jhesrhi's paint gelding were the next best thing. Even in an impoverished, sparsely settled land, horsemen weren't rare enough to attract a great deal of curiosity, and the animals would help them complete their fool's errand and escape back across the border quickly.

He studied the terrain ahead, rolling scrub dotted with the occasional stand of trees. A cold wind out of the north made him squint and drove stinging rain into his face. Bunched, gray-black clouds and flickers of lightning suggested it was raining harder in the direction they were traveling.

He glanced over at Jhesrhi. Wrapped in a drab hooded cloak that did a fair job of hiding her shining hair, amber eyes, and the other aspects of her exotic comeliness, she could have been any commoner traveling for any mundane reason. Bundled in cloth, her staff might have been the central support of a wayfarer's tent or even a fishing pole.

"I wouldn't be averse to more cover," Gaedynn said.

Jhesrhi didn't answer. He wasn't surprised. She hadn't said a word since they'd set forth from Soolabax. But he was getting tired of journeying with a mute.

"Do you think we've crossed the border yet?" he asked, and then waited for her reply.

Which didn't come.

"Good point," he said, just as though it had. "There probably isn't a clearly defined boundary. Who would bother to survey this dreary kingdom? And where would you find a Chessentan with the requisite knowledge? If they're ignorant enough to fear magic, they're likely deathly afraid of mathematics as well."

He paused. She didn't answer. He started to feel genuinely annoyed. Or perhaps concerned.

Either way, it tempted him to provoke her just to elicit some sort of reaction, even if the words picked at his own scabs too. "You know, I've been pondering what possessed Aoth to send the two of us on this mission. Of course, I remember what he said. I know how to uncover secrets in the wilderness and civilization alike. You're a wizard. Together we, and only we, have the necessary skills.

"Still," he continued, "with Khouryn headed south, this leaves the old man without any senior officers at all. In normal circumstances he would have balked at that, no matter what the object. I think sweet Lady Firehair came down from the moon and whispered in his ear. She heard you say it would never work for us to run away together, and she decided to prove you wrong."

Jhesrhi *still* didn't answer.

Now Gaedynn knew he was more worried than otherwise. He erased the grin from his face and the teasing edge from his voice. "What's wrong, buttercup? I thought I understood why Luthcheq bothered you. By the Black Bow, I'm not even a wizard, and it bothered me too. But we're out of there now, and you're still upset. If anything I'd say you're feeling worse."

"I'm all right," Jhesrhi muttered.

"The statue speaks! Astounding! But plainly you're *not* all right. Tell me what the problem is."

"No. You just want me to break down because you think that while I'm weak, you can take advantage of me."

Stung, he smirked. "Can you think of a better reason?"

It was only after the words left his mouth that it even occurred to him that he could have responded differently, with something other than a jeer. But by then she'd already sunk back into stony silence.

He told himself it was for the best. For after all, he *didn't* much care what she was feeling or why. Why should he? Keen-Eye knew, nobody, Jhesrhi included, had ever been all that interested in easing *his* distress.

The rain fell harder, and the sky darkened. Gaedynn judged it was around midday, but it looked like dusk. That was why he didn't spot the guard outpost until he and Jhesrhi were nearly on top of it. That and the fact that there was no watchtower or bastion there, just a barricade of tangled brambles across the trail and a hole in one of the hillsides it ran between.

Gaedynn reined in the black mare. "Shouldn't your damned wind have warned you we were coming up on that?"

"This is new country," Jhesrhi said. "I'm still making friends with it. But I don't see anyone. Maybe it's abandoned."

As if to mock her hope, two dwarf-sized figures with reptilian heads emerged from the opening. They were kobolds, specimens of one of the barbaric races often found in service to dragons.

Gaedynn grimaced. Had they detected the outpost in time, he and Jhesrhi could have ridden around it. But they couldn't do that now without arousing suspicion.

Oh well. Like his companion, he'd disguised himself as a shabby drifter in search of nothing more than the chance to shoot, forage, filch, or—if absolutely necessary—earn his next meal. He expected to put the deception to the test many times before his mission was through, and he supposed this might as well be the first.

He kept one hand on the reins and raised the other to show that it was empty. Then he walked his horse forward. Jhesrhi did the same, except that she lifted both hands and guided the gelding with her knees. Show-off.

They halted their mounts in front of the barricade. For an instant Gaedynn wondered how the hunched, stunted kobolds with their oversized skulls, long lashing tails, and musky stink could simultaneously be so like and unlike the dragonborn he and his comrades had come to know over the course of the past few tendays.

"Names," rasped the kobold on the left. Like his comrade, he wore the crossed-scepter-and-wand emblem of Kassur Jedea. Kassur was the nominal king of Threskel, although it was common knowledge he took his orders from Alasklerbanbastos just like everybody else.

"I'm Azzedar," Gaedynn replied, "and this is Ilzza." They were common Untheric names, and many Threskelan families descended from Untheric stock.

Two more kobolds wandered out into the rain. They must have had a sizable warren under the hill.

The black mare wasn't a war-horse. Possession of such a valuable mount would have immediately discredited Gaedynn's disguise. She was just a nag, and she tried to shy away from the reptiles. He drew back on the reins to steady her.

"Coming from Chessenta?" asked the kobold who'd spoken before. The glint in his narrowed eyes belied his casual tone.

"Abyss, no," Gaedynn said. "Or mostly no. I may have done some hunting on the other side of the line, but not lately. Too many patrols. Mainly I've been camped just a *little* south of here."

"Where are you headed?"

"My brother's farm. His bitch of a wife wouldn't let Ilzza and me winter there, but they'll need help with the spring planting."

"Well," said the kobold, "maybe they'll get it. If you can pay the toll."

"Toll?" Gaedynn asked.

"Maybe you haven't heard, wandering around in the wild, but we're going to war. And the Bone Wyrm needs coin to fight it."

Gaedynn was reasonably certain that no copper collected at this remote outpost would ever find its way to Alasklerbanbastos's coffers. But from his perspective, that was hardly the point.

"I don't have any coin," he said.

"You've got horses," the kobold answered. "True, they don't look like much, but they're something. How do you feel about walking the rest of the way to your brother's place?"

"Wait." Gaedynn rummaged in a saddlebag. "I have a little dreammist." He pulled out a bundle wrapped in a rag and leaned down to proffer it.

The kobold slipped around the end of the barricade, opened the packet, and sniffed the few bits of brown crushed leaf inside. "You don't have much."

"Enough for you and your friends to have some fun," Gaedynn said.

"Oh, take it and let them go on," a different kobold said. "We're getting soaked."

"All right," said the first kobold, evidently a sergeant or something comparable. It waved a clawed hand, and its fellows started to drag the mass of brambles aside.

"Stop," a new voice rumbled. Less sibilant and two octaves deeper than the kobolds' voices, it spoke Chessentan more clearly. Perhaps because it issued from a throat and mouth better shaped for human speech.

Gaedynn turned. Something more or less man-shaped, but as tall on its own two feet as he was on horseback, peered back at him from the darkness inside the burrow.

The big creature yawned. "What do we have here?"

"Nobody," said the sergeant. "Just vagabonds."

His superior emerged into the light and the rain. Perhaps it was a kind of kobold too. It had the same sort of claws, fangs, and greenish leathery hide. But sorcery, or conceivably mixed blood, had produced something more closely resembling one of the hulking giant-kin called ogres.

The big creature looked at the weapon clipped to Gaedynn's saddle. "That's a fine bow for a vagabond."

Wishing he'd made do with an inferior one, Gaedynn inclined his head. "The one fine thing I own, sir. You wouldn't take it, I hope. It's what keeps the woman and me alive when times are lean."

The leader grunted. "We'll see." It turned to the ordinary kobolds. "Search them. Persons and baggage both."

If Jhesrhi knew a spell to change the creature's mind, or to extricate herself and Gaedynn from this situation in some other way, now would be an excellent time to cast it. Before the kobolds unwrapped her staff or found the gold and silver they carried. Hoping to nudge her into action, he shot her a glance—then felt a pang of dismay.

Since they'd reached the barricade, she'd sat silently with her head bowed. She was trying to look cowed and submissive before the kobolds.

But now appearance had become reality. She was trembling.

By the Nine Hells and every flame that burned there, what was the matter with her? He'd watched her battle foes far more intimidating than kobolds and ogres without flinching.

"Get off your horses," the kobold sergeant said.

Gaedynn wished he could drive an arrow into the reptile's upraised snout. But an innocent traveler wouldn't have had his bow strung, and so his wasn't either. He yanked his sword from under the bundle intended to render it inconspicuous and cut.

The sergeant jumped back out of range. One of the other kobolds cast a javelin. It flew past the black mare's head.

Spooked, she reared. Caught by surprise, Gaedynn tumbled from the saddle and over her rump to slam down on the ground.

Kobolds rushed him. Luckily they had to maneuver around the barricade and the frightened horse to do it, in the moment before she galloped back down the trail. It gave him time to roll to his feet and meet his first attacker with a slash that split its belly.

Javelins jabbed at him, and he knocked them out of line. Back foot splashing down in a puddle, he retreated to keep the smaller reptiles from encircling him. Then, from the corner of his eye, he glimpsed something looming on his flank. He pivoted in that direction, and the big creature's long, brass-studded war club whizzed down at his head.

His warrior's instincts kept him from trying to parry, lest he break his sword and perhaps his arm with it. Instead, he sidestepped and slashed the officer's forearm. The brute snarled.

Instantly, before it could heave the club into position for another swing, he followed up with a second cut. A poorly aimed one—it missed the officer's torso but at least gashed its lead leg. The brute stumbled backward, and Gaedynn turned just in time to parry another javelin thrust from one of the lesser kobolds. As he did, he noticed more of the creatures running out of the warren.

"Jhesrhi!" he yelled. "Do something, damn it!"

But she just kept sitting on the paint that, eyes rolling, looked like he'd bolt as soon as he discerned a clear path through the combatants. She wouldn't even lift her head and *look* at the fight. Which likely meant Gaedynn wasn't getting out of this.

The leader dropped its war club, turned, and ran at Jhesrhi. Perhaps caught by surprise, or simply still frozen with dread, she didn't even try to resist as it grabbed her, dragged her out of the saddle, and held her up in the air like a toy.

"Drop your sword!" it bellowed. "Or I'll pull her arms off!"

Apparently Gaedynn's prowess had impressed it enough that it didn't want to risk losing any more of its warriors or getting sliced up any worse itself.

It would be idiotic to surrender. By her inaction, Jhesrhi had forfeited any claim on his consideration, and yielding probably wouldn't help either of them anyway. He'd likely be trading a slim chance for none at all.

Yet he didn't know if he had it in him to ignore the threat. He was still wondering when she finally came to life.

Perhaps it was the awareness that she was actually being held, *touched,* that roused her. She suddenly screamed and thrashed, and though her frenzy had no art in it—no precisely articulated words of command or flowing mystic passes—magic answered her anyway. The officer's face burst into flame.

The hulking thing roared and let Jhesrhi drop so it could slap at the fire as it floundered backward. It reeled into the barricade. There was little chance of the thorns piercing its thick hide to any great effect, but Gaedynn supposed every little bit helped.

Jhesrhi rounded on her horse just as the animal lunged to follow the mare back down the trail. She rattled off a brief incantation, and the paint froze, his momentum nearly pitching him forward onto his nose. Even though Gaedynn wasn't the target of the spell, for an instant his muscles bunched and locked as well.

Jhesrhi darted to the gelding and grabbed her staff. The rawhide lashings around the wrapping unknotted themselves.

A pair of kobolds rushed Gaedynn. He smeared the first one's eye down its face with a stop cut and balked the second by chopping the steel point off its javelin.

Then he scrambled to interpose himself between Jhesrhi and

as many of the enemy as he could. Now that she was belatedly making herself useful, it was his task to keep the kobolds off her while she cast her spells.

He landed a cut to a kobold's flank, then twisted aside from a javelin thrust. *Almost* nimbly enough—the steel point ripped his jerkin and shirt and grazed along a rib. Because shiftless poachers, Glasya take them, didn't wear brigandines. He killed his assailant before it could pull the weapon back for another try.

Behind him, Jhesrhi chanted a rhyme. For a heartbeat iridescence shimmered through the air. Rain fell upward, leaping from the puddles toward the clouds. A point of red light flew past Gaedynn into the mouth of the burrow—where, with a roar, it exploded into flame. The blast ripped the kobolds that were just emerging into burning, tumbling limbs.

Jhesrhi rattled off another spell. Rumbling and thudding in big chunks and little pellets, earth fell from the roof of the opening. The collapse didn't quite fill it all the way to the ceiling, but no more kobolds would be coming out that way.

When the reptiles who'd already emerged saw what Jhesrhi could do, they hesitated. Panting, Gaedynn wondered if he and his companion could get past without having to fight the rest of them.

Then the big creature bellowed. Gaedynn glanced around just in time to see it launch itself at Jhesrhi. Its face was a charred, oozing mass. But the fire was out and had spared the brute's eyes.

Jhesrhi spoke a word of command and stabbed with the tip of her staff. A fan-shaped flare of yellow flame leaped from the staff. It seared her attacker, but the creature kept charging, war club raised for a bone-shattering blow.

Gaedynn was too far away to interpose himself between the officer and Jhesrhi. So he hurled his sword.

He was no expert knife thrower, nor was the blade balanced for throwing. Tumbling, it hit with the flat, not the point, and did no more harm than if he'd tossed a stick.

But perhaps it startled the brute, for it looked around. And maybe it was that momentary hesitation that gave Jhesrhi time for one last spell. She stamped her foot, and the ground split beneath the officer's feet. It howled as it plunged into the chasm. It released the club and snatched for the edge but failed to grab hold.

Whipping out the hunting knife he wore on his belt, Gaedynn spun back around to face the remaining kobolds. It wasn't much of a weapon for a man battling multiple opponents, but to his relief, the reptiles looked even less inclined to keep fighting than they had a moment before.

One of them spoke in their own harsh, hissing tongue. Then they retreated, at first backing away with weapons leveled, then turning and scurrying into the rain.

Gaedynn watched to see if their withdrawal was a ruse. It didn't appear to be.

"Are you all right?" he asked.

"Yes," Jhesrhi said, looking around for creeping kobolds like he was. "You?"

"Scratched." And the graze was starting to sting, now. "Some healer's salve would be a good idea. What happened to you?"

"It won't happen again."

"That's not what I asked."

"But it's all I have to tell you."

"Curse it, woman, it was my life in danger too."

Her voice was ice. "*It won't happen again.*"

"How deeply reassuring." He took a breath. "Do you know a charm to help us catch the horses?"

* * * * *

The Brotherhood had conducted its first successful raid into Threskelan territory. Now they were bringing their plunder into Soolabax. Laden with sacks of flour and seed, the carts squeaked and rumbled. The skinny sheep *baaed*, and the goats bleated.

As Aoth watched from the battlements atop the gate, it occurred to him that his men had just condemned a bunch of peasants to hardship if not starvation. They'd left the wretches with nothing to eat or plant, with no better justification than that the farmers happened to live on the wrong side of the border.

For a moment, he felt guilty. Which was stupid, since he'd given the same order many times before and, if Lady Luck smiled, would give it many more. This kind of predation was just a part of war.

Better, then, to focus on the reaction of the people in the street below. Watching, grinning, chattering to one another, they seemed happy that someone had finally hurt the Threskelans as the Threskelans had injured them, even if it had taken a war-mage to lead the way.

Aoth waved his hand at the scene below. "You see, milord, with griffon riders scouting from on high, we can find what we want, hit it, and get away before the dragons and such even realize we were there."

Hasos's lip curled. "You were lucky your first time out, Captain. It doesn't mean your overall strategy is sound."

If anything, the baron seemed even colder than before. Maybe he felt that the sellswords' quick success pointed out his own shortcomings as a soldier.

If so, then Aoth agreed with him. But he didn't want Hasos to resent him. It would make his job harder. Unfortunately, he couldn't see much to do about it, except keep offering the noble the chance to participate in his endeavors and so earn a share of the credit.

"Be that as it may," Cera Eurthos said, "to me this seems a portent of greater victories to come."

Short, snub-nosed, and pleasingly plump, Cera was one of several dignitaries who'd climbed to the top of the gate to watch the plunder come into town. With curly hair as yellow as her vestments, she seemed a fitting high priestess for the sun god.

She had a warm, sunny smile too, although, after his experiences with Daelric Apathos, Aoth was surprised to find it shining in his direction.

Hasos inclined his head. "With respect, Sunlady, perhaps that's why you're a cleric and not a soldier."

"Oh, very likely, milord. Captain, now that you too are what passes for a notable in this sleepy little town, we should become better acquainted."

Aoth inclined his head. "You honor me."

"Perhaps we can start with a stroll along the wall."

He looked out to the end of the column and beyond, making sure no one was in pursuit. Nobody was. "That sounds nice."

Seeming more a coquette than the wise mistress of a temple, she reached to take his arm, then smiled at her own awkwardness when she noticed something was in her way. He shifted his spear into his other hand, and they set off down the wall walk.

He fancied he could feel Hasos's glare boring into the back of his skull.

Cera looked at the blue sky above the fields speckled with blades of new green grass. "Here in Chessenta, we have a saying. 'Precious as a sunny day in Tarsakh.'"

Aoth smiled. "The gods know sellswords have reason to dislike this time of year. You have to come out of winter quarters and start making coin. Of course, you want to anyway. You're half mad with boredom and confinement. But you always end up marching through storms and mud."

"Like the man and woman who rode out just a day after you arrived."

He started to frown then caught himself. His instincts suggested it was better to go on matching her light, casual air. "Keeping track of us, Sunlady?"

"Everyone's keeping track of you, Captain. You're objects of great curiosity. So be gallant and satisfy mine. Who were those people, anyway?"

"Just scouts."

"On horseback. When I've just heard you extol the advantages of reconnaissance from the air."

"You see things from on high that you wouldn't from the ground, but occasionally the reverse is also true."

They sauntered up on a sentry. He was one of Hasos's men and looked like he couldn't make up his mind how much courtesy he owed to Aoth. In the end he decided to salute, and Aoth acknowledged it with a dip of his spearhead.

"Interesting," Cera said. Aoth couldn't tell if she meant his explanation of the spies' mission or the sentry's reaction to him.

"Do you know, you seem like a very . . . *practical* sort of person. If I had to guess, I'd have said you weren't profoundly interested in *any* religion, let alone a mad cult like the Church of Tchazzar."

"Well, that answers one of *my* questions. Daelric sent you a message conveying his opinion of me."

"It's one of my great blessings that my superior writes me often, with an abundance of observations and instructions."

"Well, he was wrong about me. I couldn't care less about the Church of Tchazzar. I didn't let him roast the fools in that parade because I feared it would start a riot." He smiled crookedly. "Of course, before we were through, Luthcheq had a riot anyway. But at least I tried."

Down below them, sellswords started chivvying the plundered goats and sheep into the butchers' pens. The carts rolled on toward the bakers.

"That's good to know," Cera said. "In dangerous times, people need to put their faith in the true gods, and the lords the gods appoint to watch over them."

"You're sure Tchazzar's not a real god?" asked Aoth, simply to see her reaction. "Plainly, you know far more about such matters than I do. But as I understand it, it wouldn't make him the first creature to start out mortal and ascend to divinity."

"If he'd truly been a god, he wouldn't simply have disappeared."

"Didn't Amaunator? For many centuries? When I was young, he was just a distant memory without a worshiper or altar to his name."

She smiled. "When you were young, indeed! You don't look all that withered and decrepit to me. But as for the Keeper of the Yellow Sun, we now know he was with us all along, in the guise of Lathander the Morninglord."

"Then couldn't Tchazzar put on his own disguise? The stories say he was always a shapeshifter, sometimes a man and sometimes a wyrm."

"Are you *sure* you're not a cultist?"

"I promise. When I pray, it's to Kossuth."

She cocked her head. "Not to Tempus, or some other war god?"

"During the War of the Zulkirs, when my comrades and I fought necromancers and the undead they sent against us, the fire priests were our staunch allies. I've never forgotten that."

He supposed that even after all this time, he'd never quite forgotten Chathi, the Firelord's priestess, either. For a moment, sadness cast its shadow over him.

Cera's blue eyes narrowed. Apparently she'd noticed that fleeting change in his mood. But instead of asking about it, she said, "That's understandable, and Kossuth is a legitimate object of veneration. So I won't bore you with another theological argument explaining that technically, he's not a god either."

"The sunlady is as merciful as she is wise."

Cera chuckled. "Thank you. And you don't seem nearly as savage and depraved as a Thayan mage and sellsword ought to be."

"I tried to learn to bite the heads off kittens and puppies, but I have bad teeth."

"Perhaps I'll give a banquet so that others can see what I see. It might make it easier for you to conduct your business here."

"If they're willing to eat at the same table with an arcanist, that sounds good."

"Oh, they'll come if I invite them. Especially since we're all afraid of the Great Bone Wyrm, and you're here to protect us. Now, shall we head back? I'm due at the temple soon, and it looks bad if the high priestess of the supreme timekeeper turns up late."

As they strolled back the way they'd come, she chatted about the people he could expect to meet at the forthcoming feast. Humorous, gossipy, and occasionally salacious, the discourse lasted long enough to see them back to the top of the gate.

Hasos and his companions were gone. Aoth escorted Cera to the top of the stairs that would take them to the ground.

Though Soolabax was scarcely one of the great fortress cities of the East, the gate itself was a massive piece of stonework. The wooden stairs spiraled down an enclosed shaft with only a few windows narrow as arrow loops to light the way.

The dimness was no inconvenience to Aoth with his fire-kissed eyes. The cramped quarters, however, required that he and Cera stop walking arm in arm. She courteously waved for him to go first.

They were about a third of the way down when he saw something that brought him to a sudden stop. Cera bumped against his back, and he was glad she hadn't done it harder. Because he wouldn't have wanted her to knock him farther down the steps.

Just as he could see in the dark, and see even farther than a griffon, so too did he see the world in minute and exquisite detail. And thus, just as he was about to trust his weight to the next step, he'd spotted the webs of tiny cracks running through the half dozen risers immediately below him.

"Is something wrong?" Cera asked.

He reached with the point of his spear and touched the first stair below him. Most of it crumbled. He tapped the next. It disintegrated too. The fragments pattered on the undamaged steps one twist beneath them.

"They were fine when we climbed up," Cera said.

"Yes." Some spell or alchemical solution had weakened them in the brief period between Hasos's descent and now.

And if not for his inhumanly keen vision, an edge Aoth liked to conceal from the world at large, the trap might have caught him. True, he had a tattoo to provide a soft landing if he fell, but it took an instant to activate the magic. Caught by surprise and dropping a relatively short distance, he could have cracked his head or broken his leg before he managed it.

Rushing footsteps thumped risers farther down the stairwell. Someone had been lying in wait to finish Aoth off if the plunge didn't kill him. Now that it was plain that his target wasn't going to fall, the assassin was trying to get away.

Aoth wished he could see the bastard. But even spellscarred eyes couldn't peer through the plank stairs blocking the view.

He could give chase, though. He activated the tattoo, jumped through the hole created by the missing steps to the intact ones below, and charged onward.

He bounded all the way to the bottom and out into the street that ran parallel to the wall. Where people of various sorts were going about their business—they gasped and shied as he lunged into their midst with his spear at the ready.

"Did someone run out this doorway ahead of me?" he asked.

For what seemed an interminable moment, they all just gawked at him. Then a woman with the feet of a dead chicken sticking out of her wicker basket shook her head.

"Wonderful," sighed Aoth. The would-be killer had evidently either exited the gate while invisible or used a spell or talisman to shift himself through space. Either way, he'd made a successful escape.

Aoth tramped back up the stairs, and warm yellow light gleamed down at him. Cera still stood where he'd left her, but now she was glowing. She'd raised her power in case she needed to defend herself, and her resolute expression made a marked contrast to her lighthearted manner from before.

"It's all right," Aoth said. "Well, not really. I wanted to find out who the whoreson was. But anyway, he's gone."

* * * * *

"See the dragon?" Jhesrhi asked.

"What?" said Gaedynn, wrenching himself back and forth in the saddle. "Where?"

It was one of those rare moments when he seemed genuinely flummoxed. Despite the potentially dangerous circumstances and her sour mood, it gave her a moment of malicious amusement to see the master scout discomfited at having missed something as big and threatening as a wyrm.

Although if she were inclined to be fair, she'd admit that it was surprisingly easy to miss a blue dragon flying against a blue sky. Fortunately, the wind in these farmlands was now her ally, and as a result she hadn't needed her own eyes to learn of the creature's approach.

"Just keep riding," Gaedynn said. "In Threskel, a dragon's one of the nobility, not a beast of prey. It likely won't bother us unless we do something suspicious."

The remark implied that he thought she might be on the verge of panic. In light of her behavior back at the kobold outpost, he had every right to, but it irked her anyway.

"I know what to do," she snapped. She proved it by kicking the paint into motion and trotting on up the muddy road to Mourktar.

From a distance, with a number of towers jutting high above the buildings huddled around them, Mourktar looked like a fairly impressive city. Jhesrhi supposed that viewed from the seaward side, it would seem even more so. Because the town was Threskel's one deepwater port on the Alamber Sea, and by all accounts, the bustling heart of the place was the docks and the warehouses adjacent to them.

Although Jhesrhi had no reason to care about that. Not unless she gave in to the temptation to board an outbound ship and flee. She and Gaedynn were there because prospectors, trappers, and others who sought their fortunes in the hills and mountains called the Sky Riders often passed through Mourktar on their way in and out.

The blue dragon flew on toward the city, and then a second such creature soared up from among the buildings. Surprised, Jhesrhi reined in her mount. Gaedynn caught up and halted beside her.

The blues circled each other. After a while, Jhesrhi said, "I can't hear them at this distance, but I suppose they're talking."

"I'm sure they are," Gaedynn replied. "By all accounts, dragons are garrulous creatures. But they're doing more than that. I saw something like this once before and never forgot it. Each wyrm is trying to climb higher than the other. Given your affinity for the air, if you just look for the currents and updrafts, you'll see it more clearly than I can."

She reached out with her perceptions. It was only partly a matter of seeing, partly a matter of feeling at a distance. "Yes. You're right."

"And notice the smell in the air, like a storm is brewing. Notice the flicker inside their mouths. You can see it blink like a twinkling star, even this far away. I doubt there's much point to it. It's difficult to hurt a dragon with the same element it breathes itself. But it's their instinct to ready the weapon, no matter what."

"So they really are going to duel. I wonder why."

"I have no idea. But I do know I'd rather not be in the town underneath them while they do it. Let's watch from here."

And that was what they did, for what seemed a long while. Then the dragons swooped toward the buildings below. One disappeared into the streets on the north side of Mourktar, and the other into the southern part of town.

Gaedynn shrugged. "Well, whatever it was that divided them, apparently they worked it out."

"Apparently," Jhesrhi said. She felt a little disappointed. How often did a person have the chance to watch dragons fight each other?

"Then shall we?" Gaedynn waved his hand at the road ahead. Jhesrhi gave a nod, and they rode onward.

By the time they reached the outskirts of the city, the clear sky was giving way to gray clouds blowing in from the sea. The streets teemed with a mixture of races. Humans. Kobolds. Goblins no taller than Khouryn with big pointed ears and ruddy skin, and orcs with swinish tusks and, occasionally, one eye gouged out in honor of their patron deity Gruumsh.

Whatever his kind, if a person was well armed and carried himself like a warrior, he often wore the wand-and-scepter badge. Mourktar was full of soldiers, some likely sellswords arrived by sea. It was additional evidence that Threskel really did intend to mount an invasion.

In a sensible world, Jhesrhi thought, she and Gaedynn would scurry back to the Brotherhood with this valuable piece of intelligence. But in this one, they had to proceed with their pointless errand, searching for a creature who'd surely perished in the cataclysm that had killed even mightier beings and altered the face of Faerûn itself.

With the streets so crowded, it was slow going, and she worried they wouldn't find anywhere to stable the horses or to stay themselves. Gaedynn managed it, though. A silver coin and the promise of more persuaded an innkeeper that he could somehow provide care for two more nags and that it would be all right for a pair of weary travelers to sleep in the hayloft.

By that time, the sun had set. They ate a supper of fish stew, rye bread, and ale in the inn's common room, then headed back out into the streets. Jhesrhi braced herself for the press of bodies. It had been unpleasant enough on horseback, when people could only brush and jostle her legs. It would be worse when she was fully submerged in the crowd.

But she tolerated it because she had to. She caught Gaedynn glancing at her repeatedly, checking on her, and shot him back a scowl.

Which perhaps he didn't deserve, for he wasted no time leading her to a narrow, doglegged street where the taverns had names like The Five Nuggets and The Hill Man's Bliss and the merchants sold shovels, pans, sluice boxes, traps, bows, and boar spears. Since he'd never visited Mourktar before either, she had no idea how he found the right part of it so quickly. It didn't seem fair that a man raised in the woods should seem so completely at home in cities as well. Especially since she seldom felt fully at ease anywhere at all.

As they wandered from one smoky, boisterous taproom to another, he presented himself as the woodsman and hunter he was, and the hill men took him for one of their own. She looked on quietly as he bought rounds of drinks, swapped preposterous boasts and filthy jokes, and in time turned the conversation to strange tales and rumors from the wild.

It was probably because she remained aloof from the conversation that she was the one who noticed someone watching them.

A small man sat alone in the shadowy corner nearest the door. He wore the same stained, patched, rugged garb as most of the people in the room, but to judge from the pallor of his face and hands, he hadn't really spent much time in the sun and the rain. He wasn't quite staring at Gaedynn, Jhesrhi, and the hill men at their table, but his dark, pouched eyes kept returning to them.

She wondered how best to find out who he was and what he wanted. She was still pondering when he abruptly rose and headed out into the night.

She took hold of her staff, still shrouded in a layer of cloth to hide the rare, valuable blackwood and inlaid golden runes. The wrapping attenuated her mystical link to the rod, but not so much as to render it useless. She waited another moment, then rose and started for the door. Gaedynn gave her a questioning look. She raised her hand, signaling him to keep his seat.

Though she was only a few heartbeats behind the watcher, by the time she stepped out the door, he was nowhere to be seen. She whispered to the breeze that carried both the stink of the city's garbage and the saltwater smell of the sea. Unfortunately, it hadn't taken any notice of the pale man.

"What's going on?" Gaedynn asked.

Startled, Jhesrhi jerked around to find him standing right behind her. "I told you to stay put," she said. But he hadn't, because he didn't trust her nerve and judgment anymore.

"We're done here anyway," he said. "What pulled you out of your chair?"

"Someone was watching our table. I wanted to find out why, but somehow he outdistanced me."

Gaedynn looked around. "Well, he could have ducked in any of these doors, and it's not that far to the bend in the street. Who do you think it was?"

She shrugged. "Someone trying to pass for a hill man, but not. Beyond that I can't say. I hope he wasn't a spy looking for his opposite numbers from south of the border."

"Even if he was, we weren't doing anything overtly nefarious. I think it's more likely he's a spotter for the local thieves' guild. I was spreading a little coin around. And even though you have that hood shadowing your face and a cloak obscuring your shape, a perceptive fellow could still tell you'd make a lot of coin for any of the local festhalls."

She scowled at him.

He grinned back. "Facts are facts, buttercup. The point is, if we keep our guard up, we can surely handle a few toughs." He hesitated. "Can't we?"

"Yes," she said, gritting her teeth. "In your estimation, have we learned anything?"

"I assume you heard most of it. Plenty of people have stories to share about a dragon roaring in the night. The problem is, the tales are vague as to what hillside or mountaintop it's roaring on. But just now I got the name of a fellow who collects information about the

Sky Riders, then sells it to trappers looking for particularly luxuriant pelts or prospectors looking for streams that run yellow with gold."

"In other words, a swindler."

Gaedynn smiled. "I'd bet my life on it. Or at least somebody's life. But I'd also wager he gathers real information to make his lies more convincing. And that he's not averse to peddling that as well, when there's a market for it. Shall we go find out?"

Jhesrhi kept watch for the pale man, and for any lurking ruffians, as Gaedynn led her into a shabby dead-end street. She didn't see anyone suspicious. Nor, when she consulted it, did the wind. Maybe the watcher had taken their measure and decided to seek easier prey.

She noticed the structures in the immediate vicinity were smaller than average, with windows placed lower to the ground. Some builder had thrown up a dozen apartment houses for people shorter than humans.

Gaedynn rapped on one of the street-level doors, then waited. After a time it squeaked open a crack, and a halfling peered out from the darkness within.

"Good evening," Gaedynn said. "My companion and I are headed into the Sky Riders. We need information to ensure a successful journey."

"I need silver to open this door," the halfling answered. Because of their size, his kind tended to have voices higher than humans, and old age seemed to have pitched the scratchy one Jhesrhi was hearing higher still. Yet she was reasonably sure the speaker was male.

Gaedynn produced a coin and presented it with a flourish. It disappeared into the crack, and then the door opened. Despite a soldier's familiarity with wounds and scars, Jhesrhi had to suppress an impulse to stare or wince at what stood revealed on the other side.

The halfling was missing the eye, the ear, and some of the white hair from the right side of his head. In their places were deep, livid, horizontal grooves. His right hand and some of the forearm were gone too, while the right leg, though present, was twisted shorter than the left, hitching his body off center.

He turned and, limping, conducted his visitors into a candlelit, low-ceilinged room. Bearskins, wolf pelts, racks of antlers, and halfling-sized hunting weapons hung on the walls. A scatter of maps lay on a table, along with the hook and leather cuff the halfling presumably wore when he felt the need for a prosthesis.

Jhesrhi was somewhat encouraged. Judging from appearances, their host might truly have known the Sky Riders well, in the days before some beast mauled and crippled him.

He flicked his remaining hand at a bench with chipped and peeling paint that looked like he'd salvaged it from the town dump. "That's the one thing big enough for humans to sit on."

"Thank you," Gaedynn said.

The halfling flopped down in a chair. "What exactly do you want?"

"We've heard stories," Gaedynn said, "about a dragon that roars by night somewhere high in the hills."

"So?"

Gaedynn smiled. "A dragon's lair is full of treasure."

The cripple snorted. "And you think you can carry it off? Just the two of you?"

"The tales suggest this particular wyrm is inconvenienced somehow."

"It's still a dragon."

"We don't intend to fight it. Just sneak into its lair, pocket a few prize gems, and live like lords for the rest of our days."

The halfling squirmed in his chair like he couldn't get comfortable. "It sounds like you've got it all figured out already. What do you need me for?"

"The tales are either unclear or contradictory concerning the dragon's location."

The maimed hunter grinned, revealing gapped, stained teeth. "Easy to see why, if the creature only appears at night. And seeing as how fools are always getting lost in the Sky Riders. People who saw or heard the wyrm—if anyone truly did—may not have known exactly where they were."

"Do you think anyone did?" Jhesrhi asked. "See it, I mean."

"What's the difference?" The halfling shifted again. "You and your man have decided they did, or else you wouldn't be here. Nothing I say is likely to change your minds."

"You're probably right," Gaedynn said. "So, can you help us?"

"Maybe," the halfling said. "I've heard all the stories you have and more, and knowing the hill country, I can interpret details that don't mean anything to you. I can make a good guess where you ought to look. But only if you make it worth my while."

"I already gave you one piece of silver. How about four more?"

"That's piddling for information that will make you rich, or so you tell me. How about ten gold?"

"If we had that kind of coin, we wouldn't need to chase dragons. What about this? We'll cut you in for a tenth of the profits."

"Now, that sounds splendid! Because I'm confident you'll come back loaded down with diamonds and rubies, and just as certain you'll keep your word."

"I take your point. We'll pay you three gold. But I swear by the Merchant's Friend, we can't go any higher."

The halfling grunted. "Hand it over."

Gaedynn fished a purse out of the jerkin he'd mended with big, clumsy stitches after the kobold's javelin tore it. "You just need to understand one thing."

"What's that?"

Gaedynn shook coins out into his palm. "My companion is a wizard. She's going to cast a charm that will alert her if you try to cheat us."

It was a lie. Jhesrhi had mastered dozens of spells, but none that would serve that particular purpose. But other people had no way of knowing that, and she and Gaedynn had used the bluff to extract the truth from the credulous on several previous occasions.

As he took the coins, the halfling made a spitting sound. "As long as she doesn't turn me into a rat or make my manhood fall off, she can do what she likes."

Jhesrhi whispered words of power. The room grew colder. For a moment, the candles burned green, and a breeze rustled the parchments on the table. It was likely enough to create the impression that some useful enchantment was in place.

"Now," said Gaedynn, "go ahead."

The halfling leaned over the table and riffled through the maps until he found one drawn on vellum. He sketched a circle on it with his fingertip. "Somewhere in this area. And I think that if it's really there to be found, you'll find it on the western side of a hill."

Maintaining the fiction that Jhesrhi could tell if their informant was telling the truth, Gaedynn looked to her. She nodded.

The redheaded archer extended his hand. "Thank you for your help."

The halfling blinked like he wasn't used to courtesy or gratitude. "There's one more thing I can tell you. People only ever glimpse or hear the dragon at the dark of the moon."

"That complicates matters," Gaedynn said, "but at least it's not for a while yet. We have time to get to the right place. Thank you again."

After the cripple showed them out, Jhesrhi said, "You could have just given the poor fellow ten gold."

"That would have seemed very strange to him. He expected me to haggle."

"And, it's bad luck to swear a false oath by any of the gods."

"Oh, I imagine Waukeen will forgive me." He grinned. "As you know better than anyone, I'm well nigh irresistible to blondes with golden eyes."

She scowled. "Where now? Back to the stable?"

"If you like. We have what we came for."

They headed in that direction. To her relief, the crowds in the streets had thinned out. In fact, they soon found themselves entirely alone on a block lined with dark, shuttered shops at ground level. In the quiet, even the iron ferrule of her staff *bump-bump-bumping* against the mud seemed noisy. She picked up the weapon and carried it over her shoulder.

Then the wind whispered to her. She willed the bindings on the staff to loosen, and the cloth fell away. She lifted the rod into a middle guard and roused the power stored inside it. The golden runes glittered.

By that time, Gaedynn had noticed what she was doing and nocked an arrow. "What?" he asked.

"People are stalking us," she said.

"Where are they?"

"All around us. I think. They're using magic that hinders even the wind's ability to perceive them, and—"

"And anyway, the breezes in Mourktar haven't fallen in love with you yet." He shifted so they stood back to back. "I've heard the song before. If the bastards are just thieves, now that they see that we're ready for them, maybe they'll go away."

"I doubt common thieves would command such potent enchantments."

"Permit me the comfort of my delusions."

The breeze moaned, warning her. "Above us!" she said.

They both looked up at the wide, shadowy something plunging down at them. They each leaped forward, separating in the process because otherwise they wouldn't have had time to scramble out from underneath. The weighted net thudded and rustled down between them.

A figure with a white face and hands jumped off the rooftop after the meshwork like a four-story drop was nothing. And apparently for him it was. He landed like a cat, and Gaedynn drove an arrow into his chest.

That too should have killed or at least incapacitated him. But he simply staggered a step, then charged. As he did, Jhesrhi recognized him as the small man from the tavern. She also noticed his bared fangs.

Fortunately, Gaedynn did too—and after the nightmarish campaign in Thay, he knew how to fight a vampire. His next shaft punched into the creature's heart, where it would serve the same function as a stake. Paralyzed, the undead collapsed.

Jhesrhi glanced around. Other pale figures were creeping from between the houses. She hurled a blast of fire and set the nearest two ablaze.

Then she pivoted, searching for her next target. Even though she was trying to avoid it, she looked straight into another vampire's eyes.

The undead's coercive power stabbed into her head. Suddenly she couldn't move. She wanted to, but it was like she'd forgotten how. She had the terrifying feeling she'd even stopped breathing.

She strained to break free. In her mind she recited words of strength and liberation that would no longer pass her lips. Abruptly, and without realizing it was about to happen, she wrenched her gaze away and gasped for air.

Her paralysis, brief though it had been, had given her foes the chance to rush closer. She spoke to the wind, and it hurled a vampire backward an instant before his outstretched hands could grab her.

Behind her, light flashed, momentarily painting the world bluewhite. Thunder boomed, power crackled, and Gaedynn laughed a single "Ha!" of satisfaction. He'd used one of the special arrows she'd enchanted for him, evidently to good effect.

Even comparatively weak vampires—and it seemed to her that these were some of the weaker ones—were fearsome opponents, but so far it appeared that she and the archer were holding their own. Hoping to stand back to back again, she retreated a step, and then other figures stalked from the gloom behind the undead.

The newcomers weren't pale as bone, and she didn't see any glistening fangs or lambent eyes. Humans, then, wrapped in shapeless hooded cloaks much like her own.

She drew breath to cast a spell at the new enemies, then realized some of them were already chanting. A couple whirled implements resembling picks through serpentine passes with a nimbleness at odds with the weapons' obvious weight.

Jhesrhi abandoned her offensive magic to rattle off a briefer charm. A disk of golden light shimmered into existence in the air before her.

Also floating and made of glowing light, but continually rippling from one color to another, several picks abruptly appeared in front of her defense. The magical weapons hurtled at her, and though her amber shield shifted back and forth, it couldn't block them all. One red as flame whirled itself around the edge of the oval. She parried it with her staff, but at the same instant another such attack stabbed her in the back.

Wracked with pain and horribly cold besides, she crumpled. The pick that had wounded her changed from white to green and struck again before she finished falling. Her nose, mouth, and throat burned, and she started coughing uncontrollably.

Evidently recognizing that she was no longer able to oppose them, the enemy sent the animated picks streaking over her to take Gaedynn from behind. Still coughing, floundering in her own blood, she flopped over to watch the inevitable result.

Gaedynn whirled and loosed another arrow. Then, chopping relentlessly, the luminous, multicolored picks assailed him like a swarm of wasps. He fell with blood streaming from his wounds.

Between coughs, Jhesrhi caught the stink of charred flesh. Hands grabbed her and slammed her flat on her back. His skin burned black, a vampire dropped to his knees and bent over her.

Then one of cloaked men stepped into Jhesrhi's field of vision. Now that he'd come close enough, she could make out the pattern of scales on the robe visible through the gap between the wings of his outer garment. She could even discern how the folds of the iridescent vestment changed color as he moved, although in the darkness she couldn't truly see the colors themselves.

But she didn't have to see them to recognize a priest of five-headed Tiamat, the Dragon Queen. "Get away from her," the cleric said.

The vampire glared up at him. "She burned me," he said, the words garbled for want of the lips the fire had taken. "It's only fair that her blood help restore me."

"If we injure her any further, she's likely to die. As it is, we'll have to cast healings on her and the bowman before they're fit to travel."

Coughing less, no longer shaking quite so hard with chill, but still too weak to resist, Jhesrhi silently thanked the Foehammer that Gaedynn was still alive.

"You . . . mortals," the vampire snarled, like it was the foulest insult imaginable. "You priests. You order us to the fore to run the greatest risk——"

"And you obey," the wyrmkeeper said, "because our master has given us authority over you." Master, Jhesrhi noted, not mistress. Whomever he was talking about, it wasn't his goddess. "And because you know we possess the power to compel you—or at least I assume you know. If necessary, I can provide a demonstration."

Though still glowering with fangs extended, the undead rose and backed away. "Thank you," the wyrmkeeper said. He stooped and tugged the staff from Jhesrhi's feeble grasp. The runes stopped shining. He studied the tool with a knowledgeable eye. "Nice. Very nice. Now, we're going to gag you and bind your hands. Then I'll do something to restore your strength and take away the worst of—"

"Look!" someone yelped.

The wyrmkeeper pivoted and glanced around. "At what?"

One of the men armed with a pick made of ordinary steel and wood pointed at a rooftop. "He's gone now, but he was there! Somebody spying!"

The wyrmkeeper turned toward the spot where three vampires stood clustered together. "Whoever it is, retrieve him."

The pale-faced figures dissolved from bottom to top like icicles melting. Shrunken into bats with wrinkled snouts and eyes like gleaming ink, swirling around one another, they fluttered upward and vanished into the night sky.

Next the cloaked men restrained Jhesrhi, denying her any hope of using her magic. Then the wyrmkeeper prayed over her. The nasty, sibilant sound of the words made her skin crawl. But as promised, they closed her wounds, muted her pain, and brought a bit of her strength trickling back. The priest moved over to Gaedynn and did the same for him.

Shortly afterward the three vampires, in human guise once more, stalked into view. The one in the lead was carrying a motionless body in his arms. When he dumped it on the street, its cape fell open. Jhesrhi was surprised to see that under his outer garment, the dead man too wore a vestment of iridescent scales.

"Thank the Dark Lady," the wyrmkeeper said.

"What do we do with him?" asked the fellow who'd spotted the skulker in the first place.

"It's better that he should disappear than be found," said the priest. "So I suppose we'll have to drag him along with us. Get them up."

The enemy hauled Jhesrhi and Gaedynn to their feet, and she

saw that they'd disarmed, bound, and gagged the archer as well. The wyrmkeeper rubbed the black, mask-shaped ring on his finger, and she felt a powerful enchantment—no doubt the charm of invisibility—enfold the entire company, captors and captives alike.

Then they all tramped some distance through the city. Thanks to the wyrmkeeper's restorative magic, Jhesrhi expected that she'd continue to recover from her wounds with preternatural speed. But for now she was still weak and sore, and the walk taxed her severely. She might have been glad when her foes pointed her toward the entrance to the ruins of an old warehouse, except that she had every reason to be wary of whatever waited inside.

First she caught its odor, the tang of a gathering storm like she'd smelled that afternoon. Then she saw the sparks jumping and popping on the body that was simply a huge, shapeless mass in the dark. Eyes big as serving platters glowed white at the top of the murky form.

"I see you caught them," the creature said, its voice a sort of rumbling hiss.

"Yes, milord," the wyrmkeeper said. "Unfortunately, a spy loyal to one of your brothers discovered us at our work. But he won't tell anyone what he saw."

"That's all right, then. Tie the prisoners to my back."

Jhesrhi felt a pang of dread and tried to shake it off. To take comfort in the fact that at least the dragon didn't mean to torture or kill her and Gaedynn on the spot.

Someone produced a long coil of rope, and the worshipers of the Nemesis of the Gods proceeded to obey the wyrm's command. Meanwhile, Jhesrhi noticed, although she hadn't been able to tell it from the street, that most of the derelict building was open to the sky. A creature with wings wouldn't have much trouble entering from above.

Or exiting in the same manner—as the blue dragon proved by lashing its own batlike wings and carrying Gaedynn and Jhesrhi aloft. In a hundred heartbeats or so, Mourktar was left behind.

SIX

29 Tarsakh–Greengrass
the Year of the Ageless One (1479 DR)

Fires burned in the southwest. Khouryn couldn't see the flames, but no one could miss the columns of black smoke, even against a gray sky.

He clucked and urged his dappled mare forward. The dragonborn bred big, powerful horses to bear their weight, and though his was the smallest Perra had to offer, she was still an enormous steed for a dwarf. But he'd ridden all sorts of mounts since leaving East Rift, and he managed well enough.

He caught up with Medrash and Balasar, who sat silently contemplating the smoke like everyone else. "What is it?" he asked.

"War," Medrash said.

Wonderful, Khouryn thought sourly. Because his wife and home were on the far side of that war, and with Vigilant gone he couldn't just fly over it, now could he?

"Pick up the pace!" Perra called. Evidently the sight of the smoke made it seem even more urgent that she confer with her master as soon as possible.

So they rode or marched faster, and by the end of the morning, Djerad Thymar came into view. For some time afterward, Khouryn kept squinting at it. He was sure some trick of perspective was making the place look bigger than it really was.

But it wasn't so. The closer they approached, the more obvious it became that the dragonborn had built themselves a veritable mountain of a city. The structure rested on a colossal block of granite. On top of that, hundreds of gigantic pillars supported a kind of pyramid with a flattened apex. In its totality, the edifice towered more than a thousand feet high.

Since sighting the smoke, the ambassador and her retainers had been taciturn. But now Balasar noticed Khouryn staring, and grinned a fierce-looking reptilian grin. "Impressed?"

"I'd have to say yes," Khouryn replied.

"I hear you dwarves build things just as grand."

"We do. But we start with caverns and dig and carve. To begin in the open air with nothing more than a piece of ground, quarry all those big, heavy pieces of stone, haul them cross-country, set them one on top of another, layer on layer . . ." Khouryn shook his head. "Your ancestors must have been out of their minds."

Medrash looked over his shoulder. "Keep up," he said.

The paladin's curt manner reminded Khouryn that grim times had come to Tymanther, not that he needed reminding. There were numerous indications as the company crossed the fields surrounding the city. Though he couldn't quite make out what sort of beasts they were riding, he spotted several aerial cavalry patrols taking off from the platform at the top of the truncated pyramid. Meanwhile, drums thumped out a somber cadence from the open, colonnaded space underneath the bottom. He inferred the sound was a call to arms, a funerary observance, or both.

A wide ramp led up the outside of the slab. Farmers, soldiers, and other folk drew to the edges to let the ambassador's party by. At the top, Khouryn and his companions passed into shadow. The pyramid perched above them blocked out much of the sky.

Before them was an agora with rings of shops around it. The travelers proceeded along the edge of the commercial area, between the outermost mercantile establishments and a row of pillars, until they reached a rectangular structure that clearly served as a stable and likely performed other functions as well.

Grooms marked with the jade-ring piercings of Clan Ophinshtalajiir hurried to take charge of the horses and to clamor greetings. Perra responded cordially, but also with a briskness that made it clear she didn't have time for chitchat.

As everyone dismounted, Khouryn said, "I suppose I can stick here for the time being."

"Please don't," Perra said. "You were in the thick of it, just like Medrash and Balasar. The vanquisher may wish to question you."

"Whatever you want," Khouryn said.

She led the three warriors past the stalls into a tack room that smelled of leather and the oil that kept it supple. "Since we're in a hurry, I'm about to trust the three of you with a secret of my clan. Just a little one, but I expect you to keep it." Using a claw tip, she traced a right triangle on a bare section of wall.

The world seemed to flash and lurch, and then they were standing in a different room. Khouryn realized magic had shifted them through space. Up into the pyramid, he assumed.

They strode on through what proved to be a handsomely

appointed residence, where other dragonborn bearing jade rings hailed Perra with even greater surprise. As before, she didn't let anyone delay her for more than a moment or two, and when she'd shaken off the last of her well-wishers, she swept through an arch, between a pair of sentries, and into a passage that was plainly a public thoroughfare.

That in turn led to a plaza, an atrium that rose from the pyramid's floor all the way to its ceiling, where huge bats hung wrapped in their folded wings. Catwalks crisscrossed among them, a clue that the beasts weren't vermin, but rather the flying mounts Khouryn had seen swooping and fluttering across the sky outside.

Countless balconies jutted from the walls, and—rather to his surprise—beds of flowering plants flourished on the floor, suffusing the air with the scent of verdure. Evidently the magical glow illuminating the space nourished them as well as sunlight would.

"Don't stop and gawk," Medrash said. Then, possibly realizing how harsh he'd sounded, he softened his tone. "I understand the urge. I was the same way when I first got to Luthcheq. But Balasar and I will show you around later."

They marched on into a succession of chambers that—by virtue of their spaciousness and general magnificence, and the number of guards and bustling servants in evidence—Khouryn took to be the residence of the vanquisher. Perra spoke to a functionary who then hurried away, hurried back shortly thereafter, and conducted the newcomers into an audience chamber.

Khouryn's first impression was that like Shala Karanok's, the Tymantheran monarch's hall celebrated war. But here, suits of armor on stands took the place of the sculptures, and the cracked, faded frescos all depicted heroic struggles against dragons. There were wyrm heads mounted on the walls too, and old yellowed claws the size of short swords on display in trophy cases.

Tarhun, the vanquisher himself, was as hulking a dragonborn as Khouryn had yet seen, with a greatsword cradled in his hands to serve as a symbol of office. Square bits of gold studded the green hide under his eyes like teardrops. "Perra!" he boomed, as soon as she and her companions entered. "What does this mean?"

Perra, Medrash, and Balasar all bowed while sinuously sweeping their hands outward. Khouryn copied the salute as best he could.

"The war hero expelled us from Chessenta," Perra replied. "I take full responsibility."

Tarhun grunted. "Before we go assigning blame, maybe you should explain exactly how it happened."

"Yes, Majesty." Perra gave him the story as clearly and concisely as, Khouryn suspected, such a bewildering mess could be related.

When she finished, Tarhun's eyes shifted to Khouryn. Who saw curiosity and calculation there, but none of the distrust and distaste he'd so often encountered in Chessentan faces. "And you must be the sellsword officer who helped my emissaries in Luthcheq and again on the road home," the vanquisher said.

"Yes, Majesty," Khouryn said.

"For that," Tarhun said, "Tymanther thanks you. Will you and your spearmen stay on in my service, for a season or a year? I can use your skills, and I'll pay well."

"Thank you. But we're content in the Brotherhood of the Griffon, and the Brotherhood already has a contract."

Tarhun grimaced. "Which could mean that the next time I see you, it will be at the wrong end of a battlefield."

"Maybe not, Majesty. Shala Karanok expects to have her hands full with the Great Bone Wyrm."

"An enemy we dragonborn would gladly help her fight, if . . ." The monarch shook his head. In that moment, his manifest strength notwithstanding, his manner conveyed an emotion not too far removed from despair.

"Majesty," Medrash said, "if I may speak—from the smoke in the sky, I gather we have our own war to concern us."

"Yes," Tarhun said. "With the ash giants."

"They've been raiding for generations," Medrash said. "But as far as I know, no one ever gave them the honor of beating the war drums for them before."

"It's different this time. They're coming in greater numbers and in a more organized fashion. Someone has united the tribes. They certainly seem to be fighting more cleverly, although the details are sketchy. Many of those who engaged them didn't return to tell the tale." The vanquisher barked a mirthless laugh. "I know I just said I would have helped Chessenta, but in truth we could use their help just as much. And if Shala actually does attack us, or if she merely permits the genasi to cross her territory and attack, then we'll have to fight two foes simultaneously."

"Majesty," Perra said, "I need to make sure I understand what's really happening if I'm to be of any use to you. And so, though I don't wish to give offense, I'll ask directly—did you send raiders into Akanûl and simply not tell me about it?"

Tarhun glowered. "Of course not."

"Did you send assassins into Luthcheq?"

"Again, of course not. The dishonor aside, what possible reason could there be?"

"Did you lend warriors to High Imaskar to serve aboard her ships?"

"You know better than anyone how fast I've danced to stay neutral in the quarrel between Chessenta and the Imaskari. And even if my policy had changed, I need every soldier I have to fight the giants."

"You know," Balasar drawled, "the last I heard, the Imaskari have an ambassador in Djerad Thymar. Somebody could ask him what's going on in their navy, and possibly unravel one little corner of this tangle, anyway."

"That," said Tarhun, "is a sensible idea. Certainly more sensible than what usually comes out of your mouth, scapegrace. Fetch Nellis Saradexma."

They didn't have to wait long. The Imaskari ambassador probably lived in apartments handy to the royal residence. Tall and thin, he had a high, broad slab of a forehead and a receding hairline that made it seem even more prominent.

Gray lines marbled his skin. Khouryn might have taken them for scars or a souvenir of some illness that marked its victims like the pox, except that the retainers accompanying Nellis had them too. Evidently the marks were a characteristic peculiar to their race, like the patterns etching the bodies of the genasi.

The envoy wore a high-collared coat with three layers of shoulder cape attached. The silvery fabric gleamed and rippled in the light. The shirt, sash, and trousers underneath were black, as were the several rings on his fingers and the wizard's orb tucked under his arm.

He had to palm the crystal globe in one long-fingered hand to bow as the dragonborn did on entering the presence of their overlord, and he managed it deftly. "Majesty. How may I be of service?"

"You can tell me," Tarhun said, "about the Imaskari's naval operations against Chessenta."

Nellis frowned. "As Your Majesty knows, Chessenta has been raiding High Imaskar for years, with no better justification than a hatred millennia out of date. We're simply retaliating in kind. I daresay that in our place, Tymanther would do as much and more."

"Maybe," Tarhun said. "But the war hero believes there are dragonborn serving aboard your warships. I need to know if it's true before I end up in the middle of your quarrel."

Nellis hesitated. "To the best of my knowledge, Majesty, that's not true."

"What does that mean?" Tarhun replied. "To the best of your knowledge?"

"I have a guess," Medrash said, "if you wish to hear it."

Tarhun gave him a nod.

"High Imaskar has never been much of a naval power," the paladin continued. "That's why the Chessentan privateers were able to cause so much harm. And my suspicion is, the Imaskari still don't have many warships they can truly call their own. Someone else is striking back at Chessenta on their behalf, and that's why even a high official like Lord Nellis doesn't know the details."

The vanquisher turned his gaze back on Nellis. "Is it so?"

The envoy took a breath. "Essentially. As Sir Medrash says, my people have no great seafaring tradition. Nevertheless, we laid plans to defend ourselves from the war hero's pirates. Then, however, enormous worms and other creatures started attacking from the Plains of Purple Dust. We've always had some trouble with them, but in times past the Giant's Belt and Dragonsword ranges served as natural barriers to hold most of them back. Suddenly that didn't seem to be true any longer. Which meant we had to counter multiple threats, not just one. It was at that point that emissaries from Murghôm came to us with a proposal."

"Murghôm," Tarhun said. His disgust was plain, and mirrored in the expressions of other dragonborn in the hall.

"Yes," Nellis said. To his credit, his voice remained steady despite the dragonborn's sudden hostility. "As you'd expect, not all of it, but several of the principalities allied for a common enterprise. They offered to see to our naval defense in exchange for gold, free access to the Alamber, and certain trading concessions."

Khouryn had never visited High Imaskar—or Murghôm either—but he visualized the map of the East he carried in his head, and then he understood. If they chose, the Imaskari plainly could deny the merchant vessels of Murghôm passage down the Rauthenflow to the sea, or charge them a toll to traverse the river.

"I understand your need," Tarhun said, "but it still sickens me that your empress would strike a bargain with dragons. I thought better of your people."

"Majesty, I'm sorry if we've lost your good opinion. But we needed help, and neither you nor . . . anyone else who claimed to be our friend would join us in a fight against Chessenta. We took aid where we could get it. And earlier, I alluded to feuds and prejudices that persist even after they stop making any kind of sense. I respectfully suggest you consider the fact that the dragon princes of Murghôm aren't the same wyrms who oppressed your ancestors in the faraway land where you once lived. They're a different group of dragons altogether."

"A dragon is a dragon," Tarhun replied. "Your people will learn that eventually, and I hope you don't pay too high a price for the lesson. Now, since your people have helped to poison Tymanther's relationship with Chessenta—"

"Majesty, as I already made clear, that isn't so. There *can't* be dragonborn on those warships, because dragonborn only come from Tymanther. If a significant number of them had traveled to Murghôm to take service with the dragon princes, surely you'd know."

Tarhun faltered, no doubt because Nellis had made a sensible argument. Assuming it was valid, it also explained why unidentified dragonborn shouldn't be committing outrages in Luthcheq and Akanûl either. Even though Khouryn had come face to face with the former and was starting to believe in the existence of the latter.

The vanquisher started again. "Be that as it may, milord, High Imaskar professes friendship for Tymanther. Will you stand with us if Chessenta attacks?"

Nellis shifted his gleaming black orb from the crook of one arm to the other. "Majesty, we're already fighting Chessenta on the sea, and I'm confident that will continue. I can't commit land troops to Tymanther's defense without consulting the empress. I know she'd *want* to send them, but it might not be possible until we counter the threat from the Purple Dust."

"Will she also want to send them if Shala Karanok grants passage to a genasi army?"

Now it was Nellis's turn to hesitate.

"I'll spare Lord Nellis the awkwardness of answering that question," Perra said. "Toward the end of my time in Luthcheq, it came to light that Akanûl and High Imaskar have sealed an alliance."

"That's an . . . overstatement," Nellis said. "Naturally, we Imaskari want to trade with as many—"

"Dragons *and* genasi?" Tarhun snarled. "Get out, milord. I'll send for you again when I feel sure of my ability to give you the courtesy due an ambassador."

The Imaskari bowed and withdrew.

Light rippling on his emerald scales, the vanquisher turned to Khouryn, Medrash, and Balasar. "Sirs, I excuse you as well. No doubt you'd like to refresh yourselves after your journey. Perra, my deputies, and I have a long palaver ahead of us."

* * * * *

Gaedynn woke in absolute darkness. For a moment, he was confused, and then memory flooded back.

The last thing he recalled was flying tied to the blue dragon's back. His wounds throbbed and made him weak. The ropes cut off his circulation. The high air chilled him. At some point it had all been too much, and he passed out.

And ended up lying on hard stone. Thanks to the wyrmkeeper's magic, his wounds only hurt a little now. But he was parched and stiff, and when he sat up, he felt the shackles around his wrists and the weight of the rattling chains attached to them.

"Gaedynn?" asked Jhesrhi, somewhere to his left.

He swallowed away some of the dryness in his throat. "Yes."

"Are you all right?"

"More or less, as best I can judge. You?"

"Yes."

"Well, now that I'm awake, I recommend you rid us of our

chains, strike a light, and lead me to safety. While slaughtering any foes we meet along the way."

"I can't. Someone enchanted the shackles to inhibit spellcasting. If I had my staff, I might be able to overcome the effect, but I don't."

He sighed. "That's inconvenient. Do you know where we are?"

"A cave inside Mount Thulbane."

He winced. The volcano was the lair of Jaxanaedegor, the vampiric green dragon who was the Great Bone Wyrm's principal lieutenant. "I have to say, I'm a little offended we don't rate the hospitality of Alasklerbanbastos himself."

"Is there anything you can do?"

"At the moment? Just wait for a chance to present itself. Well, that and divert you with witty and erudite conversation. I referred to Alasklerbanbastos as 'himself,' but in your opinion is that accurate? I understand he started out male, but supposedly there's nothing left of him but a skeleton. Is a fellow still a fellow if his manliest parts have rotted away?"

Jhesrhi didn't answer.

"I suppose we could pose the same question about Szass Tam," Gaedynn continued. "The last time Aoth saw him, he was nothing but bone and flame. Although he probably looks more lifelike now. That's one of the advantages of being a lich *and* a necromancer, isn't it? If you need a patch job, you just find or make a fresh corpse and cut—"

"I didn't freeze," she said.

He hesitated. "What?"

"Fighting in the street. The enemy didn't overwhelm us and take you prisoner because I wasn't doing my part."

"I know that," he said. "It happened because we were

outnumbered and Lady Luck was busy elsewhere."

She was quiet for several heartbeats, then said, "I thought you might think it was my fault because of what happened with the kobolds. And the way I've been since we arrived in Luthcheq."

"I have wondered and worried about you. So has Khouryn."

"What about Aoth?"

"Well, I could tell he's not puzzled. He knows what's bothering you, although much to my annoyance he kept your secret. But he was concerned. I think it's one reason he wished we had somewhere to go besides Chessenta."

Another silence. Finally she said, "I was born in Luthcheq. I started showing signs of having a talent for wizardry from an early age."

"Were your parents mages?"

"No. They were respectable merchants who shared the general prejudice against wizards. They were afraid I was going to draw demons into their home or grow up to commit horrible crimes. Most of all they worried that other people would find out I was an abomination, and that would damage their own reputations. So they forbade me to use my gift and prayed to Chauntea to take it away."

Chauntea, Gaedynn reflected, being the goddess who oversaw natural, healthy growth. "Obviously, that didn't work."

"No. I tried to be good and obey, but I couldn't keep from experimenting with my talent any more than you could have refrained from picking up a bow after you saw your elf friends practicing archery. And so my mother and father grew ever more afraid and loved me less and less.

"And then," she continued, her voice still oddly cool and matter-of-fact, "they led a caravan north. This was during one of those times when Chessenta and Threskel were supposedly at peace. But the north country was still full of brigands, human and otherwise, and a band of elemental magi waylaid us."

Elemental magi were ogres who, somewhat like the genasi, possessed an innate affinity for fire, earth, or air. "When you half saw that big kobold-thing standing in the dark, you took it for an elemental mage, didn't you? That's what . . . rattled you."

"Yes. But let me finish telling this my own way. The caravan was better prepared than the giants expected, and the guards withstood their first attack. But the magi still posed a threat, and the creatures knew it. They demanded tribute to let my parents go on their way."

Gaedynn felt sick to his stomach. "You were the tribute, weren't you? Or a part of it."

"Yes." Jhesrhi's voice, though still soft and calm, grew bitter. "The elemental magi liked the idea of having a human child for a slave, and by that point my parents barely thought of me as their daughter anymore. I was just a problem, and this was a solution."

She took a breath. "The next several years were bad. The giants brutalized me in all the usual ways. When the shaman perceived my gift, they taught me their own kind of magic, but even that, which should have been joyous, was awful. Partly because they made me use it to help them attack other travelers."

"Knowing you as I do, I assume they must have taken precautions to keep you from turning the power on them."

"Yes. I don't know where they got it, but they had an old leather collar with an enchantment of obedience on it. And they made me wear it. But even if they hadn't, I don't know if I would have found the courage to rebel. I was so afraid of them! To some extent, that fear started trickling back as soon as I learned we were bound for Luthcheq, and it grew stronger when Aoth asked us to travel to Threskel."

"Levistus take him for that, and for dragging you to this wretched kingdom in the first place."

"He has to do what's right for the Brotherhood. The whole Brotherhood. And I have to perform the duties that fall to me, or I never should have joined the company in the first place. And I *have* performed them, except for those few moments with the kobolds."

"You performed them then too." He chuckled. "It just took you a little longer than I found comfortable. Still, for Aoth to send you on this particular mission—"

"He needed a mage, and he probably thought it might help that I spent years wandering the wilds of Threskel. Please don't be angry with him. I'd still be a slave if he hadn't rescued me."

"Oh?"

"It was pure chance, Tymora smiling on me or Ilmater taking pity on me at last. The Brotherhood was sailing to start a new commission, and storms damaged the ships. They had to put in to a port south of the Wizards' Reach for repairs, and while they were stuck there, some minor Jedea cousin wanted to hire a few sellswords to travel inland and do a job. Aoth was bored, so he decided to attend to it personally. When the elemental magi and I attacked, he and the other Brothers killed the ogres, but they let me live. Because those eyes of his could see it was the collar forcing me to fight. He got it off me and offered me a place in the company. Maybe because he realized I had nowhere else to go."

"Or maybe because he realized such a powerful wizard would be damn useful, especially after he arranged for additional training.

Still, you've made your point. Perhaps I won't shoot him when we see him next."

She was silent again.

"Jhesrhi?" he asked.

Her chains clinked. "Now maybe you understand."

"I do."

"Not about the kobolds and all that. About before, and you and me. I thought that if it could be good with anyone, it would be good with you. But when we tried, all I could think about was the ogres. They were so ugly and rough and big, and I was so little. Just the stink of them . . ." She drew a ragged breath.

Guilt twisted Gaedynn's insides. Which was completely unfair, since he hadn't known about the magi and certainly hadn't intended to put her through an ordeal, but the feeling persisted nonetheless. "I'm sorry."

"No. I am."

"Don't be. At least we stayed friends, and I finally understand I shouldn't take your revulsion personally. As for the rest, I can get that in any festhall." He faltered. "I didn't mean that the way it may have sounded."

She laughed. He couldn't remember the last time she'd done that, and it was strange to hear it sounding from the darkness of their prison, especially considering the torments she'd just revealed. "Now I know why you generally avoid saying how you truly feel. You're terrible at it."

A retort sprang to mind. But before he could voice it, a cold hand gripped his shoulder.

* * * * *

The apartments of Clan Daardendrien were high up the south wall of the pyramid, which meant Khouryn and his fellow sellswords had a long climb up stairs and ramps to get there. But the supper of roast pheasant was worth it. So was the tart white wine.

Afterward, pleasantly replete and a little tipsy, with full goblets in hand and a fresh bottle awaiting their pleasure, he, Medrash, and Balasar lounged on the balcony overlooking the atrium. The magical illumination had dimmed to match the night outside. Across the empty space, the lamps in other dragonborn homes glowed like stars. Somewhere, a lutenist plucked out an air in a minor key.

Balasar sipped from his cup. "Do you like the view?"

"Yes," Khouryn said. "Now that the light's faded, this feels very much like certain portions of East Rift."

Speaking the name of his home brought a pang of melancholy.

Evidently Medrash sensed it. "There must be some way to get you there," he said.

"It doesn't seem like it," Khouryn said. He emptied his cup and reached for the new bottle. "Your war has closed the Dustroad. Somehow, it's even stopped boat traffic on the lakes, even though I'm told the giants never bothered it before."

Balasar shrugged. "If you took control of the narrows where Lanee Lake flows into Ash Lake, it wouldn't be that hard to do."

"Apparently not," Khouryn sighed.

"Are you sure you don't want to try going the long way around?"

"Through the Shaar Desolation? I like to think I could survive the trek, but traveling through a desert would take a lot longer than using the road. And I can't stay gone from the Brotherhood forever, not with Chessenta and Threskel preparing for war. Truly, the only solution I can imagine would be for the vanquisher to lend me one of those bats. And you say that despite the warm welcome he gave me, he won't."

"I'm sorry," Medrash said. "The bats are the steeds of the Lance Defenders, the core of our army. I've never heard of anyone else being entrusted with one under any circumstances. In wartime, it's all but inconceivable." He sipped from his cup.

"Unless we stole one," Balasar said.

Medrash choked and sputtered.

"Easy," Balasar said, laughter in his voice. "I didn't say we should, or that I would. I was speaking hypothetically."

The paladin wiped his mouth with the back of a scaly hand. "That's good, since such a theft would amount to treason."

"And I wouldn't be a party to it anyway," Khouryn said. "I'll just have to resign myself to not seeing my lass this time around."

Out in the darkness, the lutenist finished his song, paused, then started another just as sad.

After a while, Balasar said, "It seems like a cheerless world all of a sudden. Bad things happening everywhere you look." Khouryn noticed that when dragonborn drank to excess, they started to slur just like dwarves and men.

"I hate sensing the pattern," Medrash said, "yet not being able to *see* it. That's the thing that keeps us helpless."

"Everything doesn't have to be connected," Balasar said. "Not in the way you mean. Maybe the stars are just in a bad configuration or something."

"No, there's a better reason than that. If the Loyal Fury would guide me again, maybe I could figure it out. But given my failure in Luthcheq, perhaps he's decided to look for a more capable agent."

"Please," Balasar groaned. "I'm begging you by the tree and the stone, don't start babbling that nonsense again."

Khouryn decided to change the subject. "What will the two of you do now that Perra doesn't need your services anymore?"

Balasar grinned, the gleam of his pointed teeth perceptible even in the dark. "You're looking at it. Strong drink and a soft chair. Throw in an amorous female or two and I'm set."

Medrash gave him an irritated glance. "It isn't only active Lance Defenders fighting the giants. Every clan has sent or will send its own troops. I'm going, and I know that whatever he pretends, this clown wouldn't think of staying behind."

"Oh, I'd think about it," Balasar said.

"How soon will you leave?" Khouryn asked.

Balasar chuckled. "I have a terrible premonition that the prig here won't even give me time for my hangover to run its course."

"In that case, I'll tag along if you'll have me. Just me. I need to send the other sellswords back to Aoth."

"Of course we'll have you," Medrash said. "But why are you doing this?"

"If Tymora smiles, maybe it won't take you dragonborn long to win a decisive victory. Then the Dustroad will open up again, and I'll be in the right place to take advantage of it."

That really was the main reason. But it was also true that Medrash's murky talk of a pattern had struck a chord with him.

Could the paladin possibly be right? Was there a common underlying cause for all the tribulations afflicting the realms around the Alamber? If so, then it could only benefit the Brotherhood to understand it. And maybe if Khouryn stuck with Medrash and Balasar and learned more about Tymanther's problems, he'd gain some insight.

More likely not. But all things considered, it was worth an extra tenday or two just in case.

* * * * *

From their icy touch, and the fact that they had no trouble moving around in the dark, Jhesrhi inferred that the captors gripping her forearms and marching her along were vampires. Once she realized that, she found their touch even more repulsive than that of the living, but all she could do was steel herself and bear it as they marched her along. They'd removed the shackles that suppressed her magic, but it was unlikely her powers could help her while she was blind and two such formidable creatures were holding on to her.

"Are you still all right, buttercup?" asked Gaedynn from somewhere behind her. Despite their predicament, his tone was no longer grave and gentle as it had been before the vampires came for them. Now it was as jaunty as usual.

"I'm well," she answered.

Light appeared ahead of them, revealing the dimensions of the tunnel they were traversing. She could tell it was magical illumination, silvery and soft, but after her time in the dark it made her squint like the glare of a summer sun.

As her eyes adjusted, her pale, gaunt guards marched her and Gaedynn into a broad, high-ceilinged chamber where glowing white balls floated in the air and slowly drifted from one point to another. Their light gleamed on the treasure below. Gold and silver coins filled open coffers or simply lay in heaps and drifts on the floor. Emeralds, diamonds, sapphires, water stars, and red tears lay scattered among the rounds of precious metal—some loose, some set in necklaces, rings, and brooches.

It could have been a spectacle to make an observer smile at its glittering beauty or drool with greed, except that there was more to it. Corpses—human, halfling, orc, goblin, and others—sprawled amid the wealth. Some were old and withered, and others still fresh enough to nourish the scuttling rats. All were mangled and had had the heads ripped from their shoulders. Their rotten stink made Jhesrhi queasy.

Suddenly a shape surged from the rear of the chamber. It was so huge that she couldn't understand how she'd missed it before, but it truly seemed to burst out of nowhere. Startled, she tried to recoil, although the cold iron grips of the vampires kept her from succeeding. Gaedynn gasped.

Jaxanaedegor was immense enough to make the blue dragon who'd carried the prisoners there seem puny by comparison. Subtly patterned with scales of lighter and darker green, his clawed feet were the size of oxcarts. The spiny crest that ran from the top of his wedge-shaped head down the length of his body was nearly as tall as a human being all by itself.

Yet the most daunting thing about him was the pale unearthly sheen in his yellow eyes, a surface manifestation of the insatiable hunger and boundless malice of the undead. Jhesrhi recognized it from her time in Thay, but she'd never seen it melded with the profound intelligence and prodigious might of an ancient wyrm before.

As she struggled to contain her fear, Gaedynn's guards brought him forward to stand beside her. He ran his gaze over the nearest corpses and said, "You might think about tidying up a bit."

Jaxanaedegor stared at him for a moment that seemed to drag on endlessly, scraping at Jhesrhi's nerves. Then the lesser vampires let the captives go and backed away. She assumed their master had given them some silent signal to do so.

It didn't matter. If she had had her staff and Gaedynn his bow, or at least some weapon and armor, they might have had an infinitesimal chance of fighting their way clear of the situation. As it was, they had no hope at all.

"I know you," the dragon said. "Jhesrhi Coldcreek and Gaedynn Ulraes. Lieutenants to Aoth Fezim."

Jhesrhi tried to keep her surprise from showing in her face.

"Who?" Gaedynn replied. "My name is Azzedar, and my woman is Ilzza. We—"

Fast as a striking serpent, Jaxanaedegor lunged forward. A flick of his forefoot flung Gaedynn backward to slam down on an old sack. It burst under the impact, and clinking coins splashed out.

Meanwhile, the same forefoot grabbed Jhesrhi around the middle and shoved her to the floor. Jaxanaedegor's scaly hide was as cold as his servants' skin, and his weight squashed the breath out of her.

She wheezed a word of power. The wyrm glared down at her. The force of his will stabbed into her head and made it throb, but failed to paralyze her. She forced out the next word of her incantation, and he shifted his stance to make her take a fraction more of his weight.

"All I have to do is bear down," he said, "to crush you into jelly."

She left the rest of the spell unspoken. The stillborn magic dispersed with a crackling sound.

Gaedynn jumped up and started toward Jaxanaedegor. The dragon's head whipped in his direction. Wisps of yellow-green vapor fumed from the creature's nostrils and between his fangs.

Jhesrhi caught a whiff of it. It seared her nose and throat and made her cough.

Gaedynn stopped.

"That's better," Jaxanaedegor said.

"Let her up," the archer said.

"Are you done lying?"

"Yes."

"You'd better be." The wyrm picked up his foot.

Jhesrhi sucked in a breath, then rose and scurried to stand with Gaedynn. She realized that putting a few paces between the dragon and herself meant absolutely nothing in terms of making her safer. But it *felt* better than lingering within arm's reach.

"If I may ask," Gaedynn said, "how is it that you know us?"

"For obvious reasons," Jaxanaedegor said, "we in the north take an interest in the soldiers the war hero sends against us." His breath weapon had stopped leaking into the air, though the little that had escaped was enough to fill the cave with an eye-watering haze. "I have an observer in Soolabax, and when he lost track of you, I told my people throughout Threskel to keep an eye out. Because you had to be going somewhere."

To Jhesrhi it seemed, if not a false explanation, certainly an incomplete one. She could understand a lord of Threskel monitoring the Brotherhood of the Griffon as a whole, or its captain for that matter. But it still surprised her that the wyrm had taken such a close interest that he knew two lesser officers by name.

"Well," Gaedynn said, "we're honored to have snagged the attention of the terror of Mount Thulbane."

"It could work out to your advantage," Jaxanaedegor said. "You could attain eternal life."

"As an eternal menial eternally creeping around in a hole in the ground, like these?" Gaedynn waved a hand to indicate the undead standing at the mouth of the tunnel.

"Servants with minor talents," the dragon said, "must content themselves with minor roles. But you're a skilled warrior, and your companion is versed in elemental sorcery. I might consider giving you the true Dark Gift of the Undying. To make you master vampires and knights of the realm."

Jhesrhi took a breath. "We had an undead comrade named Bareris Anskuld. We saw what his condition made of him. We're not interested."

"You assume you have a choice."

"I don't assume I could hurt you or fend you off for any length of time. But I do think I could raise enough fire to burn Gaedynn and me to ash."

Actually, probably not—not without her staff. But it was possible that despite his cunning, Jaxanaedegor couldn't tell that.

The dragon grunted. "Well, don't set yourself ablaze quite yet. I'm still deciding what to do with you. Tell the truth, and I might show more mercy than a spy deserves. What were you looking for in Mourktar?"

Gaedynn cocked his head. "Didn't your own spy tell you?"

"He reported you were asking about rumors of a dragon somewhere in the Sky Riders. I want to know why."

"The stories suggest the wyrm in question is inconvenienced in some way. We hoped that would make it possible for us to pilfer from its horde."

"And how would that help Chessenta?"

"It wouldn't. Jhesrhi and I have parted company with the

Brotherhood of the Griffon. Deserted, if you want to put it unkindly. We just want to get our hands on enough coin to keep us in comfort for the rest of our days."

"I find that difficult to believe. By all accounts, both you and the wizard have been loyal members of Aoth Fezim's company for several years."

Gaedynn grinned. "I don't know what accounts you've heard, but I've never been loyal to much of anything but my own self-interest. Now, Jhesrhi—I admit—is somewhat more prone to that particular weakness. But not to the point of stupidity. Captain Fezim led us to near ruin in Thay and again in Impiltur. Now he's dragged us to a kingdom where mages like her are pariahs. She doesn't trust him anymore, and wants out just like me."

Jaxanaedegor pounced as he had before. Only this time, it was Jhesrhi he flicked through the air and Gaedynn he pressed beneath his forefoot.

As Jhesrhi clambered to her feet, the dragon glared at her. "Your friend is nearly as glib as a dragon," he said. "Unfortunately for him, I *am* a dragon, and my instincts tell me he's still lying. Perhaps you'd care to speak the truth."

"Gaedynn already did," she replied.

"I don't think I want him as any sort of servant," Jaxanaedegor said. "I suspect that even bound to my will, he'd find a way of getting into mischief. But that's the point of taking the heads off—so they don't rise." He opened his mouth, and two of the upper fangs lengthened.

"Don't!" Jhesrhi cried. "I'll tell you. Nicos Corynian, the Brotherhood's employer, believes the dragon in the hills is Tchazzar."

"Tchazzar!" Jaxanaedegor said. "Why in the Dark Lady's name would he think that?"

"I'm not sure we know, entirely. Lord Nicos may have held something back. But the last anyone in Chessenta saw of Tchazzar, he was headed into Threskel. And the wyrm in the hills is supposedly a fire-breather."

"And if it is Tchazzar, you're supposed to bring him back to fight for Chessenta in her time of need."

"Gaedynn and I are just supposed to investigate and report. But if it did turn out to be Tchazzar, I suppose someone would try to retrieve him. Now, please, I've given you what you wanted. Let Gaedynn up."

"I suppose I might as well," the dragon answered. "I've already drunk well tonight. It makes sense to save the two of you until I'm thirsty again."

The lesser vampires started toward Jhesrhi. She cried to the stone surrounding her, raised one hand high, closed her fingers like she was clutching something, and whipped her arm down. Chunks of granite rained from the high domed ceiling.

But only enough to smash down on top of one of the undead. The others broke into a run that brought them into striking distance an instant later. One lashed her across the face with the back of his hand, and the blow knocked all the strength and much of the sense out of her. The world suddenly seemed a distant and meaningless place, and that kept her from resisting any further as the dragon's minions hauled her and Gaedynn back into the dark.

* * * * *

Cera Eurthos waved her hand, and sunlight pushed back the night to reveal shrubs and blueleaf trees putting forth new growth, pebbled paths, a marble bench, and what Aoth supposed was the inevitable sundial.

"Do you like it?" Cera asked.

"Yes," he said, and he didn't bother to mention that his fire-touched eyes had seen the temple garden clearly even before her magic illuminated it.

The golden glow faded and night returned. "I'm afraid I don't tend my personal patch of it very diligently. Just when the mood takes me."

They sat down on the bench. He noticed she didn't leave much space between them, and set his spear on the dewy grass. He wasn't sure how the rest of the evening would unfold, but it wouldn't hurt to put the weapon where it was out of the way.

"How did you think the banquet went?" he asked.

"You were the very model of a courtly gentleman soldier," she said.

He smiled a crooked smile. "If so, it didn't keep them from making signs to ward off evil when they thought I wasn't looking."

"Not all of them."

"Well, I hope not."

"Trust me. You won some of them over."

"But probably not the one who sent an assassin to kill me at the gate."

She frowned. "Do you really believe one of the town elders was responsible?"

"Truthfully? Who knows? Hasos resents me for taking away part of his authority and showing him up. Others may think I'll somehow bring disaster just because I'm a war-mage. But there are other possibilities. You can pretty much count on it that Threskel has an agent or two living in town. Even if they don't, how hard would it be to sneak an assassin in with the honest farmers and travelers whenever the gates are open? Especially one who knows some sorcery."

"You don't seem very worried about it."

He shrugged. "I won't say I'm used to it exactly, but sometimes assassination attempts are just a part of war."

"Well, I think you're brave. To say nothing of observant. I would have fallen through those stairs if you hadn't been with me."

He could have pointed out that if she hadn't been with him, the steps would have been undamaged, but given his hopes, that seemed counterproductive. He stroked her cheek. A bit tentatively, for she was, after all, a high priestess, and a part of him was still the Mulan who'd spent his childhood being reminded over and over that he looked like a lowly, ugly Rashemi.

She smiled and slid closer, and then he was sure they wanted the same thing. He kissed her. Her lips warmed him like sunlight.

Before long, they grew impatient with the hard narrow bench and lay together on the ground. He unhooked the top of her yellow vestment and slipped his hand inside to caress her through her shift.

Then, for just a heartbeat, he caught a whiff of something nasty and stinging through the mingled scents of the vegetation, the wet rich soil, and her lilac perfume.

He started to lift himself up to look around, and she tugged to pull him back down. He almost yielded, but then realized the new odor had smelled exactly like the acid the dragonborn had spat at him in Luthcheq.

He jerked himself out of Cera's embrace, and she gave a startled little cry of protest. Clad in hooded robes and cloaks, dragonborn were stalking toward him and his companion. A flicker of magic outlined their forms. Most likely it meant they were more or less invisible. Not to him, of course, but with his attention fixed on Cera, they'd managed to sneak up on him just fine.

The two nearest sucked in deep breaths.

Kneeling, he snatched for his spear, aimed it, and snarled a word of command to discharge one of the spells stored inside. A cloud of greenish vapor materialized around the dragonborn. They reeled and retched inside it, unable to spew their breath weapons—for the moment, anyway.

Unfortunately, there were plenty more outside the fog, and Aoth didn't even have his mail. You didn't wear armor to a banquet.

He scrambled to his feet. So did Cera. In circumstances like these, he was sometimes uncertain how much people with ordinary eyes could see. Judging from her expression and stance, she perceived some indication of the threat, maybe shadowy figures flickering in and out of view.

"I can call back Amaunator's light—," she began.

"I can already see them," Aoth snapped. "I'm also armed. You aren't. Get help!"

She turned and ran toward the arched yellow door that led back into the Keeper's house. Dragonborn darted after her. Aoth lunged to intercept them.

The reptile in the lead swung a sword down at his head. He caught the stroke on the shaft of his spear, spun the weapon, and thrust it into his opponent's throat. As he yanked it back, he saw another dragonborn spitting vitriol at him.

There was no time left to close the distance or try to deter the reptile with a spell. He could only dodge, and some of the spray splashed his left arm and shoulder anyway. Smoking and sizzling, the liquid burned like Kossuth's anger.

But he couldn't let that slow him down, or his assailants would overwhelm him for certain. He invoked the magic of a tattoo to dampen the pain and struck back with a thunderous blast of sound. The magic knocked the dragonborn off his feet, and shattered bones and ruptured organs if Aoth was lucky.

He couldn't wait and watch to see if he was. He had to pivot and blast another pair of dragonborn with an explosion of crimson flame.

Pain seared his back. Once again he invoked the magic of the numbing tattoo. It worked, but not as well as before. He turned, rattled off words of power, and crumbled the foe who'd just spat on him into a spill of dust.

Individually the dragonborn were no match for him, but there were a lot of them, they weren't attacking individually, and they weren't stupid enough to bunch up so he could catch several at once with a spell devised to smite multiple opponents. Gradually, and despite his best efforts, they surrounded him.

More acid caught him in the back. He cried out and lurched forward. Dragonborn lunged to hack and stab while he was off balance.

Then he felt a presence enter his mind and avail itself of his eyes. A shape as black as the night sky overhead plunged out of it to pierce reptiles with its talons and smash them under its hurtling weight. Jet twisted his head and decapitated another dragonborn with a snap of his beak. Startled, the rest recoiled.

Aoth tried the tattoo again and found there was still a little analgesic virtue left in it. "Were you spying on me?" he gasped.

"No," Jet replied. "I was just taking some exercise and happened to fly overhead. But I probably should have been. Why is it you can never mate without it turning into a situation?"

A dragonborn recovered his nerve and charged. Aoth ducked the swing of his axe and drove his spear into the creature's guts. Then the rest of the enemy surged forward, and there was no more time or breath to spare for talk. Not until every reptile lay torn, blackened and smoldering, encrusted with frost, or otherwise slain on the ground.

"Curse it," Aoth growled. "We really could have used a prisoner to question."

Jet grunted. "And here I thought I was doing well just to save your hide."

"Believe me, I'm grateful. It's just that it's unfortunate." Aoth studied the bodies.

"I see it too," the griffon said. "No piercings, just like in Luthcheq."

"You're right," said Aoth, "but this time I'm noticing something more. Dragonborn come in a variety of colors, but every one of these is black. What are the odds?"

"Not bad, if they belong to some sect or cadre that only takes black ones."

"All right. But they all spat acid at us, just like all black dragons spew acid. Even though the color of a dragonborn's scales has no relation to the nature of his breath weapon. So what are the chances of *that*?"

"Maybe not as good. But what does it mean?"

Aoth sighed. "I have no idea." His burns throbbed, and he sucked in a breath through his teeth.

Then the yellow door flew open, and Cera rushed out with a

mace and targe that were either made of gold or, more likely, simply looked like it. The priests and guards scrambling behind her were similarly equipped. They all stopped short at the sight of the carnage.

"Thank goodness you're here," said Jet.

Cera gave Aoth an apologetic look. "It's only been a few moments. I brought the others as fast as I could."

"I know," said Aoth, "and you're not too late to help us. We're both burned. It hurts quite a lot, actually."

She dropped her weapon and shield and came to inspect his wounds. She murmured a prayer and gently touched her hands to the burned spots, and a soothing warmth began to ease the pain.

"Did you know there were this many dragonborn in Soolabax?" asked Aoth.

Cera shook her head. "That's what I can't understand. There aren't any."

"Well," said Jet as her fellow sunlords—moving gingerly in proximity to such a formidable beast with such a gory beak and bloody claws—began to tend his burns, "maybe not anymore."

* * * * *

Gaedynn banged his shackles on the floor. It jolted his wrists and soon made them sore, but he kept at it anyway. He'd already tried and failed to squeeze his fingers together and slip a hand free, or to grip a chain and pull it free of its moorings in the wall. He didn't know what else to do.

On his left, Jhesrhi recited one incantation after another. Sometimes it sounded like she was giving commands, sometimes like she was coaxing, and sometimes growling threats. But however she tried it, she never produced more than a puff of displaced air or a momentary bitter taste on his tongue.

Finally he stopped pounding to catch his breath. That inspired her to pause as well. The darkness felt even darker without their noise to fill it.

He examined his shackles by touch. If his efforts were damaging the lock or knocking loose the hinges, he certainly couldn't tell it. He cursed.

"I'm not getting anywhere either," Jhesrhi said.

He tried to speak with his customary self-assurance. "Ah well, the chains are just a temporary inconvenience. Our escorts will remove them to take us back to Jaxanaedegor. Then your powers will return and you'll set one of the wretches on fire. The light will enable me to strike down the others."

She hesitated, then said, "Yes, I'm sure that's just how it will go. But just in case it doesn't . . ."

"Yes?"

Another hesitation. "I don't know. I shouldn't think like that anyway. We have to believe there will be something we can do."

Footsteps padded in the blackness.

Jhesrhi sucked in a startled breath. Gaedynn felt his muscles tighten, and exhaled to blow the tension out.

He only heard one person approaching. And he'd never heard the vampires at all until they laid hands on him. Was it possible that he and Jhesrhi really did have a chance?

The footsteps halted in front of him. Then something clicked against the floor.

"Food and water," rasped a voice with a barbarous accent. "Dragon want you strong." The guard sniggered. "Want your *blood* strong."

The hope bled out of Gaedynn as fast as it had come. Because this wasn't the escort who would unlock the shackles after all.

Still, he needed to quench his thirst and fill his belly. Crawling, he groped his way forward as far as his chains would let him go. There he found what felt like a ceramic bowl with a chipped rim. Inside it were water and a hunk of bread. The bread was soggy where the water had soaked into it and hard as rock elsewhere.

He forced himself to drink slowly. The water was lukewarm and tasted of sulfur. His parched body shivered with relief as it went down.

Meanwhile, Jaxanaedegor's servant padded onward. A second clack announced that he'd down set Jhesrhi's bowl.

Then there was nothing. No sound indicative of further motion. Evidently the guard was still standing in front of Jhesrhi.

Intelligent as she was, she no doubt realized it, and it likely made her as uneasy as it did Gaedynn. But she needed water as much as he had. Her chains clinked as she came forward.

Leather creaked. The guard was moving. The chains rattled as Jhesrhi scrambled backward.

"You pretty," said the guard. He paced after her. It was horribly easy to imagine him pressing her up against the wall.

Arms outstretched, Gaedynn moved left to the limits of his chains. There was nothing within reach.

From beyond his straining hands came the sounds of grunting, clinking chains, slaps smacking a face, and blows thumping solid flesh. Then the guard yelped. Something big and heavy slammed into Gaedynn's hands.

He'd thought himself poised to act if he got the chance, but in the dark the sudden impact caught him by surprise. It felt like the guard was bouncing back out of his reach before he could catch hold. He grabbed frantically. Gripped what felt like a brigandine and the body inside it.

He still didn't know what sort of creature he was fighting. But the would-be rapist could obviously see in the dark, which meant he'd make short work of his opponent if Gaedynn gave him a chance. He heaved the guard off balance, threw him down on the floor, and dropped on top of him.

There he hung on with one hand and bashed with the other, looping a length of chain to use like a flail. As he made one such attack, something sliced the skin atop his knuckles. Apparently his swinging fist had grazed a fang or tusk.

Meanwhile the guard pummeled him in turn, while also trying to break his hold and squirm out from underneath him. Until the punching stopped.

Probably because the guard had decided to reach for a knife. Something about the way his body shifted told Gaedynn which hand was doing the reaching. He twisted. The guard's arm brushed across his chest as the first stab missed.

The next one likely wouldn't. Bellowing, Gaedynn put all his strength and weight behind another blow to the face. Bone crunched, and the guard went limp.

But Gaedynn could still hear breath whistling in and out of his foe's nose. He groped, found the guard's neck with both hands, and squeezed.

"Are you all right?" Jhesrhi asked.

"Fine," he panted. "Just finishing up. How about you?"

"Just scraped and bruised, I imagine. I thought my only hope was to shove him to where you could reach them, but then *I* couldn't reach him anymore."

"Don't worry about it. You gave me all the help I needed." He loosened his grip. The whistling didn't resume. "Let's find out what sort of presents your admirer brought us."

He patted his way down the guard's body. He found the knife, the scimitar his adversary hadn't been able to use fighting at such close quarters, and then the metal ring clipped to his belt. When he felt what was attached to it, he caught his breath.

"What is it?"

He slipped the key into the shackle on his left wrist and twisted it. The lock clicked and the heavy metal ring hitched open. "Proof that Lady Luck might actually love me almost as much as I deserve." He rid himself of the other shackle. "Talk, so I can find you without bumping into you."

"My name is Jhesrhi Coldcreek. I'm a wizard and an officer in the Brotherhood of the Griffon. The name of my own griffon is—"

"Good enough." He reached and found that she had her arms outstretched. The key fit her shackles too.

She murmured a word of command and conjured a glowing amber ball into the palm of her upturned hand. At first it dazzled him and made him squint, but when his eyes adjusted, he could see for himself that she was disheveled but unharmed. He felt the urge to hug her but caught himself in time.

The light revealed that the guard had been an orc. By rights one such creature shouldn't pose much of a problem for a soldier who'd stood against wraiths, nightwalkers, and the steel scorpion of Anhaurz, and Gaedynn grinned at the thought that this foe had given him one of the most desperate fights he'd ever fought.

"What are you smirking at?" Jhesrhi asked.

"I'll tell you later. Look, somehow we managed to dance with the guard without overturning either of our bowls. So drink and eat. We're going to need it."

After he finished his own meal, he appropriated the orc's weapons and—his mouth twisted in distaste—the brigandine. The reinforced leather stank of the brutish warrior's sweat, but armor was armor.

As he buckled it on and found he couldn't tighten the straps enough to make it snug on his lean frame, he asked, "Can you disguise us?"

"To a degree," Jhesrhi said. "But we'll never find a way out without light."

"I know. But since Jaxanaedegor's more or less a grandee of the realm, maybe he has servants or occasional visitors who need light as much as we do. If so, then using it won't necessarily unmask us."

"We can hope." She set the orb of light afloat in midair as if she were setting it on a shelf. Then she murmured a rhyming incantation and stroked her fingertips from the midline of her face outward like she was streaking it with paint. When she did the same to Gaedynn, his cheeks and forehead tingled.

"There," she said.

He looked at his hands. They appeared clean, pale, and devoid of hair. Tattoos peeked out from under the sleeves of what now appeared to be a finely made mail shirt with hammered brass runes and sigils riveted to the links.

Jhesrhi was tattooed and hairless too, even her eyebrows and lashes shed to leave her bald as an egg. Her golden eyes had changed to a less distinctive gray, and the patched, ragged garb of Ilzza the vagabond had become a crimson robe.

"We're Thayans," he said.

"Supposedly Szass Tam sometimes sends envoys to the lords of Threskel. If so, then Jaxanaedegor's lesser servants have learned to bow and scrape to them. They also wouldn't expect them to know their way around. Both those things could work to our advantage. So I'm a Red Wizard and you're my knight."

He smiled. "Almost like real life."

Thanks to the golden glow, it was now plain that Jaxanaedegor's servants had imprisoned them in a hollow where a dozen sets of shackles dangled from the walls. A single passage ran away into the dark. Jhesrhi sent the light drifting in that direction, and she and Gaedynn followed.

As they paced along, he kept hoping for a branching passage. Because there was a guard station, barracks, or something similar up ahead. He hadn't been able to see it in the dark, but he'd heard the murmur of voices as the vampires marched Jhesrhi and him back and forth.

But it appeared fickle Tymora had forgotten him again. Or, to be fair, maybe it was a bit much to ask her to reach back in time, trespass in the business of Kossuth and Grumbar, and alter the way lava carved rifts in the volcano just to smooth his path. In any case, no alternate route presented itself before he heard voices once again and caught the smells of wood smoke and roasting meat. His hunk of stale bread hadn't been all that big or satisfying, and the latter aroma made his mouth water.

"They're going to think it odd that two Thayans are coming out of the prison," Jhesrhi whispered.

"Especially when they didn't notice two Thayans going in," Gaedynn answered. "That's assuming they bother to think about it. Maybe they won't. But if they do, well, you're magical and too important and arrogant to take kindly to answering questions from the likes of them."

"Right." They walked on.

The way widened, and openings led off the passage to interconnecting chambers on either side. Taken altogether, the honeycomb was large enough for a garrison of dozens, but Gaedynn was glad to see there didn't appear to be that many warriors currently.

There was at least one, though. Frowning, a one-eyed orc peered out into the passage. Gaedynn gave him a stare, and he retreated into the darkness. But as soon as the supposed Thayans passed by, the guard shouted something in the language of his kind. Gaedynn didn't speak it, but assumed the echoing call pertained to Jhesrhi and himself.

Other voices replied, and footsteps scurried. Five other orcs emerged from openings up ahead, then gathered together to form a single group.

It didn't look like they meant to attack. Not yet anyway. But they evidently didn't intend to let the strangers pass without a word or two of explanation either.

Still, it didn't seem all that dire a situation until the light floated close enough to show them clearly. Then Gaedynn saw that while four were warriors, one wore a voluminous robe and carried a staff. He was some sort of sorcerer or shaman, and likely more cunning and difficult to bluff than his fellows.

Oh well. Gaedynn would just have to strive for words that flew as true as Keen-Eye's arrows.

When Jhesrhi and he came close enough to converse without difficulty, he gave a brusque nod. "We'll return to our accommodations now."

"Accommodations?" the shaman asked. He spoke Chessentan

without an accent, and although his staff was carved of shadow-wood rather than blackwood and the rune-engraved rings that banded it at intervals were made of some exotic red metal instead of gold, it appeared as handsomely crafted and civilized an artifact as the one Jhesrhi had lost in Mourktar.

"The quarters Lord Jaxanaedegor assigned to Lady Azhir," Gaedynn said.

One of the soldier orcs turned to mutter in the sorcerer's pointed ear. In the process, he gave Gaedynn a better look at the longbow he carried on his back. It was as superbly made as the staff, and to Gaedynn as enticing as the smell of the roasting meat.

"We understand," the sorcerer said. "But how did you get into the cell?"

Gaedynn sneered like it was a stupid question. "My lady doesn't need to move around as common people do." *And let's not dwell on the fact that no wizard in her right mind would shift herself around blindly in an unfamiliar tunnel system without a compelling reason.*

"But why go to the cell at all?" the shaman persisted. "I wouldn't ask, but the prisoners are my responsibility."

"We didn't hurt them," Gaedynn said. "When Lord Jaxanaedegor mentioned them, my lady thought she detected a resemblance to a pair of sellswords who caused trouble in Thay last year. She was curious to see if these were the same two knaves. It turns out they're not. Now, orc, have I satisfied *your* curiosity, or will you keep us here until the dragon starts wondering what busybody is detaining his guests?"

"You're free to go, of course," the sorcerer said, "and I'm sorry if I gave offense." He and the other orcs shifted to the sides of the passage.

As Jhesrhi and Gaedynn strode forward, he glimpsed motion at the periphery of his vision. Trying not to be obvious about it, he glanced in that direction.

An eyeless black rat crawled out of the sorcerer's collar and perched on his shoulder. Where it sniffed repeatedly like a bloodhound.

Would Jhesrhi's disguises deceive the nose as they did the eyes? Gaedynn had no idea.

He drew the scimitar, pivoted, and cut. The sorcerer fell backward with blood gushing from his throat. The familiar tumbled from his shoulder.

Gaedynn turned, slashed, and dropped another orc. So much for the easy part. The other three had their weapons ready.

They drove in, and he gave ground before them. Jhesrhi slashed her hand from right to left and raked them with a flare of flame. One caught fire and reeled. Though barely singed, the other two faltered. Taking advantage of their distraction, Gaedynn pounced at them and cut them down.

The burning orc dropped too. Gaedynn turned to give Jhesrhi a smile. Facing back the way they'd come, she rattled off words of power and thrust out her hand. Darts of yellow light shot from her fingertips. They plunged into the torso of the orc who'd called to the others. The one that Gaedynn had to admit, to himself if never to Jhesrhi, he'd forgotten all about.

The orc pitched forward. His finger still pulled the trigger of his crossbow, but the bolt merely hit the floor a pace or two in front of him.

"I thought we were trying to trick our way through," Jhesrhi said. "It still might have worked."

"Maybe," Gaedynn said, "but I didn't feel like giving up the advantage of surprise to find out. Besides, you need a staff, and I a bow. We both need some of that meat."

Which turned out to be goat. It was still half raw, but they didn't have time to linger and turn the spit. They gobbled their fill and moved on.

In time they found their way to a broad shelf where the ceiling rose high enough to permit a huddle of stone buildings and stubby towers. Beyond was a gray sky.

The sight of any sky would have excited Gaedynn, but this one all but elated him. Because it was a daytime sky, and not so shrouded in fumes from the volcano as to mask every trace of the sun. No vampire could pursue fugitives under such a sky, and even living but nocturnal creatures like orcs might find it inconvenient.

"What's the plan?" Jhesrhi allowed her floating light to blink out of existence. "Try to walk out like we have every right to?"

Gaedynn grinned. "Why not? We're bound to fool *somebody*, eventually."

They headed into the cluster of buildings. Gaedynn tried to look like a haughty Thayan warrior having a casual look at the area and finding it contemptible. As opposed to a twitchy escapee, his nerves frayed to rags by fumbling his way through a dark maze of tunnels.

A stooped, dirty man stepped into the sellswords' path, noticed them, hesitated as though trying to decide whether they were close enough that he needed to bow or kneel, and then settled for scurrying on his way. A sentry, also human, watched their progress from the battlements atop one of the towers, but not with any show of suspicion or even much curiosity.

Beyond the edge of the shelf, the mountainside fell away in a slope shallow enough to permit cultivation. Slaves bent in freshly plowed fields, planting peas or beans in the furrows and grain on the ridges. Overseers with whips sauntered among them.

Nearby was a barn, and horses standing in a paddock. Gaedynn led Jhesrhi in that direction. "Grooms!" he shouted.

Two thralls scrambled into view. They had the same cringing demeanor as the man back on the shelf, and sets of scabby double puncture wounds on their throats.

"The lady and I are going for a ride," Gaedynn said. "Saddle two horses."

The men hesitated. Then one said, "The countryside can be dangerous. I can ask the soldiers in the towers to—"

"Now!" Gaedynn snapped.

The slaves flinched, then hurried to obey. He could see they were hurrying, even if the task seemed to drag on endlessly. But finally he and Jhesrhi were in the saddle and, moments later, trotting down the trail that meandered among the fields.

Jhesrhi shook her head. "Strange."

"What?" Gaedynn asked.

"I wouldn't have said it while we were doing it, but now that we're out, escaping almost seemed too easy."

He laughed. "By my estimation, we have about half an afternoon to put distance between Mount Thulbane and ourselves. Before you make up your mind how easy it was, let's see how we fare come nightfall."

SEVEN

GREENGRASS–7 MIRTUL
THE YEAR OF THE AGELESS ONE (1479 DR)

The scent of flowers filled the air. The prayers of druids and sunlords made it possible to grow them in time for the spring festival. Usually they went to decorate public places, or to worshipers to use as offerings, but Cera had diverted two bouquets to fill the vases in her bedroom.

At present, she lay on her stomach with the tangled covers concealing her from the small of her bare back down. Aoth studied her, and she reassured him that she truly was asleep by giving a soft buzz of a snore.

Moving carefully, he stood up, put on the clothes he'd left strewn on the floor, and picked up his spear where it leaned against a chair. She kept snoring.

So far, so good. Now what?

He could rummage through her personal effects, but it would be unfortunate if she woke and caught him. And it seemed likely that if what he was looking for was there at all, he could find some sign of it elsewhere.

He prowled through the rest of her apartments and peeked out into the corridor beyond. It pleased him that some thrifty soul had extinguished the oil lamp. The gloom would obscure him without hindering his own vision.

He skulked on past the chambers of Cera's subordinates. Moans sounded from one and a rhythmic *slap-slap-slap* from another. For a moment he smiled. When he was young, the priests of Lathander had been a famously amorous lot, and although Amaunator was supposed to be a more staid and dignified god, perhaps their successors had inherited the same proclivity.

Or maybe it was just Greengrass sparking carnal urges in one and all.

He slipped from the cloister into the sanctuary, where it wasn't quite as dark. Votive flames burned in one place and another, and the moon and stars shone through the skylights. He didn't know a great deal about Amaunatori customs, and—concerned that he might encounter a priest performing some late-night ritual, or perhaps a ceremonial guard—he crept even more warily. But there didn't appear to be anyone else around.

He trusted his fire-touched eyes to reveal the presence of concealed doors and the like, but there didn't seem to be any of those either. Just stone stairs in plain sight descending into the floor. He headed down and came to a door in the form of a wrought-iron grille. He tried it, and it was locked.

He scowled. Jhesrhi could likely have opened the lock without breaking it. Gaedynn might have found a way as well. Both were better suited to spying than their commander, which was why Aoth had sent them into Threskel. But he regretted their absence now.

Well, he'd just have to proceed as best he could. He slipped the point of his spear into the crack above the latch, then pried, releasing a bit of the power stored inside the weapon to make the action more forceful. The grille lurched open with a snap.

He swung it shut again behind him. With luck, no one would notice the damage before morning at the earliest. He climbed down the remaining steps.

Which put him in a musty-smelling room with brick walls and a few old boxes scattered around. He stalked through an arch into a second rectangular space like the first.

Another grille separated the second room from a third. On the other side were coffers, jars, urns, and icons, some of the latter depictions of the Morninglord and thus no longer suitable for veneration. The wealth of the temple, locked away for safekeeping.

Aoth broke open the new barrier and explored the repository. No matter how intently he peered at the contents, and at the ceiling, walls, and floor, he still couldn't find any trace of what he sought. And there was nowhere else to look, not down here anyway.

Warm golden light bloomed at his back. As he pivoted toward the doorway, it brightened. By the time he faced it, it was like looking directly at the sun.

Unfortunately, glare was one thing that could still impair his vision. Shielding his eyes with one hand, he leveled the spear with the other. "Stop what you're doing. I don't have to see you to hurt you."

"I vouched for you," Cera said, from inside the dazzling light or beyond it. "I told everyone you were honorable and came here to protect us. And you get up *out of my bed* and slink down here to steal Amaunator's treasure!"

He wondered if she truly believed that. "You're wrong. That's not what I'm doing."

"Then drop your spear and surrender, and afterward we'll sort it out."

"I can't do that." She might kill him once she had him disarmed.

"Then this is your own fault."

The blaze in the doorway seemed to leap at him, engulf him, and pain seared him. He willed a tattoo to life, and its enchantment dulled the agony. Maybe it even kept him from bursting into flame.

He growled a word of power, and a thunderclap boomed through the cellar. Hoping it had at least staggered Cera, he charged the doorway. And slammed into the grille. He'd left it open, so the priestess must have closed it and the glare kept him from noticing.

He rebounded and fell on his rump. The grille squeaked on its hinges and clanked against the wall. Footsteps pattered in his direction.

Cera evidently hoped the impact had left him dazed or disoriented, but though his head throbbed, it hadn't. He could judge where she was, and he raised the spear to spit her. Then he flung himself to the side instead. Something, likely her golden mace, banged against the floor.

He scrambled, turned, and then he was facing her with his back to the glare. He was still half blind with floating smears of afterimage, but at least he could make out her silhouette and see that she had indeed armed herself with her mace and targe.

As he sprang to his feet, he feinted at her face with the spear. The round shield jerked up to block in a way that more or less blinded her. She was resourceful and commanded potent magic, but she was no expert at hand-to-hand combat.

He reversed the spear and swept her feet out from under her with the blunt end. She thumped down on the floor. He spun the weapon again and touched the point to her throat.

"Let go of the mace and shield," he said.

She did.

"Now push them away."

The articles scraped along the floor.

"Now put out the light in the doorway."

She blinked. "I won't be able to see."

"That's all right. I will."

The glare went out.

"This isn't over," she said.

"It is if I kill you and nobody finds out who did it."

Her voice quavered, but only a little. "Is that what you're going to do?"

He sighed and rubbed the sore spot on his forehead. "I don't know yet. I'm poking around down here because I don't know much of anything. And at first that was fine with me. I figured, let the nobles have their secrets and conspiracies. Let them plunge the whole East into war, for any stupid reason or none at all. From a sellsword's perspective, nothing could be better."

"But after two attempts on your life, you changed your mind."

"Basically. Like I told you, assassination is just a move in the game we soldiers play. But dragonborn assassins, in a town where there have never been any dragonborn? And a special kind of dragonborn at that? It's just too odd. Even leaving my own safety out of it, it shows there's too much going on that I don't understand. And that could lead to problems on the battlefield."

She frowned, evidently mulling over what he'd said, then asked, "Given the magic they use, couldn't the dragonborn have sneaked into the city from outside?"

"Maybe," said Aoth, "but from *where* outside? Threskel? As far as we know, there aren't any there either. All the way from Tymanther? And why are the damn reptiles targeting me anyway? I'm a good soldier, but not all that important. By the Hells, if you heard how I broke my contract with Aglarond, marched into Thay, took heavy losses, and retreated without seeming to accomplish anything—and then suffered another defeat in Impiltur—you might not even realize I *am* good."

"It's a puzzle," she said, "but what prompted you to look for answers in my temple's cellars?"

"I'm working on the assumption that unlikely as it sounds, someone in Soolabax is hiding the dragonborn and aiding them in general. Now, who was surprisingly friendly and flirtatious with me from the start?"

"I was, but not to deflect suspicion or trick you into lowering your guard. Because you intrigued me. I grew up in Luthcheq, not a sleepy farm town. I've come to like the people who live here, but to be honest, they often bore me too. And you were an exotic stranger who'd consorted with kings and archmages and fought his way across the world."

"When you took me for that stroll on the battlements, it gave the first assassin a chance to weaken the steps. And when I stopped short, you bumped me from behind. It almost pitched me forward and made me fall."

"But only almost, because I wasn't trying. And as for the other, well, it wasn't the first time you'd climbed to the top of the gate to look out over the countryside. The dragonborn just lurked nearby and waited for his chance."

"Well, he and his friends got a second chance when you hosted the feast and then drew me out into the garden. You even held me down so I wouldn't see them coming. And then, after I sent you for help, you and the other sunlords didn't make it back till the fight was over."

"Because Jet arrived to help you, and then the two of you finished it quickly. And as for the rest, I swear by the Yellow Sun it was only coincidence or the reptiles watching and waiting for their chance. The banquet was no more a secret than your visits to the gate."

"No matter what you say, it doesn't change the fact that the dragonborn have come at me twice, and you've been there both times."

"And if I'd used my magic against you, they would have killed you for certain."

"Not for certain. And if I survived, I would have known you for my enemy."

She scowled. "Listen, idiot. I'm a priestess of the lord of Eternal Sun. One of the supreme powers of righteousness. I wouldn't do something treacherous and evil."

"You might if you thought it served a greater good. Like your superior believes it's his duty to persecute wizards and lay curses on marchers in the street."

"Earlier tonight, couldn't you *feel* how much I truly liked you?"

She must have been running out of arguments, because that was the weakest one yet. No man could live a hundred years without learning how many women could feign affection convincingly.

Yet taken altogether, her arguments carried more weight, especially considering that his search hadn't turned up anything. And who knew, maybe he *had* felt something genuine between them. Just not strongly enough to negate what seemed abundant reason for suspicion.

"All right." He lifted the spear away from her throat and roused the power in it to make the point glow and give her light. "I guess that whoever's out to get me, it isn't you." He extended his hand to help her up.

She swatted it away and stood up on her own.

He frowned. "I thought you 'truly liked' me."

"I did. Before you seduced me to create an opportunity to ransack Amaunator's house."

"I seduced you?"

Her mouth twitched. Like a smile had momentarily tried to replace the glower? "I suppose that isn't fair. Still, you tricked me!"

Aoth sighed. "For what it's worth, I honestly liked you too, before I started to worry about you. If you want revenge, you can complain to Hasos and write to Nicos, Daelric, and the war hero."

"And if it got you and your cutthroats kicked out of Soolabax, or out of Chessenta entirely, how would that help us when Threskel comes in force?"

"Well, there's that."

She brushed some of her tousled blonde curls away from her eyes. "You have your own little army. Instead of sneaking around looking for dragonborn by yourself, why not use it to search the whole town house to house?"

"The enemy might see us coming and get away. Or they may not really be here in the first place. And if I didn't turn up anything, it would anger people who already didn't trust me to begin with."

"Hm. I see your point."

"Also, when my comrades and I tracked down the Green Hand Killers in Luthcheq, the bastards burned their papers and mystical insignia. I don't want the dragonborn in Soolabax to have the same opportunity."

"I already said I see your point, and I'll help you. It's my duty as a sunlady and one of the town's protectors."

"I appreciate the offer. But if you mean you'll help me with some sort of divination, we tried that in Luthcheq and it didn't work."

"With the Keeper's help, we'll think of something. Just don't imagine it means I want you back in my arms. You spoiled that for good and all."

"I understand."

Her scowl deepened. Turning on her heel, she willed a flood of golden light into being as if to spurn even the glow he'd conjured for her convenience.

* * * * *

The mare's eyes rolled. Gaedynn whispered reassurance, clung to the animal's halter with one hand, and stroked her neck with the other.

He and Jhesrhi had ridden their stolen mounts past the point of exhaustion. She'd laid charms of calmness and obedience on them. By rights they should have been stolid as a pair of stones, but they weren't. Not under the circumstances. And if they made too much noise, or bolted out from under the oak that shielded them from the sky, Jaxanaedegor would surely spot them.

He might do it anyway. Dragons had keen senses, and Gaedynn suspected those of a vampiric dragon were sharper still. Conceivably sharp enough to pierce Jhesrhi's spell of concealment.

Gaedynn abruptly realized the wyrm was overhead again. Perhaps, peering through the tangled branches, he saw a star vanish as the undead hunter glided in front of it. But mostly he *felt* the proximity of a malice profound enough to turn his mouth dry and make him shudder.

His horse trembled too. She tried to toss her head, and then whickered. He wondered if he should kill her, or if that would make even more noise.

Then, up in the sky, leathery wings cracked like a whip. The overpowering sense of vileness faded. Either Jaxanaedegor was a little deaf by dragon standards, or else Jhesrhi's magic had kept him from hearing the whinny. In any case, he was flying away.

The sellswords kept silent. If the wyrm was still looking for them, he might swing close again, depending on the search pattern. But that didn't happen, and Gaedynn finally decided it wasn't going to.

"I have to admit," he said, "there are moments when it looks like you're starting to get the hang of sorcery."

Jhesrhi grunted. "We were lucky. Can you find us something to eat?"

"If you'll take charge of my horse, I'll be happy to try."

"Do you want light?"

"Let's not lean too hard on that luck you mentioned." Wishing it were later in the year, alternately standing straight and stooping low, he started examining the tree limbs, shrubs, and roots in their vicinity.

"So what now?" Jhesrhi asked abruptly.

He glanced back at her. "I thought you just requested a late supper."

"I mean tomorrow."

"We flee back to Soolabax, I suppose."

"What about our mission?"

He thought he glimpsed the round pale caps of mushrooms, took a step closer, and saw they were actually toadstools. Damn it. "Our mission is considerably more dangerous now that Jaxanaedegor knows about it."

"He didn't seem to think it likely that the dragon in the Sky Riders really is Tchazzar. And he may not think we're reckless enough to still go there."

Gaedynn smiled, not because of anything she'd said, but because he spotted helmthorn vines. He took another pace and, as he'd hoped, saw berries. They were still in the process of ripening from green to indigo, but in a pinch a person could eat the tart fruit anyway.

Trying not to prick himself on the long black thorns—he already had one gash on his hand!—he started picking them and putting them in the pouch on the orc guard's sword belt. "Then our former host is right on both counts. The dragon, if there even is one, *isn't* Tchazzar, and I'm *not* foolhardy enough to keep looking for it."

"Let's assume the worst."

"By all means, since it's what keeps happening."

As usual, the interruption annoyed her—he could hear it in her voice. "Jaxanaedegor will go look for the dragon or send someone to do it. But he never got around to asking us exactly where in the Sky Riders it is. That means we can find out the truth and get away before anyone else shows up."

As he finished picking the berries, he spotted something else interesting and headed for it. "That's insanely optimistic, but let's continue in the same spirit and see where it leads us. Say we do find Tchazzar. Say he is still interested in protecting Chessenta. Do you really think Lord Nicos or anyone else will be able to free an ancient wyrm from whatever it is that's strong enough to hold him?"

"I don't know. I just know Aoth entrusted us with a task."

"Are you sure you aren't just bent on testing yourself against Threskel? On proving you're a courageous, capable person here or anywhere? Because you already did that, in Mourktar and again inside the volcano."

Jhesrhi kept silent for several heartbeats. When she spoke again, her voice was ice. "That has nothing to do with it."

He sighed. "Of course it doesn't. And we'll go to the Sky Riders if you think it best." He straightened up and, keeping one hand behind him, walked back to her. "I've got helmthorn berries. And these." He bowed and held out the violets he'd found. "I'm not entirely sure how long we were chained up in the dark, but I think it may be Greengrass night."

Making sure her hand didn't come into contact with his, she took the flowers. "You never stop striking poses."

Gaedynn grinned. "Well, as you pointed out yourself, it serves me better than sincerity."

* * * * *

The giants had raided deep into Tymanther, burning villages and fields to raise the smoke Khouryn and his companions had noticed on their way to Djerad Thymar. But—so far at least—the marauders kept retreating back to the Black Ash Plain, and so the vanquisher's warriors had gone to seek them there.

Which was to say, to a gray wasteland where only sparse grass and twisted shrubs grew and smoke rose from cracks in the ground. The air stank of combustion, and drifting flecks of ash stung the eye. To either side towered freestanding columns of solidified ash. Though as a dwarf, Khouryn had a reasonable knowledge of earth, stone, and fire, he couldn't imagine what natural process created the things. Or set a couple of the more distant ones sliding like tokens on a game board without toppling over or breaking apart. It couldn't be the wind. They were moving in opposite directions.

Riding on Khouryn's left, Balasar turned his head and smiled. "Like the scenery?"

"I've seen it before," Khouryn answered, and that was more or less true. He'd traveled the Dustroad. But it had become clear that if a person kept to the highway, he never quite found out just how strange and unwelcoming these particular badlands actually were.

The Lance Defenders were on the road or near it, where they hoped to engage the largest horde of ash giants. Like most of the companies fielded by one clan or another, the thirty Daardendrien warriors and their one dwarf ally were ranging through the heart of the barrens to intercept smaller bands of enemy raiders before they reached the dragonborn lands beyond.

Riding on the other side of Balasar, his black surcoat marked with the six white circles of Daardendrien but his heater shield bearing the right-hand gauntlet emblem of Torm, Medrash asked, "Are you sorry you came?"

Khouryn assumed some note of glumness or sourness in his voice had prompted the question. "I won't be if our side defeats the giants fast enough for me to pay a visit home."

But he suspected that was unlikely. And as for the notion that he might penetrate sinister secrets opaque to everyone else, well, that had seemed a *little* plausible back in Djerad Thymar, when he was a little drunk. But now that he'd sobered up it seemed ridiculous, and not just because a fellow wasn't apt to learn much about schemes and conspiracies while stuck in the middle of a godscursed wasteland.

Khouryn knew he was far from stupid. He understood warfare and siegecraft better than almost anyone he'd ever met. And he could concoct a clever battlefield ruse when the situation called for it. But in the main, he thought in a straightforward manner ill suited to unraveling intrigues.

To the Abyss with it, he thought. I'll stick with Medrash and Balasar for the length of this patrol. But then, unless I've found a better reason to stay, I'm heading back to Chessenta.

Balasar pointed. "Look."

A speck moved across the hazy sky. Khouryn squinted and could just make out that it was a Lance Defender riding one of the giant bats. A scout or messenger, he assumed. The sight gave him a fresh pang of sadness for the loss of his own winged mount.

The Lance Defender plunged earthward.

"Is he diving?" Balasar asked

"No," Khouryn said. A bat didn't fly exactly the same as a griffon, but he was still sure he knew how to interpret what he was seeing. "His mount is hurt. Shot from below, I imagine. It isn't dead, at least not yet, but it can't stay in the air. He's trying to put it on the ground before its strength gives out."

And maybe the rider succeeded. It appeared to Khouryn that the bat wasn't *quite* plummeting when it vanished behind a low rise.

"We have to get to him." Medrash kicked his horse into a canter, and everyone else followed his lead.

They rode most of the way to the rise, then dismounted. Leaving a couple of warriors behind to guard the horses, they stalked up the slope on foot. Khouryn had learned that given a choice, dragonborn rarely fought on horseback, and maybe his companions hoped a quieter approach would catch any enemies by surprise.

Whatever they were thinking, he was glad to be on his own two feet again. He could manage his enormous mare under normal circumstances, but if he tried to do so in the midst of battle, he might well get the both of them killed.

He peered over the top of the rise. The bat lay crumpled a stone's throw beyond the base of the shallow descent on the other side. An arrow the size of a javelin protruded from the animal's flank. Neither it nor the dragonborn slumped on its back were moving. Nor were the three pillars of ash looming in a semicircle behind them.

"Is he alive?" Balasar whispered.

Medrash whispered a prayer. For a moment, power warmed the air. "Yes. I feel his thoughts. But I think he's badly injured."

"Where's the tail-waggling son of a toad that shot him?"

"That I can't tell."

"Even a giant could hide behind one of those spires," Khouryn said. "But that's just a guess. The enemy could be anywhere, and there may be more than just a lone archer."

"It doesn't matter," Medrash said. "I have to get down there if the Lance Defender is to have any chance of living." He stood up straight and headed down the hillside.

"What about my chances of living?" said Balasar to his clan

brother's back. But he followed without hesitation. So did Khouryn and everyone else.

Peering one way and another, weapons at the ready, they prowled halfway down the slope. Then the column of ash to their right shuddered. Grit broke off and showered down the sides. Then it slid forward.

"We've got an adept!" Medrash shouted. He meant a giant shaman capable of magically pushing the spires around to serve as ponderous but powerful weapons.

Though few dragonborn possessed a knack for spellcasting, the Daardendriens had brought along one of the exceptions, an old fellow with a scarred snout and bronze scales who wore six wands sheathed on his belt like a collection of daggers. He drew one carved of alexandrite, greenish in the light here, pointed and spiral-cut to resemble a unicorn's horn. He stabbed it at the advancing column and snarled words of power.

The spire kept coming. As Khouryn tried to predict its course and poised himself to dodge as need be, he thought, I'll bet Jhesrhi could stop it.

At which point it did stop, and he decided he hadn't given the dragonborn sorcerer enough credit. Then the pillar shredded apart, the demolition proceeding from top to bottom as quickly as a sword stroke.

It filled the air with much more ash than before. Khouryn felt like he was choking on the stuff, and his smarting eyes were so filled with tears that he could barely see.

Balasar coughed. "The giants have learned a new trick."

It hurt, but Khouryn forced himself to take a deep breath anyway. So he could shout. "They're coming! Be ready!"

A dragonborn started to curse, and then the obscenity warped into a scream. If not for the warning, Khouryn might never have noticed another spire gliding in on his left.

Fortunately, it wasn't too hard to dodge if you did see it coming and had somewhere to go. But he winced to imagine such a weapon plowing and crushing its way through a close formation of infantry.

He jabbed it with his spear as it shuddered past. He didn't really expect the attack to accomplish anything, and as far as he could tell it didn't. The pillar didn't fall over or anything like that.

The dragonborn wizard began another incantation. Peering through the murk of floating ash, Khouryn saw that the magus had swapped out the alexandrite wand for one made of rose red phenalope. He jabbed it insistently at the ground as he recited, in a manner that reminded Khouryn of someone ordering a dog off a piece of furniture.

The spire crumbled. That had the unfortunate consequence of setting even more ash adrift in the air, but the wizard wasn't done. He recited a final rhyming couplet, and all the gray-black flakes and particles fell to the ground like they'd become as heavy as lead.

The sorcerer smiled a fierce reptilian smile of satisfaction. Then an arrow as big as the one that had felled the bat punched into the center of his chest. He collapsed, the red wand tumbling from his hand.

Khouryn spun around and saw his first ash giants.

Technically speaking. About twice as tall as the dragonborn, with gray, hairless flesh, cadaverous faces, and deep-set black eyes, they appeared to be an offshoot of the race known as stone giants in other parts of Faerûn. It was hard to credit that so many big creatures—six at least—had hidden themselves so well and sneaked so near before being detected. But their natural coloration no doubt helped, and they'd smeared their bodies with ash to camouflage themselves even better. And the limited visibility aided them too.

Balasar half roared, half hissed a battle cry and rushed the nearest. Sword glowing, encircled by floating phosphorescent runes, Medrash charged just a stride behind him. Their clan brothers spread out to flank other foes.

Khouryn doubted that either the adept or the archer had advanced to fight hand-to-hand, so he held back and tried to spot them. He located the bowman first, peeking out from behind a boulder and, by the looks of him, waiting for a clear shot at Medrash.

Khouryn charged. A giant sweeping a greatclub back and forth drove three dragonborn into his path, and he veered around them.

The archer didn't notice him coming until he'd nearly closed the distance. But then the hulking creature turned, drew his arrow back to his shoulder, and let it fly.

Khouryn covered up with his shield. It was well made and enchanted as well, and even an oversized arrow streaking from an enormously powerful bow failed to penetrate it. But the impact jolted it back against his body.

He couldn't let the shock make him falter. The giant was already reaching for another of the arrows stuck in the ground. Khouryn hefted his spear and threw it.

It wasn't meant to be used that way. It was too long and heavy. But he was strong even for a dwarf, and he'd practiced when none of his men were around to watch and decide that if an officer thought casting one's spear away was a sensible tactic, they should consider using it too.

The giant tried to dodge, but the spear still pierced his thigh. Blood flowed, looking redder than red on his gray skin in that gray place.

The archer yanked the weapon out. That made the wound bleed more copiously, but it would keep him from tripping over the spear as he moved around. Meanwhile, Khouryn dropped his shield, pulled the urgrosh from his back, and pounded on.

The ash giant resumed reaching for an arrow. Then he registered just how close Khouryn had gotten and snatched up the greatclub leaning against the boulder instead.

The club was a length of wood as tall as a man, with sharp chunks of flint jutting from the top. The giant swung it in a low arc. Khouryn hopped backward, and the end of the weapon whizzed by a finger length in front of him.

It was time to rush in close, where the larger combatant's reach became a handicap and the smaller one found it easier to strike. But unfortunately, the archer seemed to understand that as well as Khouryn did, and the wound in his leg wasn't doing much to impair his mobility. He retreated, and that gave him the time and room to shift the greatclub back into a threatening position. Khouryn had to stop short to keep from running onto the jagged flint sticking out of the top.

The giant advanced and attacked with short, vicious strikes that kept the club between Khouryn and himself. As Khouryn gave ground, he waited for the archer to overcommit, to open his guard or throw himself off balance. It didn't happen.

To the Abyss with it, then. Khouryn stopped retreating and so invited an attack. The greatclub whipped at his head. He ducked beneath the blow, jumped back up, pivoted, and chopped at the weapon at the end of its stroke, in that precious instant before the giant could put it in motion again.

The axe blade cut the rock-studded crown off the club. It also broke the giant's grip on what remained, and he fumbled to regain a firm hold on it.

Now! Khouryn charged up to the giant's legs and cut repeatedly. Blood gushed, and the archer fell forward.

He wasn't done, though. He tried to heave himself around, presumably to jab at his foe with the stub of his broken weapon or simply seize him in his enormous gray hands.

But Khouryn found a vital spot before the ash giant located him. He reversed the urgrosh, stepped in, and thrust the spike between two ribs. It punched deep enough to reach the heart. The giant made a croaking sound, shuddered, and then slumped motionless.

Panting, wiping giant blood off his face, Khouryn turned to see how the rest of the battle was going.

Not too badly, he decided. A few of the dragonborn had fallen, but two of the giants' frontline fighters had too. At the moment, the adept looked like the most serious problem. Either he'd emerged from hiding on his own, or Medrash and Balasar had finished their first opponent and flushed him out. Then they'd charged him.

They hadn't reached him though, because he'd turned the solid ground beneath them into loose ash and cinders, and they were floundering in it like it was quicksand. Meanwhile, the adept stood with his arm stretched out to the remaining spire. Moving slowly for now, but accelerating as it started to come out of its turn, the column was looping around to make a run at the two dragonborn.

Fortunately, the adept was fairly close. Khouryn charged.

The giant heard or glimpsed him coming. He turned, growled words of power, and lashed his arm like he was throwing a stone.

In reality, he was throwing several. Appearing in midair, the conjured barrage hurtled at Khouryn, who threw up an arm to shield his face.

Some rocks missed. One bounced off his helmet with a clank. Two others cracked against his mail, stinging him but doing no actual harm. He ran on.

The shaman backpedaled and slashed his hand through the opening zigzag pass of another spell. But he was so focused on self-defense that he lost control of the spire. As Khouryn understood it, the peculiar landforms rarely fell over when they wandered around on their own, but that wasn't the case here. The pillar was moving as the giant wanted it to move, and deprived of his psychic guidance, it toppled.

Happily, it wasn't yet close enough to land on Medrash and Balasar as it crashed to pieces, and a moment later they succeeded in dragging themselves out of the soft ash. Both were now covered in the stuff, and the filth made an odd contrast to the pearly radiance of Medrash's sword and the glyphs of light still hovering around his body.

The two dragonborn and Khouryn advanced on the adept. We've got this, Khouryn thought. It's been a hard fight, but we're going to win.

Backing away, the shaman reached inside his horsehair tunic and brought out a gray, gleaming egg-shaped object. He raised it over his head and chanted. Power groaned through the air. But that was all that happened, and Balasar laughed a short, derisive laugh.

As if in response, something bellowed. Khouryn looked over his shoulder.

Big gray creatures were bursting out of the pocket of ash the shaman had created, and the piles and drifts the fallen spires left behind. The things were as big as ogres, and lizardlike, but something about their shapes made Khouryn think of bears as well. Diseased bears, for sores and pustules dotted their scaly hides.

One of the lizard things charged Balasar. Khouryn took a stride toward his friend, then saw from the corner of his eye that a second creature was racing at him. He pivoted to face it.

It lunged, jaws open wide to reveal a mouth full of blisters and slime. It snapped, he sidestepped, and its fangs clashed shut on empty air.

But drops of its slaver spattered his exposed skin and, smoking and popping, burned him. Snarling at the pain, grateful that none of the viscous stuff had landed in his eyes, he cut at the creature's head.

The urgrosh split hide and flesh and cracked the skull beneath. But it wasn't enough to kill the lizard-bear. It turned and sprang at him, and he dodged and chopped at it again.

It still wouldn't go down, and then the ground crumbled beneath his feet. As he plunged down into the powder, he realized that the adept had played the same trick on him that he'd used on Medrash and Balasar. He also realized he couldn't defend himself while half drowning in the dry, hot quagmire. All the lizard thing had to do was lean down and nip his head off.

It started to. Then Medrash rushed in on its flank and cut its neck. His luminous blade bit deep, and the beast collapsed.

Then Medrash stuck his sword in the ground. He had to grab Balasar to heave Khouryn out of the ash, because Medrash's off hand was useless. A different lizard thing had torn away his shield and shredded the arm that supported it. The wounds fumed and made a sickening sizzling sound as acid continued to eat its way into his flesh.

"Heal yourself!" Khouryn said.

Medrash swayed. "The others . . ."

"You can't help anybody if you pass out!"

"You're right." Medrash pressed his good hand to the injuries and recited a prayer. Light shone between his fingers.

Meanwhile, Khouryn surveyed the battlefield, then cursed. The advent of the lizard creatures had shifted the balance of power disastrously. He and the dragonborn likely could have handled either them or the ash giants, but not both together. Half the Daardendrien warriors had fallen already, and the rest were hard pressed.

"We have to make a run for it," he said.

Medrash gave a curt nod, and then he bellowed, "Retreat!"

Retreating was particularly difficult for him and Khouryn with most of the enemy between them and where they wanted to go. But, miraculously still unscathed, Balasar came to fight alongside them, and that helped. Together they killed one lizard-bear, lamed another, and scrambled away faster than it could follow. The adept filled the air around them with embers, but the sparks only singed them a little before they sprinted clear. Maybe Medrash's circle of runes protected them.

Then Khouryn felt the slant of the ground beneath his feet. He and his friends had reached the slope, anyway.

Eventually, they reached the top too, and at that point Medrash stopped running and glared back at the pursuing giants and lizard things. Balasar and Khouryn stopped to stand to either side of him.

The paladin shouted, "I'm right here! Kill me if you can!" Khouryn could tell the declaration carried a charge of divine power. Even though he wasn't the target, the words echoed inside his head. They certainly set hooks in several of the enemy, who left off chasing other dragonborn to veer toward Medrash. And his two companions.

"Now how is this a good thing?" Balasar asked. Then an ash giant pounded up to him, and he caught the first chop of a stone axe on his shield.

He probably riposted too, but Khouryn didn't see it. He had to turn and contend with a giant of his own.

The next few moments were a frenzy of bashing, hacking giant weapons and the blades that leaped and darted in reply. Chanting a prayer, Medrash began to shine like his sword. Lacking any comparable mystical resources of his own, Khouryn simply kept in constant motion and used every skill and trick he'd mastered in training yards and battles across the East.

Somehow it kept him alive until Balasar yelled, "Everyone's gone past us!"

Medrash thrust the point of his sword into the ground. "Torm!" he bellowed. Brighter light flared from the weapon. Khouryn didn't feel a thing as it washed over him, but it slammed giants and lizard-bears reeling backward.

Which enabled the three defenders to break away. As they turned and ran, the glow in Medrash's sword, the radiance shining from his body, and his ring of floating runes all winked out together. Which likely meant that for the moment, he'd exhausted his ability to channel his deity's power.

Below them, one of the guards they'd left with the horses was still waiting, still holding a string of the animals ready. Balasar, who'd evidently noticed that it took a dwarf a bit of time to clamber up into the saddle, picked Khouryn up and dumped him there before springing onto his own mount.

Medrash swung himself onto his horse. The guard started to do the same. Then something cracked, and he collapsed, his head abruptly misshapen inside his dented helm. Blood gushed from under the rim. Khouryn realized one of the giants had thrown a stone with lethal force and aim.

The guard appeared beyond help, and the riders spurred their steeds and left him sprawled in the dirt. They had to. Because giants and lizard things were charging down the slope like a wave rushing at the shore.

For the next several heartbeats, Khouryn wondered if reaching the horses was actually going to be enough. It was possible that the giants with their long legs could run just as fast, or the lizard creatures for that matter. Or one of the rocks whizzing through the air could kill or lame a horse.

But he and his comrades gradually pulled ahead, and one by one the giants gave up the chase and shouted after them. Khouryn didn't speak their language, but the mockery in their tone was unmistakable.

And maybe they deserved to feel superior. Because when Khouryn and his companions caught up with the dragonborn who'd ridden away before them—the warriors whose lives they'd bought with their seemingly suicidal rearguard action—they saw there were only three of them. That meant Clan Daardendrien had lost twenty-five of its finest.

Balasar looked around at what little was left of their war band, then made a spitting sound. "And we never even got to the scout on the bat!"

* * * * *

Hasos glared at Aoth. "A man is dead!" the noble said.

"I regret that," Aoth replied. "But war really is coming. Threskel is moving more and more of its strength to the border. You'd better get used to the idea that before this is over, a lot of men will be dead."

"The other farmers are afraid to work the fields."

"All the more reason to help me stop the raiders in their own territory before they slip into yours and hurt people."

Hasos's mouth twisted. "We've been though this, Captain. I won't provoke the Threskelans into attacking any more aggressively than they are already. I won't risk men I may need later."

Aoth studied Hasos. Please, he thought, show me a sign that this whoreson sent the killers after me. Do it and I'll arrest him, take sole command of all the soldiers hereabouts, and worry about justifying my actions to the war hero later.

But the scene before him didn't change. He could depend on his fire-kissed eyes to see through darkness or mirages, but providing some intimation of a man's secret thoughts was a more difficult trick.

Of course, it was entirely possible he was staring at the wrong man anyway. He wanted Hasos to be guilty. It would make life simpler, and he didn't like the aristocrat any better than Hasos liked him. But that didn't mean the Chessentan really was sheltering dragonborn assassins.

"All right," said Aoth, "you keep your men patrolling your own lands, I'll keep sending mine into Threskel, and maybe together we can keep any more peasants from catching arrows. Now, if we've talked about everything you wanted to discuss, I have something too."

Hasos scowled like he wasn't done witlessly trying to blame the plowman's death on the sellswords' incursions into enemy territory. But then he evidently decided to let it go. "What's that?"

"I need to walk this keep from top to bottom."

"Why?"

"Obviously, my lord, if the Threskelans lay siege to Soolabax and succeed in getting inside the walls, your residence will become crucial to our defense. So I need to be familiar with it. I should have looked it over before this, but I had even more urgent things to do."

"I suppose I can have someone show you around. Or do it myself, if you think that would be better."

And then, if there was something Aoth wasn't meant to see, his guide would steer him away from it. "No need. I can find my way around a fortress. I just wanted your permission."

"Very well. You have it."

Aoth left Hasos's study and proceeded to explore the smallish castle from battlements to cellars. He took inventory of its strengths and weaknesses, just as he'd said he would. But he also looked for signs of secret passages and hidden chambers.

Which evidently didn't exist.

He finished in the wine cellar. Exasperated by his failure, he found a dusty old bottle and picked at the cork with his dagger. He got some of it out and pushed the rest down the neck into the red liquid inside. Hoping he was pilfering something expensive, he took a swig.

Not bad, in a sour sort of way.

When he'd drunk his fill, he left the bottle on the floor, departed the keep, and walked to the temple of Amaunator. He had to wait while Cera completed a ceremony, but then she received him in a study considerably brighter and cheerier than the one where Hasos conducted business. The costly glass windows and skylights let in the warm afternoon sunlight.

Cera lifted off a round golden mask and set it on a table. "You look awful." She sounded slightly hoarse from her praying and chanting.

Aoth snorted. "Thanks so much. Lack of sleep will do that to a person. The war is starting. I have to spend most of my time in the field. Then when I do make it back to town, instead of resting I walk the streets or fly over them, looking for some sign of the dragonborn."

"From your manner, I take it you still haven't found one."

"No."

She removed the topaz-studded cloth-of-gold stole hanging around her neck. "I guess 'true sight' doesn't live up to its reputation."

"It doesn't make me omniscient, if that's what you mean. You jeer at me. Have you had any better luck?"

She poured water from a pitcher into a goblet and took a sip. "Not yet. There's a ritual that enables me to tell if another person's speaking the truth. When I have the chance, I perform it before I talk to someone we decided was a likely suspect." She smirked. "By the way, you're reimbursing the temple for the incense I have to burn."

"Even though you're telling me I won't be getting much for my coin."

"I'm afraid not. Even if a person is guilty, the trick is steering the conversation in such a way that he needs to lie. I can't just say, by the way, are you hiding dragonborn in your house? Or, how's the plan to murder that ugly little sellsword commander going? What's that all about, anyway?"

"And who's to say you're even talking to the right people? Or that anyone is sheltering the reptiles? Maybe they've taken refuge in an empty building."

"Now that I doubt. To say the least, Soolabax is no metropolis, but it's grown since Hasos's ancestors built the walls. It's crowded now, especially since we locals had to find space for you sellswords. There just aren't that many vacant houses."

"I suppose not." He felt a yawn coming on and smothered it. He considered using a tattoo to stave off fatigue and decided not to bother. "It sounds like I just have to keep looking over my shoulder."

"Not necessarily."

"Oh?"

"I assume that even a devil-worshiping Thayan is aware that among his other attributes, Amaunator is a god of time."

"You mean Bane. It's Bane my countrymen all worship since Szass Tam drove the other zulkirs out. But yes, I know that."

"Then it may not astonish you that under certain circumstances, the Keeper gives his clerics a measure of power over time. Not enough to visit the past in the flesh—there are excellent reasons why no one can ever be allowed to do that—but to travel there in spirit and watch what unfolds."

He frowned. "You're saying our souls could lurk outside your garden and see where the dragonborn came from. Get a direction, anyway."

"Yes."

"I don't know. It sounds like a form of divination, and I told you what happened when the wizards tried that in Luthcheq."

"It's not divination in a technical sense. It *is* a unique way of directing divine power, one that most people outside my order have never even heard of. That gives us reason to hope that we could do it without triggering the assassins' mystical defenses."

"All right, let's try."

"Don't make up your mind quite yet." She took another sip. "The sacred texts warn that the ritual is dangerous and should only be attempted to achieve something of extreme importance."

Aoth smiled a crooked smile. "More important than saving the hide of one devil-worshiping Thayan, you mean."

"Yes. But if your survival or learning the truth about the dragonborn is necessary to keep Chessenta from falling to the armies of an undead dragon, then perhaps I would be justified. I've prayed and meditated, and I don't feel Amaunator telling me no."

"How reassuring."

"If it's not good enough for you, you may also want to consider that I've never tried this before, or even watched anyone else do it."

He shrugged. "You understand Amaunatori mysteries better than I ever could. If your instincts say go forward, then I'm game."

She smiled, and it struck him again just how much he liked her round, impish face. "Then shall we do it now, before we come to our senses?"

"Right now?"

"The sun is bright and high in the sky. I just came from worship. I'm about as powerful as I'm going to get." She picked up an old book bound in crumbling yellow leather, then waved her hand at a wooden chest. "You carry that."

It turned out to be heavier than he expected, enough that it was awkward to manage it and his spear too. He had a feeling she was waiting for him to grunt and stagger, and he did his best to hide the fact that he was straining.

Cera led him through the temple to the door that opened on the garden. She instructed an acolyte to stand watch and make sure no one disturbed them, and then they stepped out amid the winding paths, green grass, and fresh red and yellow blossoms.

Aoth set the chest on the bench he and Cera had used on the night of the attack. She opened the box, and when she unpacked the four items inside and removed their velvet wrappings, he saw what had made it so heavy. About as tall as his forearm was long, each of the objects was a golden statue of Amaunator standing with an hourglass, a calendar stone, or some other device emblematic of time. The sculptor had fashioned the figures in an elongated style that made the god look skinny.

"I trust you can find the cardinal points," Cera said.

"My men and I would have spent a lot of time wandering around lost if I couldn't."

"Then set the icons out on the ground to define a circle. It doesn't matter how big, as long as we can both fit inside comfortably."

He did as she'd directed. "Now what?"

"Now I stand at the center of the circle, you stand toward the edge, and you don't speak or move till I say you can."

They took their places.

Cera stood up straight and took a breath. Up until then, despite the fact that she and Aoth were engaged in serious business, there'd been an edge to her that might have signified playful teasing, lingering anger, or a mixture of the two. Now, even though she'd stopped talking, he somehow felt that quality fall away. Suddenly she almost seemed like a holy image herself, her whole being focused on drawing down the power of her god.

She opened the old yellow book and started to read aloud. At first Aoth only heard the words. Then, though a kind of synesthesia, he also perceived them as pulses of warmth and light.

Even he shouldn't have been able to see the latter in a garden already awash in spring sunlight. Nor should he have seen the arcs of radiance that flared into existence to delineate the sacred circle, and the lines that stabbed outward through the grass. But, as if they were more real than anything around them, the magical phenomena possessed a transcendent vividness that would have made them visible in any circumstances whatsoever.

The icon to the east shimmered and faded away. Then the ones to the north and south disappeared, and lastly the figure in the west. The ritual had consumed them like fire ate wood.

Suddenly, Aoth felt light as air and sensed his essence trying to rise. For a moment something held him like sticky strands of spiderweb, but then the adhesion broke and he floated clear of his body. Which stood like a statue beneath him—except with the heart and lungs still working, he assumed.

Cera flowed up out of her body. Her spirit wore a semblance of her vestments and carried an analogue to the yellow book just as he still appeared to possess his mail and spear. "Do you feel disoriented?" she asked.

He shook his head. "I've experienced astral travel before." At the Dread Ring in Lapendrar—he hoped this venture would prove less dangerous and more productive than that one had.

"Then let's get outside the walls." She soared over the one on the east and disappeared behind it.

He willed himself after her, and simple intent was enough to launch him like an arrow from a bow. The sensation of effortless, weightless flight was as exhilarating as he remembered, for the instant before he touched down in the street.

Several boys were playing catch in the center of the thoroughfare while a black dog scampered around their feet. A man—a potter, judging from the clay stains on his hands and clothing—scowled, apparently at the momentary inconvenience of having to detour around the game.

Nobody reacted to Cera and Aoth's arrival. Because no one had the magic or spellscarred eyes that would have allowed him to perceive disembodied spirits.

"What now?" asked Aoth.

"If I performed the ritual properly," Cera replied, "it should work more or less on its own from here."

The leather ball halted in midair, then flew back into the hand that had thrown it. Putting his feet exactly where he had before, the potter backed up.

At first, even though everything was regressing, it didn't move any faster than it normally would. Aoth wondered if he and Cera would have to wait for what would feel like actual days before they reached the dragonborn attack.

But then the world sped up until all he could see was flickers and blurs in the street. Occasionally he felt a cool tingle as something streaked through his insubstantial body.

The sun dropped toward the eastern horizon, and dawn gave way to night. The darkness only lasted a few moments, and when the sun rose in the west it was racing even faster. Daylight and star-dappled blackness alternated as quickly as the beat of clapping hands.

Until he felt the rapid regression come to a sudden halt. It left them in the dark, which was a good sign. Still, he asked, "Are we where—or rather when—we need to be?"

Cera smiled. "Listen."

He did. He could just make out the rippling music of the harpist she'd hired to play at the feast.

"When the dragonborn appear," she continued, "I think I can back up time a little more, at its normal speed. Then we can follow the assassins back to their lair."

"This is . . . impressive."

"I certainly am. I'll bet you're sorry you trampled on my maidenly feelings now, aren't you?"

He was still trying to figure out how to respond to that when his eyes throbbed. He grunted and raised a hand to them.

"What's wrong?" she asked.

"I don't know. I'm not in pain. But I have a strange sensation."

"Let me see." She came closer and peered up into his face.

"It doesn't hurt. It's not interfering with my vision either. It's just—"

The sky resumed flickering from night to day and back again. Then Cera and Aoth hurtled upward like leaves in a tornado. He instinctively tried to resist, but the force that gripped them was far stronger than his ability to move or stay by force of will.

In fact, he was afraid it would rip Cera and him apart. She plainly had the same concern, for she reached out at the same instant he did. He grabbed her hand, pulled her close, and wrapped his arm around her. Caught between them, the sacred book pressed into his chest.

"What's happening?" he asked.

"I don't know."

"In that case, maybe I'm not as impressed as I thought."

He had a sense they were streaking along fast as lightning, and that combined with the flashing madness that was the sky made it impossible for him to judge where they were headed or how much farther in the past their destination lay. But the journey only took a moment or two, and then they were at rest again. It seemed like a relief until he took in their surroundings.

They stood on a ledge midway up one side of a sort of bowl in the ground. Crags rose all around the low place like the points of a crown. They looked natural, but not entirely so. Someone had dug and carved to make sure that the balconies were spacious and plentiful enough for all the enormous creatures that perched here under the stars, and that the openings in the rock were sufficiently high and broad to admit them to what must be a warren of tunnels within the spires.

Everything was silent. An animal odor hung in the chilly air.

"That smell," Cera said. "Is something here?"

"Dragons," said Aoth.

She stiffened. "What?"

"Dozens of them, perched all around. They must have some spell of concealment in place. That's why you can't see them."

"What are they doing?"

"Not much. Talking, I think."

"About what?"

"The enchantment that hides them makes them quiet too. And the Blue Fire changed my eyes, not my ears."

"I don't understand any of this!"

"I don't either. But since we're here, let me watch for a while."

"If I call on Amaunator, maybe I can see them too."

"Or maybe they'll sense the use of power. I'm sure it's frustrating, but leave the spying to me."

For all the good it was likely to do when he couldn't hear anything. He noted a preponderance of blues, greens, reds, and the other dragons collectively called chromatics, fewer gem wyrms, and only a couple metallics. Then all the behemoths in front of him raised their crested, wedge-shaped heads, and he turned to look where they were peering.

When he did, he felt a stab of fear, as well as incredulity that he'd only now noticed what perched on a balcony to his right. The entity was at least as huge as any of the other dragons, but made of nothing but bare bones, the sparks that danced on them, and the spectral blue light in its eye sockets. A horn jutted from its snout and bobbed a little as its jaws worked. Aoth could feel its malice and cruelty as plainly as he could see its scythelike talons, or the naked armature of its wings.

"By the Flame," he whispered, "it's Alasklerbanbastos."

Up until then, he'd imagined he and Cera had a good chance of going undetected. But suddenly it seemed all too likely that an undead wyrm would notice the presence of discarnate spirits, and probably sooner rather than later.

It made Aoth glad that like every other ledge, the one he and Cera occupied had an opening to the tunnels. "We're retreating into the caves," he said. "And as soon as all the dragons are out of sight, you're going to pray us back where we belong."

She nodded. "If I can."

They backed up. Given their status as living ghosts, they shouldn't have needed to tiptoe or creep slowly, but they did anyway. With dragons and a dracolich only a stone's throw away, Aoth found it impossible to do otherwise.

But even if his attempt at stealth made sense, it wasn't good enough. On the other side of the bowl, on a shelf near the jagged top of the rim, a dragon sat up abruptly. A dull, mottled red with a black ridge on its spine—Aoth wondered exactly what sort of wyrm it was—peered at them with eyes like burning coals. Then it exhaled a cloud of vapor and cinders with a care that reminded him of a pipe smoker blowing a smoke ring.

The exhalation writhed and billowed, forming legs, batlike wings, and a serpentine head, neck, and tail. Becoming a vague, semitransparent parody of its creator. Then the smokelike image hurtled straight at Aoth and Cera. Startled, puzzled, other dragons and even the Great Bone Wyrm himself twisted to follow its flight.

Aoth had no doubt that the wyrm with the rust-colored scales realized the intruders were spirits, give or take, and had unleashed a magic capable of harming them. Kossuth grant that meant a living phantom could hurt it in return. "Run!" he rapped. He leveled his spear and spoke a word of power.

Wind howled out across the bowl. It didn't disturb so much as a particle of dust existing solely in the material world, but it hurled the smoke-thing backward, frayed its limbs, and stretched them out of shape.

Still, the blast of air didn't tear it apart as Aoth had hoped it would. The creature, if that was the right word for it, pulled itself more or less back into shape and kept coming.

As it set down on the ledge, he threw a pearly blast of frost at it. Seemingly unaffected, it sprang forward and lifted a forefoot to claw at him.

Then warm golden light shone from behind him. To him it felt pleasant, bracing, but the smoke-wyrm flinched.

"Its maker is undead," Cera said, "so sunlight burns it as well."

"I don't care!" snapped Aoth. "I'll hold it off. You concentrate on getting us back where we belong."

The breath-entity plunged forward. Aoth sidestepped a silent snap of its hazy jaws, charged the point of his spear with destructive force, and thrust it into his adversary's neck.

But had the attack actually hurt it? He couldn't tell.

The smoke-thing clawed at him. He thought he jumped back far enough to avoid the raking stroke—although with the limits of the entity's body so poorly defined, it was hard to be sure about that either. In any case, a chill stabbed through his body, weakening and numbing him. Tiny red droplets burst from his pores to drift up and merge with the swirl of sparks and vapor.

He drew strength from a tattoo to stave off feebleness, shouted words of evocation, and hurled a bright, twisting bolt of lightning into his foe. It faltered and shuddered, but only for an instant. Then it snapped at him again.

Aoth dodged. As, visible through the swirling vapor that was the breath-entity's substance, Alasklerbanbastos crawled into the cave. Aoth looked into the seething blue light that was the dracolich's gaze. Suddenly he couldn't move, *absolutely could not move*, while the smoke-wyrm lunged—

Aoth shot upward through the solid rock above him and high into a sky flashing from dark to light and back again. He looked for Cera and found her to his right, just beyond arm's reach. It occurred to him he ought to try to take his bearings, but it was too late. They were already hurtling through time and space.

He returned to his physical form with a sort of mental jolt, like he'd jumped out of a tree. For an instant, solid flesh and bone felt heavy as lead. He stumbled to the bench, shoved the box off onto the grass, and flopped down.

Looking as exhausted as he felt, Cera sank down beside him. "Are you all right?" she panted.

He realized he was winded too, even though his body hadn't done anything. He pulled off his gauntlets and saw his hands looked the same as always. At least, unlike his spirit form, the physical Aoth hadn't bled.

"The breath-thing hurt me a little," he said, "but now that we're back, I imagine I'll shake it off. I'm just glad it didn't take you any longer to end the spell."

"So am I." She closed her eyes, whispered something, and kissed the flaking yellow cover of her book.

"Do you have any idea where we were, or when?"

"No."

"I didn't recognize anything either. Well, nothing but the Great Bone Wyrm. I mean, I assumed it was him. Damn it! Why didn't we stay where we wanted to be?"

She sighed. "I don't know. Maybe the dragonborn's defenses did interfere. Maybe I didn't perform the magic properly. Or . . ."

"Go on."

"Maybe I really had no business trying it at all. Perhaps the circumstances didn't warrant it. One thing's certain—I broke the rules of my order by doing it without asking Daelric's permission."

"Because you knew he wouldn't give it."

"Well . . . yes. And I believed my judgment in the matter was better than his. Perhaps what we just experienced was the Keeper rebuking my arrogance."

"It seems like an odd sort of punishment. Why not just send an angel to give you a spanking?"

That tugged a slight smile out of her. "I don't know."

"Is it possible that Amaunator, or whichever of his exarchs took control of the magic, meant to help you? That he showed us what he thought we ought to see, as opposed to what we believed was important?"

Cera frowned. "I suppose it's conceivable. But if so, *why* was that more important?"

"I don't know. Finding the reptiles who want to murder me strikes me as extremely important. But come to think of it, there's even another possibility."

"What?"

"You were trying to cast what's essentially an enchantment of seeing. My eyes already carry a magic of seeing that, even a century after the Spellplague, no one truly understands. Perhaps the two powers combined in a way we couldn't anticipate."

She shrugged. "I guess it's possible."

"There's doubt in your voice. But either of my ideas is more plausible than the notion that your god is angry with you."

"I hope you're right. More than once I've heard it whispered that I'm nowhere near as solemn and dignified as a sunlady ought to be. But I do love Amaunator and try to walk in his light."

"Of course you do. I feel the strength of the bond you share every time you invoke his power."

She smiled. "As if a devil-worshiping Thayan would recognize holiness when he saw it."

He grinned back. "Well, you've got me there. Do you think we dare try that particular magic a second time?"

"It doesn't matter what I think. We don't have a second set of statues."

"Next you're going to tell me they were worth thousands and thousands of trade bars, and you expect me to pay for them too."

"Maybe I can think of a way for you to work off the debt." Using her fingertip, she traced the shape of the tattoo on the back of his hand.

EIGHT

7–8 MIRTUL, THE YEAR OF THE AGELESS ONE (1479 DR)

The night darkened. Or at least it seemed to. Jhesrhi assumed that in reality, the enchantment she'd cast to enable Gaedynn and herself to see on the moonless night was wearing off. She'd have to renew it soon.

Fortunately, that shouldn't pose a problem. Though she still regretted the loss of the staff the wyrmkeeper had taken from her in Mourktar, the new one was a worthy tool in its own right, and her bond with it grew ever stronger. The red alloy rings were even turning yellow, apparently just because she was used to carrying a staff trimmed with gold.

"Do you know," Gaedynn murmured, "I have to give credit where it's due. You said Jaxanaedegor wouldn't bother sending a search party into the Sky Riders, and we haven't seen any sign of one."

"Don't start," Jhesrhi said.

"On the other hand, I have to give credit to the dragon too. He didn't send anyone because he believed there was nothing to find. And again, evidently—"

"It's the last night of the new moon," Jhesrhi said, gritting her teeth. "If we don't find anything, we'll head back to Soolabax in the morning. Meanwhile, stop complaining and look."

"I am looking. I can do that and complain at the same time."

But he fell silent again as they prowled through the pines that grew along the ridge. The horses, lucky beasts that they were, were presumably sleeping back in camp. Even with his sight sharpened, Gaedynn didn't want to ride through the dark for fear he'd miss signs he would have noticed on foot.

A long, echoing, inhuman cry sounded from somewhere to the west. As one, Jhesrhi and Gaedynn pivoted in that direction.

"On the other hand . . . ," the archer said.

Her heart thumping faster, Jhesrhi took a breath. "I can't tell if the creature making that noise is a dragon. I certainly can't tell if it's Tchazzar. But we've found the reason for the stories."

"Come close to finding it, anyway. Let's hope it keeps wailing to draw us in."

It did, and its call reminded her of wounded men crying out in agony on the battlefield. As, stalking up one hillside and down the next, she and her companion approached the source, her staff warmed in her grip. The sensation made her even more eager.

Because the arcanist who'd fashioned the implement had been particularly interested in fire magic. And now it was reacting to the presence of a mighty blaze—or, given the absence of any telltale glow, something capable of producing one. Like a red dragon.

A hand grabbed her forearm, arresting her progress, startling her, and bringing the usual reflexive spasm of loathing.

"Sorry," said Gaedynn, releasing her again, "but you have to watch where you're stepping."

She looked down at the patches of pale, whorled fungus in front of her. He was right. If she'd stepped on them, the spores would have stuck to her legs, producing painful pustules or worse.

"Thank you," she said.

"I'm not sure if you've noticed, but this is about the most unpleasant bit of the Sky Riders we've wandered into so far." He waved a hand, inviting her to inspect the gnarled, blighted-looking trees and thickets.

"I noticed," she lied.

"Was it poisoned by the same power that's making our friend caterwaul?"

"I can't tell. Maybe."

"Well, I guess we'll find out soon enough."

They stalked on. Over hills and through hollows where noisome fungus flourished and other vegetation didn't. The leaves on the trees were sparse and spotted, and bark had flaked away to reveal pockets of slimy rot in the sapwood.

Shadows shifted at the edges of her vision, settling when she turned her head to look at them directly. She'd seen the same phenomenon in Thay, on battlefields where necromancers had conjured. The darkness was struggling to give shape to something vile. It just wasn't strong enough.

Her staff went from warm to hot until its touch would have blistered anyone else. Another cry sounded, and she could tell the source was close. Maybe just over the next rise. She and Gaedynn climbed to the crest of the hill and, lying on their stomachs, peeked over.

A dragon sprawled on the barren slope below. It was huger even than Jaxanaedegor, but also profoundly emaciated, although lack of food didn't seem to be the problem. A scatter of bones suggested that it ate from time to time.

Or, more precisely, that someone fed it. For staples of some black substance clasped its legs and tail to the ground.

"It looks sick," Gaedynn whispered, "but even so, I'm surprised those restraints can hold it."

"They're enchanted." She could feel the magic inside them like an itch on her face. "Still, it surprises me too."

"Have we seen enough to be sure that against all probability, you and Lord Nicos were right, and that's Tchazzar?"

"We've seen all that we safely can, that's for certain. Let's get out of here."

They started to crawl backward. Then something snapped and rustled overhead. They froze.

A wyrm almost as big as the prisoner plunged down to land beside it. Short horns encrusted the newcomer's head, and rows of spines ran down the length of its body. The membranes connecting them looked puny and awkward compared to the wings of any dragon Jhesrhi had seen before, but she assumed that somehow they must suffice to carry it through the air.

It moved in what appeared to be a haze of grit, and as soon as it landed, several dust devils swirled up from the ground around its feet. Its eyes were pits of shadow with a sort of oily shimmer in the depths.

The prisoner raised its head and tried to spit fire at the newcomer, but the attack was too feeble even to reach its target. The brief, wavering glow revealed that the scales of both dragons were dull red.

The newcomer snarled. Jhesrhi thought she heard a kind of

laughter in the noise. Then the wyrm snatched with a forefoot, caught the prisoner's serpentine neck just behind the skull, slammed its head to the ground, and held it there.

The master wyrm stared down at the other. The prisoner withered a little more. Meanwhile, branches on the trees adjacent to the bare earth dropped their sickly leaves like it was autumn instead of spring. Blades of grass turned brown and dry.

And Jhesrhi felt a sudden weakness and gut-twisting sickness. She gripped the staff and recited a charm of protection to shield Gaedynn and herself, and the sensation passed.

"Thanks," he gasped. "When we got out of Thay, I hoped we were done with vampires. Now I can't empty my bladder without hitting some kind of vampire dragon."

She wished he'd shut up. The terrible thing below them might hear even a whisper. Although it didn't appear to; maybe it was too intent on its meal.

It seemed to go on feeding for a long time, while its victim shuddered and shriveled, and newly dead branches cracked under their own weight. At last it turned away. That would have been a good time for the prisoner to attempt another attack, but it was evidently too drained.

The life-drinker trotted a few steps, lashed its peculiar wings, and sprang into the air. In flight, it wobbled in a way that made it look unsteady, like it might plummet at any moment. But it gained altitude almost as quickly as a griffon.

Jhesrhi waited for it to disappear, and for one hundred heartbeats afterward. Then she turned to Gaedynn. "Now?"

"Now," he said. "Let me lead, and stay under the trees as much as you can."

Where it's darkest, she thought, but he was right. The shadows' impotent yearning for mayhem was a paltry threat compared to what was soaring on the night wind.

She and Gaedynn started down the hill. And ran straight into what was climbing up the other way.

The people, if that was what they were, had scarred, tattooed gray skin, dark braided hair, and eyes a featureless black like the dragon that had just flown away. Their garments were black as a crow as well, and the gloom seemed thicker in their vicinity than elsewhere, even though there was nothing hanging over them to cast a shadow. They weren't walking like they were trying to be especially quiet, but they were anyway, and Jhesrhi sensed that silence came as naturally to them as to a cat.

"Easy, friends," Gaedynn said. "We're just peaceful travelers."

The gray people appeared to laugh, although Jhesrhi couldn't actually hear it. The darkness around them thickened, and the two men in front pulled off the chains wrapped around their waists. The links didn't rattle. The warriors vanished and instantly reappeared almost within striking distance of Jhesrhi and Gaedynn. Preparing to attack, they spun their weapons.

Then arrows pierced their chests and they stumbled backward. As Gaedynn spoke his placatory words, he'd also gotten ready to shoot, and neither the chainfighters' sudden shift through space nor their shroud of gloom had thrown off his aim.

The rest of the gray people—Jhesrhi still couldn't make out exactly how many that was, but she thought at least half a dozen—howled in fury. She heard them at last, although the sound was faint and thin, like it was coming from miles away. They glided and flickered forward, while also spreading out to flank their foes.

Gaedynn and Jhesrhi gave ground. His hands were a blur as he loosed arrow after arrow. She shifted her staff into a central guard, and a rhyme to conjure fire leaped into her mind.

That was the influence of the staff. Though it was neither alive nor sentient, in its own way it yearned for the element to which it was most attuned.

But it would have to go unsatisfied at the moment. Flame in the dark could catch the eye of the wyrm that had flown away, or of something else she didn't want to meet. She rattled off a different incantation and made a stabbing motion with the staff, and a dozen small knives appeared in the air around two of the chainfighters. They too stabbed. One gray warrior fell. The other scrambled clear of the effect, but with blood staining part of his shirt a different shade of black.

Jhesrhi hesitated, trying to decided whether to finish off the wounded man or attack someone else. In that instant, she sensed motion on her left, something different from the fast but steady rhythm of Gaedynn's shooting.

She turned. A gray man with a dagger in either hand was lunging in on Gaedynn's flank. And she couldn't hit the enemy combatant with her magic, not in time to stop him from attacking, because the archer was in her way. All she could do was yell, "Watch out!"

Gaedynn pivoted. The gray man slashed, first with one blade, then the other. The archer tried to dodge. Standing behind him, Jhesrhi couldn't tell if he succeeded either time.

But bands of darkness wrapped around him like a constricting serpent, crushing his arms and bow against his torso and binding his legs together. Off balance, he toppled to the ground.

That at least got him out of Jhesrhi's way. Terrified that the gray warrior would bend down and finish him off, she jabbed the staff at the attacker and snarled a word of command. Raw force smashed in the dark man's face and blew out the back of his skull.

At her feet, Gaedynn squirmed and strained. Good, he was still alive and able to struggle, but she couldn't take the time to help him free himself. Despite the losses they'd already sustained, more of the gray people were advancing in their flitting, deliberate fashion. It was like they didn't fear death at all.

She softened the earth beneath a chainfighter, and he plunged in up to his waist. Then suddenly, everything got even darker. She assumed it meant one of the enemy had crept in close to her.

Jhesrhi turned, looking for the threat. For a moment she saw a vague figure. Its dark eyes stared into hers, and then it was gone.

Hands grabbed her throat from behind. The iron grip cut off her air and seared her flesh as well.

She could no longer afford to care whether she showed a light in the darkness. Suddenly bereft of speech, she had to use the only magic she could still access quickly. She clutched the staff and, in her thoughts, recited words of command.

Flame erupted over her body like she'd soaked herself in oil. It didn't hurt her, but it presumably burned her attacker, because the hands let go of her neck.

She pivoted to face the strangler, then felt a twinge of surprise because it was a gray *woman*. Not that that mattered. She threw the dark figure backward with a bolt of force.

But the strangler only flew a couple of paces. Then she slammed into one of the chainfighters who, plainly undaunted by Jhesrhi's mantle of flame, were rapidly closing in on her.

She hated their single-minded bloodlust, their sheer uncanniness, and the prospect of them pressing in from all sides. She wanted the fight to be over, and the conjured fire responded to her desire. It lashed out all around her like the spokes of a wheel to blast and burn gray flesh. Her assailants reeled and dropped.

She took a deep breath, willed her own fiery halo and the patches of flame still dancing on the corpses to go out, and turned to see how Gaedynn was faring. A gray man crawling on the ground leered up at her and thrust a dagger at her belly.

Gaedynn heaved himself free of the loops of congealed darkness, scrambled, and grabbed the enemy warrior's arm just before the blade could plunge home. The two combatants thrashed and rolled while Jhesrhi looked for a chance to smite the scarred man without hurting Gaedynn. Then the archer landed a short jab to his opponent's throat. The gray man stopped struggling; suddenly all he could do was shake and choke. Using the heel of his palm Gaedynn hit him again, this time smashing his nose, and he stopped moving altogether.

Gaedynn turned and pulled his bow clear of the coils of darkness. "Are you all right? Those marks remind me of Thay, when a ghost would get its hands on somebody."

She cautiously touched what she surmised to be hand-shaped bruises or discolorations on her neck. Now that the battle was over, they were really starting to sting. Still . . . "I don't think they're all that bad. How are you?"

"I wish we still had that healing balm, but really, the knife just scratched me. The brigandine stopped the worst of it." He pulled the arrows from his quiver. He'd used a lot of them during the fight, and the pressure of the dark coils and rolling around on the ground had broken some of the rest. "Curse it! What were these bastards, anyway? Shades? Shadar-kai?"

"They were a long way from home if they were." The Empire of Netheril, which bred men infused with the essence of darkness, lay two thousand miles to the west.

"True." He grinned. "I just think it would be nice to have Netherese running around our part of the world. Because things aren't nearly complicated enough already."

"We should move out. In case something saw the flames."

"Whenever you're ready."

Farther down the hill, they found yokes with buckets of water attached, and the carcasses of slaughtered deer. Jhesrhi inferred that the gray folk had dropped them when they decided to attack.

"Our foes were Tchazzar's jailers," she said, "charged with bringing him food and drink. They cleared out when the other dragon came to feed, for fear it would leech the strength out of them as well. When we met them, they were coming back."

"Maybe." Squatting beside it, Gaedynn was clearly more interested in examining one of the deer. "Look at this!"

She walked over and stood beside him. "What?"

He pointed. "Look at the striped pattern on the hindquarters." He indicated one of the legs. "And here—no dew claw. During your time in Threskel, did you ever see a doe like this?"

"I don't know. The elemental magi weren't like your elves. They didn't devote any time to teaching me woodcraft."

"Well, I know I haven't seen one before. It's . . . peculiar."

"You can ponder the mystery of its existence when we're well away from here."

He smiled. "I suppose that might be the prudent thing to do."

They hurried onward, while the pain in the front and sides of her neck waxed and waned. Until Gaedynn finally halted and, turning in a complete circle, peered around.

"What is it?" Jhesrhi whispered.

"I think I must be lost," he replied.

Jhesrhi wondered if he was making another poorly timed and pointless joke. "You don't get lost."

"No. I don't. But we've walked far enough that we should be clear of the poisoned area. Yet we're not."

The hill rising in front of them wasn't as utterly and obviously blighted as the dragon captive's immediate vicinity. But when she looked closely, it was obviously tainted. Shadows seethed when they thought no one was looking. Twisted oaks sweated a pale, viscous fluid that reminded her of pus.

"And I can't get my bearings," Gaedynn continued. "The shape of the hills is off."

"Keep walking," Jhesrhi said. "We'll come to something we recognize."

They didn't, though, and in time she began to suspect what had happened. But she had an irrational dread that somehow, saying it aloud would make it true. So she waited until what she supposed she could still call dawn. When the sky lightened from black to slate gray, but nothing recognizable as a sun rose to brighten it any further.

* * * * *

Columns of smoke ascended from behind a rise. Just the thought that someone might be cooking breakfast there made Khouryn's mouth water and his belly growl.

Following their disastrous clash with the ash giants, he and the dragonborn survivors had tried to head east. Medrash wanted to tell the Lance Defenders about the threat of the lizard-bears, which apparently the enemy had never used before. But unfortunately, the riders kept spotting other giant war bands blocking the way to the Dustroad. Sometimes the giants spotted them too, and then they had to flee. Meanwhile their rations ran short, and only occasionally did they find potable water, or grass for their steeds. Two of the animals went lame.

"Fried ham," said Balasar. "If your friend Torm truly takes a benevolent interest in the affairs of mortals, then let him prove it by providing fried ham."

Medrash gave him a sour look. "The Loyal Fury has nothing to prove to you or anyone. And you might want to remember that giants have been known to build fires of their own."

"And that smoke sometimes rises from holes in the ground in this foul kingdom," Khouryn said. "Still, that does look like it's coming from somebody's campfires. Let's find out." He pointed to the left. "If we swing that way, we can come up on high ground overlooking whatever there is to see. And if it's giants, we'll be far enough away to disappear before they can bother us."

Medrash nodded. "Onward."

On the way up, rocks slid and clattered under the hooves of Khouryn's mare, and for a moment he feared the tired beast was going to fall. She didn't, though. She regained her footing and carried him up onto the ridge with his companions.

Where the view was well worth seeing. Although tiny with distance, the figures in the camp below were plainly dragonborn. He felt a surge of elation, which faded when he noticed his companions didn't appear to share it.

Their attitude was a peculiar mix of emotions. Like him, they were relieved. But also surprised, and to varying degrees disgusted.

"What's wrong?" he asked.

For a moment no one replied, as if the answer was shameful. Then Medrash said, "Look at the banner."

Khouryn did. The black flag had a silvery squiggle on it. Trying to make out what it represented, he squinted, then blinked in surprise. "Is that a dragon?"

"Yes," the paladin said. "And as you've heard, dragons are the tyrants who held our ancestors as slaves. Yet there are those among us who preach that we're kin to wyrms and that we should celebrate that kinship and forget the ancient debt of blood."

Khouryn decided he'd just learned whom dragonborn spat at in the street.

"Or to put it another way," Balasar said, "they fixated on one of the gods of this new world—Bahamut, is that what they call him?—the same way you did."

Medrash glared. "If anyone but a clan brother made that comparison, I'd challenge him."

"Then it's lucky for you I am one."

"So anyway," Khouryn said, "these . . . cultists?"

"They call themselves the Platinum Cadre," Balasar said.

"So anyway, this Platinum Cadre apparently fielded its own company to fight the ash giants. And we need help. So I assume we're going down there, even if you find their creed objectionable."

Medrash sighed. "We have no choice." He urged his horse down the slope that led to the camp. Everyone else followed.

Khouryn rode beside Balasar. "He's really not happy, is he?"

"No," Balasar replied. "When the giants defeated us and killed so many, he put the blame on himself. And needing to ask dragon-lovers for help? That's yet another disgrace. You can see that everybody else feels it too, although not as keenly. The rest of us are a little less fanatical about our honor and a little more interested in getting off Black Ash Plain alive."

The dragonborn of the Platinum Cadre gathered to watch the riders approach. The majority wore mismatched bits of armor or none at all. Some carried axes intended for chopping wood and spears designed for hunting boar. A number had only round little scars where their piercings should have been.

They all stared, and Khouryn discerned that a good deal of their curiosity focused on himself. But he didn't sense anything hostile about it.

Two dragonborn stepped forth from the crowd to greet the newcomers.

The one on the left was a big warrior with crimson scales, and scars where, at some point in the past, a blade had hacked away some of the frills around his left cheek and ear. Three silver chains dangled from the studs pierced into his lower jaw like a sparse, clinking excuse for a beard. Judging from the expert workmanship of his plate, Khouryn thought it likely that one of his own people's armorers had made it. The deep blue surcoat bore the platinum-colored head of a dragon.

The one on the right was a female. Her brown hide was freckled with gold, with a pale, puckered spot on the left side of her brow ridge to show where she'd once carried her piercing. She wore a dark purple robe embroidered with silvery sigils and held the shadow-wood staff of a spellcaster. Unlike most dragonborn of either gender, who generally gave the impression of massive solidity, she swayed lithely, ever so slightly, as she swiveled her head to study the riders one at a time.

"Well met," said Medrash, and whatever his true feelings, his tone was respectful. "Clan Daardendrien and Sir Khouryn Skulldark, our trusted ally, request assistance."

"You'll have it," the warrior replied. "I'm Shestendeliath Patrin. I'm in command here. This is Yrjixtilex Nala, my lieutenant."

"It's just Nala now," the wizard said.

"The day will come," Patrin said, "when your clan will be proud to take you back."

"I pray you're right," said Nala, "but either way it's the last thing these people care about. Climb down from your horses, friends. By the looks of you, you need water, food, and rest. Perhaps the aid of a healer as well."

"Thank you." Khouryn clambered down off his steed.

"I understand supplies are hard to come by in this wasteland," Medrash said. "But if you can do anything for our horses, that will place us even deeper in your debt."

"Of course," Patrin said. "We're mostly a company of foot soldiers, but we have a few horses and feed for them in the supply carts. We can spare a little."

As it turned out, breakfast wasn't ham. It was lukewarm gruel, biscuits that needed the mold trimmed off the edges, and strips of jerky. But it was filling, and even Balasar appeared content with it.

Nala and Patrin sat at the dying fire along with Khouryn and the Daardendriens. At first the pair kept quiet and let the newcomers eat in peace. But as they were finishing up, the warrior in the blue surcoat said, "I know there must have been more than six of you when you rode onto Black Ash Plain. I'm sorry if it's a painful subject, but what happened to the rest?"

Where Medrash was concerned, "painful" was surely an understatement. But he also no doubt recognized that a fellow defender of Tymanther, even a member of the Platinum Cadre, both needed and had a right to the information. He told the story of the fall of the bat, and of all that followed, in a calm, clear manner.

"So you see," he concluded, "the ash giants have learned new tricks. They're even more dangerous than they were before. And I hope you won't take it badly if I repay your hospitality by presuming to give you some advice."

Nala smiled. Even sitting cross-legged in the dirt, the skirt of her robe puddled around her, she still had the trick of swaying almost imperceptibly from side to side. "You don't need to," she told Medrash. "We can guess what you're going to say. If a company of Daardendrien's finest couldn't defeat the giants, then plainly we perverse, crazy outcasts have no hope of doing so."

"That's not what I was going to say," Medrash replied. "I don't share your beliefs and never could, but I wouldn't answer kindness with an insult. What I will say is that most of your troops are nowhere near as well armed as Sir Patrin. Some don't appear in the best of health. I'll hazard a guess that those same fellows haven't spent much time in the training yard in recent years, nor has your company had much opportunity to drill together as a unit. So perhaps you're not ready to march deep into enemy territory. Maybe you could better serve Tymanther by garrisoning a post along the border."

Patrin rose. "I regret dragging you to your feet again so soon, but I want to show you something."

They all tramped over to one of the carts the cadre officer had mentioned. He picked up a sack that smelled of rot. The stink grew stronger when he dumped the contents out.

Those contents were severed ears, too big for a dwarf or human head, and the gray was their natural color. It was the brown and purple spots that betrayed decay.

"I know taking this sort of trophy is a little barbaric," Patrin said. "But after the war is over, we need to be able to prove what we accomplished."

"And then the doubters will see the truth and value of our path," Nala said.

Medrash shook his head. "How did you accomplish this?"

"I just told you," the wizard said, her upper body weaving a fraction of an inch from side to side. Khouryn wondered if the rhythmic motion was a symptom of some malady or just a nervous tic. "With Bahamut's aid. By embracing the dragon nature inside us."

"If you say so," said Balasar, "but I think my clan brother was asking about tactics."

Patrin shrugged. "Well, as to that, I doubt they're different from what anyone else would use. But if you'd like to see us in action, I'm glad, because I have a proposition for you."

"What's that?" Medrash asked.

"You came to the Plain to fight and so did we. So join us."

Medrash hesitated. "None of us wishes to accept your faith."

Patrin smiled. "Well, I certainly don't expect *you* to. I recognize the device on your shield, just as I know that when a paladin pledges himself to a god, the commitment lasts forever."

Plainly even more perplexed than before, Medrash narrowed his eyes. "How do you know I'm a paladin?"

"Because like speaks to like. You might feel it too if not for your . . . preconceptions. But here's the point. We won't press you or any of these others to embrace our beliefs. If they come to Bahamut, let it be in their own time and for their own reasons. I want you because Clan Daardendrien has a reputation for valor, and so do the dwarves of East Rift. And because you have horses. They're in sad shape now, but it's nothing feed, rest, and a little magic won't cure—and I need outriders."

"We intended to head east," said Balasar, "to report our experiences to the Lance Defenders."

"Perfect," Nala said. "That's the way we're headed. Now that we've tested ourselves in a couple of battles, we're going where the giants are thickest."

"I'd like to discuss this with my comrades," Medrash said. "Would you excuse us for a moment?"

A scowl flickered across Nala's face, but Patrin said, "By all means."

Medrash led his clan brothers and Khouryn several paces away from the Bahamut worshipers and the cart. "What do you all think?" he asked.

"I'll do whatever you and Sir Balasar want," said an umber-scaled Daardendrien warrior. "But can it be honorable to fight alongside dragon-lovers?"

"It might be more honorable than slinking home with nothing but defeat to report," Balasar said. "Lunatics or not, this war band is winning its battles."

"And if we ride with them," Khouryn said, "we'll share in any future victories. And even if they don't locate any more of the enemy, it's safer than traveling this wasteland alone."

"I've always looked down on the Platinum Cadre," Medrash said, "and now I feel ashamed. These warriors have done us nothing but good. Maybe saved our lives. Perhaps they aren't mad or depraved but simply misguided."

Balasar grinned. "So we accept Patrin's offer."

"If everyone agrees."

Khouryn looked around the circle and saw that everyone did.

* * * * *

The day never brightened past a kind of filthy twilight. Even Jhesrhi's golden hair and eyes couldn't shine. In fact, for the first time Gaedynn could remember, she didn't look beautiful.

Or maybe that was just because he was angry.

"Are you sure?" he asked, realizing even as the words left his lips just how stupid they were.

Jhesrhi waved a hand to indicate the wooded slopes around them. "You yourself told me that a lot of the trees and bushes are different, and even the contours of the hills. By all accounts, shadar-kai live in the Shadowfell as well as Netheril. *And there's no sun in the sky.* What do you think?"

"That we're in the Shadowfell." From what he understood, it was a distorted shadow the mortal world cast to give form to an adjacent universe. Or something like that. "Even though the wizard in our little band never sensed we were going astray until it was far too late."

She glared. "If your stories aren't all lies, you and your elf friends used to visit other worlds on a regular basis. Voices of the Abyss, you actually used the trick to shake the Simbarchs' army off our tail when we were marching through the Yuirwood. So don't make out that I'm the one who should have noticed the transition!"

Her refusal to take the blame had the paradoxical effect of dissolving his annoyance. Perhaps because it was likely the way he would have responded himself.

"The elves took me to the Feywild." A reflection of the mortal world as fair as the Shadowfell was foul. "Well, and on one unpleasant occasion, the Sildëyuir. But even then it was hardly the same thing as blundering into the Shadowfell. Still, it's remotely conceivable you have a point. Perhaps we're both to blame—or neither. Let's agree on neither. But tell me this. *How* did it happen? We didn't pass through a circle of standing stones or anything else that looked like a portal to me."

"Or to me. But scholars say it's possible for two worlds to overlap, often intermittently."

"So in this case, a bit of the hills becomes a bit of the Shadowfell on the darkest nights. Because that's when the two places are most alike."

"I think so."

He grinned. "I should have been a scholar myself."

"It's possible Tchazzar blundered into the Shadowfell during the time of Blue Fire, when all the worlds were in upheaval and congruencies were more common. Then the blight dragon—"

"That's the wyrm that's leeching his strength away?"

"I believe that's what they're called. Now that I've had time to think, I seem to recall reading about them in a bestiary, in the school where Aoth enrolled me to finish my training. Whatever it is, it somehow took Tchazzar prisoner and has been feeding off him ever since. I suspect the process degrades reality and helps keep the breach between the worlds from healing."

"Very interesting, and I'd love to hear more about it. But preferably after you whisk us home."

Jhesrhi shook her head, and a lock of her tangled hair flopped down over her forehead. "I can't."

"Nonsense. Don't expect to hear this often, but you can do damn near anything. I've seen it."

"You've seen me do impressive things with elemental magic. I don't know how to shift us between worlds."

"Didn't you do it at the Dread Ring? Twice?"

"Wizards who truly understood the magic essentially just carried me along like baggage. And we only traveled in spirit. Our physical forms stayed put."

"Still, I know you. You were paying attention, and you must have learned something."

She hesitated. "Not enough. Besides, such rituals generally involve special articles, other spellcasters lending support—or, ideally, both."

"So improvise. Our poor horses are wondering what's become of us."

She frowned. "I suppose I can try. It will be dangerous, but maybe no more dangerous than trying to survive in the Shadowfell for a whole month. Or longer. We don't know that the planes mesh every new moon without fail, or that we'd succeed in finding our way from one to the other when they do."

"What can I do to help?"

"Just stand watch—the Foehammer only knows what the magic could attract—and be ready to hurry to me when I call you."

He looked around for a suitable sentry post and decided a little elevation might help him spot a potential threat before it noticed him. He ran to a twisted tree that resembled a white elm, jumped, clutched for handholds, and tried to haul himself upward. Bark tore and crumbled beneath his fingers, and he almost fell, but not quite. He balanced in the lowest fork and laid one of his few remaining arrows on his bow.

Jhesrhi prowled around below him. He suspected she was looking for a bare, level piece of ground. When she found it, she started chanting under her breath and drawing lines in the dirt with the metal cap on the butt of her staff. Like the rings that encircled the wood at intervals, the ferrule was mostly golden now, with only a couple of flecks and streaks of red.

The soil shifted a little even after her staff moved on. It looked like it was trying to fill in the ruts she'd just inscribed. She recited her words of power a trifle louder and the subtle crawling stopped.

It only took a relatively short time to complete the pentagram, which was noticeably less elaborate than others Gaedynn had watched Jhesrhi draw. He wondered if that was because she didn't know what she was doing. Since she was uncertain what figure was truly appropriate, she'd settled for a basic emblem of power and protection.

She stood in the center of the star and circle, took a deep breath, then started a new incantation. She spoke in a language Gaedynn didn't know, so he had no idea what she was saying. But some of the words created a sort of itch inside his head.

She spoke for a long while before reaching the end. He sensed she was waiting. When nothing happened, she took a breath, shifted her stance, and—speaking a little louder—started over again. She punctuated certain phrases by lifting her staff over her head, then jamming the ferrule back into the dirt.

After several repetitions, each performed in a somewhat different fashion, Gaedynn noticed that the air felt thick and it seemed an effort just to draw a breath. But it wasn't only the air that was different. He had a sense that the whole world, or at least the part of it within view, was heavy and sore like a boil that needed to burst.

She's doing it, he thought, and waited eagerly for her to call him to her side. He was still waiting when a gray-black bat hurtled down from the sky.

Its head and body were the size of a dwarf's, although its leathery wings made it look bigger than a man. As it streaked at Jhesrhi, its long tail stopped whipping and curled into stiffness. The animal was readying a blow like the strike of a whip.

The bat's dark coloration made it hard to see in the shadowy world. Despite his vigilance, Gaedynn hadn't spotted it until it had nearly closed the distance to its target. He only had time for a single shot.

He drew and released. The arrow plunged into the bat's torso. Spasmodic, it veered, tumbled, and slammed to the ground several strides to the right of the pentagram. Where it flopped and flopped, but appeared capable of nothing more.

Gaedynn looked back at the sky and spotted another bat. It was diving at Jhesrhi too, and he dealt with it as he had the first, only better. The shot was a clean kill, and the beast plummeted like a stone.

He looked for a third bat. He didn't find one, but abruptly heard a fierce baying that clawed at his nerves. He took a breath and willed fear away, and then the big black hounds surged over a rise.

Like the shadar-kai the previous night, they flickered ahead through space as they charged, gaining ground faster than should have been possible. It made them difficult to aim at too. Gaedynn invested a precious moment studying the unnatural motion so he could guess where they'd reappear.

He dropped one and then another. It wasn't good enough. There were still too many and they were still advancing too fast. Jhesrhi needed to turn her magic on them.

But she just kept chanting. Either she was in a trance, like the wizards mired in their own ritual back in Luthcheq, or she didn't dare interrupt the spell for fear of what the forces she'd raised would do if she relinquished control.

Damn you, woman, he thought. He sprang down out of the elm and shouted, "Over here, you filthy beasts! I'm the one killing you! Attack me!" He loosed at another hound. The shaft punched deep into its neck.

His ploy worked, if one wanted to think of it that way. The hounds turned and charged him.

He shot two more, and then had to drop his bow and snatch out his scimitar. The remaining four or five—everything was happening too fast for an accurate count—encircled him. They lunged and snapped, snarling, gray foam flying from their jaws.

He turned, slashed, and dodged—and somehow kept himself from being bitten and dragged down for the first couple of heartbeats. He even split the skull of one of the beasts.

It gave him a surge of satisfaction but not of hope. Khouryn could probably have cut his way clear of the nightmare, but he was the best hand-to-hand combatant Gaedynn had ever seen. He himself was merely good, and he suspected that wasn't going to be enough.

He hoped he was buying Jhesrhi enough time to get home.

Then something whistled. And, mad with rage as they'd

appeared, the hounds drew away from him. Panting, he turned in the direction of the sound.

A little way up the slope, a shadar-kai sat on a black horse. By the light of day—or what passed for it there—Gaedynn saw that the rider's raised facial scars formed geometric patterns and must have been cut deliberately. He held a lance and wore a chain coiled on his hip.

Gray-skinned, black-haired, and clad in dark garments like the horseman—but hunched, stunted, and coarse-featured—small figures stood to the sides of his steed. One held the wooden syrinx that had evidently called back the hounds.

Gaedynn realized the shadar-kai was a hunter. And the halfling-sized creatures were servants charged with the management of his coursing beasts.

The rider lowered his lance and spurred his horse. Either he was worried that his intended prey would hurt more of his animals, or he'd decided it would be more fun to kill Gaedynn with his own hands. Either way, he must have been confident of his prowess.

The black horse accelerated to a gallop. Gaedynn forced himself to stand still while the shadar-kai and the point of his lance raced closer. Dodge too soon, and his foe would compensate.

The dark horse and rider vanished and reappeared immediately, just an arm's length short of striking distance.

Gaedynn hurled himself to the side. He avoided the lance, but not quite the horse. The animal's shoulder clipped him with bruising force and knocked him staggering. As he fought to regain his balance, something brushed his head, and he realized the shadar-kai was trying to catch him by the hair. He managed to twist away from that too, and the steed and rider pounded past.

As he regained his footing, Gaedynn felt angry with himself for not guessing that the horse might be able to shift through space like half the other creatures in the vile place. But that particular anger could only hinder him, so he took a breath and tried to exhale it away. I know now, he told himself. That's what's important.

Even so, the same trick nearly served to surprise him again. As the shadar-kai wheeled his mount, a subtle flicker lined it up with Gaedynn an instant sooner than mere conventional movement would have allowed. It started forward, disappeared, and reappeared.

Right where Gaedynn had estimated it would. He stepped diagonally, past the head of the lance and to the side of the horse, and sliced its foreleg just above the knee.

The beast pitched forward onto the ground, and the shadar-kai tumbled out of the saddle. He landed on the wrong side of his thrashing horse, and Gaedynn moved to scramble around it.

From the corner of his eye, he glimpsed something small rushing in on his flank. He wrenched himself around and parried a low thrust from a jagged-edged dagger that would have crippled him as he'd crippled the horse. His assailant was one of the stunted servants—who could apparently blink through space too, or maybe he was just sneaky. Gaedynn slashed his neck and his body dissolved in a puff of cold, black vapor.

The stuff got in Gaedynn's eyes, and for one terrifying instant he was blind. Then he blinked his vision clear.

Just in time to see the fallen rider vanish and reappear, still sprawled on the ground, among his servants. His face contorted; he spoke. Gaedynn couldn't hear his voice, but he saw his lips move.

He did hear it when the little hunchback with the pipes blew a different note. And when the remaining hounds bayed and ran at him again.

He wondered if he had time to kill the horse and put it at his back, but decided the dogs wouldn't have much trouble climbing over the carcass even if he did. Then a red spark flew into the midst of the onrushing beasts and exploded into a ragged burst of flame. The detonation tore the hounds apart.

The shadar-kai and his servants turned toward Jhesrhi. Too late. She snapped a word of command and jabbed the head of her staff at them. The hunter burst into flame. Then fire leaped from his body to the servant with the syrinx, and from him to another stunted creature, in a manner that reminded Gaedynn of water cascading down a series of ledges. In a moment, all the dark figures were burning. And flailing.

When they stopped doing the latter because there was little left of them but smoldering black husks, Gaedynn turned to Jhesrhi. "It wouldn't have hurt my pride," he said, "if you'd done that a little sooner."

She shook her head, perhaps to convey that she hadn't been able to—or simply that as usual, she didn't appreciate his sense of humor. "Are you all right?"

"Somewhat miraculously, yes." He looked around and retrieved his bow. He checked his quiver and found he had two arrows left.

"Do you think this shadar-kai was hunting us specifically? Because of what happened last night?"

"I don't know and don't particularly care. I just want you to get back to work before someone or something else shows up to bother us."

"It's no use."

"What are you talking about? I felt something happening."

"That was all you were going to feel. I just don't know how to break through."

He tried not to let the depth of his disappointment show in his face or his tone. "Ah, well. I'm sure we can last a month here if we have to." And maybe afterward they could take a pleasure cruise on the River Styx.

Cheeks puffing, Jhesrhi exhaled sharply like she was blowing out a candle. For an instant, wind gusted and howled and all the little fires left by her two attacks died. "I have thought of one other thing that might get us home sooner."

"Then tell me, please."

She did, and when she finished, he felt a mix of dismay and admiration.

"Bravo," he said. "That's as crazy a scheme as I've ever heard. Easily crazier than invading Thay with nothing but the strength of the Wizards' Reach behind us."

She scowled. "Then you don't want to try it?"

He grinned. "Actually, I do. But right now we need to clear out of here. Then we should find a place where we can go to ground, at least temporarily. We'll proceed with your idea come nightfall."

Waiting until night wouldn't ensure they went undetected, not in a world populated by creatures that saw well in the dark. But he hoped that like the orcs and goblin-kin with which he was familiar, they couldn't see as far in the dark as a man could in the light.

Once the Shadowfell was black as a coinlender's heart, with just a few faint stars gleaming in the sky and a feeling of sheer poisonous wrongness suffusing the air like a stench, he and Jhesrhi crept back to the hill where Tchazzar lay imprisoned. They kept watch long enough for him to start feeling hopeful that the dragon truly was alone, with nothing but his weakness and the staples to prevent his escape.

Then suddenly, one of the shadar-kai's small servants appeared on the hillside. Then another. Gaedynn peered closer and discerned that the dark little men were emerging from a hole in the ground like a line of ants.

Once he and Jhesrhi spotted the mouth of that tunnel, they soon noticed others, and the traffic that came and went, shadar-kai and other things that looked stranger and more dangerous still. Evidently, most of the time the hill was full of them, although they cleared out when the blight wyrm came to feed.

"Curse it," Jhesrhi whispered. "It won't work."

"Yes it will," Gaedynn replied. "It's just that you only came up with half a workable plan. Fortunately I, clever fellow that I am, have now devised the rest."

"Which is?"

"Do you remember wondering if the shadar-kai huntsman was hunting us specifically?"

She scowled. "Of course."

"Well, if they weren't before, we're going to make them start."

NINE

9–10 Mirtul, the Year of the Ageless One (1479 DR)

Aoth and Jet floated on a northerly wind and studied the fortress. Other griffon riders glided to either side but surely couldn't see the outpost, not at such a distance in the feeble predawn light.

To the untrained eye, the stronghold with its palisade walls might not have looked impressive. But it had a warren of tunnels underneath it, and a garrison large and varied enough to fill up both the above ground and subterranean barracks.

"You don't like this, do you?" asked Jet.

"I don't *dis*like it," Aoth replied, "but it's about the limit of what we ought to tackle by ourselves, especially with Gaedynn, Jhesrhi, and Khouryn absent."

"Then why do it?"

"The Threskelans have a lot of supplies stored there. On top of that, it's supposed to be a mustering point for troops bound for Chessenta. So let them arrive and find the place burned, its provisions stolen, and its garrison slaughtered. It might give them second thoughts, particularly the sellswords."

"Let's get on with it, then."

Aoth peered down at the rolling scrubland and the foot soldiers and horsemen making their way across it. In theory, a ridge higher than the surrounding terrain shielded them from the view of the sentries in the fortress. "We'll give our comrades on the ground a little more time to maneuver into position."

As he waited, his thoughts drifted back to the events of the day before the previous one. He'd eliminated Cera as a possible traitor—to say the least—but otherwise he was no closer to flushing out the dragonborn assassins or figuring out why they wanted to kill him.

In fact, the jaunt into the past had left him with new questions. Why had all those dragons been palavering? Were they all Alasklerbanbastos's allies? Was every single one of them going to attack Chessenta at the dracolich's behest? If so, then how could the war hero's forces possibly withstand them?

He scowled and tried to set such puzzles aside. He needed to focus on winning *this* battle. Everything else could wait.

He looked at the pale gleam on the eastern horizon and decided he'd delayed long enough. He willed power into the head of his spear to make it glow yellow, then swept it forward to point at the fortress. All around him, wings snapped and flapped as riders urged their griffons toward the objective.

Men laid arrows on their bows. Aoth pondered whether to start with fire or lightning and decided on the latter. Griffons furled their wings and swooped lower.

Then a horn blatted in the watchtower at one of the corners of the palisade. Aoth had hoped sentries who'd watched through the night would be tired and inattentive at the end of it, but evidently one was still alert.

Annoyed, Aoth rewarded the fellow's vigilance by hurling a bright, booming lightningbolt at the tower. It blew apart the clapboard roof and, he hoped, fried whoever was underneath.

Meanwhile, arrows whistled down at the wall walks, stabbing into other sentries as they tried to ready their own bows. Orcs and kobolds toppled from their perches to smash down in the courtyards below.

But what came next wouldn't be as easy. Warriors scrambled from the buildings below. They scurried for their various stations and started shooting back at the attackers in the sky. A crossbow bolt whizzed past Jet's beak, and he screeched in irritation.

Then an expanding glimmer of force leaped upward. Jet lashed his wings, flung himself to the side, and avoided all but the edge of the flare. Still, cold bit into Aoth's body. Hit squarely and encrusted with frost, another mount and rider plunged toward the ground.

Aoth roused a tattoo to warm him and looked for the source of the magic. At first, even his fire-touched eyes couldn't spot it. There was just too much happening. Then the tip of a white wand poked out an arrow loop at the top of one of the towers.

Jet dodged, and the next shimmering blaze missed him entirely. Aoth rattled off words of power and pointed his spear. A dark cloud materialized around the top of the bastion. The boards sizzled and crumbled as the acidic vapor ate into them. Inside the structure, people screamed.

As Aoth turned Jet toward the gate, he noticed the watchtower he'd blasted apart was barely burning. The flaming arrows some of the griffon riders were loosing weren't doing much to set the fort on fire either. Some treatment evidently kept the timbers from burning easily.

Oh well, he'd half expected as much. Once they won the battle, the Brotherhood could still turn the place into a useless ruin. It would just take a little more sweat.

He threw a lightningbolt at the gate—which jumped in its frame, but weathered the assault without a mark. It definitely possessed protective enchantments.

But fortunately, the men and orcs poised to defend it didn't. He bloodied them with a barrage of fist-sized hailstones, and while they were still reeling, he and three other griffon riders plunged down into their midst.

Beaks snapped and talons snatched, tearing the Bone Wyrm's warriors to gory tatters. Aoth looked for an enemy to stick with his spear, but Jet didn't give him the chance. The familiar was still angry from the blast of cold that had chilled him to the marrow, and this was a good opportunity to take it out on someone.

When all the defenders were dead, Aoth and his human companions dismounted, shoved back the bars securing the gate, and swung it open. The sellswords massed outside came streaming in.

After that, the combat became a chaos of packed bodies and slashing, jabbing blades, with aerial cavalry shooting from on high and occasionally diving to pick off some particularly appealing target. Aoth circled with the other griffon riders. It made it easier to oversee the progress of the battle as a whole and to use his spells to best effect.

Gradually the sellswords cleared the courtyards and bastions until only stubborn pockets of resistance remained. Khouryn's spearmen regrouped, lighting lanterns and unpacking everburning torches with their heatless, greenish flames as they prepared to venture into the tunnels. It might well turn out to be the most dangerous part of the attack, but they knew what they were doing. A dwarf had trained them to fight underground.

Still, Aoth wondered if he should lead them personally. Then something burst out of one of the buildings with access to the burrows below. It could have fit through the doorway, but only just, and only if it had been moving carefully. In its haste, it smashed loose scraps of wood and sent them flying.

The beast was an enormous blue lizard with big frilled ears and a spike on its snout. It moved in a glittering haze that also shrouded the creature on its back. The rider was a kobold with a single enormous azure scale seemingly grafted in the center of his chest. The scale flickered repeatedly, like lightning was flashing inside it, and pus seeped around the edges.

The blue lizard crashed into the front ranks of the spearmen. Dipping and tossing its head, it caught sellswords on its horn and flung them into the air. At the same time, small lightning bolts leaped from its massive body to sear one soldier, then another. The men so afflicted danced spastically in place, and the kobold howled with laughter.

Aoth wondered why this terror was only entering the battle now. He was lucky it hadn't shown up earlier, before the balance tilted in the attackers' favor.

He rattled off words of power and hurled darts of light. They vanished when they touched the seething aura. Other griffon riders loosed arrows. The shafts broke on contact with the haze.

Still laughing, the kobold raised a length of blue metal. Lightning crackled from the tip and burned into a griffon. The beast dropped, then spread its wings and arrested its fall. Plainly injured and struggling, it flew beyond the walls, no doubt looking for a safe place to set down. Aoth couldn't tell if the man now slumped on its feathery neck was still alive or not.

Meanwhile, the stormlizard went on bulling, rending, and trampling its way through the lines of spearmen. Aoth decided its master might not have waited too long to unleash it after all. If somebody didn't find a way to stop it, it could still win the fight for Threskel.

He cast a rainbow from his spear. Each colored beam had the potential to smite the reptile in a different way. None of them pierced its halo.

"There's no way to hurt it except close up," said Jet. "Of course, then the halo burns us. But I'm game."

"Wait." Aoth rattled off charms of protection against lightning in particular and hostile magic in general. He activated tattoos with similar functions. "There. That might help. Now yank the kobold off the beast's back."

Jet poised his talons and swooped.

The kobold twisted and pointed his wand. Jet dived even lower and streaked along mere inches from the ground. Aoth ducked, and lightning crackled over his head.

Jet lashed his wings and bobbed back up to the kobold shaman's level. Aoth aimed his spear, just in case the griffon's claws somehow missed the target.

Then, faster and more nimbly than Aoth had imagined it could move, the stormlizard spun around and reared up onto its hind legs like a horse. One of its forefeet struck at Jet.

Through their psychic link, Aoth felt his mount's determination to swerve and avoid the blow, and then the shock when it hit him anyway. They lurched off balance and nearly tumbled over, and the griffon fought to stay right side up and regain control of his trajectory.

He managed the former but not quite the latter. He jolted to earth amid a scatter of dead orcs, and momentum pitched him off his feet.

Fortunately, Aoth could feel that neither the stormlizard's claws nor slamming into the ground had hurt Jet badly. Mostly they'd made him angry. He drew breath to let out a screech and plunge back into the fight.

"Wait!" Aoth snapped. "Pretend you're hurt. Stay here. When they've forgotten all about you, then come at them again." He swung himself out of the saddle.

As he started to run, he saw that the stormlizard had resumed tearing into the spearmen. No doubt realizing that even if they avoided the jabbing horn, the flares of lightning would sear them where they stood, the sellswords were falling back, their ranks disintegrating.

"That's right!" Aoth yelled. "Get clear! Leave it to me!"

Charging his spear with destructive power, he poised himself in front of the stormlizard. He was close enough to attack it—close enough too that the kobold would have difficulty casting spells at him past the enormous blue reptile's head.

Which was good as far as it went, but it also put him within easy reach of the stormlizard's horn. It surged forward and tossed its head, and the spike nearly caught him even though the creature had done exactly what he expected.

Still, he did sidestep the blow and riposted with a thrust. His spear leaped through the sparkling haze without difficulty and stabbed the stormlizard in the face. It roared, and he grinned. He'd finally hurt the thing.

The trick was hurting it enough. Over the course of the next several heartbeats Aoth inflicted several wounds on its snout and jaws, but the superficial punctures only made it more eager to rend him. And he couldn't get past the tossing, jabbing horn to attack a different part of its body.

Meanwhile, lightning leaped repeatedly from the stormlizard's body to his. At first he couldn't feel it. Then it stung like insect bites. His protective magic was wearing away.

Trying to line up a shot, the kobold leaned from side to side. He slashed the wand through a zigzag pass and started a lengthy incantation. Aoth inferred that while lightning was the shaman's favorite weapon, he knew other magic as well and had decided now was the time to use it.

Then Jet hit the kobold like a bolt from a ballista. His talons pierced the scaly little body all the way through, and his momentum whisked the corpse off the stormlizard's back, all in the blink of an eye.

Enraged by Aoth's stabbing spear, and his refusal to stand still and let himself be gored, the stormlizard didn't even seem to notice its rider was gone. It just kept striking at the man on the ground.

Jet streaked in, plunged his claws into almost the exact spot where the kobold had sat, clung, and ripped away scaly blue hide and the muscle beneath with his beak. The stormlizard bellowed and rolled, trying to crush the griffon beneath it.

But Jet beat his wings and sprang clear. And when the stormlizard flopped over, it exposed its underside. Aoth willed fresh power into the head of his spear, charged, plunged it into the spot where he judged the beast's heart ought to be, and instantly yanked it out for a second thrust.

Hot blood sprayed and spattered him from head to toe. He swiped the blinding gore from his eyes.

Just in time to see the stormlizard heave itself around, and its horn rip upward. He tried to jump away. The point caught him anyway and flipped him through the air to smash down on his back.

His chest ached, but when he looked down he saw the horn had only grazed him. It hadn't breached his mail to cleave the flesh beneath.

And that had been the stormlizard's final effort. Now it simply lay shuddering, more blood pumping out in diminishing spurts and its shimmering corona fading. One final arc of lightning crackled from the tip of a claw to the ground.

At that same instant, an idea popped into Aoth's head.

He had no idea why. He'd resolved to concentrate solely on the assault, and he had. But apparently without him even being aware of it, some buried part of his mind had kept on worrying at his other problems, and now it was making a suggestion.

It was a suggestion he couldn't take if his men still needed him. But when he glanced surreptitiously around, that didn't appear to be the case. There were no more stormlizards coming out of the tunnels, and in general the Brotherhood seemed to have things under control. In battle, few things were ever absolutely certain, but he was willing to gamble they could carry on without him.

Smelling of singed feathers, wings rustling, Jet landed beside him. "Why aren't you getting up?" the familiar asked.

Because, Aoth replied, speaking mind to mind, *I'm horribly wounded. Don't you see all the blood?*

It's the lizard's blood. Its horn just bumped you.

You're right. But no one else was standing close enough to tell.

Using his spear as a prop and doing his best to move like a man in hideous pain, Aoth rose and clambered onto the griffon's back.

* * * * *

The staff seemed to quiver in Jhesrhi's hand like a dog straining at a leash. She willed it into quiescence.

Patience, she thought. If this idiot scheme works, you'll get the chance to make plenty of fire. But in the meantime, she needed to avoid sparking big, telltale flashes of light in the midst of all the gloom.

She peered from the brush Gaedynn had chosen to serve as their blind at the trail meandering down the hillside several yards away. Tchazzar's captors traversed it often to take gray crawfish as long as her forearm and black eyeless pike from the murky river at the end.

Though she and Gaedynn were waiting for the dark men, their silence and the dusk that shrouded the wooded hills even by day kept her from spotting them until they were unnervingly close. One was a shadar-kai with a bow in his hand, a chain around his waist, and triangular scars on his forehead and cheeks. The other six were hunched servants carrying cast nets and baskets.

Jhesrhi whispered to the earth, and the patch of trail beneath the creatures' feet turned to muck. They all plunged in up to their knees or deeper.

Gaedynn sprang to his feet and loosed his last two arrows. The first pierced the shadar-kai's torso. The second stabbed all the way through a servant's throat.

She willed the soil to well up higher around the foes who were still alive, like waves in a stormy sea. Dirt flowed over one and covered him entirely.

But the other three vanished, leaving holes in the ground. Prompted by instinct, Jhesrhi spun around. Two of the servants were right behind her. Covered in mud, ugly faces contorted, they sprang at her with their knives raised over their heads.

She spoke to the wind, and it howled and shoved them back. That gave her time to rattle off a charm of slumber, each syllable softer than the one before.

The little gray men collapsed. She killed one by ramming the butt of her staff into his forehead. His scimitar already bloody—from dispatching the servant who'd shifted elsewhere, presumably—Gaedynn trotted up beside her and slashed the throat of the other. The bodies exploded into dark vapor, and their killers stepped back to avoid it.

"Well," Gaedynn said, "that was easy enough."

"It will get harder once their friends find the corpses and realize we're still in their territory. And hunting them as they hunted us."

"Oh, I'm sure we'll cope." He strode to the mired corpse of the shadar-kai and removed the dead man's quiver. He pulled out one of the many black arrows, sighted down the length of it, and smiled.

* * * * *

Cera sat cross-legged on a flat portion of the temple roof. The elevation brought her closer to the sun.

Amaunator's radiance was shining just as brightly at ground level, so her ascent was purely a symbolic gesture. But every acolyte learned early on that where meditation was concerned, symbolism helped the practitioner achieve the proper frame of mind.

She studied the golden light reflecting from the rooftops around her. Then, when she felt centered, she lifted her eyes and gazed directly at the sun. No layman could have done so without pain and, if he persisted nonetheless, permanent damage to his sight. But the blaze simultaneously calmed and exalted her. It made her feel the majesty of her god.

Until a screech split the air, and a big black shape with outstretched wings cut between her and the object of her adoration. She felt a pang of dread, but the emotion disappeared when she recognized Jet for what—or, according to Aoth, who—he was.

"Sunlady!" cried the griffon.

"Yes?" she replied, thinking that even though she knew the beast could speak, it was a marvel to hear it nonetheless.

"Meet me in your garden! Now!"

She started to ask why. But then Jet swooped level with her rooftop, and she gasped at the sight of a crimson figure slumped on his back.

She clambered down her ladder and scurried through the interior of the temple with no regard for the dignity of a high priestess. As she burst out into the garden, Jet said, "A drake, or some creature like a drake, hurt him bad! I think he may be dying!"

Cera tried to put dismay aside and think with the calmness befitting a cleric and healer. "I'll call my people to carry him to a bed."

"No," Jet said. "This town is full of people who want to be rid of him. You're the only one I trust. You open doors for me and I'll carry him."

She trusted her own subordinates, but it wasn't worth arguing about, certainly not when Aoth was in urgent need of care. "Whatever you say."

People either recoiled or goggled to see the enormous black mount with his scarlet eyes stalking through the temple at her back. Prayers and litanies stumbled to a halt.

She had Jet bear his rider to her own chambers and her own bed. Then she checked the saddle for straps securing Aoth in place. There weren't any. Either he wasn't worried about losing his seat and falling, or magic prevented it. She took hold of him to ease him onto the bed. He was heavy, particularly in his mail, but she'd had a lot of practice lifting patients.

"Boo!" he whispered.

She jumped back.

"Some healer," he said, grinning and swinging himself off Jet's back. "You couldn't tell the blood isn't mine?"

She took a breath, and her heart stopped thumping quite as hard. "Not before I examined you."

"Good. If the ranking sunlady of the temple couldn't tell close up, then I doubt anyone else did from farther away."

"What is the matter with you? If this is a joke—"

He raised a hand. "It's not. Well, the boo part was, but the rest no. This is me taking advantage of a chance to catch our elusive dragonborn."

"How?"

"In Luthcheq, when we couldn't find the Green Hand killers, we set a trap to flush them out. We're doing it again, and this time the bait is me. We'll spread the word that I got badly hurt on the other side of the border. And that you think you can save me, but even with your strongest prayers mending me, I'll be a helpless invalid for a couple of days. That should prompt the dragonborn to come after me while I can't fight back."

She frowned. "I suppose that could work."

"I'm glad you think so, because obviously I need your help to make it work. For one thing, we have to provide a lure that really is enticing. My being wounded won't look like such a perfect opportunity if Jet and a bunch of sellswords are standing guard over me. There has to be a credible reason why they're not."

Cera nodded. "I can handle that."

* * * * *

"I want to fight," Medrash said.

Patrin smiled. "But?"

"But it's a bigger party than the one that defeated us Daardendriens." The admission still tasted bitter in his mouth. "They've already seen us just as we've seen them, so we can't surprise them. I think it would be wiser to avoid them if we can."

Her upper body swaying ever so slightly, Nala said, "The blood of dragons flows in our veins. We can kill these giants like we killed the others."

"I agree," Patrin said. He looked back at Medrash. "But we won't think less of you if you stay behind and guard the carts and horses."

"We'd think less of ourselves," Medrash said. "We said we'd stand with the Platinum Cadre. So if you fight, we will too."

Patrin grinned and gripped Medrash's shoulder. "I knew I could count on you. How could it be otherwise, when your god and mine are staunch friends and fellow lords of Celestia?"

The suggestion that Torm willingly associated with any sort of dragon deity struck Medrash as blasphemous, but he did his best to hide his distaste. "I look forward to fighting alongside you as well."

"Then let's go kill some giants."

As the warriors of the company fell into a loose formation, Balasar said, "It's a funny thing. *I* wouldn't think a bit less of myself if I stayed behind."

"Yet here you are," Medrash answered. Patrin flourished his sword, and everyone started forward.

"Here we all are," Khouryn said, his urgrosh in one hand and a crossbow in the other. "Me, because I want to see how this ragtag band accomplishes what a better company couldn't."

"Let's hope the answer isn't pure luck," Balasar said. "Or if it is, let's hope this isn't the day the luck runs dry."

When they reached the top of a rise, they saw the giants awaiting them. Several ash spires towered in the enemy's vicinity, three with horizontal branches interconnecting them, two others sliding sluggishly. Medrash couldn't actually tell if the enemy had a shaman capable of pushing the landforms around, but he assumed so.

The dragonborn jogged forward. Khouryn broke stride for a moment to discharge his crossbow. Other warriors loosed their bows.

Medrash just had time to see some of the shafts hit their marks. Then one of the giants—clearly the adept he'd been trying to spot— swung a long stone rod in a circle over his head and growled a word of power. The interconnected spires exploded into ash. The wind howled and blew the grit into the oncoming dragonborn's faces.

Medrash's eyes burned, and he coughed. The ground shuddered under his feet, surely a sign that the giants were charging and perhaps that other ash spires were sliding toward the Tymantherans as well.

He raised his sword over his head and chanted a prayer. Off to his left in the streaming murk, visible only by virtue of the white light shining from his blade, Patrin did the same. Nala chanted a spell.

The wind died, and the blinding, choking ash simply vanished from the air. Someone had countered the shaman's power. Or perhaps they'd all three done it working together.

But unfortunately, the ash storm had lasted long enough to neutralize the advantage afforded by their bows. The giants were closing fast. So were two ash spires, looping in on either flank.

"Swords!" bellowed Patrin. "Charge!" Medrash saw it was the right move. At least once the Tymantherans closed with their foes, the spires couldn't threaten them anymore. Not without running into the giants as well.

The attackers raced forward. An enormous javelin flew at Medrash. He threw himself flat, it hurtled over his head, and he leaped up again.

His allies were as eager to close as he was, and the momentary break in his advance allowed the foremost to reach the giants ahead of him. As a result, he had a good view when they spat their breath weapons.

Then he nearly faltered in amazement. A dragonborn's breath attack could be formidable but, in his experience, rarely as devastating as this. The blasts of fire, frost, or what have you hurled the gray giants reeling backward.

About half the dragonborn pressed their foes and spewed a second attack. That was astonishing too. The ability almost never renewed itself so quickly. In that moment, Medrash almost believed the Platinum Cadre had found a way to invoke a "dragon within."

But only almost, because the notion of such a kinship was obscene. And, combined with the shame attendant on all his previous blunders and defeats, the illusion of it fueled his determination to show every deluded follower of a false creed like Patrin, and every scoffer like Balasar, what the servant of a true god could do.

"Torm!" he bellowed. "Torm!"

A giant ran at him with a sword made of stone held in a middle guard. The edges of the weapon glowed and threw off heat like a bed of red-hot coals.

The ash giant cut. Medrash caught the blow on his shield, and sparks flew. It was a hard impact, but not hard enough to rob him of his balance.

He shifted forward and slashed the giant's knee. As the huge barbarian pitched off balance, he shifted behind him and cut the same leg again. The giant toppled, and he drove his sword point into the knobbed ridge of his spine.

He glimpsed motion from the corner of his eye and pivoted toward another giant rushing to avenge his comrade. The creature hadn't quite closed to striking distance, so Medrash used the time to chant a prayer.

White light flared from his sword. The giant cried out and stumbled as a spasm wracked his body. Hoping to strike him before he recovered his balance, Medrash rushed in.

The giant managed to jab the tip of his greatclub at Medrash's head. Medrash slipped the attack and slashed. His sword bit into his opponent's flank.

And hurt him badly too, if Medrash was any judge, but he didn't seem to feel the effects as yet. He twisted, pulling free of the sword in the process, and swung his club straight down at Medrash's skull.

At another moment, Medrash would have dodged out from underneath. Now, however, instinct prompted him to hold his shield over his head and depend on his god.

Composed of hazy luminescence, the form of an upturned hand in a metal gauntlet flickered into being around the shield. The greatclub hit the combined defense and shattered into three pieces. Medrash scarcely felt the jolt.

The phantom gauntlet vanished, but its power didn't. That burned down Medrash's arm and through his body, and he cried out in exhilaration. He felt strong as one of the Brotherhood's griffons and light as air.

He sprang high enough to make it easy to strike at the startled giant's neck. His sword sheared through slate-colored flesh. The huge creature toppled backward, blood leaping like a geyser from the gash.

"Torm!" Medrash shouted. He turned, seeking another foe, and spotted the adept. He still had his wand, but now he was holding up an egg-shaped crystal in his off hand. Unlike the gray talisman the other shaman had used, this one was red.

Medrash charged the adept. But before he could close the distance, a drift of ash churned, then exploded. A creature lunged out of the flying grit.

Massive enough that it almost seemed to waddle on its four thick legs, the gigantic lizard had scales of a mottled, dirty red. Its piggy eyes gleamed white, and a pair of horns swept back from the base of its skull. Rows of fangs lined its beaklike jaws, and fire flickered at the back of its mouth. Its body threw off heat like an oven.

It immediately oriented on Medrash, either because the adept wanted it to or simply because he was the nearest foe. It opened its jaws wide and, with a thunderous belching noise, spewed a plume of fire.

Medrash threw himself down, and the flame washed over him. The red lizard charged, and he rolled aside to avoid the champing, fiery jaws and stamping feet.

The firebelcher turned, trying to compensate, and bumped him as he started to rise. The beast was heavy enough that even that slight contact flung him reeling off balance.

Meanwhile, the huge lizard completed its turn and put him in front of its jaws again. It spewed more flame, and a shock ripped through him. For an instant, he couldn't see, couldn't move, couldn't breathe.

"Torm," he croaked, and a cool surge of vitality restored him. It didn't heal all his burns and blisters, or quite take away the pain, but it turned it from something that hindered him into a source of righteous fury.

And fortunately, it did so quickly enough for him to dodge when the firebelcher tried to catch him in its fangs. He spun aside, and the triangular teeth clashed shut on empty air. He cut. His blade split scaly hide and grated on the bone beneath. The lizard thing kept coming.

And coming. As the fight progressed, he channeled Torm's power repeatedly, using it to augment his natural might and to smite the brute with attacks that cut both flesh and spirit, until he simply couldn't draw down any more. Still, the creature wouldn't stop—and soon, heart pounding, breath rasping in his throat, he felt his physical might flagging as certainly as his mystical talents had.

Then Balasar and Khouryn rushed in on the firebelcher's flank. Medrash's clan brother spat frost at the creature. The dwarf chopped it with his urgrosh. The lizard spun in the direction of the attack, taking the pressure off Medrash for what felt like the first time in days. He wanted to retreat and catch his breath. He snarled Torm's name and swung his sword instead.

"Do you . . . want us . . . to back off?" Balasar panted. "You seemed so . . . keen . . . to kill giants all by . . . yourself!"

"You can . . . have a piece of this thing," Medrash answered.

"That's . . . very generous."

As the three of them fought on, circling in an effort to stay away from the firebelcher's jaws, Medrash caught glimpses of the rest of the battle. Giants and dragonborn slashed, battered, and stabbed at one another. Piles and pits of ash churned as the adept tried to summon more reinforcements. But no more creatures burst or clambered into view—probably because Nala stood chanting with her shadow-wood staff sketching **S** curves in the air. Patrin stood protectively before her, his sword uplifted to kill whatever threatened her. Light shone through the red blood on the blade like sunbeams through stained glass.

Evidently Nala's countermagic was holding the shaman's power in check. That was useful, but Medrash couldn't help wishing she'd started a little sooner. Because even with three warriors hacking at it, the firebelcher still wouldn't drop.

Suddenly it heaved itself around in an arc, spewing fire as it spun. The jet washed over all three of them, but Balasar caught the worst of it, reeled, and fell. The firebelcher lunged at him. Medrash and Khouryn scrambled to intercept the beast and, striking furiously, held it back.

Risking a glance over his shoulder, Medrash saw Balasar coughing and stirring feebly. He was trying to get up but couldn't manage it.

"We have to end this," growled Khouryn, voice tight with the pain of his burns. "Can you keep its attention on you for a few moments?"

"Yes." Medrash hurled himself at the lizard.

He struck and dodged repeatedly, evading the snapping, fiery fangs by inches, unable to retreat more than a step or two lest he leave Balasar exposed. Then suddenly, Khouryn appeared on the beast's humped back. Medrash realized he must have run up its tail.

As he was still running, while avoiding the spikes jutting at intervals from the firebelcher's spine, the lizard lunged at Medrash. Khouryn staggered and appeared on the brink of losing his balance, but then somehow recovered. He scrambled onward, grabbed one of the creature's horns, and used it to anchor himself in place while he jabbed and scraped at its eyes with the spearhead on the haft of his urgrosh.

For a moment, the firebelcher didn't seem to notice him. Then the spearhead skated across one of its eyes, and it shrieked and spewed flame straight at Medrash, most likely without even intending it. He caught the jet on his shield.

The firebelcher lashed its head back and forth, trying to shake Khouryn off. Most dragonborn would have lost their grips and gone flying, or else had their arms jerked out of their sockets. But the dwarf, though bounced from side to side, kept himself steady enough to go on fishing for an eye.

With everything shaking, he wasn't able to gouge one out. But while he kept the firebelcher preoccupied, Medrash rushed in and thrust his sword point deep into the hollow where its neck jointed its body.

The red lizard froze, then shuddered. Seeming to topple with a dreamlike slowness, it flopped over onto its side. Khouryn jumped clear and landed with a clink of mail.

"Help Balasar," gasped the dwarf. "I'll keep watch."

Medrash dropped to his knees beside his clan brother. Please, Torm, he thought, grant me just a little more of your grace. He rested his hand on Balasar's shoulder, then felt power flow through the point of contact. New scales covered raw, seeping burns.

"That looks better," Khouryn said, his voice sounding from behind Medrash's back. If he could stand there and talk, it must mean the firebelcher really was dead, and that no other threats were advancing on them.

Balasar grinned up at the dwarf. "That was a good trick." He wheezed. "Were you a ropewalker in a carnival, to keep your balance like that?"

"I'm a dwarf," Khouryn answered. "We have low centers of gravity."

* * * * *

Even with an invasion looming, Hasos couldn't completely neglect the mundane business of the barony. On market day, that meant he had to sit in judgment on his dais in Whistler's Square.

It wasn't a permanent platform. Workers set it up in the morning and dismantled it again in the evening, and in recent years it had started to creak and quiver at odd moments.

Hasos tried to stop wondering if and when it might actually collapse, and at what cost to him in dignity and bruises. Tried to focus instead on the two peasants squabbling over where one's farm ended and the other's began.

It was an effort, because he despised boundary disputes. In the wake of the Spellplague and the changes it wrought, his great-grandfather had ordered the fief surveyed. That should have settled every conceivable conflict in advance. Yet somehow the glib and the greedy still found arguments to challenge the placement of markers, hedgerows, and fences.

"The stones have always marked the line," said the farmer nervously twisting a soft, broad-brimmed hat in his hands.

"You dug them up and moved them!" said the plaintiff, an old fellow seemingly bedizened with every religious trinket he could lay his hands on, either to persuade the gods to favor him or to convince Hasos he was devout and thus, surely, honest. "Do you think people can't see the fresh-turned dirt?"

"*Has* anyone else seen it?" Hasos asked. Or would he have to send someone to look?

The pious peasant hesitated. "Well . . . not exactly. The wife has bunions. She can't—"

Hasos spotted a stirring at the back of the crowd of waiting disputants and spectators, and a flash of bright yellow clothing. He raised his hand to silence the plaintiff and craned for a better look at what was happening. Followed by a pair of her subordinates, Cera came bustling toward his platform.

His feelings for Cera were complicated. They'd been lovers for a season, and he'd liked her well enough to start considering whether a priestess of her rank could possibly make a suitable wife for a baron. Then she'd told him that as far as she was concerned, their affair had run its course.

It had probably saved him from making a foolish decision, but it still stung, and kept stinging at odd moments over the three years since. It was worse when he knew she was keeping company with another man, and had been particularly bad since she'd taken up with the very scoundrel—a soulless mage, no less!—who'd come to Soolabax to subvert his authority.

Yet there was a part of him that always craved her company, even when he felt most jealous and resentful—even when he expected it to hurt. And besides, whatever she wanted, it was bound to be more interesting than the trivia on the docket.

He rose and gave her the shallow bow appropriate to their stations. "Sunlady. This is an unexpected pleasure."

"Milord." Cera was a little out of breath, and her golden vestments hung slightly askew. "I realize others have been waiting for their turns, and I apologize for shoving in ahead of them. But the dignity of Amaunator demands immediate action!"

"What do you mean?" Hasos asked.

"You're aware Captain Fezim is badly wounded."

"Of course. It's a pity. Although I did warn him that his forays into Threskel were reckless in the extreme."

"I assume you know too that I'm tending him myself in the temple."

Just kick me in the stones, why don't you? Hasos thought. "Yes, I heard."

"Well, I don't mind doing it. Since the war hero herself sent the sellswords to us, it seems only right that a senior priest or priestess should take the responsibility. But I won't have the Keeper's worship and rituals disrupted!"

She seemed so put out that Hasos wondered if he could have been mistaken about her interest in the Thayan. Or maybe that too had already *run its course*. Small wonder if it had. With his tattoos and glowing eyes, the man was positively freakish.

"Actually," he said, "the way I see it, it was Nicos Corynian who sent the sellswords. But I take your point. Well, part of it. How does the presence of one invalid interfere with temple business?"

"If it was only Captain Fezim," Cera answered, "it wouldn't. But his soldiers insist on standing guard over him, and they're a pack of thieving, blasphemous ruffians. Worse, his griffon is there! A huge, black, man-eating beast roaming among the altars! People are afraid to come and pray! My clerics can't perform their sacred offices!"

For a moment Hasos enjoyed her distress and thought that if he refused to help her, it would only be what she deserved. But whatever his personal feelings, public order was his responsibility. And anyway, even though he realized the notion was probably stupid, he couldn't help wondering if this was a chance to win back her affections.

"I assume you want me to clear out the riffraff," he said.

"If you can," she said.

"Certainly I can. While the mage was well, he and I shared command. But now that he's incapacitated, every soldier in Soolabax, whether loyal Chessentan or sellsword, answers to me." And didn't that assertion taste sweet in his mouth!

So sweet, in fact, that he left his humbler petitioners to wait while he helped Cera shoo the surly outlanders and the black griffon—which truly was an enormous, terrifying brute—out of her domain. She gave him a hug and a light little kiss when they finished.

* * * * *

His burns aching, but not as badly as before Medrash healed him, Balasar looked up at his clan brother and Khouryn. Both were blistered, and Khouryn's black beard was singed and smoking. Their chests heaved as they sucked in air.

"Help me up," Balasar said.

Khouryn held out a hand. "Sure you're ready?"

Balasar gripped the dwarf's hand and dragged himself upright. He felt a trifle unsteady on his feet, but it was nothing he couldn't manage. "That patch of ground would make anyone ready. It's hard, and it smells like rotten eggs."

"Balasar's not one to stay down while the outcome of a battle's still in doubt," Medrash said. Which was true, but it sounded idiotic when spoken aloud.

"That does Daardendrien credit," Khouryn said. "But I'm not sure it is. In doubt, I mean."

Balasar took a look around and decided the dwarf was right. Most of the giants had already fallen, and the Platinum Cadre was pressing the others hard. It really didn't appear that there was much left for his companions and him to do.

Medrash's face betrayed little, but Balasar thought he knew what was going on behind it. His clan brother was undoubtedly glad the dragonborn were winning, and if he had any sense, he must realize he'd acquitted himself in a manner that brought honor to his peculiar creed. Still, on some level, it bewildered and even rankled him that their demented new allies had performed so much better than a war band of Daardendriens.

"Look." Khouryn pointed with the axe head of his urgrosh.

Nala and the ash giant adept now stood a stone's throw apart, staring fixedly at each other. Light rippled up and down the rods they swung and shifted like swordsmen cutting and parrying. The space between them seethed and shimmered with the forces contending there.

Meanwhile, Patrin fought to keep a giant warrior away from

the dragonborn wizard. A huge greatclub crashed repeatedly on his shield.

Balasar decided Patrin's adversary had the right idea. Kill the enemy spellcaster while he and his opposite number were busy tossing magic back and forth. He ran toward the adept, and Medrash and Khouryn followed.

But they were only halfway to their objective when Nala cried out in a voice as loud as thunder, and rainbows swirled around her body. The shaman froze in position, and a kind of discoloration ran through his flesh, staining it a different shade of gray. Then his outstretched arms crumbled under their own weight, because Nala had turned him into a figure of solidified ash like the spires. The red crystal egg fell to the ground.

An instant later, Patrin roared, "Bahamut!" His sword streaked in a high horizontal slice that opened his opponent's belly. Guts bulged out, and the giant dropped his weapon and clutched at the wound to hold himself together. While he was working on that, Patrin thrust his point up under the rib cage into his heart.

Khouryn had been right the first time. There truly wasn't much more to do. Balasar felt an odd mix of anticlimax and relief.

As the giant warrior fell, Nala trotted toward the gradually eroding remains of the adept. Patrin followed, but he was a pace behind her.

She bent at the waist and straightened up with the scarlet egg in her hand. She glared into its translucent depths, and Patrin said, "Stop!"

But she didn't look away. And the talisman suddenly blazed with multicolored light bright enough to make Balasar squint and avert his eyes. When the glow faded, the egg was gone.

"Curse it!" Patrin exclaimed. Balasar realized it was the first time he'd heard the fellow sound upset. Up until then, he'd projected the same annoying calmness that Medrash so often displayed. "I told you, if we kept one of those intact, the vanquisher's wizards could study it and maybe learn something useful."

"And I told you," said Nala, "the stones are evil." She still sounded calm. In fact, Balasar thought he heard a trace of amusement lurking in her tone. "Bahamut wants them destroyed."

"I'm his champion, and I don't sense that."

"I'm his champion too, in my own fashion, and he talks to me about different things." She gazed into his eyes. "I hope you aren't going to start doubting me now. Not after we've come so far."

Patrin sighed, his glare softened, and Balasar's suspicion that the two of them were lovers as well as fellow fanatics strengthened into certainty. "Of course I trust you."

"Then let's talk of other things. If you can draw down more power, the wounded could use your healing touch. And we need to get everyone organized again."

"All right." Patrin turned toward Balasar, Medrash, and Khouryn. "Can you help?"

"I don't know that I can work any more magic," Medrash said. "Not for a while. But I can knot a bandage."

"That's something at least." Patrin led them toward two dragonborn, one lying on his back, the other applying pressure to his comrade's bloody chest wound.

When they'd left Nala several paces behind, the dwarf murmured, "For what it's worth, I agree with you. We should have kept the talisman for study."

Patrin shook his head. "No. No. Nala's wise. You see what we can accomplish with her powers backing up our swords and bows." He peered down at the wounded warrior. "I can handle this. You help someone else."

Medrash led the rest of them onward, toward another injured cultist. Meanwhile, other dragonborn sank to their knees.

In itself, that wasn't strange. Combat was exhausting. Soldiers often flopped down where they stood when it was over.

But the members of the Platinum Cadre also rocked their upper bodies from side to side. It was the same repetitive motion that kept Nala's frame perpetually writhing, only more pronounced.

"Do you see this?" Balasar asked.

"Yes," Medrash said, "but I also see something more pressing." Evidently perceiving just how badly his prospective patient was hurt, he broke into a trot and left his companions behind.

"Fair enough," said Balasar, "but I want a closer look." He headed for the nearest swaying cultist, a ruddy-scaled female with the silver falcons of Clan Clethtinthtiallor pierced into her right ear and the back of her right hand. Khouryn tramped along at his side.

Suddenly the Clethtinthtiallor turned and scuttled to the nearest giant corpse. Her sway becoming more pronounced, and she clawed the foe's gray, ash-smeared flesh with alternate swipes of her right and left hands.

Balasar and Khouryn faltered in surprise and distaste.

The cultist tore out a handful of flesh, then peered down at it as though entranced. She opened her mouth.

Balasar lunged, grabbed her by the shoulders, and gave her a shake. "No!"

She tried to twist free of his grip and bring the raw flesh to her face at the same time. But by then Khouryn was there too.

He seized hold of her wrist with one hand and dug most of the meat out of her fingers with the other.

Then a feminine voice murmured a string of words, each softer than the one before. For a moment, Balasar's eyelids drooped. The Clethtinthtiallor went limp in his grasp and started snoring.

"Thank you," Nala said, stepping closer. Her hand trailed a blur of power as she lowered it to her side. "We wouldn't want her to do something that might embarrass her later."

Balasar laid the sleeping cultist on the ground. "What's wrong with her? With all of them?" He waved his hand to indicate the other swaying warriors. Some of them had started tearing at giant bodies too, although it didn't look like they necessarily meant to eat them.

"Nothing's wrong," Nala answered. "It's just . . . well, you saw how powerful their breath attacks were, and how fiercely they fought in general."

"Yes."

"That's because the Platinum Dragon exalted them as Torm grants power to Medrash. And it isn't always easy for ordinary people to channel the might of a god. Afterward, they sometimes experience a brief period of . . . altered consciousness."

"I understand why you're taking the ears. But it's degrading to oneself to desecrate the body of any enemy, even an ash giant, in some sort of frenzy. And sick to want to eat it!"

"I assure you," Nala said, "the urge to eat is unusual, and we stop those few who feel it. But even if we didn't, you can't condemn what a person does while under the control of the divine. The gods are beyond your judgment."

Balasar smiled. "With respect, wizard, not even Medrash's special god matters a flyspeck to me, and I don't consider anything beyond my judgment."

"You may yet," Nala said. "You may yet."

TEN

12 Mirtul, the Year of the Ageless One (1479 DR)

Gaedynn straightened up and loosed two arrows. Jhesrhi looked in the direction they flew and belatedly spotted the black silhouettes of two sentries, each of whom collapsed with a shaft in his chest.

The humans waited until it seemed plain that no one else had noticed the shadar-kai falling. Then they crept onward until they had a clear view of the hillside where Tchazzar lay manacled to the ground.

"Are you ready?" Gaedynn whispered.

"Of course," she snapped.

Actually, she wasn't certain. Since arriving in the Shadowfell, she'd gradually discerned that even the elements here had a filthy, alien feel. In her own world, they leaped to do her bidding. In the Shadowfell, they balked and looked for ways to turn her magic against her.

It didn't matter as long as she was working an ordinary sort of spell. But it might when she tried to exert her powers to the fullest.

Essentially it was a problem of attunement, and she'd spent the better part of a day meditating, striving for a better fit between her consciousness and the shadow world she currently inhabited. It had helped, but the only way to find out just how much was to attempt a truly powerful spell and see what happened.

But first she had two lesser ones to cast. "Hold out your hand," she said.

He did. She poised a fingertip over his palm and sketched a rune there. For a second it glowed yellow, and the pseudomind inside her staff experienced a pang of pleasure.

"It tickles," Gaedynn said.

"Shut up. Get ready."

She spoke to the fire implicit in the air, in all that could burn, and to the fire locked inside her staff. It cloaked her in warmth and wavering yellow light. Across the hillside, shadar-kai and their stunted servants jerked around toward the radiant figure suddenly burning in the dark.

Gaedynn shot the three nearest, dropping them before they had a chance to recover from their surprise. Giving Jhesrhi time to cast the first major spell without interference.

Fortunately, it had been possible to cast part of it in advance. If she tried, she could feel the forces she'd invoked balanced and aligned like the works of a mill, waiting for a final push to set the waterwheel turning and the stones grinding. She chanted words of power.

As she'd feared, when the process was at its most precarious, the earth tried to deny her. She could feel its spite and defiance as an ache in her feet and ankles.

But she knew how to talk to it now. She promised to satisfy the love of pain and destruction festering in everything in the

Shadowfell. She wallowed in fantasies of slaughter by crushing and suffocation.

It didn't make earth and stone despise her any less. It did, however, persuade them that she could help them lash out at other soft, scurrying mites they hated just as much. It beguiled them into using her as she was using them.

She pounded the butt of her staff repeatedly on the ground. Rings of swell flowed outward from the point of impact like ripples in a pond.

She kept hammering, and the ripples rose higher and swept farther. She could feel the disturbance, but had no trouble keeping her balance. The sensation in her feet had changed from gnawing pain to one of pure connection, like she'd set down roots as deep as a mountain's. Gaedynn, however, staggered, fighting to keep his feet, then fell down anyway. He wasn't alone. No shadar-kai could stand up either. The ones struggling free of the burrows had to crawl.

The captive dragon stared at Jhesrhi, but she had no idea what it was thinking. Nor, at that moment, did it matter. She had to stay focused on jolting the ground harder and harder and harder.

Cracking and crashing, trees toppled against their neighbors. Sections of hillside, and thinner strips connecting them, fell in on themselves. The earth laughed a rumbling laugh as it squeezed the shadar-kai caught in the tunnels in its murderous grasp.

Jhesrhi realized it was time to stop, but it took three more stamps of the staff before she managed it. Her will was entangled with the earth's, and her mad collaborator wanted to go on quaking until it knocked down, shattered, or buried everything—even itself.

Gaedynn sprang to his feet. "Keep moving!"

He was right. That was exactly what they had to do, no matter how tired she felt. They turned and ran into the trees.

There, she willed her blazing cloak to go out. Gaedynn waved the hand where she'd drawn the rune. A tongue of flame leaped from his skin to become a tall, slender figure with a feminine shape. From a distance, the elemental ought to pass for a mortal woman wrapped in fire.

Gaedynn dashed onward. The living flame sprang after him.

Jhesrhi stepped behind an oak and whispered charms of silence and concealment. Invisibility was largely a magic of the mind, and she was nowhere near as proficient at it as she was at elemental wizardry. But since she'd given the enemy a nice, bright lure to follow, perhaps they wouldn't even bother to look elsewhere.

It was only a few heartbeats before, moving in eerie quiet even now, the first shadar-kai came racing after Gaedynn and the fire spirit. Had they been human, some of the dark men might have stayed behind to dig for survivors or simply because they'd succumbed to grief for those presumably lost. But she and Gaedynn had learned that malice and bloodlust were the shadar-kai's ruling passions even when unprovoked, and they'd done everything in their power to enrage them. They hoped the final outrage would goad every last one of them into giving chase. Leaving Tchazzar unattended.

It looked like it was working. Dozens of the gray-skinned, black-clad folk, and the other creatures that dwelled alongside them, hurried past her hiding place.

But she wouldn't know for certain until she returned to the hillside and determined what was waiting for her there. She let a final band of the dark little servants flicker by, then took a breath, shifted her grip on her staff, and headed in that direction.

* * * * *

Aoth sat inside the wardrobe with Cera's garments dangling all around him. He peered out the peephole he'd bored and reflected that he was like a lover in a bawdy tale hiding from the jealous husband or suspicious father.

He was trying to find the humor in his situation but was too impatient to feel truly amused. Come on, he thought, what are you waiting for?

He was impatient because he'd decided that whatever did or didn't happen, he couldn't continue the ruse beyond that night. It had seemed pretty clever when he'd first hit on it, but now that it was underway, he realized that he couldn't allow a do-nothing like Hasos to have sole charge of the defense of the barony for very long, nor could he leave the Brotherhood without a single one of its senior officers in command. Any number of his men might decide that their obligations to their unlucky company had died with its leader and that they preferred to seek their fortunes elsewhere.

He reached out with his mind and made contact with Jet, who was skulking on the gabled roof of a building adjacent to the temple. He could tell immediately that the griffon hadn't noticed anything suspicious.

He scowled in frustration. But at that moment, the door swung open and a figure in a hooded robe slipped into Cera's bedchamber. Aoth wasn't surprised that this time there was only one assassin. It should only take one to kill an invalid, and a single murderer could sneak into a sickroom more easily than a larger number, even with a kind of invisibility aiding the endeavor.

The black-scaled dragonborn took a wary look around. Then he strode to the bed and pulled back the blankets, revealing the motionless form beneath. Aoth held his breath. This was the moment when the scheme could all too easily fall apart.

The dead sellsword had perished taking the same fort where Aoth allegedly received his terrible wounds. He'd been short and burly, and with his head shaved and his skin painted with false tattoos, he made a fair approximation of his commander.

Cera had used cosmetic and magical tricks to mask the appearance of death. It was Aoth's good fortune that little Soolabax had no temple of Kelemvor and that in the absence of doomguides, other clerics had to learn how to prepare the dead for their funerals.

Still, despite the plotters' best efforts, it was entirely possible the dragonborn would realize the man lying before him wasn't Aoth. Or that he was no longer alive and therefore this must be some sort of trap.

But it didn't happen that way. As soon as the dragonborn had the corpse uncovered to the waist, he whipped out a poniard, drove it into his victim's heart, then turned and headed for the door. He was eager to finish his task and get well away before anyone discovered his handiwork.

Too late, thought Aoth. I've got you, you son of a whore.

He gave the assassin time to exit the temple. Then he ran through the building, startling yellow-clad sunlords who were astonished to see him up and around and fully armed. He plunged out into Cera's garden. Aware of his need through their psychic link, Jet swooped down in front of him.

Aoth swung himself into the saddle. "The dragonborn didn't spot you, did he?"

"He shouldn't have," said the familiar, "but I can't be sure because I still haven't seen him."

"Go," said Aoth. "Stay high and be quiet."

Jet grunted. "I know how to hunt." He loped forward, beat his wings, and carried Aoth aloft.

Once they were well above the rooftops, the griffon flew in a spiral search pattern. At first Aoth couldn't see any sign of their quarry and feared that somehow the dragonborn had already gotten away. Then he spotted a robed figure hurrying down a narrow, crooked alley.

Got him, said Jet, speaking mind to mind. Now that his master's fire-kissed eyes had spotted the assassin, he could see him as well. *I wonder where he'll lead us.*

* * * * *

Gaedynn considered himself proficient at evading pursuit. But in the past, his goal had generally been to leave the enemy far behind as expeditiously as possible. It was trickier when he needed to stay just a little way ahead so they wouldn't get discouraged, give up, and go back to their captive dragon. Trickier too, when he was fleeing with a living beacon to draw his pursuers on.

Fortunately, it wasn't necessary to have the fire spirit constantly burning at his side. He could make her disappear when his foes drew as near as they were now. He held out his hand.

The elemental's features were a vague, inconstant blur, but he thought he saw her pout. Then she thinned to a long sliver of flame, which leaped into his palm and vanished. The contact stung for an instant—further evidence, perhaps, that she didn't want to go.

He slipped between two stands of brush, on a course at right angles to the one he'd been following before. He climbed a steep hillside, then looked around.

Dark figures stood clustered together not far from the point where he'd started his ascent. As usual he couldn't really hear shadar-kai voices, but he suspected they were trying to figure out what direction he'd taken. The elemental's abrupt disappearance had confused them.

Well, Gaedynn thought, maybe I can help them out with that. He nocked an arrow, drew it to his ear, and let it fly. One of the shadar-kai reeled and fell.

Without even pausing to check on him, the others swarmed up the slope. Gaedynn turned and scurried into a tangle of gnarled, scabrous-looking oaks.

Something whispered from behind one of the trees. A slim, shadowy hand beckoned. It filled him with a yearning so keen that when he strode on anyway, it was like tearing free of a barbed hook. His would-be seducer giggled after him.

He didn't think the haunt was an ally of the shadar-kai. It was just one of the many small perils infesting the Shadowfell. In fact, for an instant as he peered around, he wondered if he was leaving the chase too far behind. Then a pair of gray-black figures skulked out of the gloom.

Naked, genderless, and hairless, virtually identical, at first glance they looked less like creatures of flesh and blood than living sculptures—and unfinished ones at that. They had empty pits for eyes and a vertical groove to suggest both a nose and a mouth. Otherwise their heads were featureless bulbs.

Gaedynn had seen such things in the company of the shadar-kai.

But he had no idea exactly what they were or how they went about attacking a foe, and he hoped to avoid finding out. He snatched out an arrow and drove it into the nearest creature's chest.

The dark thing frayed apart to nothing. Maybe it was its nature to dissolve when it died, or perhaps the black arrows carried an enchantment that made them particularly deadly to such beings. Pleasantly surprised that the kill had been so easy, Gaedynn pivoted toward his remaining foe.

It was gone. And when it suddenly rematerialized, it was standing right in front of him. Its empty sockets stared into his eyes.

Pain ripped through Gaedynn's skull. His guts churned. His legs buckled and dumped him to his knees. The faceless creature grabbed his bow, jerked it out of his hand, and tossed it aside.

Hard as it was to think with his head throbbing, Gaedynn realized it was his enemy's gaze that was hurting him. He tried to avert his eyes. The creature caught his chin in cold, leathery fingers and held his head in place. He struggled to grip its forearm and break its hold, but could only paw and fumble feebly.

He held out his hand and the fire spirit leaped into existence. The dark thing automatically turned its head to track the apparition.

Gaedynn still felt weak and sick, but not quite so much as before. He yanked an arrow from his quiver and stabbed it into his enemy's stomach like a dagger.

The creature didn't fall down or break apart, but its grip on Gaedynn's chin loosened. He knocked its hand away and scrambled to his feet. The ground tilted beneath him, but then he caught his balance.

The dark thing's head turned back in his direction. Making sure not to meet its gaze, he pulled out another arrow and thrust, aiming for the spot where a human would carry his heart.

Made of a substance that resembled polished obsidian, the black point punched into his adversary's chest. The creature stumbled backward, but he had the feeling it still wasn't ready to drop. He drew his scimitar and slashed three times. That made it fall down and start unraveling too.

He just had time to grin. Then a cold hand grabbed him by the wrist of his sword arm and jerked him around.

He could tell from the arrow still sticking out of its chest that it was the first faceless creature, not slain after all. Even though strips of its body had dissolved all the way through from front to back and it was impossible to understand how the remaining pieces maintained their proper positions with nothing but empty air between them. Its eyeless gaze reached out for his own and, startled as he was, he waited an instant too long to start resisting.

He felt compulsion take hold of him. He was going to look, and the fire sprite, now simply standing and watching the struggle from several paces away, wouldn't save him a second time.

He shifted the scimitar to his off hand and cut at the dark creature's head. At the same instant, its power blazed into his eyes, and the world exploded into agony.

When the pain ebbed, he was sprawled on his belly. He looked around. The faceless thing was gone again. For good this time, he hoped.

Suddenly the nausea he was suffering became irresistible, and he retched up the contents of his stomach. It left a foul taste and burning sensation in his mouth and nose, but even so he felt better afterward.

Not well, though. He supposed it would take time for the faceless things' poisonous influence to work its way out of his system completely.

Unfortunately, he couldn't wait. Sick or hale, he had to move or more of his pursuers would catch up with him. He sheathed the scimitar, retrieved his bow, and loped onward. The living flame fell into step beside him.

* * * * *

Though it was difficult to be certain from high above, Aoth thought that he and Jet were looking down at an apartment house. The assassin slipped through the easternmost in a row of doors.

Aoth decided to descend. Sensing his intent, Jet furled his wings, swooped, and set down lightly in the empty, darkened street, far enough away from the apartment in question that no one looking out a window was likely to see them.

Although Aoth doubted anybody was. The shutters were closed, and no light gleamed through the cracks.

"What now?" asked Jet.

Aoth swung himself off the griffon's back. "I go in after him." He considered taking his shield, then left it clipped to the saddle. He'd rather have both hands available to grip his spear.

"Is that wise?" asked Jet. "You could watch the place from here while I go for reinforcements."

"When someone breaks in in force, the enemy will know it. It will give them another chance to destroy their papers and such. If I sneak in alone, it increases the odds of finally getting some answers."

"It increases the odds of somebody tearing your head off too."

"We killed a number of dragonborn that night in the garden. There can't be an unlimited supply hiding here in Soolabax with nobody noticing. Even if one of them spots me, I expect I can contend with however many are left until you get back with those reinforcements you mentioned."

"All right. I'll be back as soon as I can." The familiar trotted, lashed his wings, and soared up toward the stars.

Aoth invoked the magic of one of his tattoos, and for a moment the design felt cold as ice on his chest. The charm didn't grant actual invisibility, but it made the bearer easy to overlook.

Then he skulked up to the door the dragonborn had entered. He couldn't hear anything on the other side. He tried the handle. As he'd expected, it was locked.

He slipped the point of his spear into the crack beneath the latch and released a bit of power from the weapon. The door made a sharp snapping sound and lurched open.

He peered into an unfurnished hallway with doorways opening off it and stairs leading upward. He neither saw nor heard anything moving, which suggested that no one had caught the noise of his forced entry.

Aoth prowled onward. None of the rooms on the ground floor was furnished or showed any signs of recent occupancy. It made him wonder if he and Jet actually had killed all the dragonborn but one.

In a small room at the back, his fire-kissed eyes saw the square outline of a low concealed panel that evidently connected the apartment with another. He reached for it, and then it started to slide. Somebody was opening it from the other side.

He turned and scrambled through the doorway to an adjacent room. Then he peeked around the corner.

Stooping, a man with bushy salt-and-pepper side-whiskers, eyebrows to match, and a mole at the corner of his narrow mouth came through the low opening, then closed the panel behind him. He wore a slashed velvet doublet with turned cuffs, like a prosperous merchant, and Aoth realized they'd actually been introduced at some point. Although he couldn't recall the fellow's name.

Whoever the whoreson was, he walked on without noticing anything amiss. Aoth considered jumping him, then opted to follow instead.

The man headed down the cellar stairs. Aoth gave him time to reach the bottom, then crept down just far enough to see what lay below.

Someone had done a fair amount of work to turn the basement into a proper shrine to Tiamat, the five-headed Dragon Queen. Votive candles burned before a bronze statue of the goddess. One flame glowed red, one white, one blue, one green, and one was a quivering teardrop of shadow. The sculpture's necks almost appeared to weave in the soft, wavering light.

A portrait depicting the Nemesis of the Gods in her human guise as a beautiful woman with long black hair hung on the wall beside an intricately painted, multicolored pentagram. The smell of bitter incense hung in the air.

Dark scales glinting in the candlelight, the dragonborn assassin stood naked before the pentagonal bloodstone altar. His robe lay discarded on the floor.

He glared at the man with the side-whiskers. "I don't like mortals in general," he said. "I definitely don't like it when they keep me waiting."

Aoth frowned. Mortals? What in Kossuth's name was that supposed to mean?

"I have an ordinary life," the man replied. "I have to devote some time to living it. Otherwise people will get suspicious."

"Just restore me to myself."

"I'm working on it." He took down a robe from a peg on the wall and pulled it on over his other clothing. Its shimmering scales changed color whenever he moved. He slipped on five rings, each bearing a stone the hue of one of the candle flames, and picked up an implement or weapon like a miner's pick.

Evidently he himself was the wyrmkeeper of this particular sanctuary.

He faced the dragonborn. "Stand still." He recited sibilant words of power and swung the heavy, unwieldy-looking pick through a looping figure with a dexterity that would have done credit to a juggler. The five wedge-shaped heads of the Tiamat statue seemed to cock forward ever so slightly, although that was likely just Aoth's imagination.

And the assassin changed form.

His features remained reptilian, but twisted from a dragonborn's rather handsome lineaments into ugliness. Batlike wings sprouted from his back, and a long tail with a spike on the end writhed out from the base of his spine. He—or it—dropped into a crouch.

Aoth wasn't a scholar of demons. But he'd met a fair assortment on the battlefield, and knew an abishai when he saw one. And it made sense that with the aid of magic, one of the devil-like spirits could assume the form of a dragonborn. Both races were kin to wyrms and thus to each other, whatever the Tymantherans might care to believe.

In fact, a lot of things suddenly made sense. Like why the dragonborn murderers, raiders, and pirates had no clan piercings and why knowledgeable Tymantherans like Perra were unable to account for them. Why they possessed supernatural abilities ordinary dragonborn didn't, and how they could lurk unnoticed in the heart of a city between atrocities. In point of fact, they didn't. They went home to Tiamat's domain in the astral world called Banehold until a human spellcaster saw fit to call them forth again.

Aoth felt a swell of elation. This truly had been a puzzle worth solving. When he reported what he'd discovered, it would save the alliance between Chessenta and Tymanther.

Its metamorphosis complete, the black abishai said, "Good. Now send me—" It whipped around toward the stairs.

Aoth realized it had glimpsed him from the corner of its eye. His veil had sufficed to fool it while it wore its dragonborn shape, but not now when its senses were evidently somewhat different.

The abishai charged up the risers. Sweating drops of fuming acid, its tail reared over its shoulder to strike like a scorpion's stinger.

Aoth hurled darts of green light from his spear. The devil-kin twisted aside, and they missed. It resumed its climb. He charged the head of his weapon with destructive power and thrust it at the creature's chest.

The abishai dodged that attack as well. Its tail whipped at Aoth's shoulder. The bony point clanked against his mail and rebounded, although just the track of vapor it left in the air was enough to sting his eyes and make them water.

Meanwhile, the wyrmkeeper chanted.

Aoth feinted to the abishai's foot. It leaped upward, beating its leathery wings as well as it could in the cramped space of the stairway, to rise above the attack. He whirled his spear—another maneuver that wasn't easy in the confines—and smashed the butt into his opponent's fanged, snarling mouth and snout.

The blow knocked the abishai back down the steps. He hurled more darts of light and, deprived of its balance, the creature couldn't dodge. The missiles plunged into its body. It jerked and then lay still.

Aoth immediately looked for the wyrmkeeper. Whatever magic the bastard was attempting, he needed to put a stop to it.

But it was too late. The man with the pick had finished his incantation, and the pentagram, and the section of wall on which he'd painted it, had disappeared. In their place, a hole opened on a bleak, rocky landscape and a red sky mountainous with black thunderheads. Abishais were swarming through.

* * * * *

Jhesrhi studied the hillside with all its new pits and ditches to show where the underlying tunnels had collapsed. The dragon lay motionless, his head between his forefeet like a dog's, as though merely looking around at all the commotion had exhausted him.

As far as she could tell, nothing else was moving either. That didn't mean there wasn't someone lying in wait—if there was one thing for which the denizens of the Shadowfell had a natural gift, it was sneaking and hiding—but if there was, she'd just have to wait for him to reveal himself and kill him when he did.

She strode out into the open. Drew breath to hail Tchazzar. Then a patch of earth heaved as something started to force its way out from underneath.

All right, she thought, let's get this over with. She lifted her staff and felt its pleasure that she finally meant to use it in the manner it preferred.

Huge hands, their skin the same color as the surrounding dirt, gripped the edge of the new hole and heaved. A head with brutish features and curved taurine horns surged into view. Beneath it were massive shoulders armored in bands of sculpted stone.

Jhesrhi started backing away. She tried to stop.

I'm not a coward, she told herself. It unsettled me to return to Chessenta, and then to Threskel, but I got better. Gaedynn said I was better.

But evidently she wasn't, because she couldn't stop retreating. She couldn't stop shaking or gasping either. Although she knew it couldn't really be there, she seemed to feel her stiff, scratchy, filthy slave collar half choking her neck.

The elemental mage—a ken-kuni, one of the giants with an affinity for earth—sneered, drew himself to his feet, and lumbered toward her.

* * * * *

Abishais of various colors rushed the stairs. Aoth knew that like the dragons they resembled, each was largely immune to the force that infused its nature. The reds couldn't burn, the whites couldn't freeze, and so forth. So he hurled a rainbow of destructive power down the steps in the hope that multiple varied attacks would kill them all.

The barrage blasted them back and smashed the wooden risers beneath them. Some then lay motionless, charred and shriveled or transformed into stone. Another, plunged into dementia, looked around in confusion.

But others picked themselves up and snarled at the man who'd hammered them. And more of the vile things were still coming through the hole.

Maybe if Aoth killed the man who'd opened it, the gate would close. He pointed his spear, rattled off words of power, and hurled a jagged bolt of shadow. Like the abishais, the wyrmkeeper might be impervious to an attack resembling one or even all of his goddess's breaths. But Aoth hoped the pure essence of death would knife through any defenses.

The magic pierced the wyrmkeeper's torso. He dropped his pick and fell, patches of his flesh dissolving into slime before he even hit the floor.

But the hole didn't close. And hands locked around Aoth's ankles. While he'd focused his attention on the priest, one of the abishais had jumped up through the splintered wreckage of the stairs and grabbed him.

The devil-kin's weight nearly dragged him over the edge. Its green stinger stabbed repeatedly against his reinforced boot, and the haze that surrounded the creature seared his mouth and nose and made him cough. The section of staircase beneath him, hanging with little or no support from below, swayed like it was about to give way.

He struggled not to cough. To articulate instead a word that swelled into an unearthly howl. The green abishai lost its hold and fell away. Three of its fellows dropped dead too.

But an instant later, Aoth heard banging and crashing at his back. He glanced around and saw the ruddy dancing glow of flame.

Instead of attempting a frontal assault up the stairs, some of the red and blue abishais were smashing, burning, and blasting their way through the basement ceiling. If he stayed where he was, he'd be trapped with foes assailing him from the front and rear simultaneously.

He hurled another rainbow at the opponents below him as he scrambled backward. He didn't like doing it. Even a master war-mage didn't command an inexhaustible supply of magic, and he was burning through his most powerful spells too quickly. But he had to hold back the creatures still in the cellar for at least another moment while he got clear of the stairs.

He felt searing heat and pivoted toward it. Shrouded in flame, a red abishai reached for him with hooked talons and whipped its stinger at him. He blasted it with a booming flare of lightning.

An instant later, a lightingbolt struck him, almost like his own magic had bounced back. Every muscle clenching and spasming, he shuddered in place for a moment, then dropped to his knees.

The power would likely have killed him if not for the protective enchantments bound into his mail and tattoos. As it was, it left his head empty and ringing like a bell. A light crawled in the blue abishai's eyes, sparks popped and sizzled on its scaly hide, and a part of him realized it was gathering its strength to throw more lightning. But at first he couldn't make himself react.

Even when his mind snapped back into functionality, his still-twitching muscles didn't want to obey it. But somehow he pointed his spear and sent a blade of white light leaping from the point. The floating sword slashed, and the abishai toppled backward. Its lightningbolt shattered a section of the ceiling.

Panting, heart pounding, Aoth rose and retreated through the empty rooms. The flying blade finished killing its first target. He called it back to hover close by and strike at whatever popped out at him.

But the sword couldn't keep all the abishais away. There were too many. There were ragged, smoldering holes gaping in the floor of every room, waiting to punish any misstep, and devil-kin lurking around every corner. When he was lucky enough to spot them while still a step beyond their reach, he blasted them with flame and frost. Otherwise he drove his spear into their vitals.

Suddenly he smelled a scent like a gathering storm, and a stray spark fell in front of his face. He wrenched himself aside, and a dazzling lightningbolt roared down from above. One of the blue abishais had gone up to the second story, clawed a hole in the floor there, and waited for him to pass underneath. He sent the flying sword streaking at it to shear the fiend's head from its shoulders.

He realized he had no idea of his direction. He'd turned and dodged so often that, ridiculously, the handful of interconnecting rooms now felt like a maze. Clamping down on a surge of panic, he glanced around and spied a window.

He blew the shutters to splinters with a blast of sound, then ran toward the opening. Shrouded in mist and bitter cold, a white abishai lunged at him. He stabbed it in the eye with his spear, jerked the weapon free, and leaped through the opening—into the street where Jet had set him down.

No help was in sight, and he realized he shouldn't have expected any. He'd only been inside for a little while, even if it had felt like all night to him.

He took a breath and aimed his spear at the abishais springing and clambering out after him. Come on, then, he thought.

* * * * *

Gaedynn loosed his last arrow, dropped his bow, pulled his scimitar out of the ground, and lunged from the thicket. He closed to striking distance before the shadar-kai he'd shot finished falling down.

He cut the second one across the kidney. By then the remaining two had their chains whirling. He jumped back, and the ends of the weapons streaked past him. He instantly stepped in and sliced into the torso of yet another silent, scar-faced opponent.

He looked for the last one and couldn't find him. Pain smashed through his ankle, and then something yanked his leg out from under him. As he slammed down on his belly, he realized the last shadar-kai had shifted behind him and caught his leg with his chain.

Gaedynn heaved himself over onto his back and slashed. The shadar-kai was diving down at him with a wavy-edged dagger in his hand, and the scimitar sheared through his throat. Blood gushing from the wound, he fell on top of Gaedynn, shuddered, and then lay still.

Gasping, his ankle throbbing, soaked in gore, Gaedynn rolled the corpse away, rid himself of the chain, and crawled to the shadar-kai he'd shot. He relieved that body of a full quiver of the black arrows.

It was actually rather ridiculous how glad he was to have them. He was still ill from the poisonous gaze of the faceless men. If anything, fatigue was making the sickness steadily worse. Most likely, thanks to the stroke of the chain, he'd be limping from now on.

His flight had taken him to a patch of relatively low ground where flickers of shadow told him his pursuers were on the wooded slopes and ridges to every side. Despite his best efforts they'd somehow managed to surround him, and now they were going to converge on him.

And there was still no sign of a rescue in the offing. Taken all together, it meant that unless Lady Luck truly loved him today, the arrows could only extend his life for a little longer and make the shadar-kai pay more dearly for the honor of snuffing it out.

Still, that was better than nothing. It just might mean the mad gamble would pay off—for Jhesrhi anyway—and in any case, better to go down drawing a bow than swinging a blade. That way, Keen-Eye would know to welcome his spirit into his camp.

Just to make sure the enemy stayed eager, he flicked the living flame out of his hand and into visible existence. "If you can fight," he told her, "this would be a perfect time to show me."

He wasn't certain, but he thought her glowing, fluid features smiled derisively.

* * * * *

As Jhesrhi backed up, she told herself, I don't have to cringe and run. I can kill this brute. My magic is stronger than any kenkuni's ever was.

Her staff too implored her to stand her ground. It promised that if she only unleashed its power, she could incinerate any foe.

Still, she kept retreating. Leering, the giant came after her in a leisurely manner, evidently so unimpressed with her that he didn't see any urgency about closing the distance.

She realized he hadn't even bothered to draw the enormous sword strapped across his back. Perhaps he didn't even mean to kill her. Maybe he planned to keep her, put his collar on her neck, *touch her* in all the dread, unbearable ways.

So fight! Don't let him! But instead, she merely gasped and whimpered.

He waved his massive, dirt-colored hand. A tremor ran through the ground and tossed her off her feet. Then suddenly he ran, and before she could even scramble up, he was looming over her. He bent down.

I'm sorry, Gaedynn, she thought. I tried. She imagined the archer fleeing and fighting in the dark.

And somehow that—or that combined with the urgings of the staff and all the things she'd already tried to tell herself—brought her to the tipping point.

She'd *tried*? And that was how it ended? That was all she had to offer one of the only true friends she'd ever had? Rage and hatred welled up in her like lava, burning her panic away, excoriating the elemental mage and herself in equal measure.

But the torrent of flame that leaped from the staff only targeted the giant. It caught him square in the face and hurled him backward.

When he caught his balance, she saw that the attack hadn't seared his body exactly as it would char human flesh. But it had plainly hurt him. Parts of him looked hard, discolored, and cracked, like badly made pottery.

He bellowed and stamped his foot.

She disregarded the staff's yearning for fire and reestablished her connection to the earth. When the shock reached her, it simply lifted her and set her back down. It didn't even stagger her, let alone snap her neck or jolt her limbs out of their sockets.

The giant snarled, and bits of his contorted features broke loose. She laughed at him.

He pulled his sword from his scabbard and charged. She spoke to the wind, and it carried her upward, her magic in a race with his long legs and reach.

A close race—he leaped as high as he could, swung the sword in an overhand cut, and it whistled by just a finger length under her feet.

But after that, there was nothing more to fear. Hovering above him, she hurled down gout after gout of flame. While he staggered around and screamed, and his body broke and broke again.

By the Nine Dark Princes, it felt good! So good that when it was over, a part of her just wanted to keep raining fire on the shards of the corpse.

But she had a job to finish. So she struggled to control her ragged breathing and put her thoughts in order. Then she asked the wind to carry her to the prisoner.

Despite his shackles and extreme emaciation, he was still a colossal red dragon, and she floated down in front of him with a pang of trepidation. But all he did was study her with his smoldering golden eyes.

"Are you Tchazzar?" she asked.

"You see that I am," he answered. His voice was more of a wheeze than either a rumble or a hiss, like it strained him just to talk.

"People say you were a great wizard."

Despite his debility, his eyes burned brighter, and she found herself taking a step back. "I'm a *god*!" he said.

"I beg your pardon for misspeaking," she said, holding her voice steady. "But my point is this. If I set you free and restore your strength, can you take my comrade and me back to the mortal world?"

"I'd do so gladly," Tchazzar said, "if you could truly keep your end of the bargain."

"I believe I can. You've seen I have an affinity for fire, and that's the essence of life to you. I'm going to pour it into your blood and sinews."

Tchazzar hesitated like she'd surprised him. "That might actually work, assuming you can channel a prodigious quantity without losing control. If you're willing to try, you'd better get started."

"Before the shadar-kai come back?"

"Before Sseelrigoth—the blight dragon—himself arrives. It's our good fortune that he can't actually live here, lest he drain the life from his subjects. But I'm sure that by now, he's sensed all the commotion and is on his way."

* * * * *

Pivoting constantly, alternately targeting the abishais at street level and those flying overhead, Aoth rattled off words of power and worked his way through his last remaining attack spells. He'd killed plenty of his foes and meant to kill more. But he suspected that when he finished casting his flares of fire and howls of bone-shattering vibration, there would still be enough left to swarm on him and tear him to pieces. He never did get that damn gate in the cellar to close.

Either way, it looked like he was going to die fighting for Chessenta. A place he decided he detested almost as much as it detested people like him.

Galloping hoof beats clattered behind him. He glanced over his shoulder.

Armored in a gilt helmet and breastplate, Cera charged in his direction. He realized she too must have been waiting for the assassin to make a move, and when Aoth had gone running through the temple, she'd tried to follow him. She couldn't have kept on Jet's track in any normal way, but maybe some trick of divine magic had made it possible. Or maybe all the thunderclaps and flashes had drawn her. Now that Aoth thought about it, it hadn't been a particularly inconspicuous fight.

Her golden-colored mare balked well short of the action. The animal tried to turn around and run the other way, and Cera struggled to reassert control.

"Get out of here!" Aoth croaked. Then he heard the flap of leathery wings and whirled back around.

A green abishai leaped at him. Holding his breath and squinting against the stinging haze that surrounded it, he ducked a sweep of its tail, drove his spear into its midsection, pulled it free, and scrambled back out of the cloud.

When he glanced back again, Cera was picking herself up off the ground. She didn't look hurt, but she didn't even have a weapon. Her mace was still slung on the saddle of the mare now racing away as fast as she could go.

"Run!" said Aoth. "You can't fight these things!"

"You don't need a fighter!" Cera said. "You need an exorcist!" She started to chant.

Apparently recognizing the power in her words, the abishais charged or flew at her. Draining his power to the dregs, Aoth created walls of flame and hovering, spinning blades between the priestess and her assailants. Anything to hold them back.

Or at least he did so during the fleeting moments when one or more abishais weren't trying to burn, blast, or stab him to death. The rest of the time he thrust the spear at what seemed an endless succession of snarling, clawing monstrosities. The weapon felt strangely heavy and dead in his hands, and not just because of his exhaustion. Because there was no magic left inside it anymore.

Then a glow flowered at his back and lit the street as bright as day. Some of the abishais charred away like dry leaves in a bonfire. The rest faltered, and when they came forward again, they appeared to struggle like swimmers fighting against a current. They seemed to grope and fumble too, as though they were half blind.

It helped. Aoth killed three more of them. But then he spotted a blue abishai that had gotten past him. Now it was soaring over Cera. Sparks jumped on its scaly hide as it prepared to hurl a lightningbolt.

Aoth rattled off words of power and hurled a ray of freezing cold from his outstretched hand. It was as powerful a ranged attack as he had left, and it wasn't enough. The devil-kin jerked and wobbled in flight but survived. Its body lit up from the inside—

And then Jet swooped at it and drove his talons deep into its back. Its power discharged in a crackling flash that made Aoth wince, but when the griffon shook the lifeless body off its claws and flew onward, it was plain he'd survived the shock.

More griffons dived out of the night sky into Cera's light. The sellswords on their backs loosed arrow after arrow, and the abishais fell. Aoth had fought so hard and for what had felt like such a long time that there was something dreamlike about how quickly the battle ended.

It wouldn't have been as quick if there were still fresh abishais rushing out of the apartment house, but he now saw that at some point that had ended. Something—either the wyrmkeeper's death, Cera's exorcism, or simply the magic running out of power—had finally closed the opening to Tiamat's domain.

Smelling of singed feathers, Jet set down in the street. "Surely," he said, "there can't be too many enemies left hiding in Soolabax. Even if worst comes to worst, you can cope with however many remain."

Aoth snorted. "It sounded reasonable when I said it. You must have thought so too, the way you took your time getting back here."

"That was because humans are idiots. I don't know how many times I had to repeat myself to make the men understand you were well and needed—"

Cera's incantation cut off abruptly.

Aoth and Jet whirled in her direction. There were no abishais anywhere near her, and no blood on her person. But she was collapsing, and as she did, darkness reclaimed the street.

Aoth ran toward her. Jet started a heartbeat later, but outdistanced his master with his first prodigious bound.

* * * * *

The embrace of fire was as glorious as the touch of a mortal lover had always been vile. It filled Jhesrhi with ecstasy and the yearning to open herself even more completely.

She didn't know what would happen if she did. Maybe she'd simply burn to ash. Or perhaps her humanity would melt away like dross, leaving a being like an efreet, more truly a creature of flame than even a red dragon could ever be. Either possibility would be a blissful consummation.

But she was a wizard, with a wizard's trained intellect and will, and she refused to surrender wholly to mere sensation, no matter how pleasurable. She maintained her awareness of the other aspects of her nature—of earth, air, water, and spirit, or identity, memory, and purpose—even as she drew the rarified essence of flame from the Elemental Chaos, gathered it in her staff, and then hurled it forth into Tchazzar's body.

Strangely, the result reminded her of the action of water, specifically of the explosion of life that came when rainfall ended a drought. Glowing like a hot coal but without heat—every bit of that was turning into muscle—the dragon's form swelled, and new scales closed old sores. Head thrown back at the end of his long neck, he gasped and groaned. Perhaps his transformation hurt, but if so it was clearly a pain he welcomed.

It looked to Jhesrhi like he was nearly restored. Then nausea and vertigo stabbed through her, and her control over her magic wavered. The fire from beyond clutched at her, trying to claim her, and her treacherous staff rejoiced.

She couldn't bend the element to her will again. She could only break the flow. The roaring, twisting jet of flame went out, and Tchazzar roared as it suddenly stopped playing over his body.

His progress more like a manta ray swimming than a bat flying, shrouded in a cloud of dust, Sseelrigoth twisted and rippled down from the sky. Newly dead leaves whispered as they dropped from the trees adjacent to the hillside.

"By the Lady of Loss," said the blight dragon, "are *all* my slaves killed?" He sounded amused rather than upset. "We'll have to find a way for you to pay for that, wizard. Right after I eat this wonderful meal you provided."

"I was weak when you bound me to the earth," Tchazzar growled. "You kept me weak for all the years since. But I'm not weak anymore." He heaved, and the staples securing his limbs tore out of the ground.

Sseelrigoth's black eyes widened in shock, but he reacted quickly. A flick of the writhing membranes on his flanks backed him farther away from the red dragon. He opened his jaws and spewed a jet of grit.

Sick and spent as she was, Jhesrhi managed to lift her staff and ask the wind for help. It howled, swirled around her, and kept any of the dragon's breath from reaching her.

But it reached Tchazzar. Some of the particles scoured his hide like a sandstorm. Others stuck to him and burned.

Then Sseelrigoth snarled, and dust devils sprang up around Tchazzar's head, no doubt to blind and confuse him. The red wyrm whipped his head back and forth, but the whirling clouds moved with it. Meanwhile, Sseelrigoth sucked in air.

Jhesrhi focused past her grinding sickness and whispered words of command. The wind screamed and tore the dust devils apart.

Vision restored, Tchazzar lashed his gigantic wings and sprang into the air. The tip of his tail whirled in Jhesrhi's direction and she threw herself flat so it wouldn't hit her.

Tchazzar slammed into Sseelrigoth and assailed him with his jaws and the talons on all four feet. He whipped his tail around him like a python. The blight wyrm responded in kind.

So entangled, they couldn't fly. They crashed to earth and rolled toward Jhesrhi. She scrambled clear just in time to keep them from crushing her.

She scurried until she was well clear and, panting and trembling, simply leaned on her staff and watched thereafter. She was too ill and tired for more and doubted she could help Tchazzar any further even if she weren't. As long as the wyrms were entwined together, it would be difficult to cast elemental magic at one without hitting the other as well.

The struggle shook the ground, and the bits of the warren that her earthquake hadn't collapsed now caved in on themselves. Chunks of ripped flesh arced through the air. Flame leaped around the dragons' fangs as they snapped and bit. Tchazzar's fire was blue and bright gold. Sseelrigoth's was a murky red, the poisonous grit he'd spat before superheated by his rage.

For a time it looked like Tchazzar was gradually tearing his adversary apart. Then Sseelrigoth's eyes grew even blacker, and his shroud of dust darkened. Tchazzar bellowed and his wounds widened, rotting at the edges while the blight dragon's hurts began to close.

Finish it! Jhesrhi thought. Before he leeches away everything I gave you!

As if he'd heard her, Tchazzar strained with every limb to loosen Sseelrigoth's coils. Unequal to the pressure, a bone in his left wing snapped and a jagged end stabbed through the membrane. But then he broke free of his adversary's grip.

At once he opened his jaws wider than Jhesrhi would have imagined possible. Taking advantage of his regained mobility, he launched himself at Sseelrigoth fast as an arrow leaping from a bow. And she perceived for the first time just how much bigger he was than the other wyrm. Big enough for his fangs to crash shut on Sseelrigoth's head from the snout to just behind the eyes.

Tchazzar's jaw muscles bunched as he bit down with all his might and wrenched his head from side to side. Flexible as a serpent, Sseelrigoth whipped his coils around his foe and clawed. In some places, his talons sliced to the bone. Meanwhile, his tail whipped up and down, battering a section of Tchazzar's neck.

Jhesrhi held her breath. She couldn't imagine the battle lasting much longer. No one, not even a dragon, could endure such punishment for long. One of them was going to succumb.

It turned out be Sseelrigoth. A splintering crunch sounded from inside Tchazzar's jaws, and then the blight wyrm's neck lashed back and forth. Nothing was restraining it anymore. Blood sprayed from the jagged bowl that was all that remained of Sseelrigoth's head.

His decapitated body raked and bashed Tchazzar another time or two. Then, the spurts of gore abating, his neck flopped to the ground and his limbs went limp as well.

Tchazzar spat out several pieces of Sseelrigoth's head. Jhesrhi took note of the short horns that encrusted them, realized the inside of the red dragon's mouth must now be a mass of sores, and winced. Still employing every bit of his strength and speed, Tchazzar kept clawing his foe's corpse.

Jhesrhi frowned. Surely Tchazzar realized Sseelrigoth was dead. But he looked like he didn't mean to stop until he'd reduced the blight dragon to tiny specks of flesh and bone.

And that wouldn't do. Gaedynn needed them now.

She stepped forward. "My lord!" she called.

Eyes blazing, flame leaping from between his fangs, Tchazzar whirled in her direction. A shock of terror jolted her as she sensed he had no idea who she was. He crouched to spring—

And then he evidently remembered her. She was no expert at reading the features of dragons, but even so she saw some of the radiant fury go out of his eyes.

He straightened up into a less threatening posture. He started to speak, grimaced, spat out a mix of blood and flame, and then tried again. "My daughter."

"My comrade Gaedynn," she said. "The shadar-kai are hunting him."

"Yes. I saw the chase begin."

"If we don't help him soon, it will be too late."

Tchazzar turned and dipped a wing to touch the ground.

She realized she was supposed to climb it like a ramp. Thinking of the broken bone and all his other wounds, she asked, "Can you still fly?"

He laughed. "I could fly to the stars for a chance to burn those maggots."

So Jhesrhi scrambled up the wing into a smell compounded of combustion, blood, decay, and a sort of dry reptilian musk. The act of climbing didn't repulse her. Though intelligent, Tchazzar was so different in form from a giant or a man that she could touch him as easily as a griffon.

She seated herself between two of the dorsal frills at the base of his neck. At once he lunged forward, lashed his wings, and carried her into the sky.

As they hurtled along, she studied the hills below. All she saw was earth and trees. She asked the wind for news of the pursuit, but this was one of those occasions when it hadn't taken any notice of the doings of creatures of flesh and blood.

Then Tchazzar dived lower, and she spotted the living flame she'd conjured shining in a depression among the hills. Shadar-kai flickered down the slopes toward the lure at the bottom. One of them fell. She couldn't actually see the arrow that had pierced him, but she was sure it was there, and she smiled.

Tchazzar didn't roar to announce his coming. He swooped at the dark men like an owl descending on a mouse. The first ones didn't know he was there until a plume of his fiery breath seared them from existence.

He wheeled and burned a second group. By the time he made a third pass, the rest were ready to fight, but it didn't matter. Their javelins and arrows couldn't stop a creature that had survived Sseelrigoth's fangs and claws. Most of the weapons glanced off Tchazzar's scales, and, all but berserk with the joy of vengeance, he didn't even seem to notice the ones that stuck.

To Jhesrhi's surprise, she felt a pang of pity. Run, she thought. Some of you might get away.

But none of them tried. And when the last of them was dead, and Tchazzar set down on the ground, Gaedynn limped out of the stand of gnarled spruces where he'd taken cover. Gray-faced, his hair plastered down with sweat, he grinned and said, "That went better than I expected."

EPILOGUE

13 Mirtul, the Year of the Ageless One (1479 DR)

Khouryn knew at a glance that the army less camped than huddled on the shore of Ash Lake had suffered a serious defeat. It wasn't just the presence of the wounded slumped on the ground, some moaning or calling out for help, although there were plenty of them. It was the absence of straight lines and organization, and the paucity of tents and baggage carts. It was the almost palpable air of misery.

Khouryn sighed with a sorrow of his own. I won't get home this season, he realized. Most likely not this year. He touched his truesilver betrothal ring through his steel and leather gauntlet.

"Those are the Lance Defenders down there," Medrash said.

"Yes," Khouryn said. "I figured that out."

"Well," Balasar said, "at least nobody's going to pay much attention to the fact that our band of Daardendriens lost its own little battle."

Medrash turned his head to glare. "This is really not funny."

"I agree," Nala said, swaying ever so slightly from side to side in the saddle. "It's a sacred moment. The turning of the tide."

"What do you mean?" Khouryn asked.

"Surely it's obvious," the wizard replied. "This proves that *only* the Platinum Cadre can stand against the ash giants, and that means our people won't be able to scorn us anymore. To the contrary. Come on. We need to talk to the commander." She kicked her horse into motion.

Patrin smiled at Medrash. "It's a great day for you too, brother," he said. "When Tymanther starts honoring Bahamut, I'm sure it will pay homage to Torm as well." He rode after Nala.

Khouryn didn't, and neither did Medrash and Balasar. Plainly they all felt the same impulse to sit on their mounts and confer quietly while the foot soldiers of the cadre passed on either side.

"I've always hoped more of our people would take up the worship of Torm," Medrash said, "but not at such a cost. And I don't say it just because Bahamut's a dragon god, despicable as that is. There's something more wrong with all this. And something sick about what happens to some of these cultists in battle."

"I agree," Khouryn said. "And I've come to believe what you do—that somehow it's a part of something bigger, although don't ask me what." He chuckled a mirthless chuckle. "From the start I've known I don't have a head for intrigue, and all my bewilderment since has only gone to prove it. But it occurs to me that if I took the vanquisher up on that offer of employment, maybe I could help your troops win without joining in Nala's prayers. I don't know if you've heard, but dwarves are good at fighting giants."

"You'd do that?" Medrash asked.

"For a little while. If our hunches are right, it might be the most useful thing I can do for the Brotherhood."

"Then that's the plan," Balasar said. "You two go win battles while I infiltrate the cult."

"What?" Medrash asked.

Balasar grinned. "They're not going to believe that a dwarf wants to discover his dragon nature. Or that *you* want to worship their god when you never stop prattling about the one you've already got. Who does that leave except me to do the hard part as usual?"

* * * * *

Cera floated in the midst of warmth, light, and an order sublime in its perfection. All things revolved in relationships that, though complex, were so stately and invariant that only peace was possible.

She understood that everything she was experiencing was Amaunator. He'd received her into his presence, even if he hadn't chosen to reveal himself in anything approximating human form.

She rejoiced until luminous spirits—bright against brightness but somehow, in this place, visible nonetheless—appeared. They took hold of her and gently urged her toward a dim spot that hadn't been visible before.

She knew they were doing Amaunator's bidding, and so resistance was inconceivable. Still, she grieved as they guided her down into coarseness, gloom, and inconstancy.

For a moment, she felt heavy as lead and knew her spirit had fused with her flesh once more. She opened her eyes and, though her vision was blurry, spied Aoth sitting beside her bed.

"You're crying," he said. Using a callused fingertip, he brushed the tears away from her eyes.

"I was sad," she said, "but it's better now."

"Does that mean you're all right? The other sunlords said you strained yourself drawing too much of Amaunator's power. They prayed over you."

"And you sat with me."

He snorted. "I even argued for the privilege. There's already a story going around that it was the evil Thayan mage who unleashed abishais on the town, and even some of your own people seem to suspect there's some truth to it."

She smiled. "Well, they are good judges of character."

He handed her a cup of water. "Thanks so much! Apparently I'm *not* a good judge of character, because I had no idea you were going to follow me. Why in the name of the Firelord didn't you tell me?"

She sat up, felt momentarily dizzy, and decided she wouldn't try standing up just yet. She sipped from the cup, and the cool water felt wonderful in her dry mouth and throat. "Would you have agreed to it?"

"I doubt it."

"Then there's your answer. It all worked out, so don't complain. Tell me what you discovered."

He did, although when he finished she felt little wiser than before.

"Was it just a few wyrmkeepers stirring up trouble," she asked, "or is it the entire Church of Tiamat? And either way, why? Chessentans have a dragon for a hero, so they ought to like us."

"On the other hand," said Aoth, "Threskel has dragons, undead and otherwise, for lords."

"There's that, I suppose. But didn't you find any papers or . . . something?"

He grinned. "Some convenient document revealing everything there is to know about the plot? I'm afraid not. Be satisfied that we learned something and that there probably won't be any more imitation dragonborn trying to murder me so long as I'm based in Soolabax."

"There has to be more we can do to solve the puzzle."

"I don't see what. We've reached the end of the trail here in the barony. And remember, nobody's paying me to figure it out. My job is to fight Threskel. I'll send word of what we learned back to Luthcheq. Lord Nicos and the war hero can decide what to do with the information."

She shook her head. "And curiosity won't drive you crazy?"

"Somehow I'll bear up under the strain."

Maybe he could at that. But he wasn't a priest of the god who'd granted them a vision of a council of dragons. It was her sacred duty to find out what it meant, and how it related to wyrmkeepers, abishais, and all the trouble that had overtaken her kingdom.

And that was just as well. Because unlike Aoth, she *was* too curious to stop pondering and prying. So it was good to know Amaunator approved.

* * * * *

His wounds already half healed, his deep voice growing louder with each syllable, Tchazzar chanted the final couplet of the incantation. Although his feet didn't leave the ground, Gaedynn had a paradoxical sensation of soaring. Then sunlight washed away the murky dusk that was as close as the Shadowfell ever came to day.

The Sky Riders were dangerous in their own right, but in comparison to the dark world they seemed like paradise. Jhesrhi looked around at the flourishing, green-leaved trees and the patches of blue sky visible through their branches with a rare smile on her face.

Gaedynn knew she had reason to smile. They'd succeeded in their mission beyond anyone's wildest expectations. Now that he'd come home, Tchazzar could well prove to be the key to victory. And on top of that, Jhesrhi had somehow purged herself of the old fears that had afflicted her ever since her return to Chessenta. She hadn't talked about it, but Gaedynn could see the difference.

So he ought to share her happiness. He was trying. But when he looked at the colossal red dragon looming behind her, gazing at the world he'd lost and regained in a sort of ecstasy, a thought came to him that made elation difficult. He told himself he had no reason to think such a thing, but the question persisted nonetheless.

What exactly have we done?

From the Ruins of Fallen Empires, A New Age of Heroes Arises

It is a time of magic and monsters, a time when the world struggles against a rising tide of shadow. Only a few scattered points of light glow with stubborn determination in the deepening darkness.

It is a time where everything is new in an ancient and mysterious world.

Be There as the First Adventures Unfold.

The Mark of Nerath
Bill Slavicsek
August 2010

The Seal of Karga Kul
Alex Irvine
December 2010

The first two novels in a new line set in the evolving world of the Dungeons & Dragons® game setting. If you haven't played . . . or read D&D® in a while, your reintroduction starts in August!

ALSO AVAILABLE AS E-BOOKS!

Dungeons & Dragons, Wizards of the Coast, and their respective logos, and D&D are trademarks of Wizards of the Coast LLC in the U.S.A. and other countries. ©2010 Wizards.

WELCOME TO THE DESERT WORLD
OF ATHAS, A LAND RULED BY A HARSH
AND UNFORGIVING CLIMATE, A LAND
GOVERNED BY THE ANCIENT AND
TYRANNICAL SORCERER KINGS.
THIS IS THE LAND OF

CITY UNDER THE SAND
Jeff Mariotte
OCTOBER 2010

*Sometimes lost knowledge is
knowledge best left unknown.*

FIND OUT WHAT YOU'RE MISSING IN THIS
BRAND NEW DARK SUN® ADVENTURE BY
THE AUTHOR OF *COLD BLACK HEARTS*.

ALSO AVAILABLE AS AN E-BOOK!

THE PRISM PENTAD
Troy Denning's classic DARK SUN
series revisited! Check out the great new editions of
The Verdant Passage, *The Crimson Legion*,
The Amber Enchantress, *The Obsidian Oracle*,
and *The Cerulean Storm*.

DARK SUN, DUNGEONS & DRAGONS, WIZARDS OF THE COAST, and their respective logos are trademarks of Wizards of the Coast LLC in the U.S.A. and other countries. ©2010 Wizards.

RETURN TO A WORLD OF PERIL, DECEIT, AND INTRIGUE, A WORLD REBORN IN THE WAKE OF A GLOBAL WAR.

TIM WAGGONER'S
LADY RUIN

She dedicated her life to the nation of Karrnath. With the war ended, and the army asleep—waiting—in their crypts, Karrnath assigned her to a new project: find a way to harness the dark powers of the Plane of Madness.

REVEL IN THE RUIN
DECEMBER 2010

ALSO AVAILABLE AS AN E-BOOK!

Eberron, Dungeons & Dragons, Wizards of the Coast, and their respective logos are trademarks of Wizards of the Coast LLC in the U.S.A. and other countries. ©2010 Wizards.

R.A. SALVATORE & GENO

STONE OF TYMORA TRILOGY

Sail the treacherous seas of the Forgotten Realms® world with Maimun, a boy who couldn't imagine how unlucky it would be to be blessed by the goddess of luck. Chased by a demon, hunted by pirates, Maimun must discover the secret of the Stone of Tymora, before his luck runs out!

Book 1 — THE STOWAWAY
Hardcover: 978-0-7869-5094-2
Paperback: 978-0-7869-5257-1

Book 2 — THE SHADOWMASK
Hardcover: 978-0-7869-5147-5
Paperback: available June 2010:
978-0-7869-5501-5

Book 3 — THE SENTINELS
Hardcover: available September 2010:
978-0-7869-5505-3
Paperback: available in Fall 2011

"An exciting new tale from R.A. Salvatore, complete with his famously pulse-quickening action scenes and, of course, lots and lots of swordplay. If you're a fan of fantasy fiction, this book is not to be missed!"
—Kidzworld on *The Stowaway*

FORGOTTEN REALMS, DUNGEONS & DRAGONS, WIZARDS OF THE COAST, and their respective logos are trademarks of Wizards of the Coast LLC in the U.S.A. and other countries. Other trademarks are property of their respective owners ©2010 Wizards.

Books for Young Readers